Copyright 2018 Sebastian De Angelis
ISBN: 978-0-9679947-0-3
What Is It Series start date: 11-26-2001
Book (1) revised on: 07-19-2018

Description: What Is It Book 1, Drawings 1 to 250
ASIN: B07FM7PMVN, ISBN: 978-0-9679947-0-3

The What Is It Series of Books is a compilation of over a thousand drawings by Sebastian De Angelis. The drawings are interesting, fascinating and sometimes humorous. They're in black & white and are available in paperback. The whole family should enjoy hours of viewing these detailed drawings. De Angelis' unique, unusual style will leave you wondering What Is It?

Although there doesn't seem to be a rhyme or reason as to what the artist is drawing, small creatures appear randomly throughout the books. These humanoid looking beings (unnamed or purpose described) come in all shapes and sizes. They typically are involved with things of a malicious nature, throwing levers, pressing buttons and all-out getting in the way of normality.

So where do all the wild ideas come from that sets the artist's pen in motion? Most of the work tells me that De Angelis is delivering a message that life is not as perfect under the facade surface as we imagine. And that situations in the world around us are a lot more ironic then we assume. The nuts & bolts, chewing gum & duck-tape that holds it all together is the World's way of evolving. Then the practicality fades due in part to those pesky humanoids! So be careful (xiao xin) out there, it's much more precarious then you think! Heee heeee…

Books in the What Is It Series

Book (1) Drawings 1-250
Book (2) Drawings 251-500
Book (3) Drawings 501-750
Book (4) Drawings 751-1000

What Is It

Book 1

Drawings 1 to 250

Sebastian De Angelis

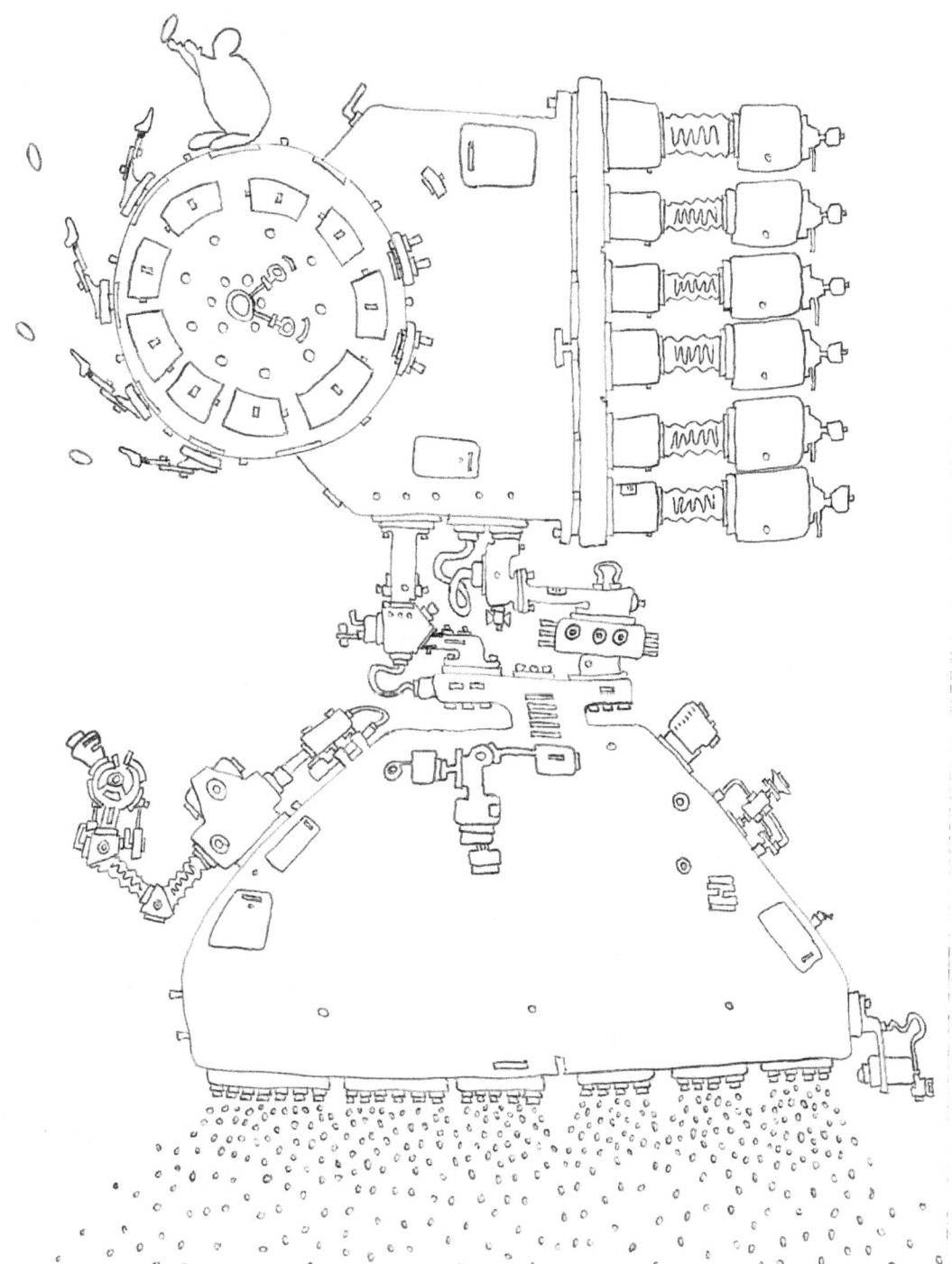

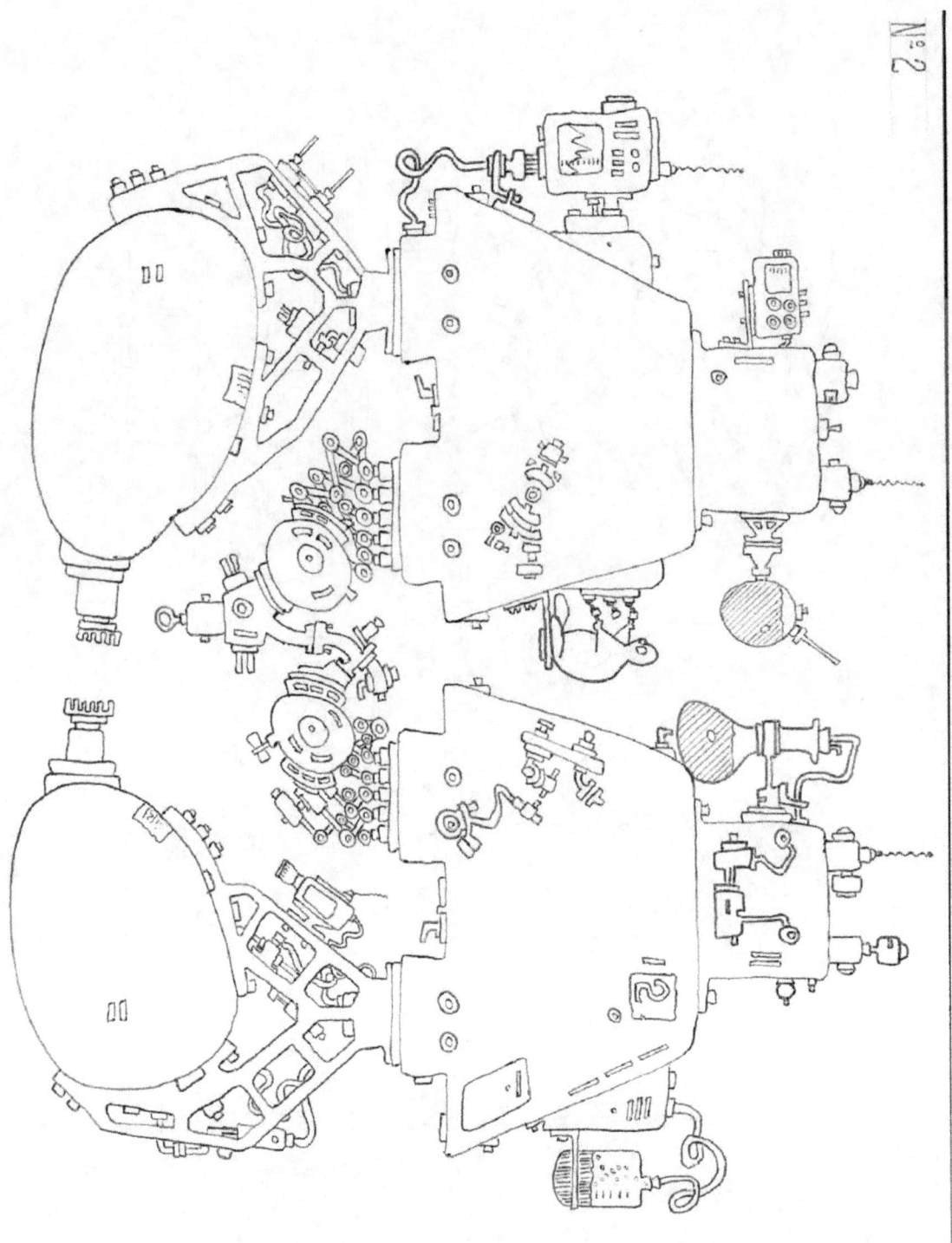

№ 3

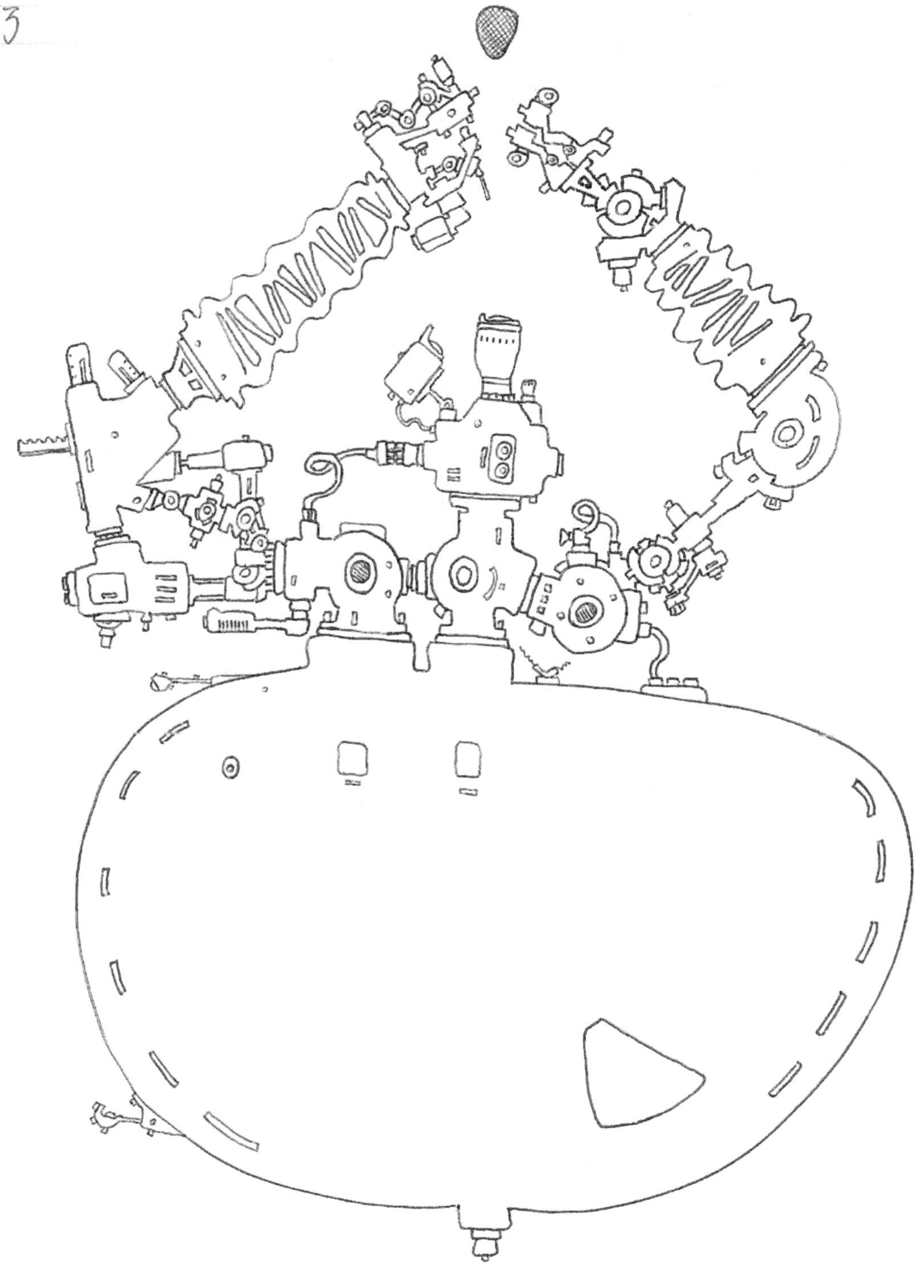

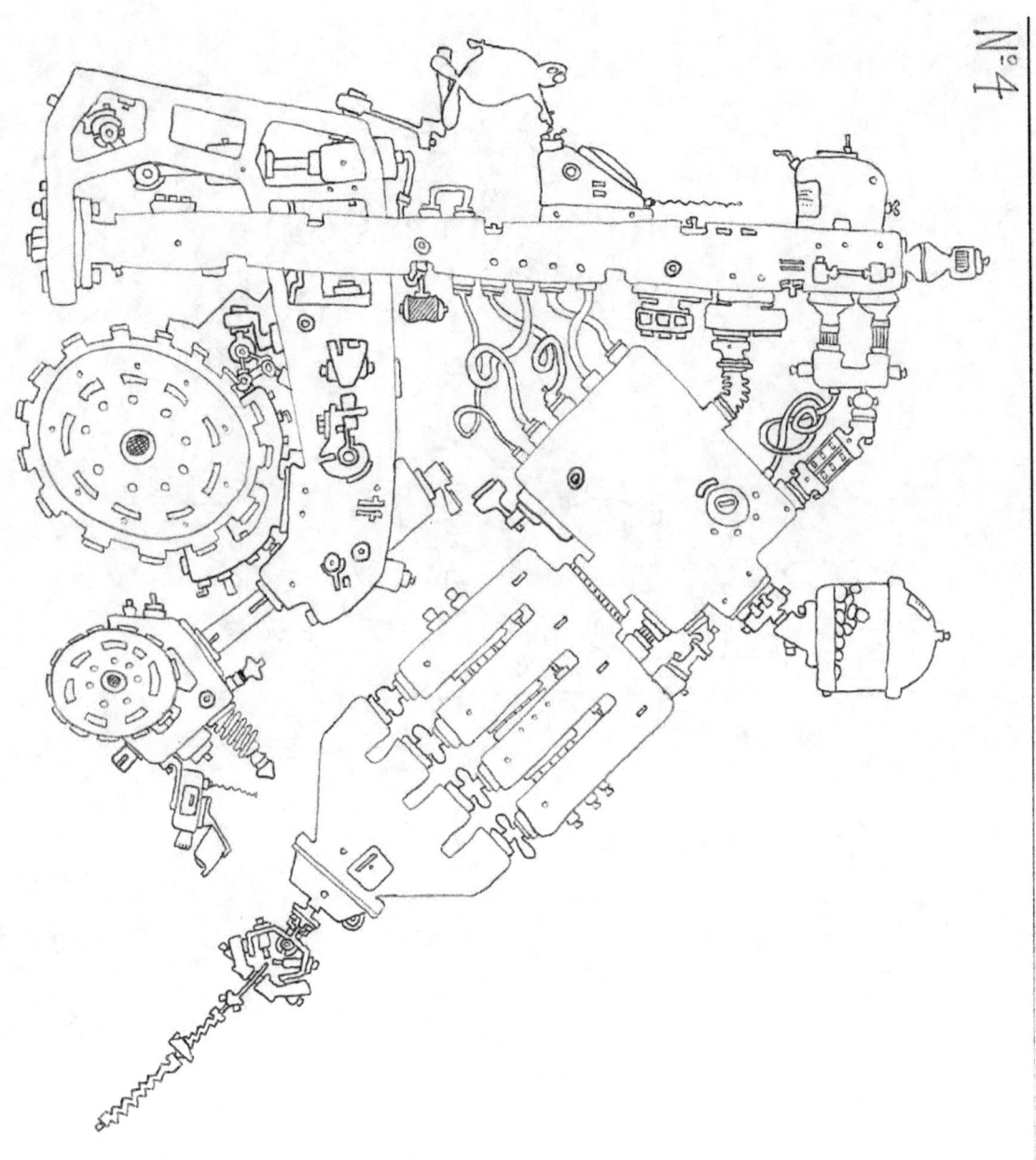

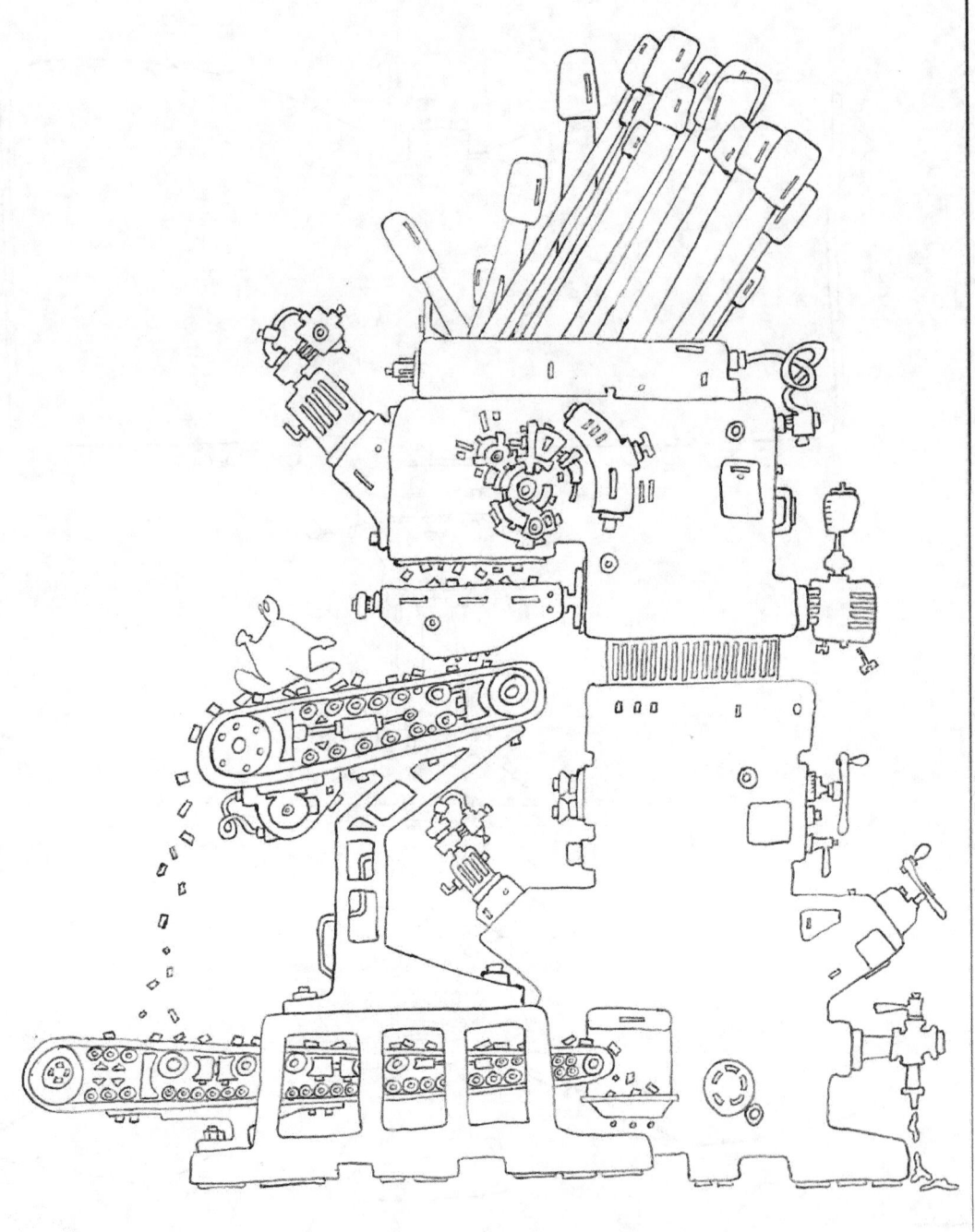

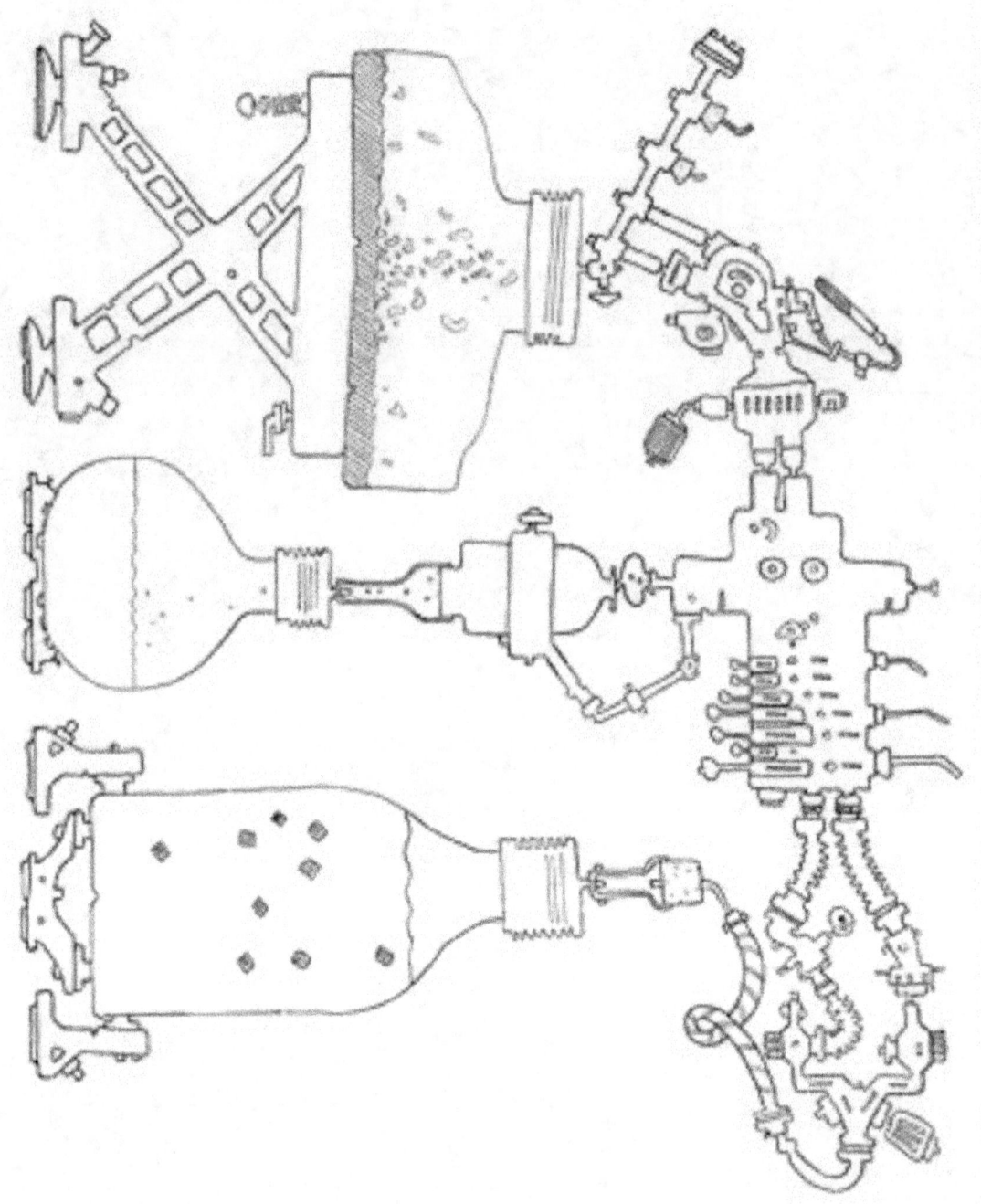

N°29

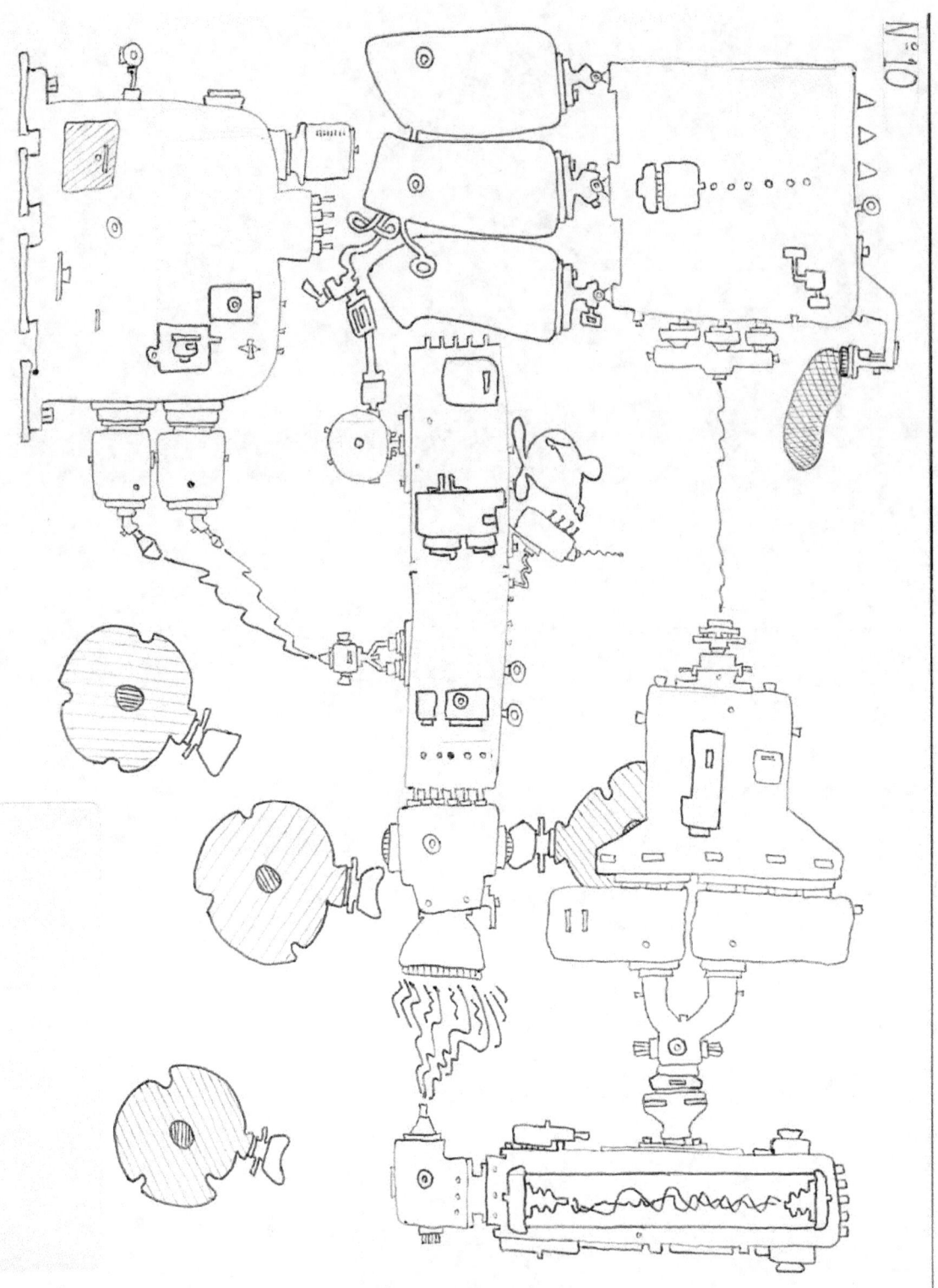

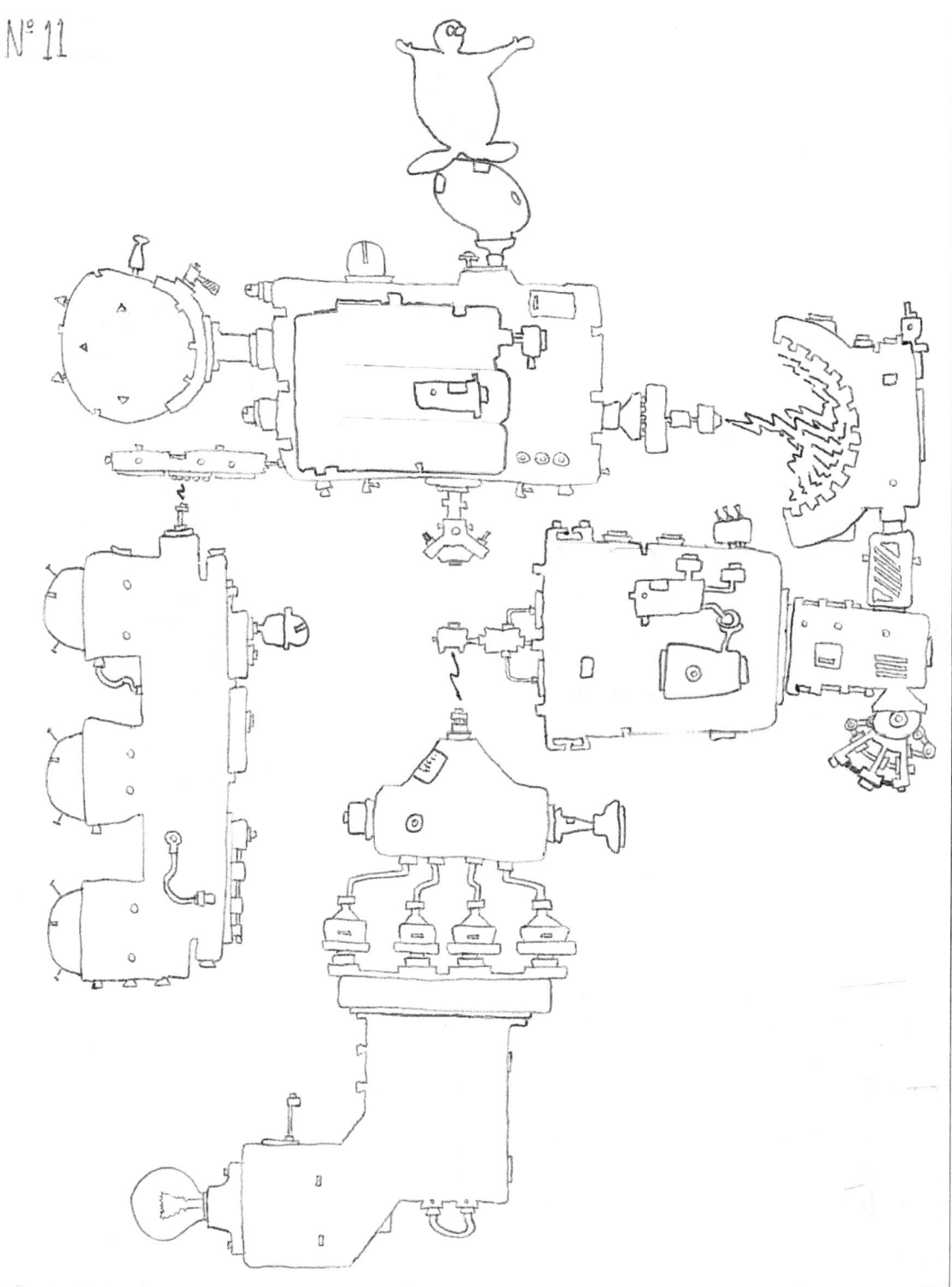

Nº 12

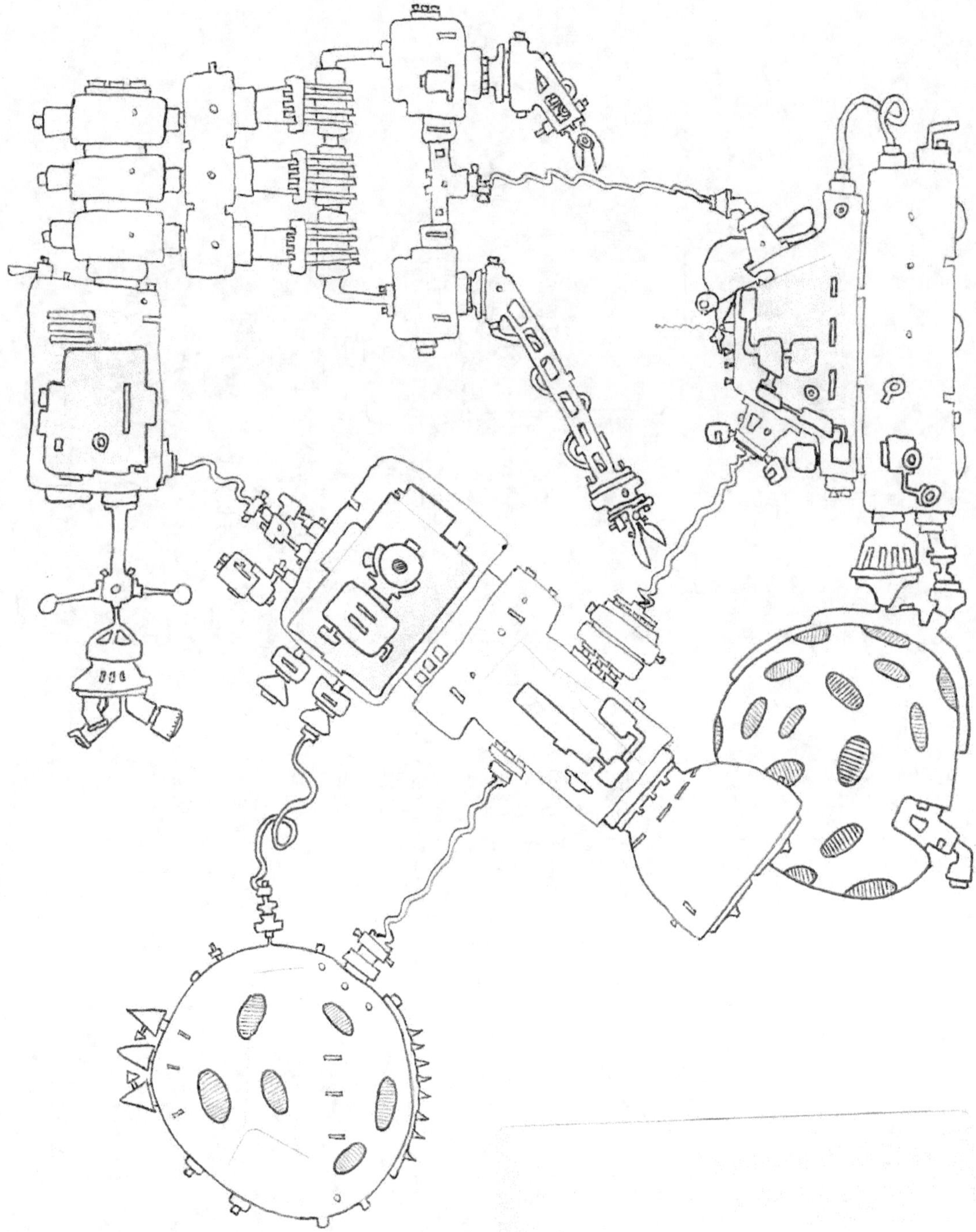

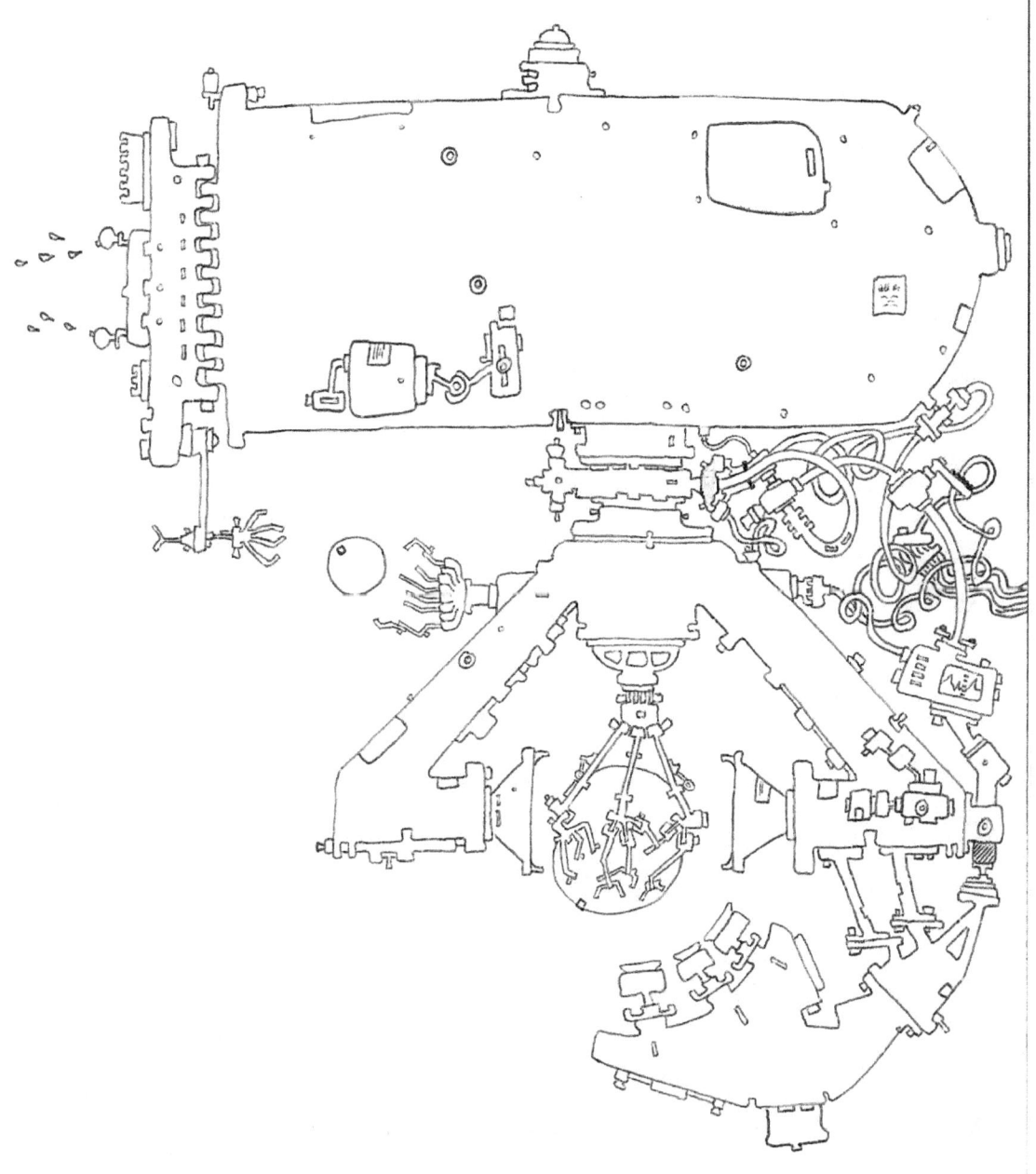

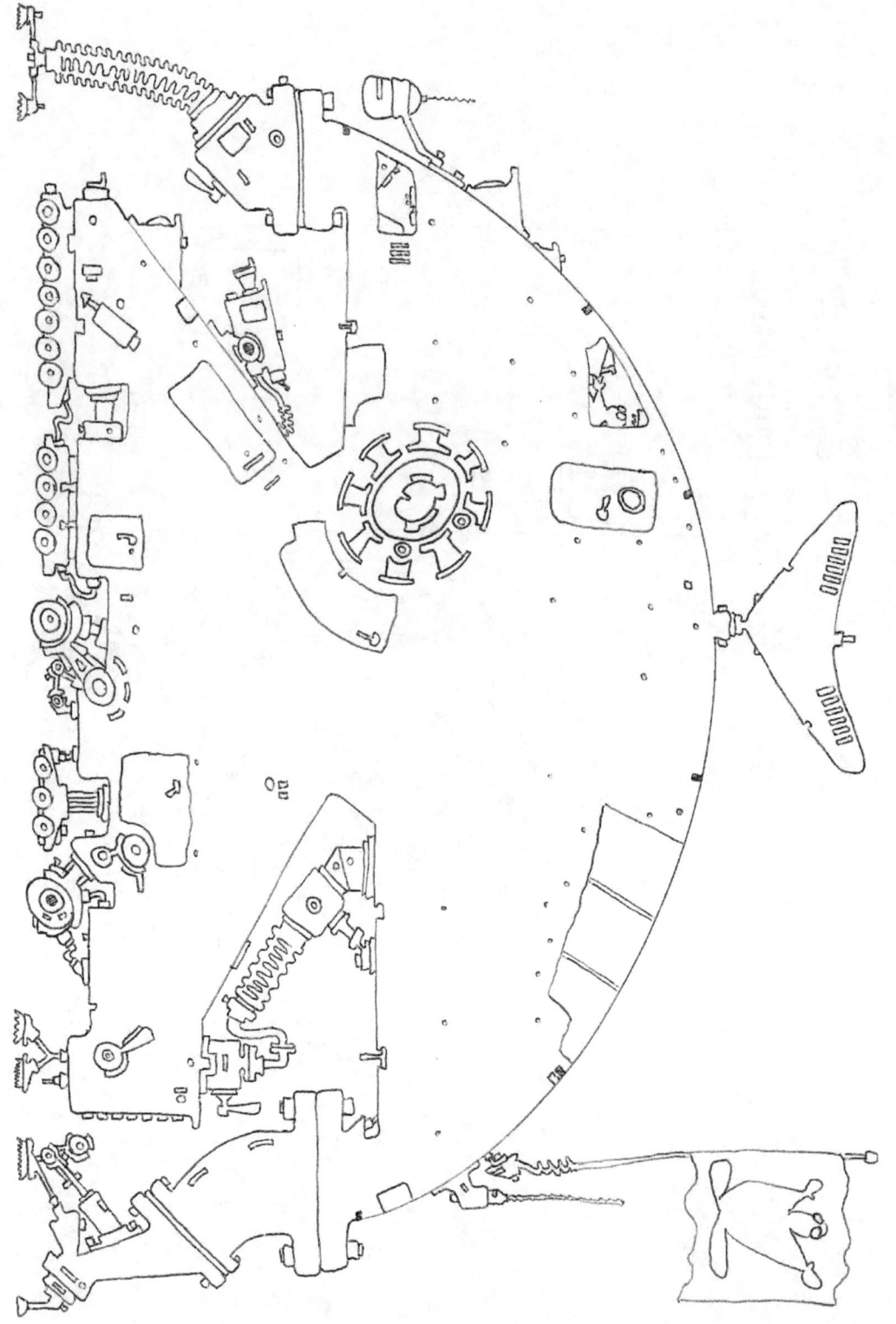

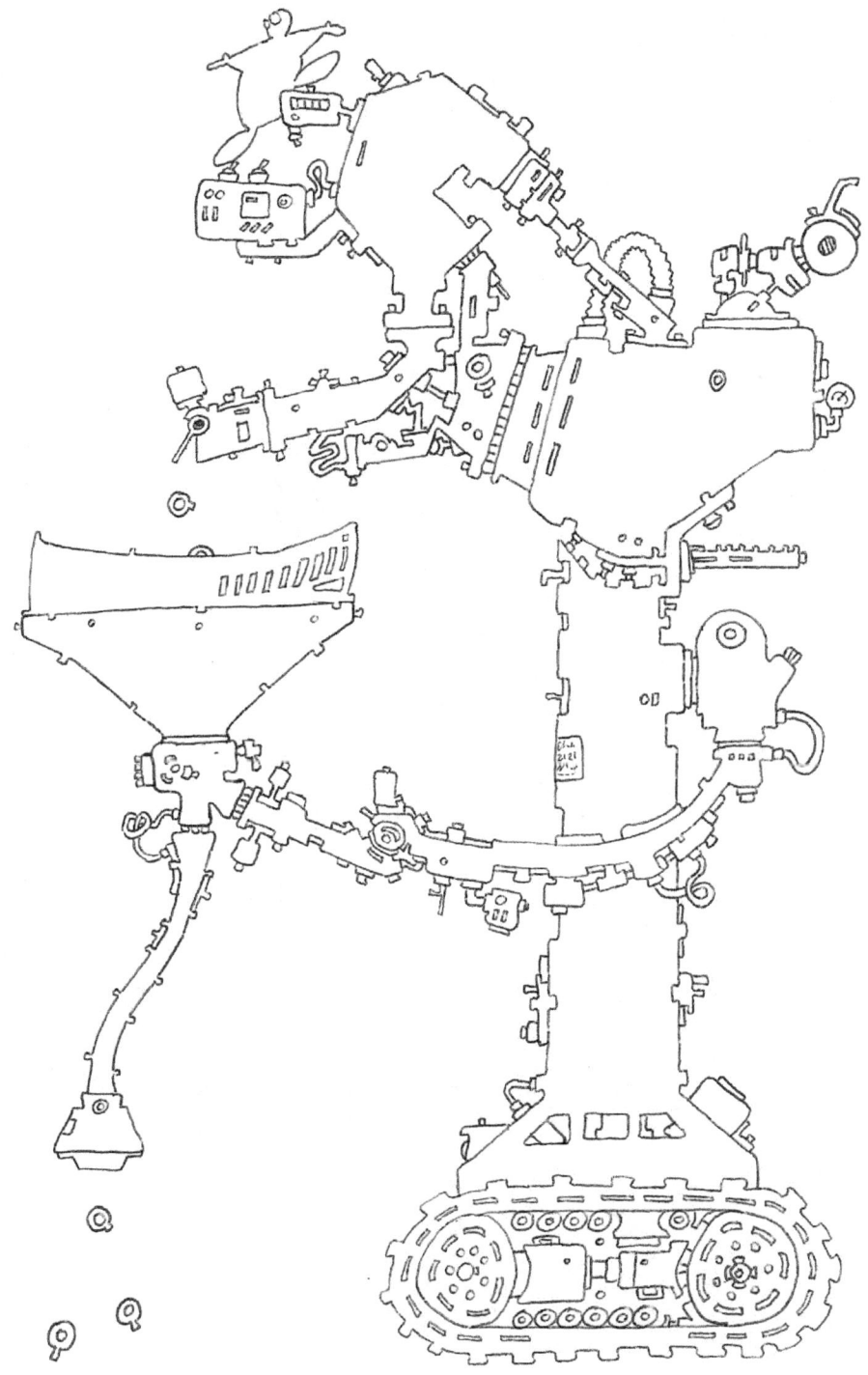

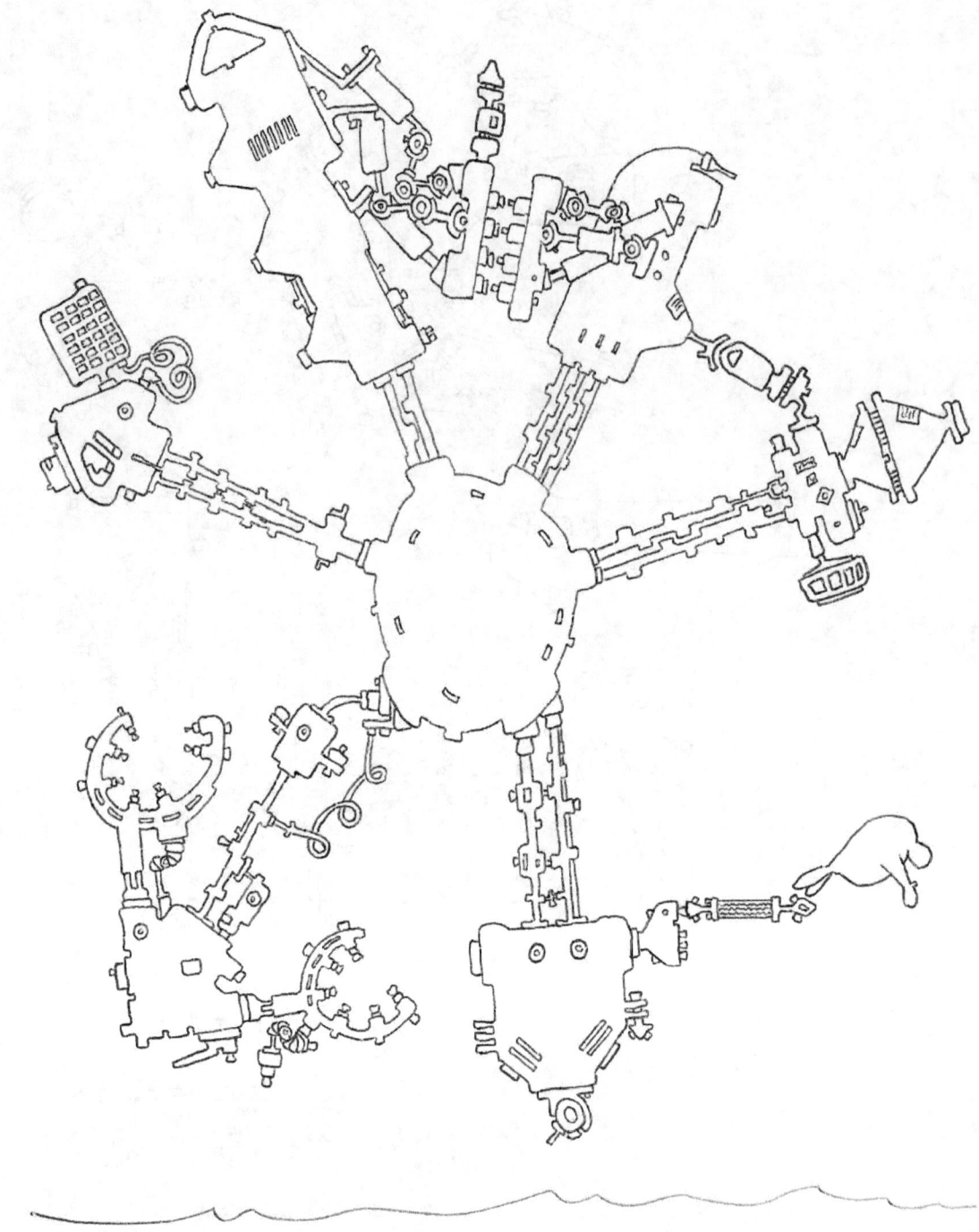

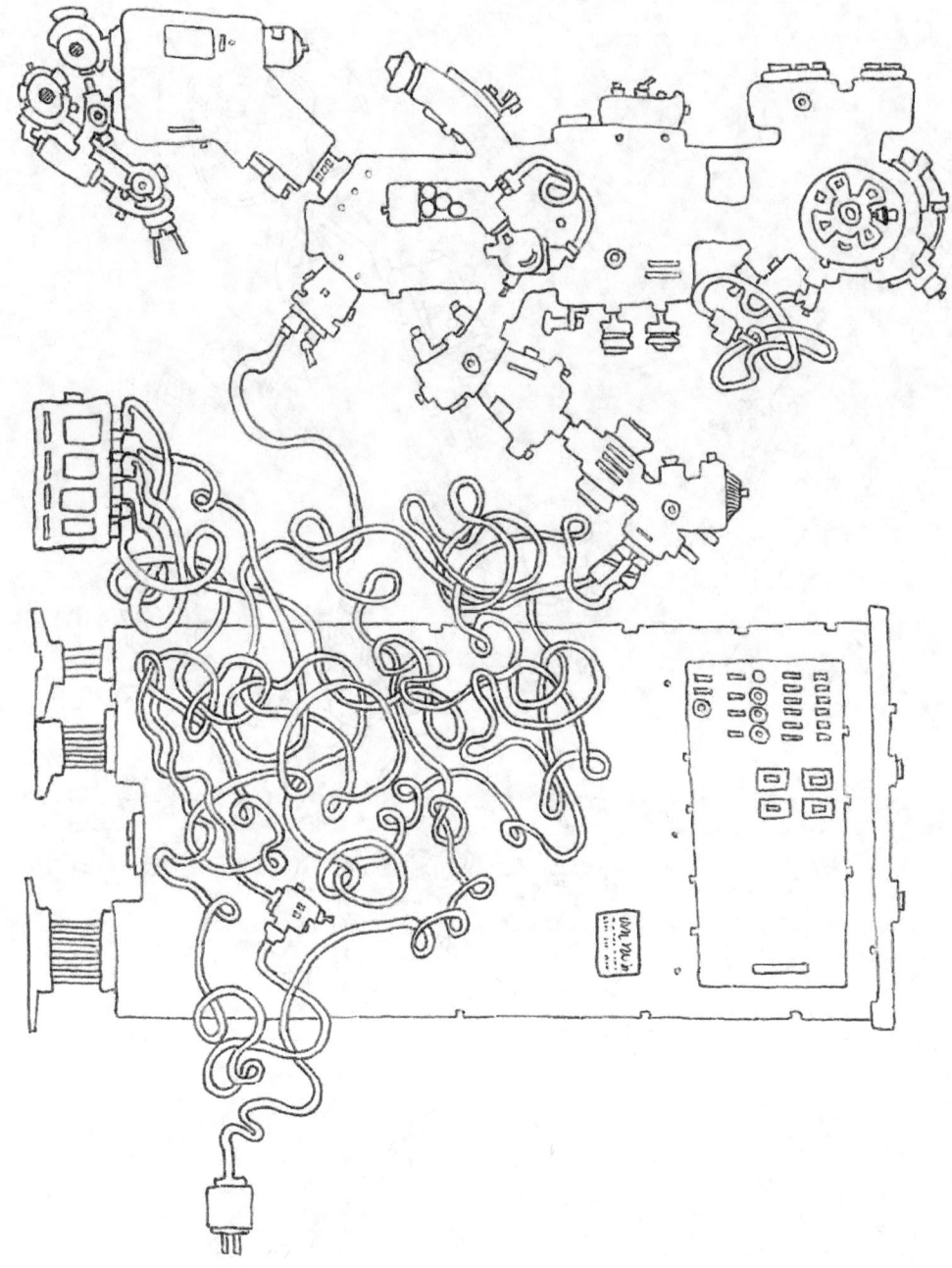

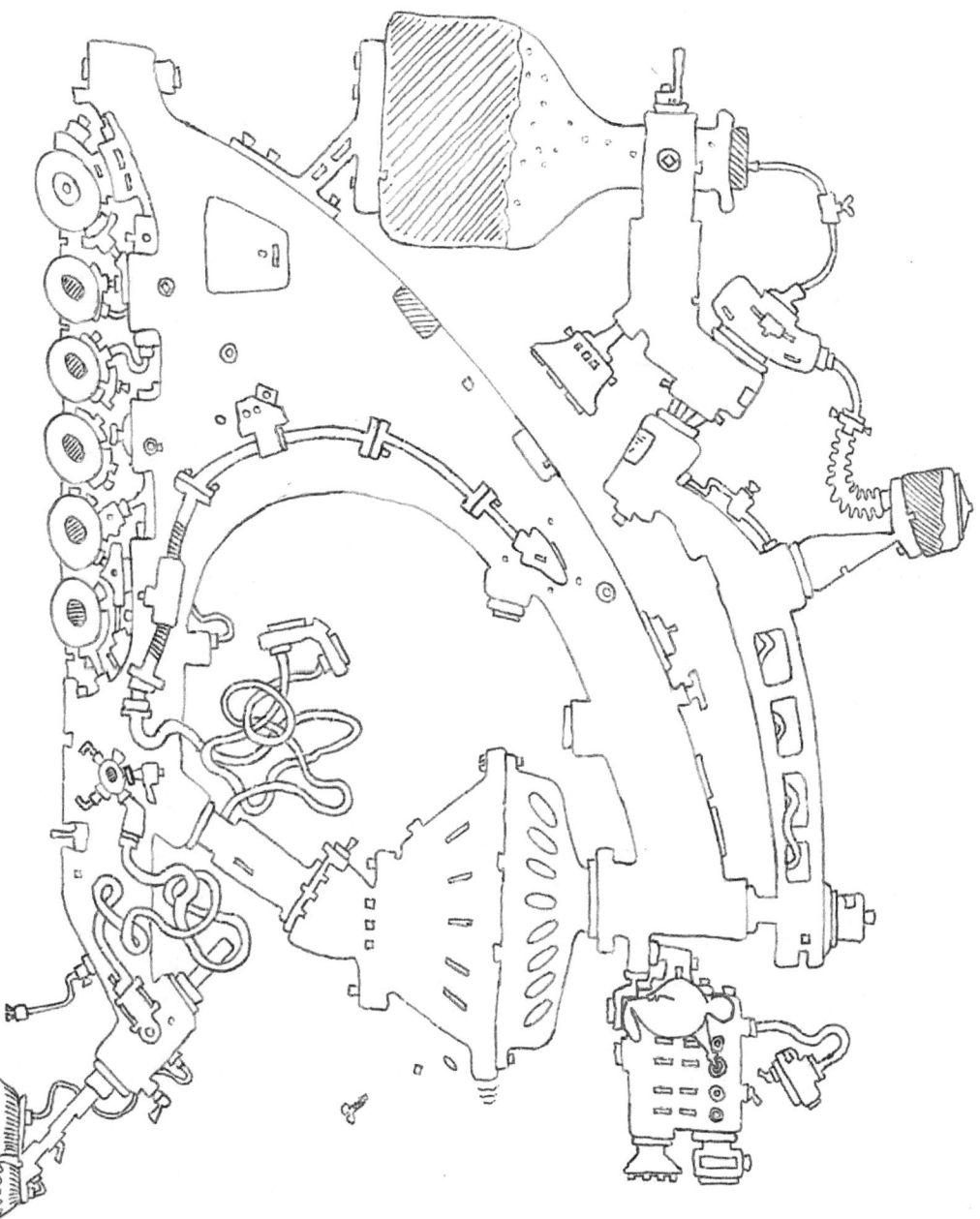

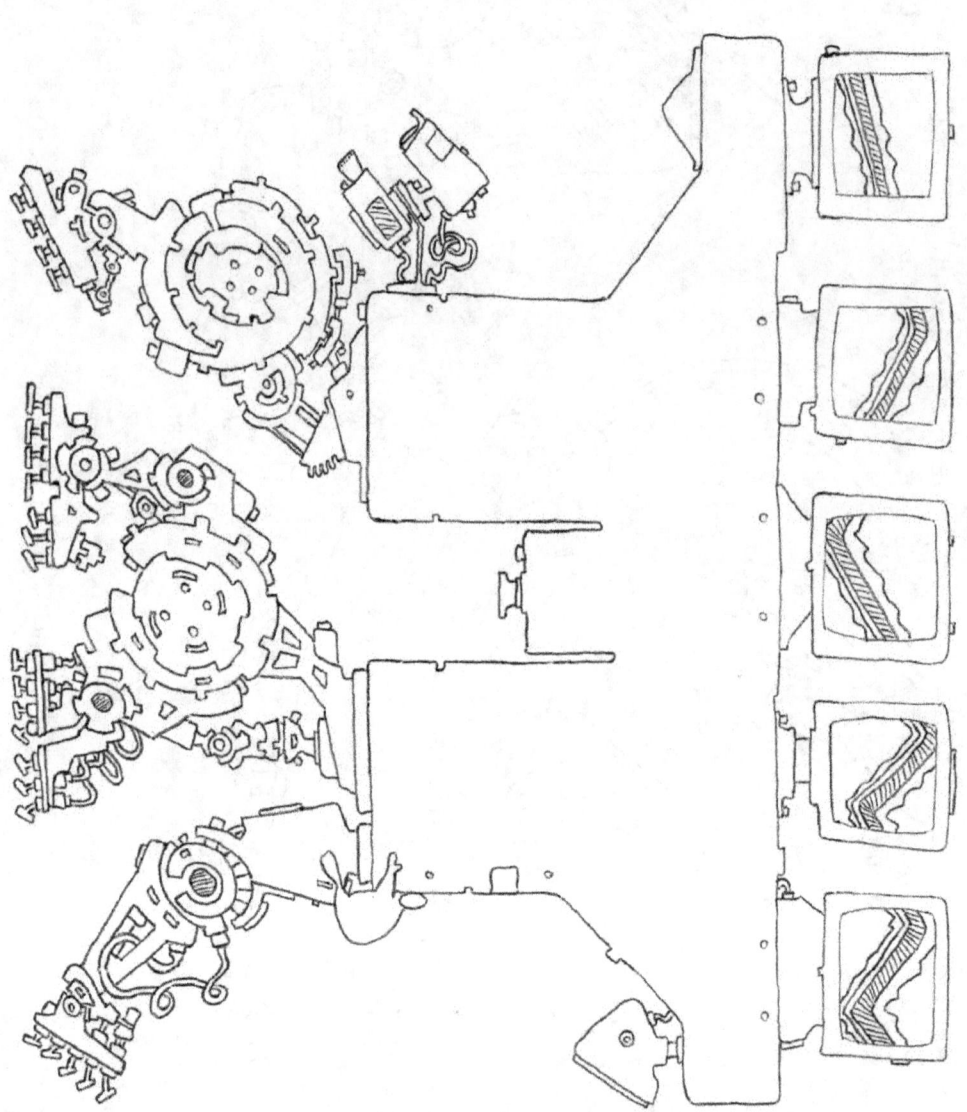

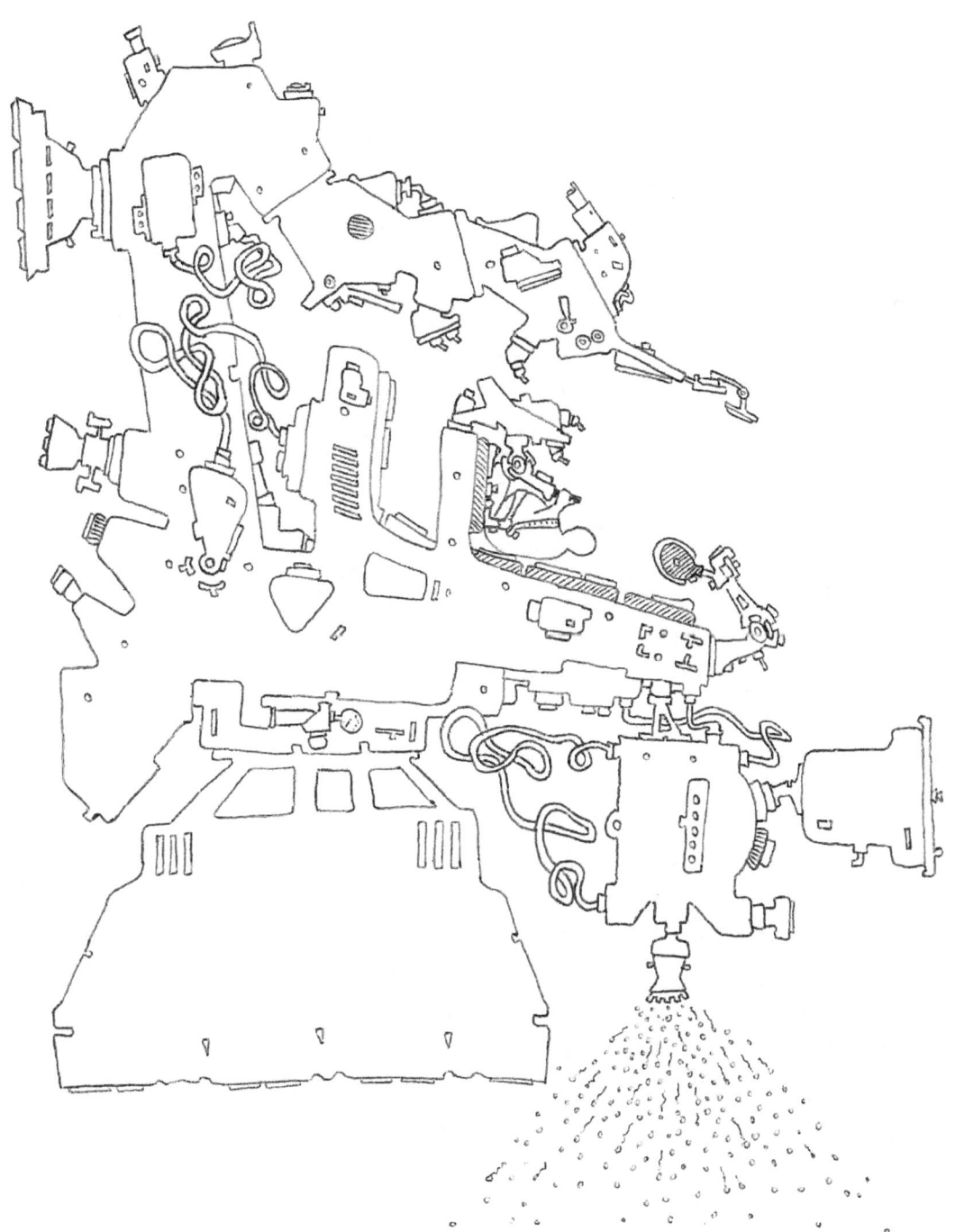

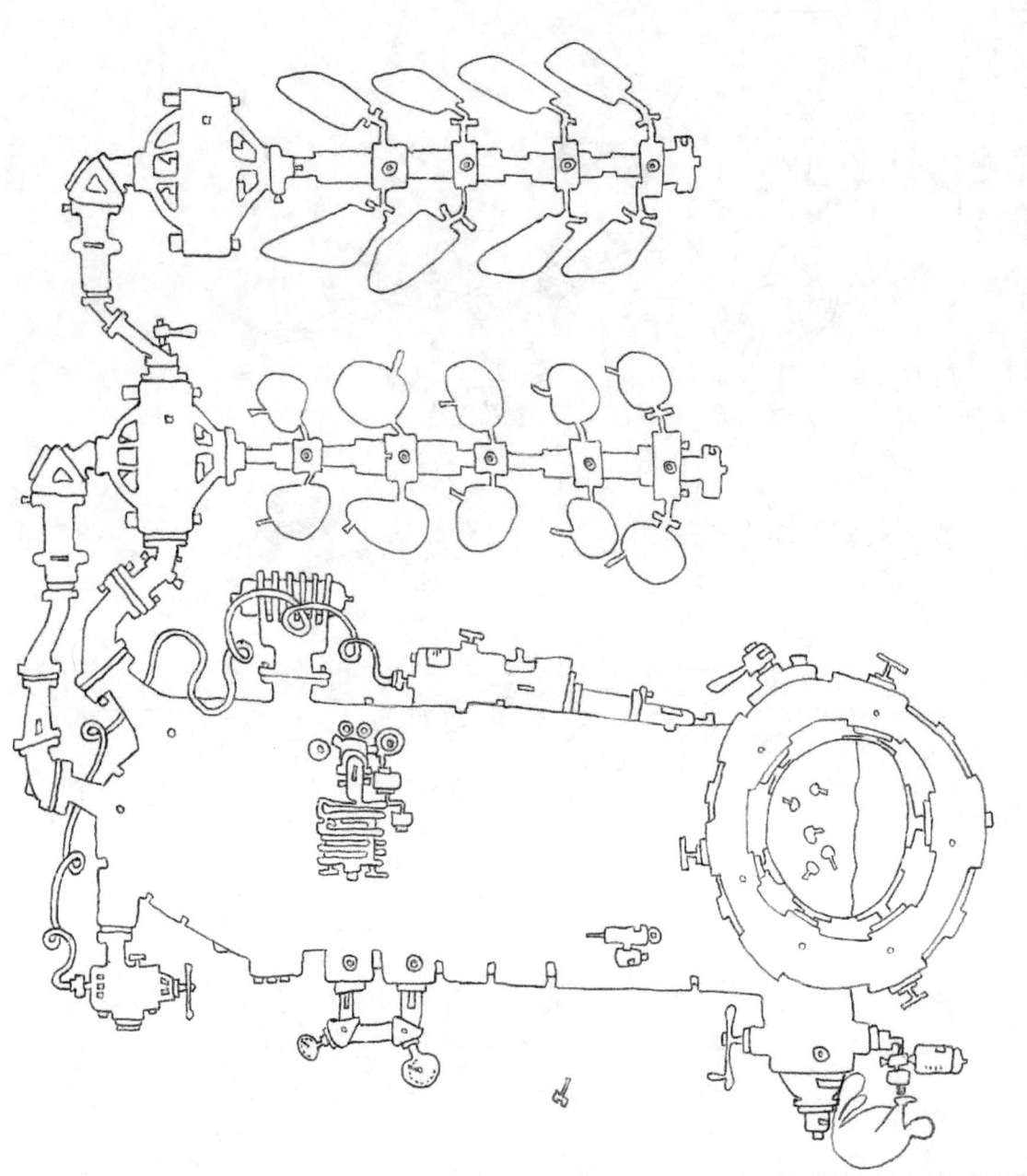

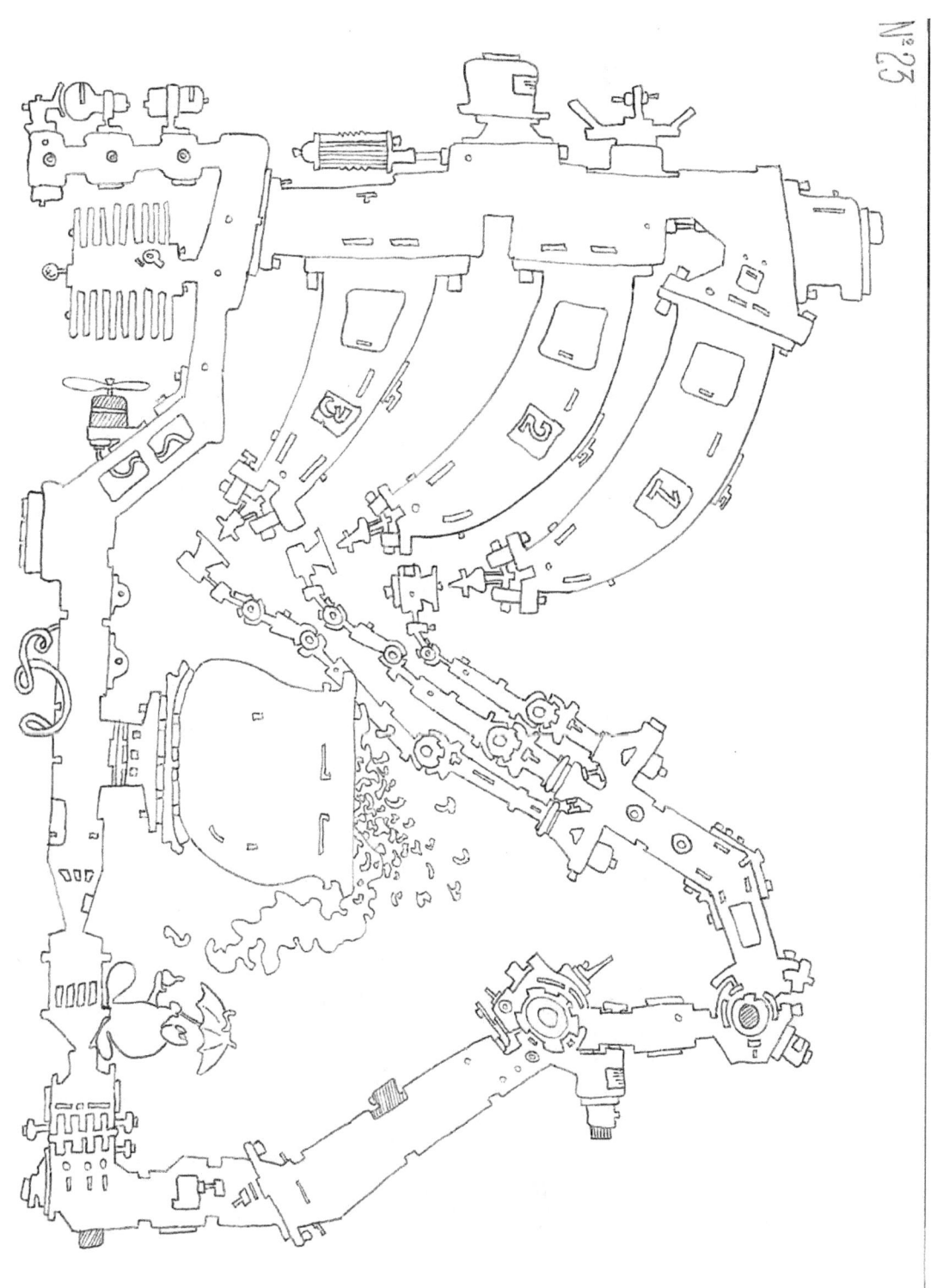

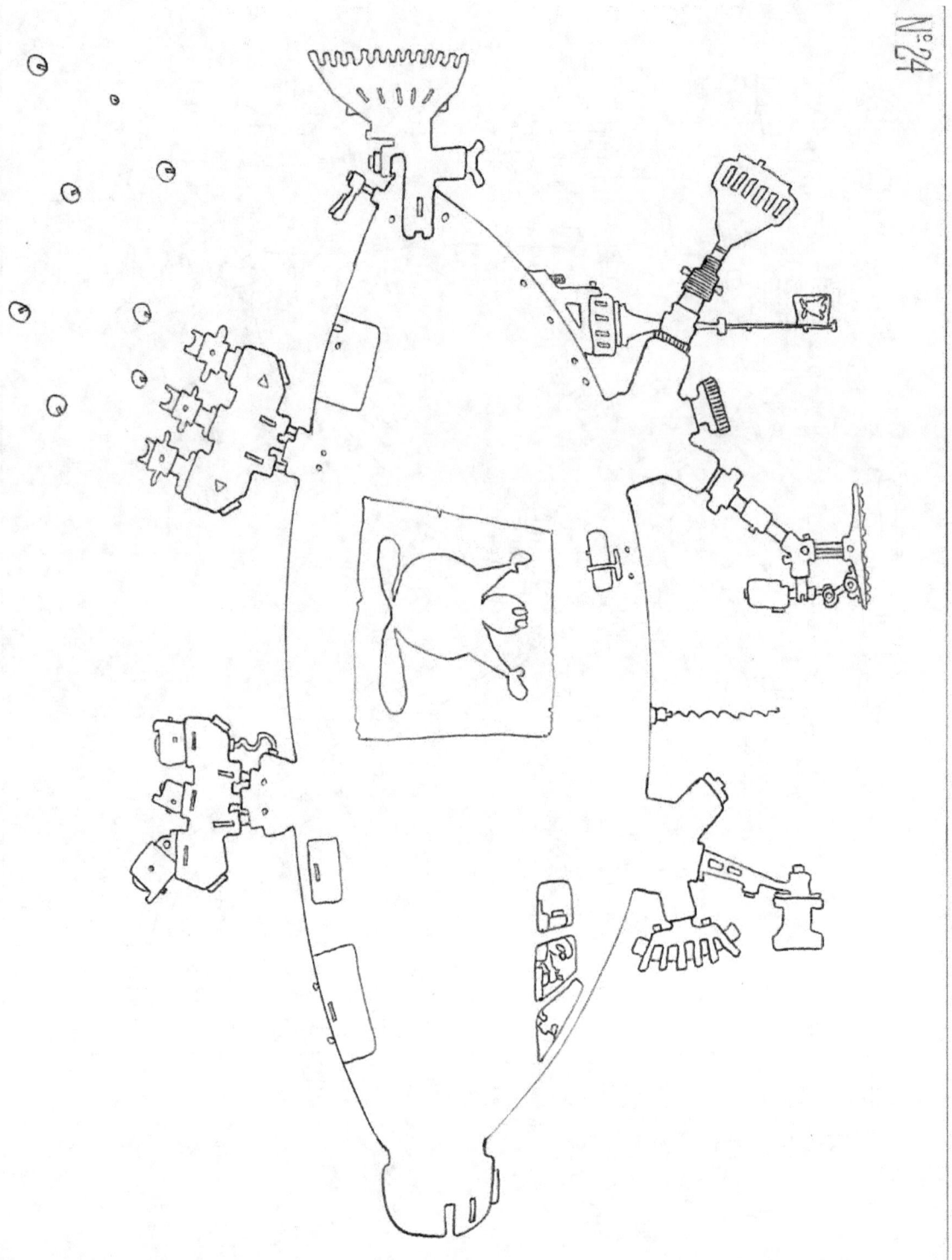

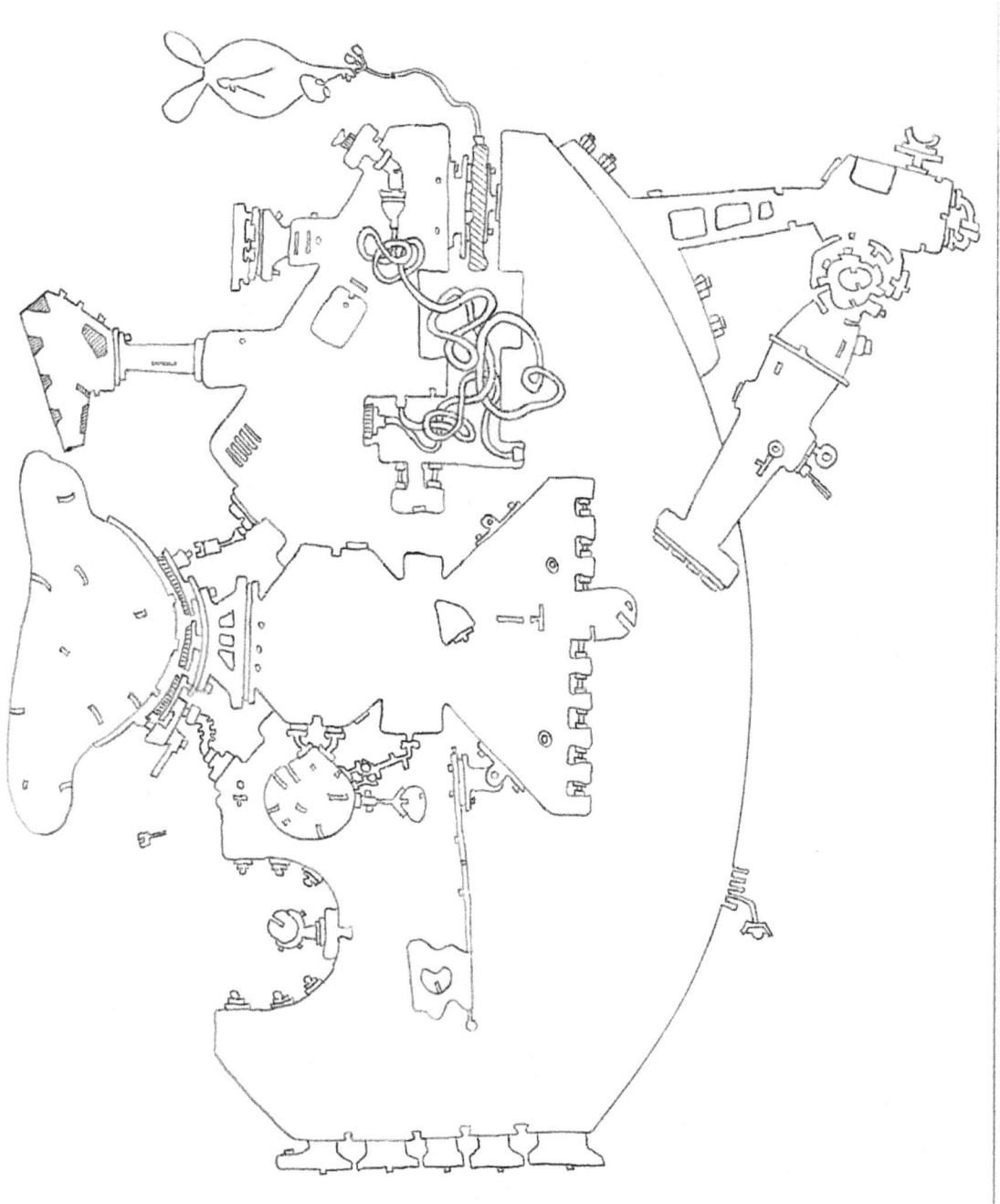

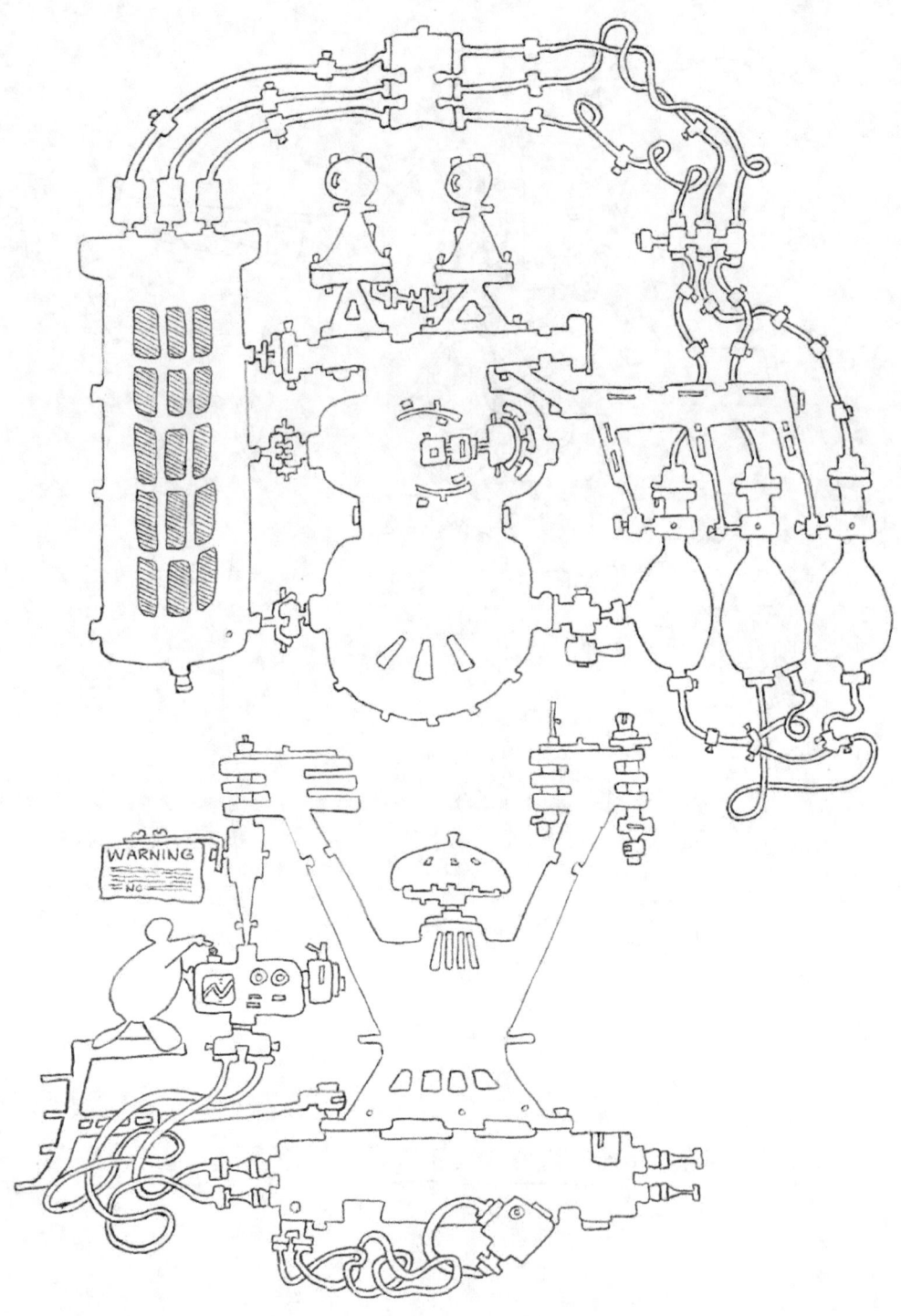

WARNING
═ NO ═

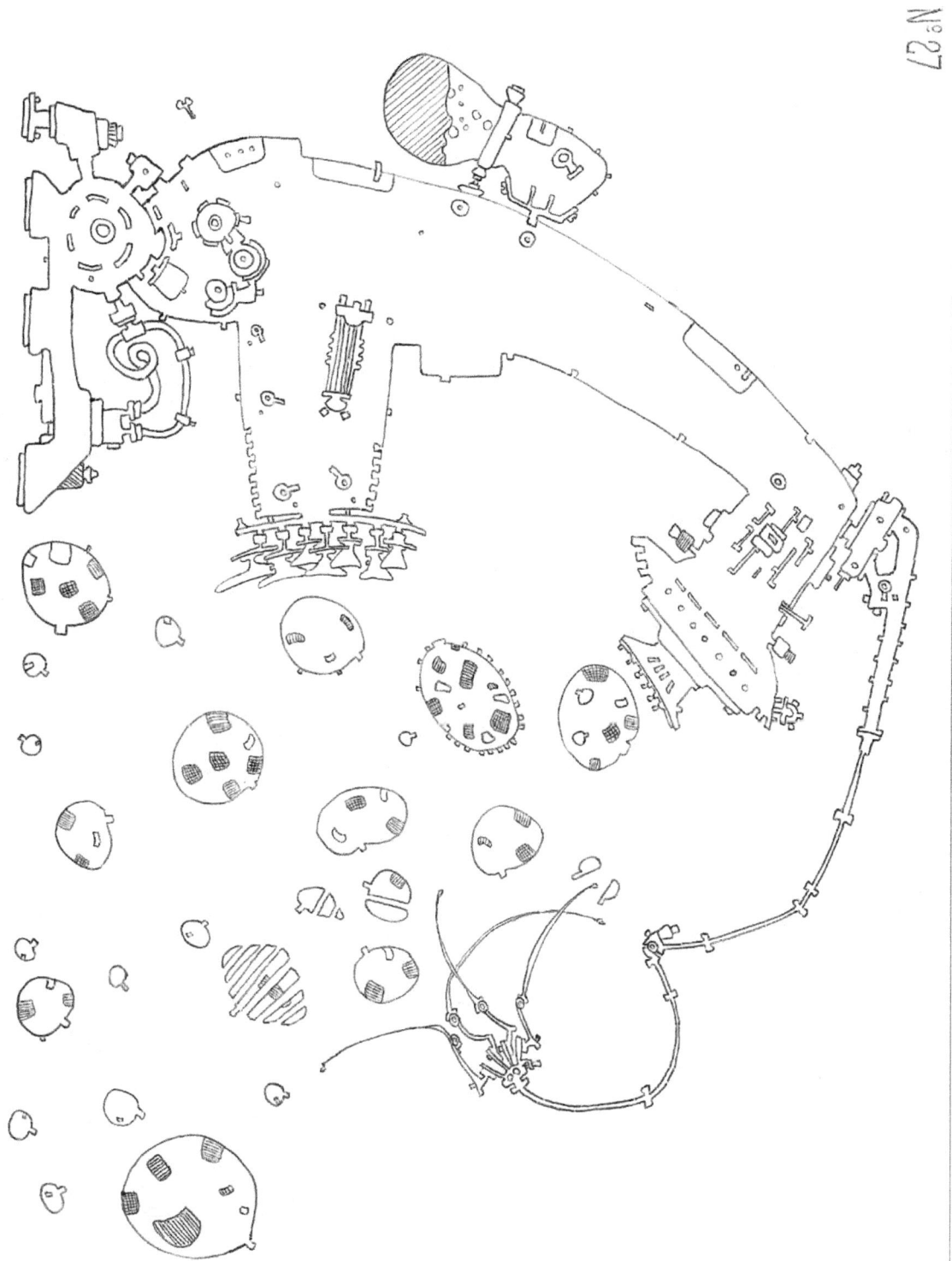

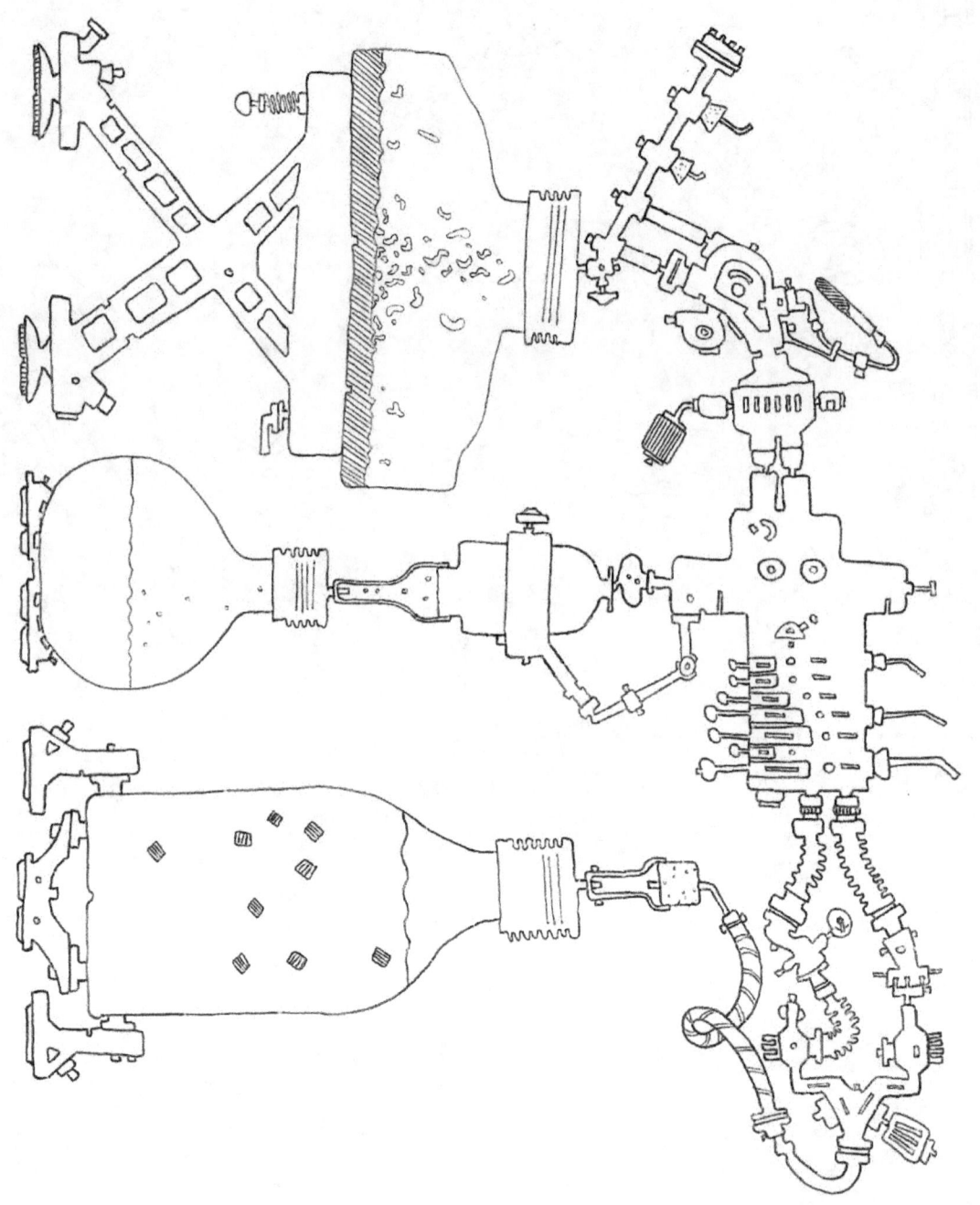

N° 29

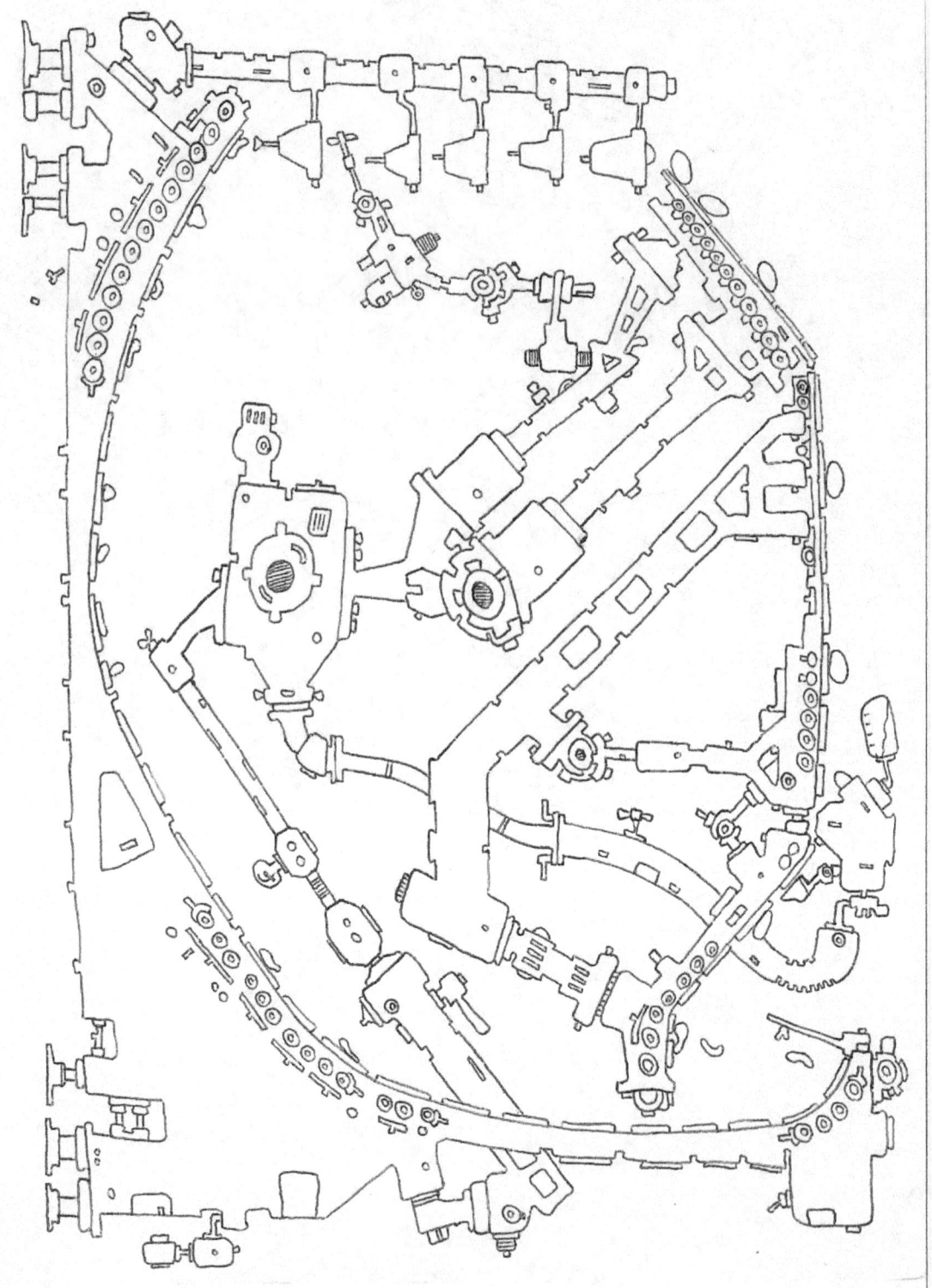

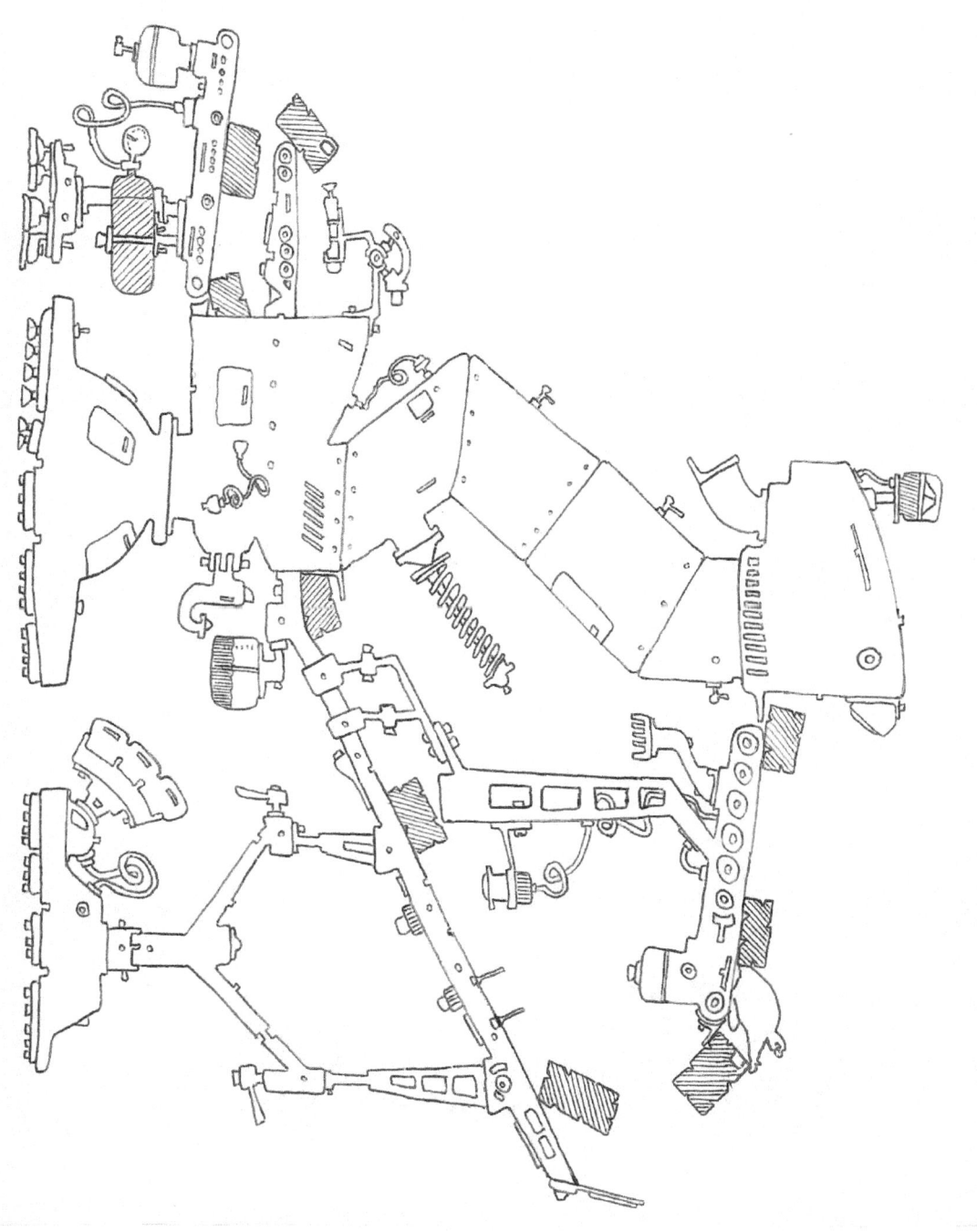

N° 32

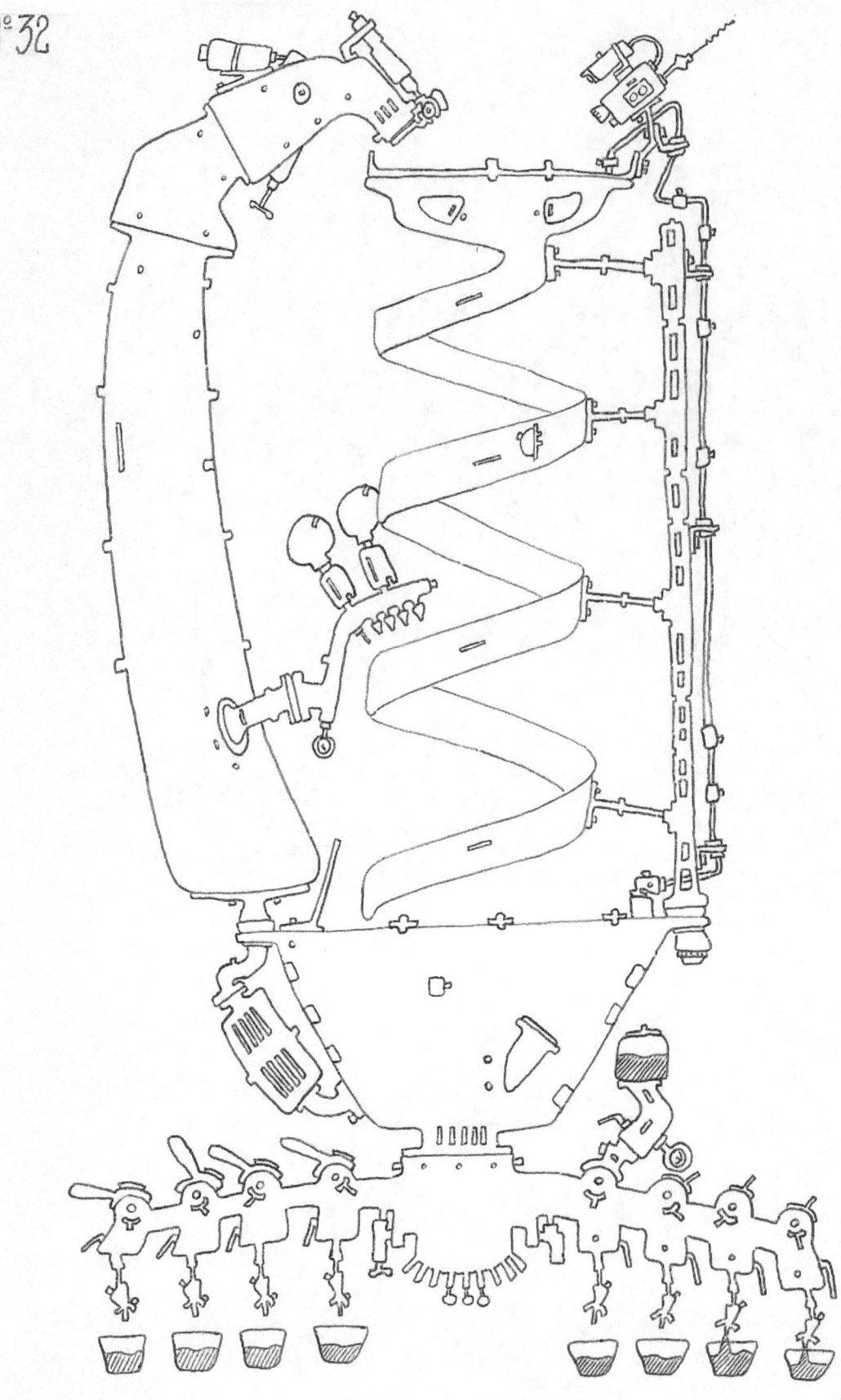

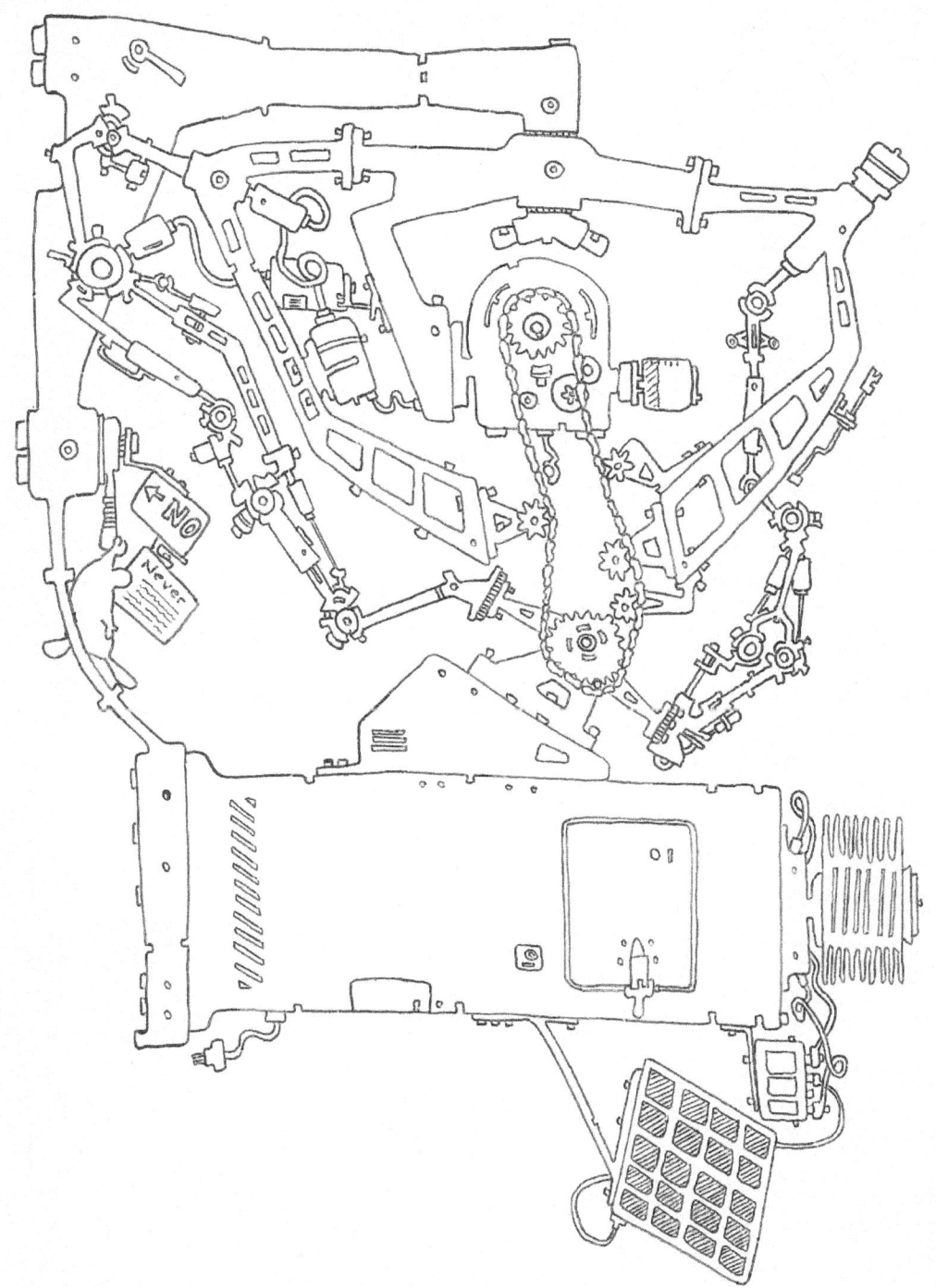

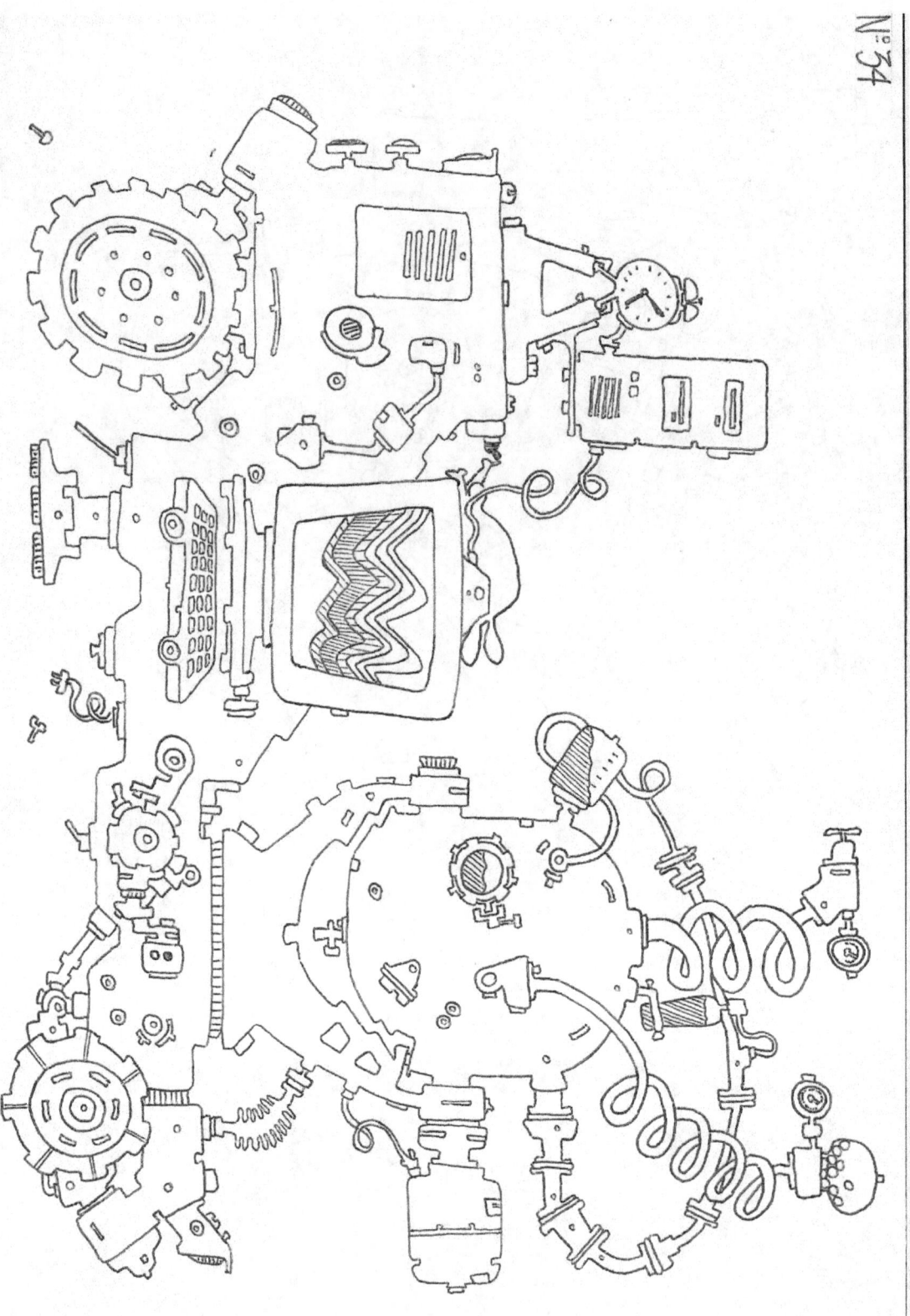

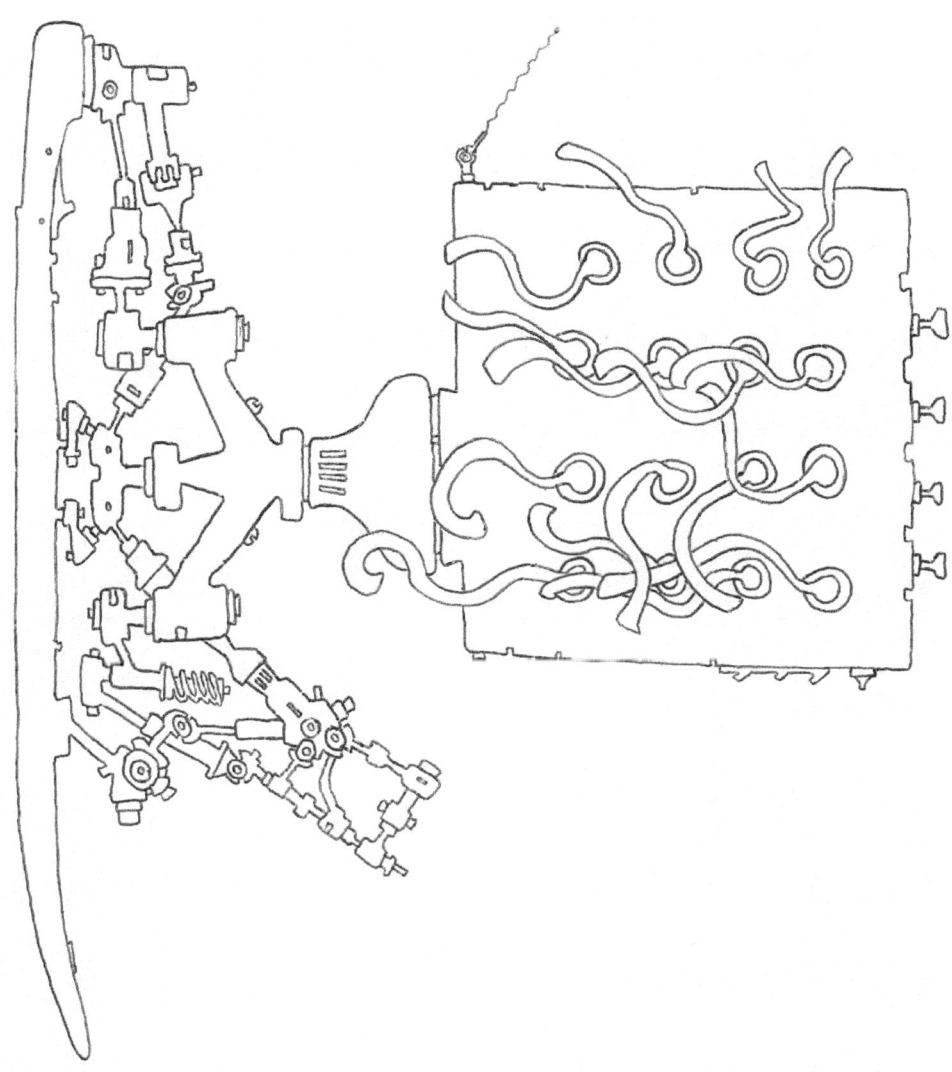

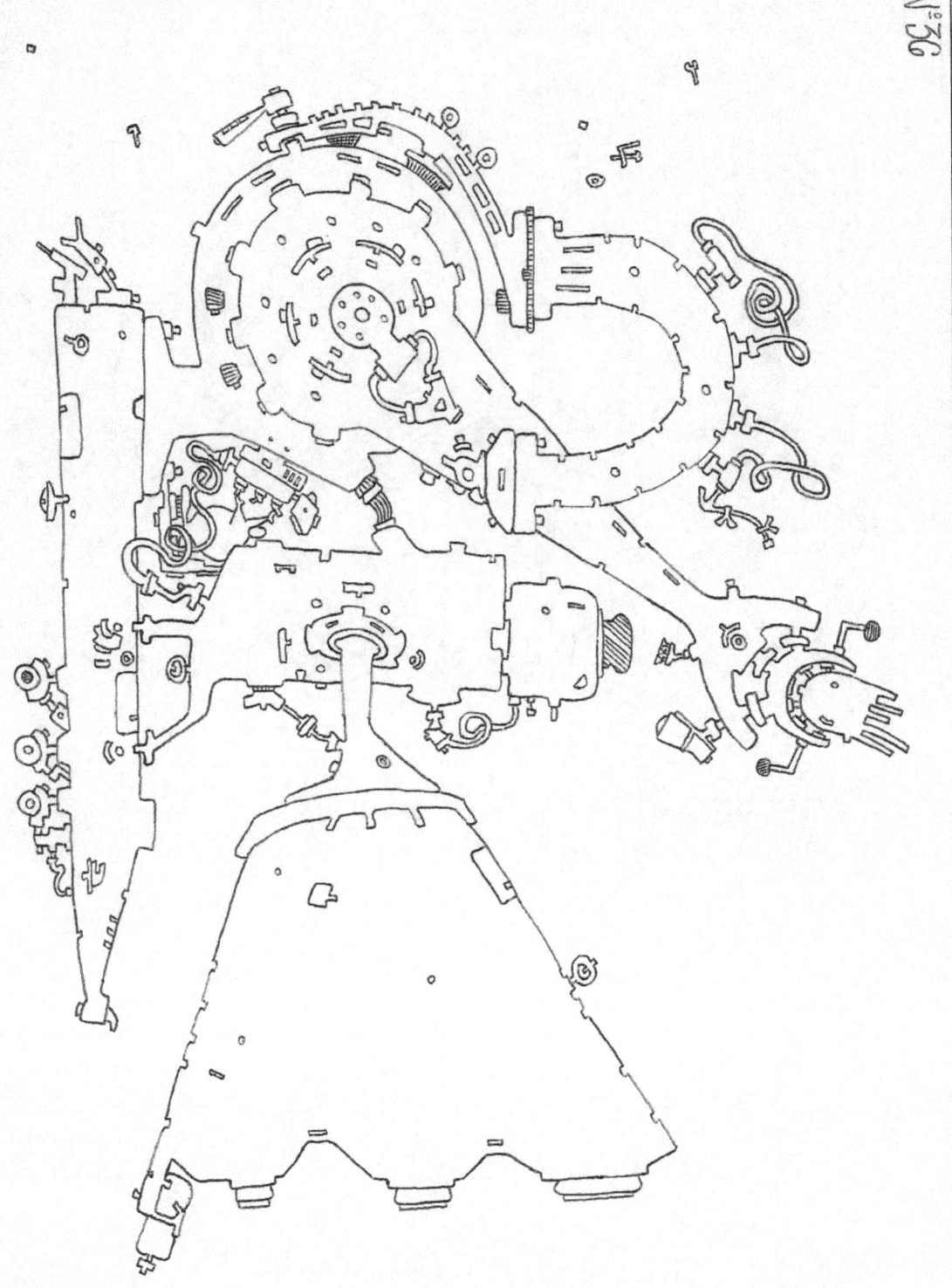

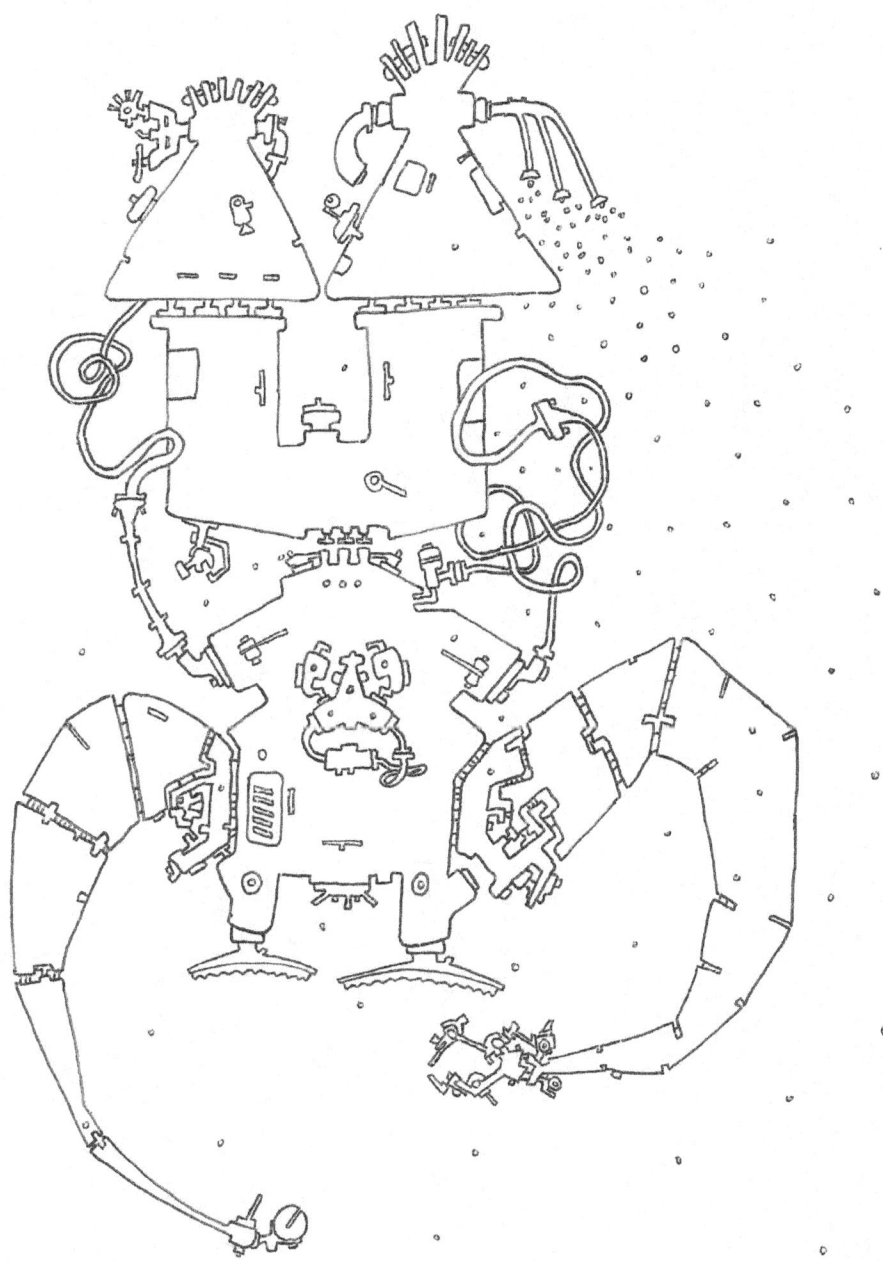

N° 38

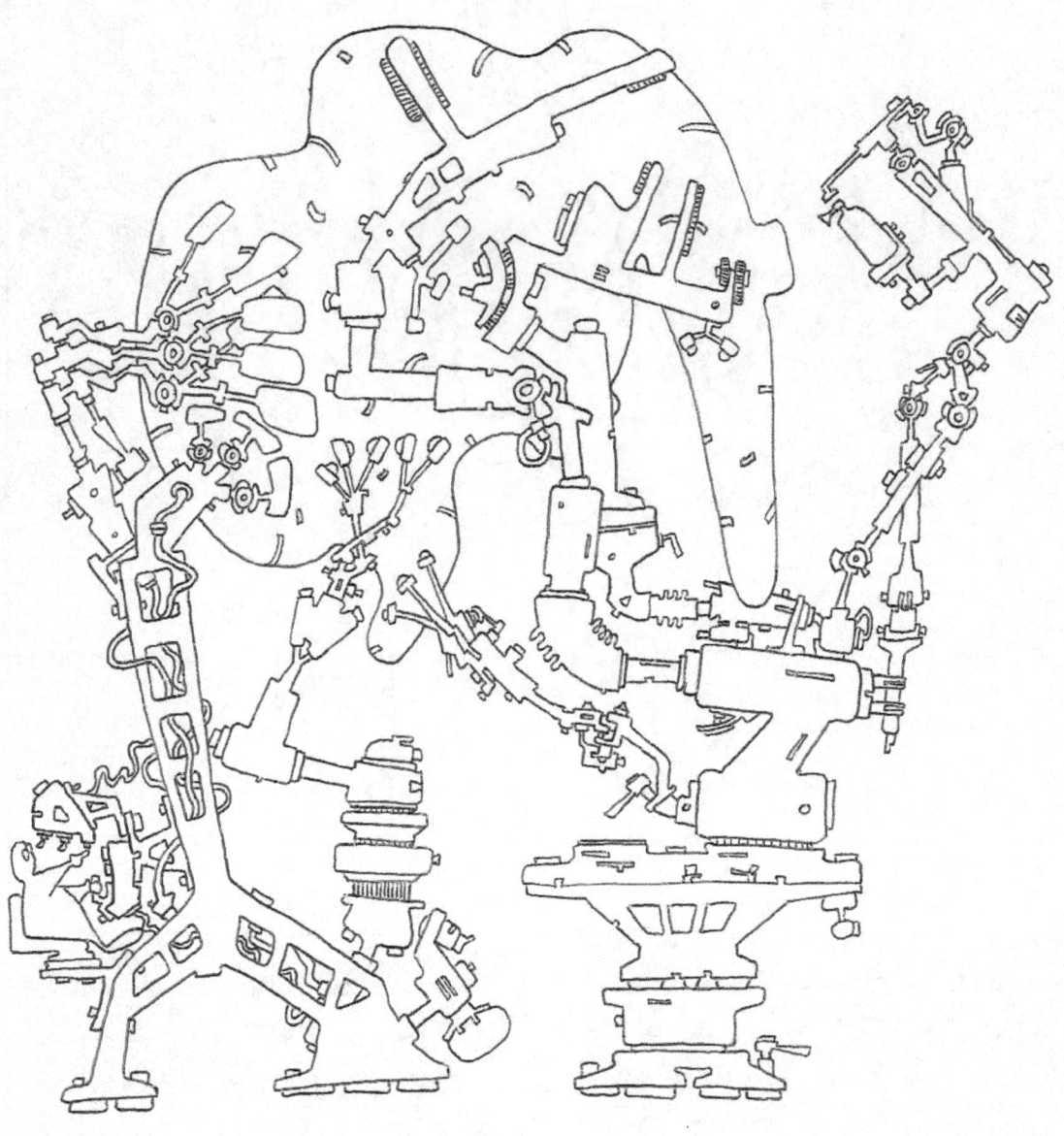

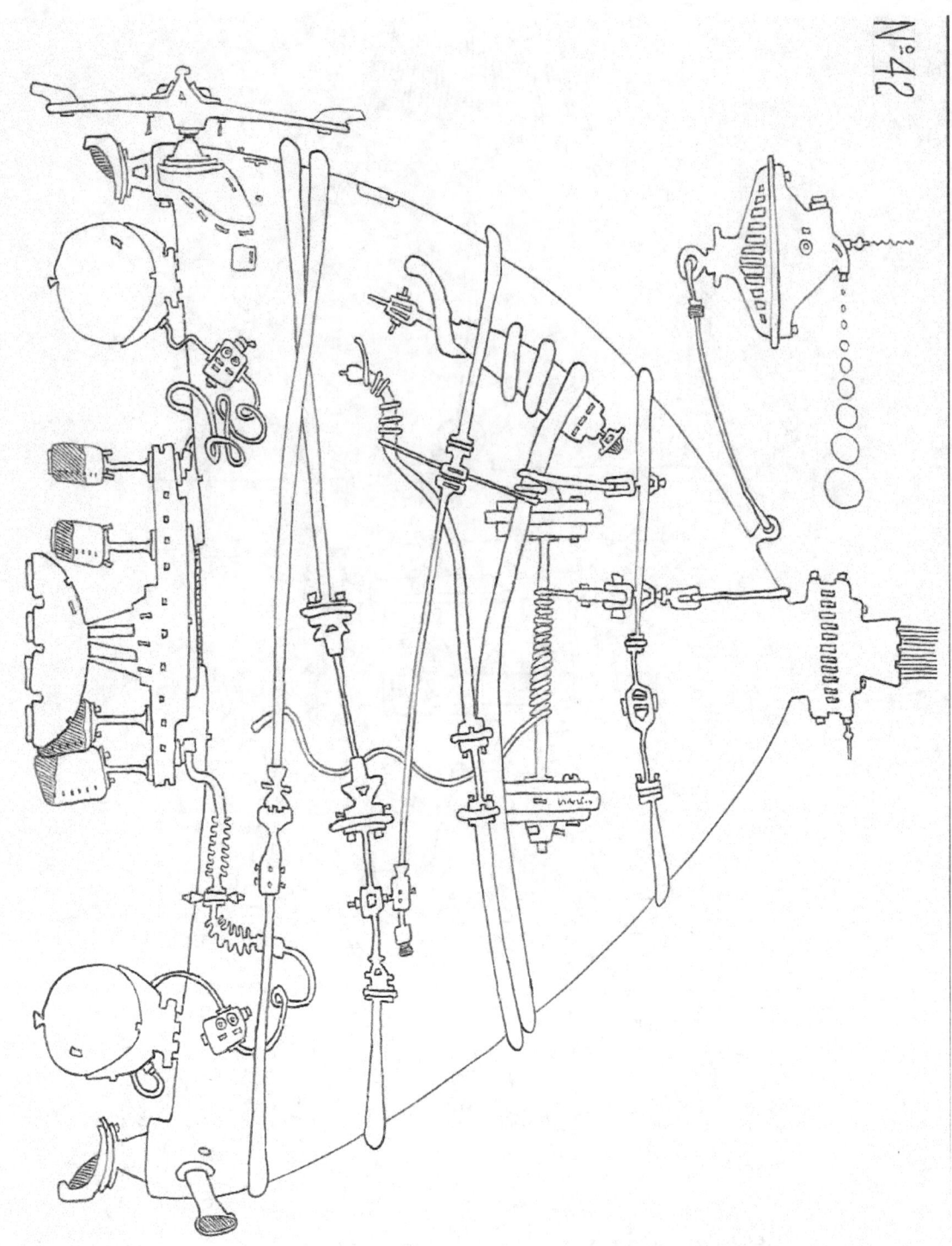

N°43

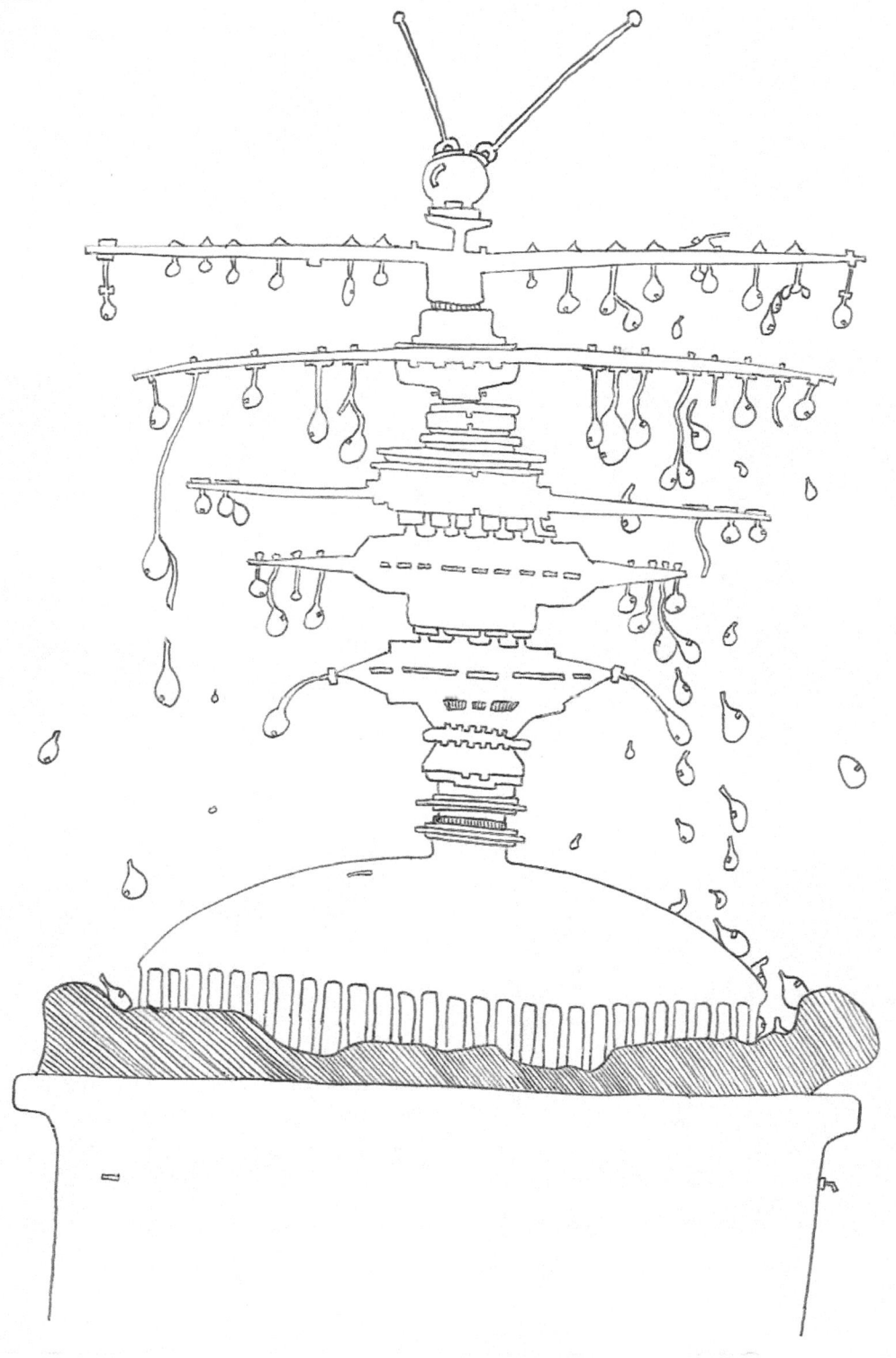

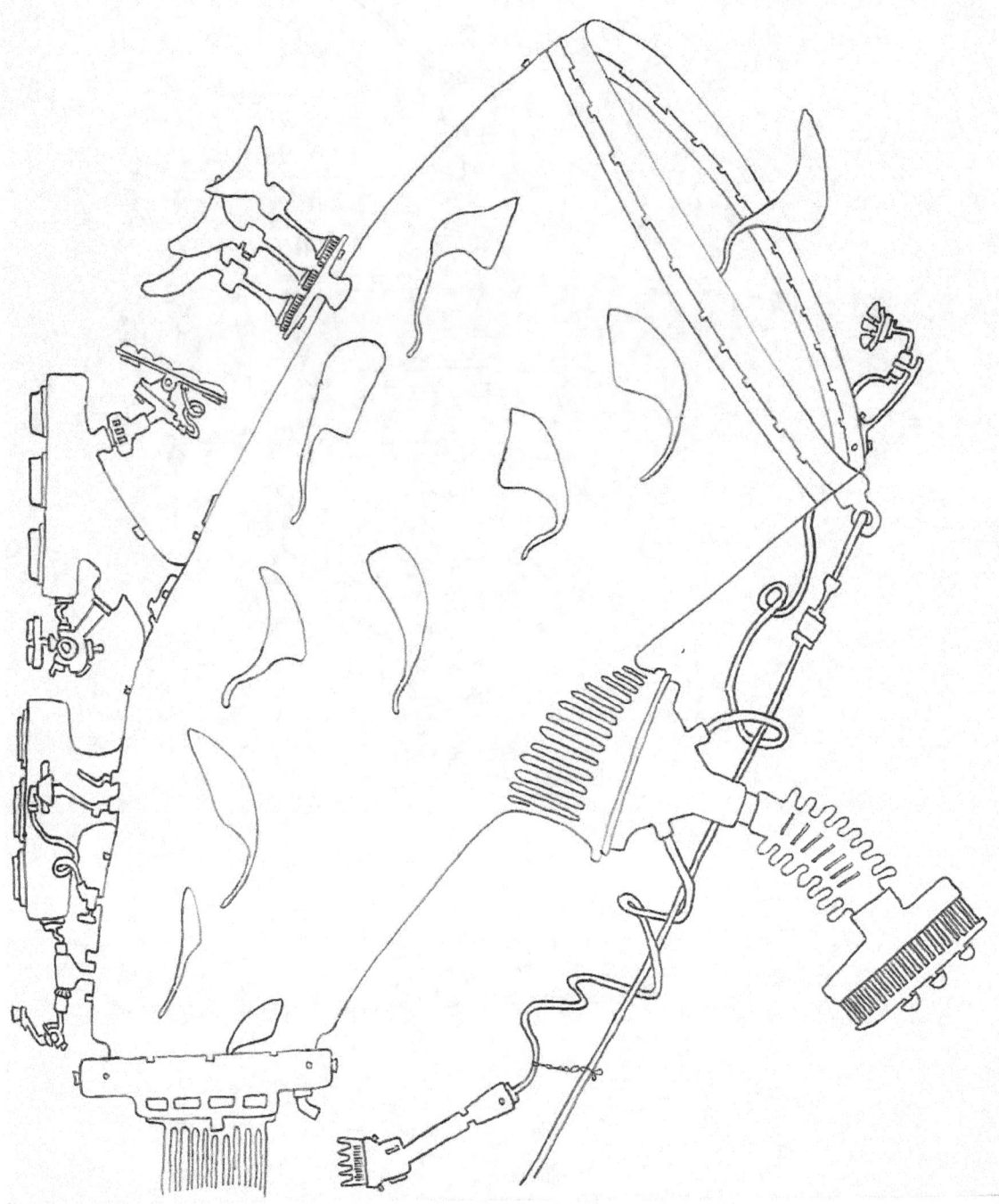

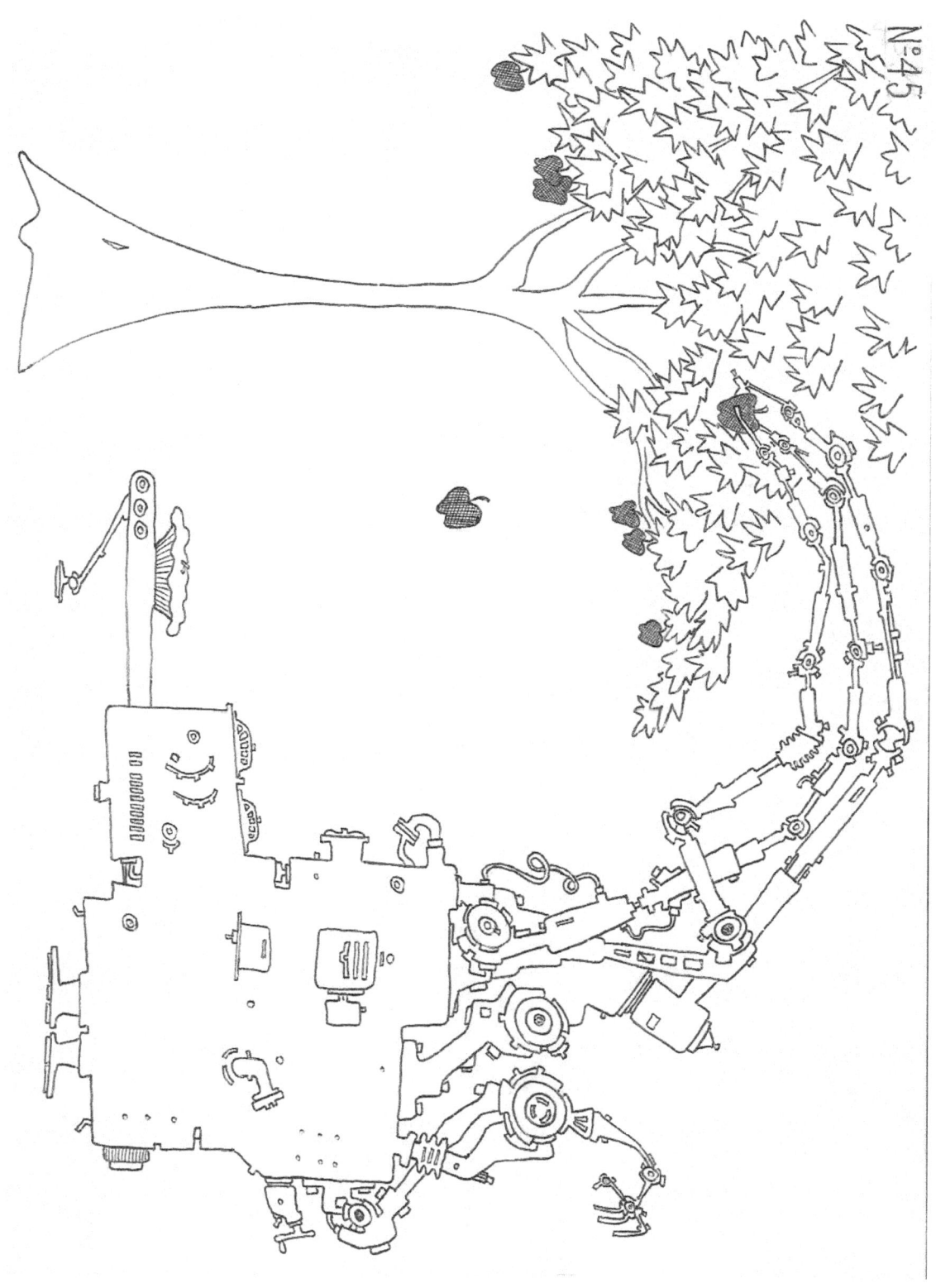

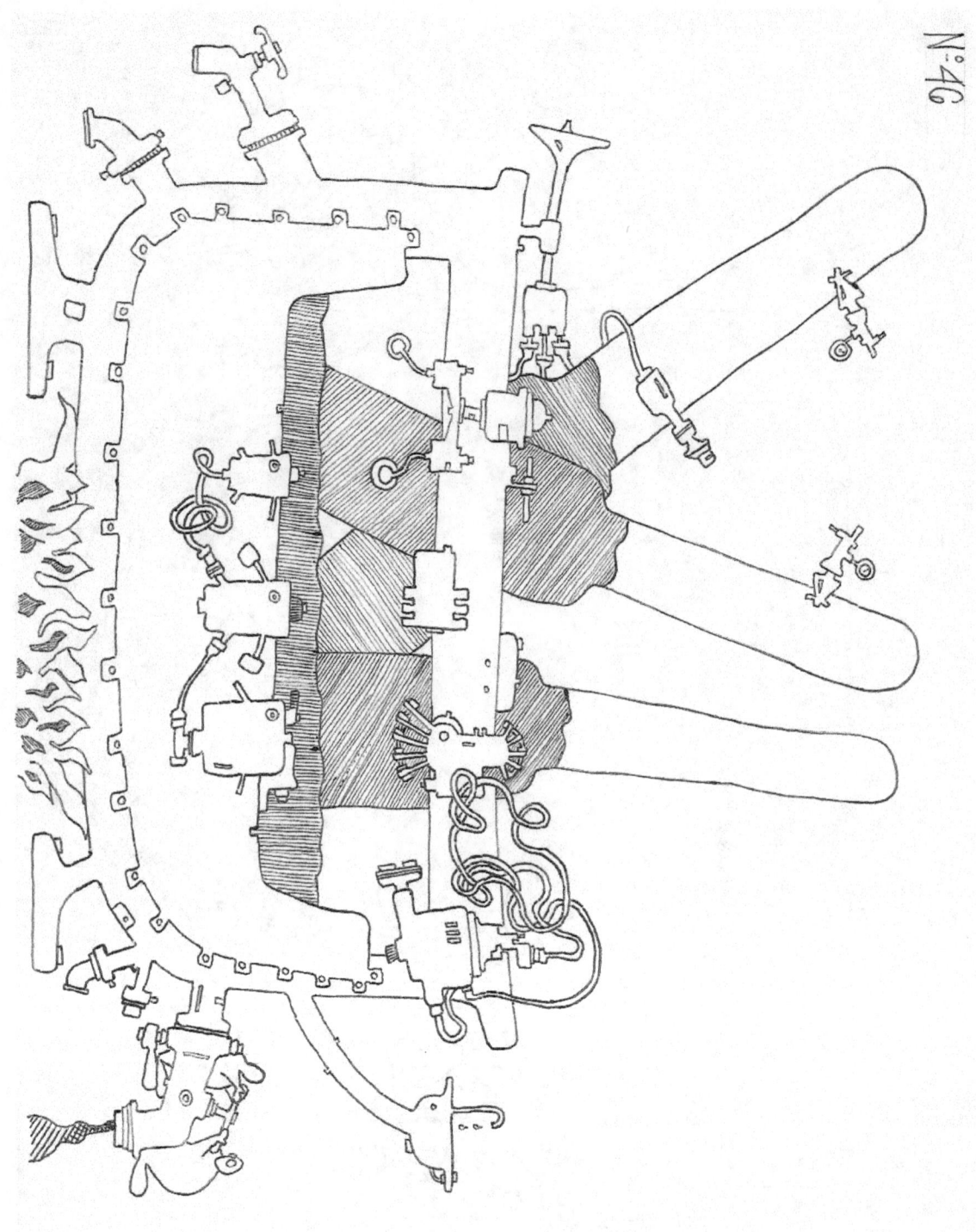

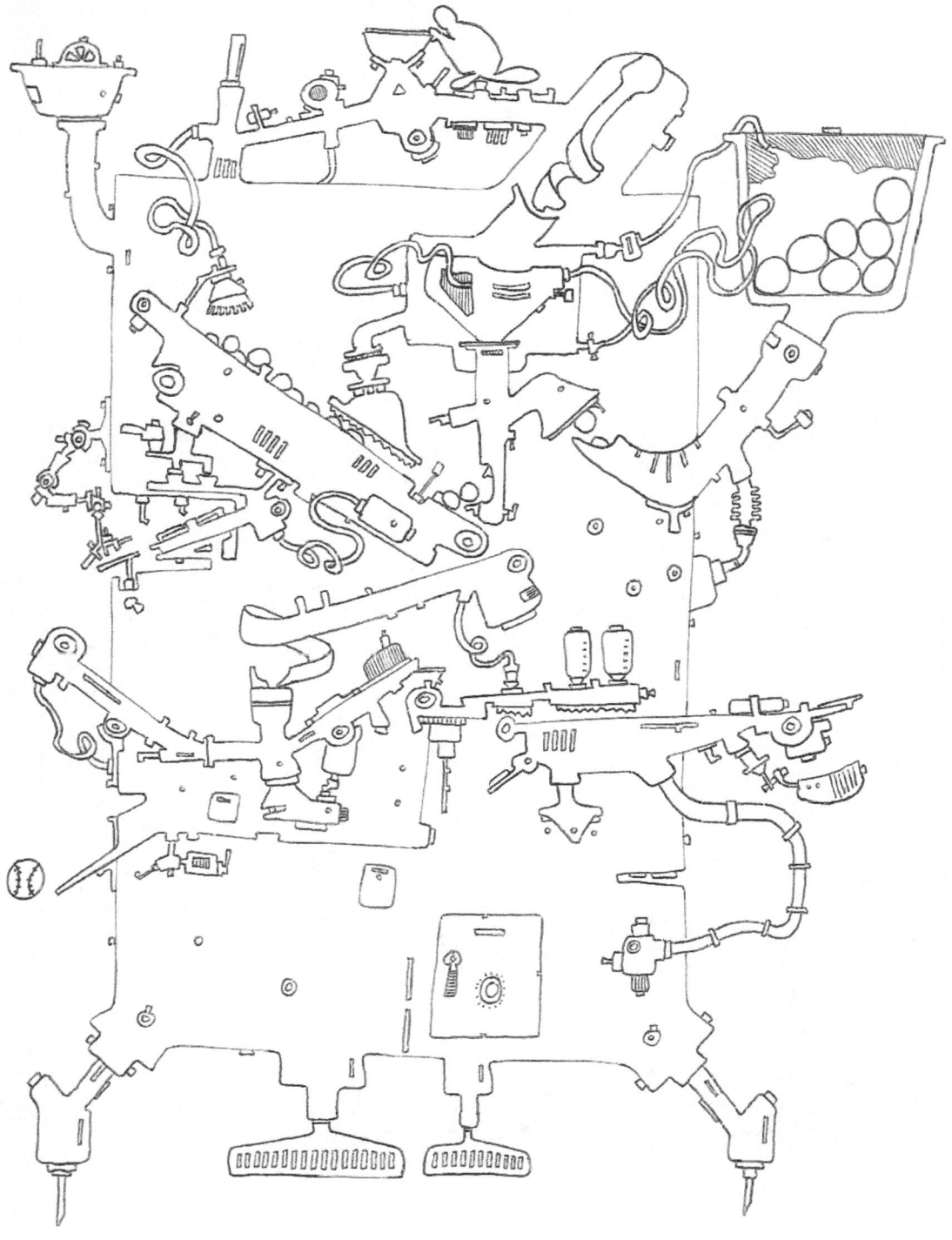

N° 48

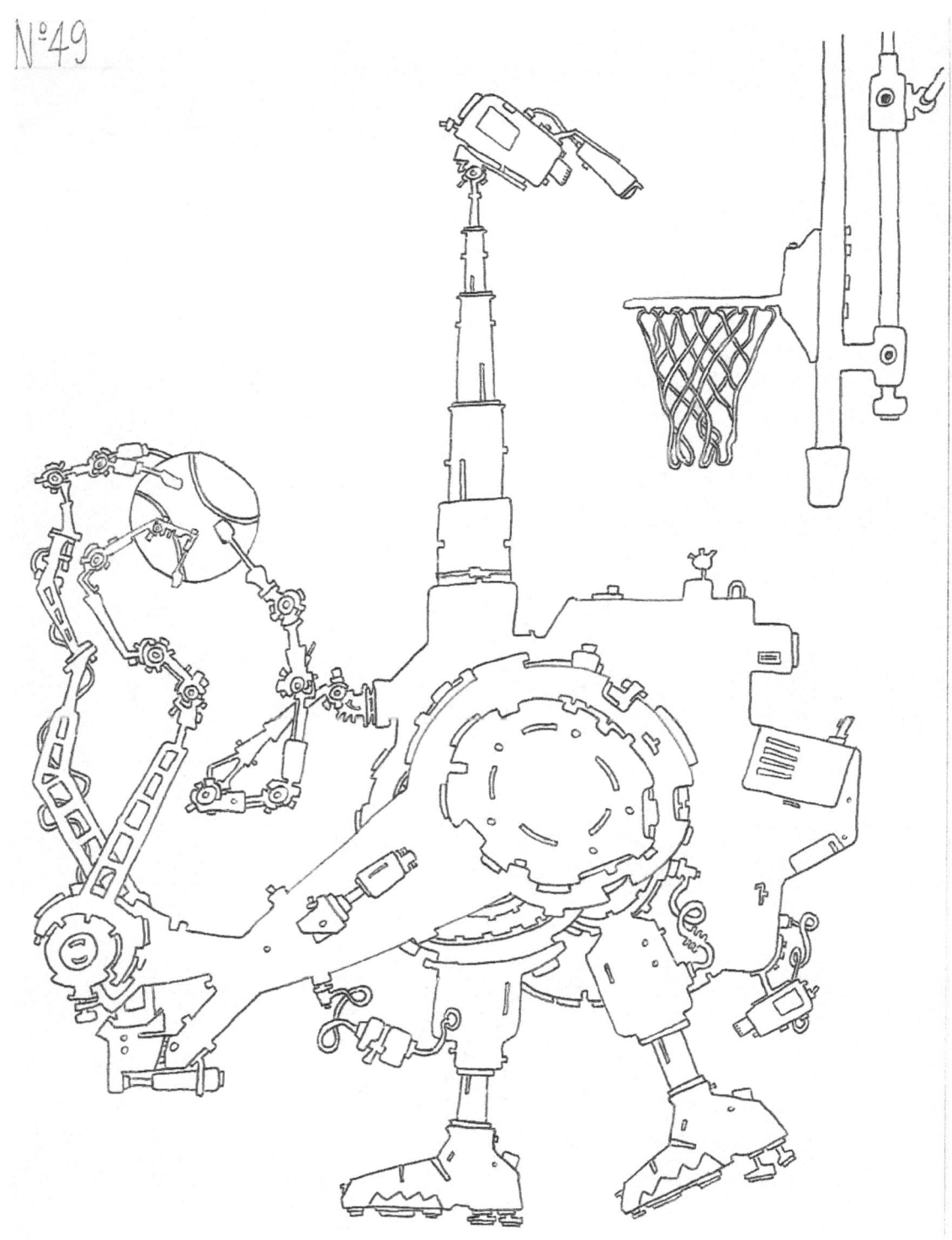

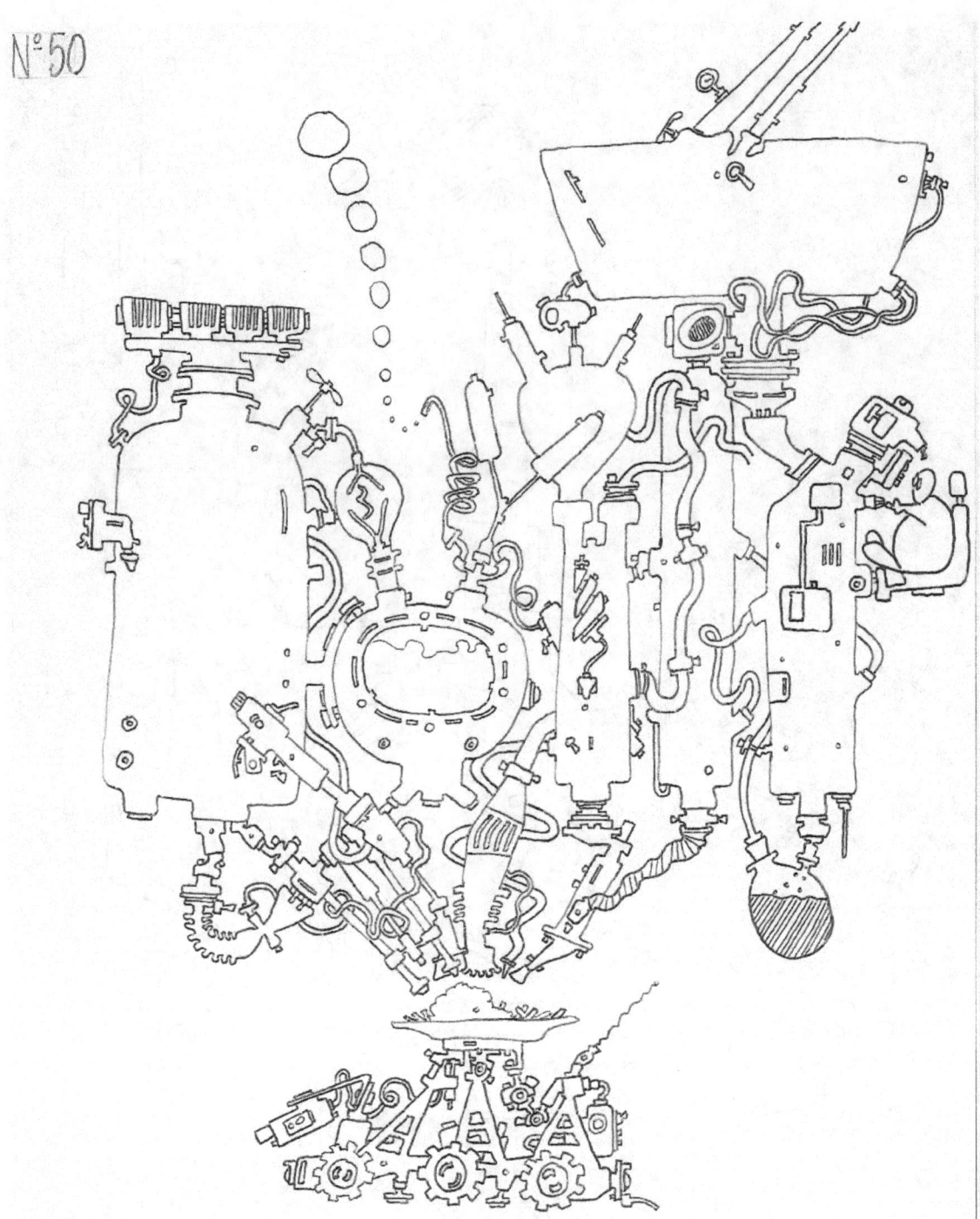

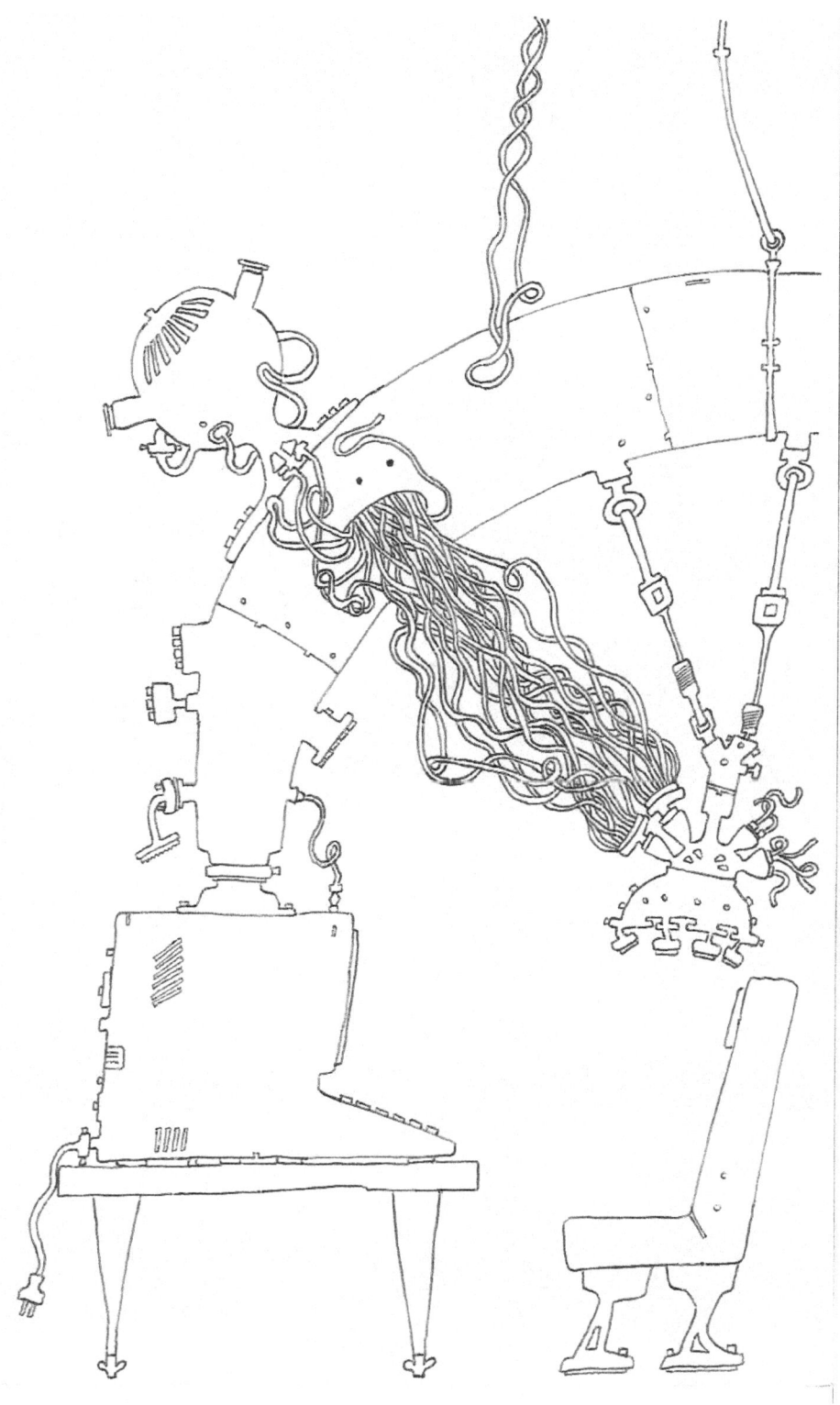

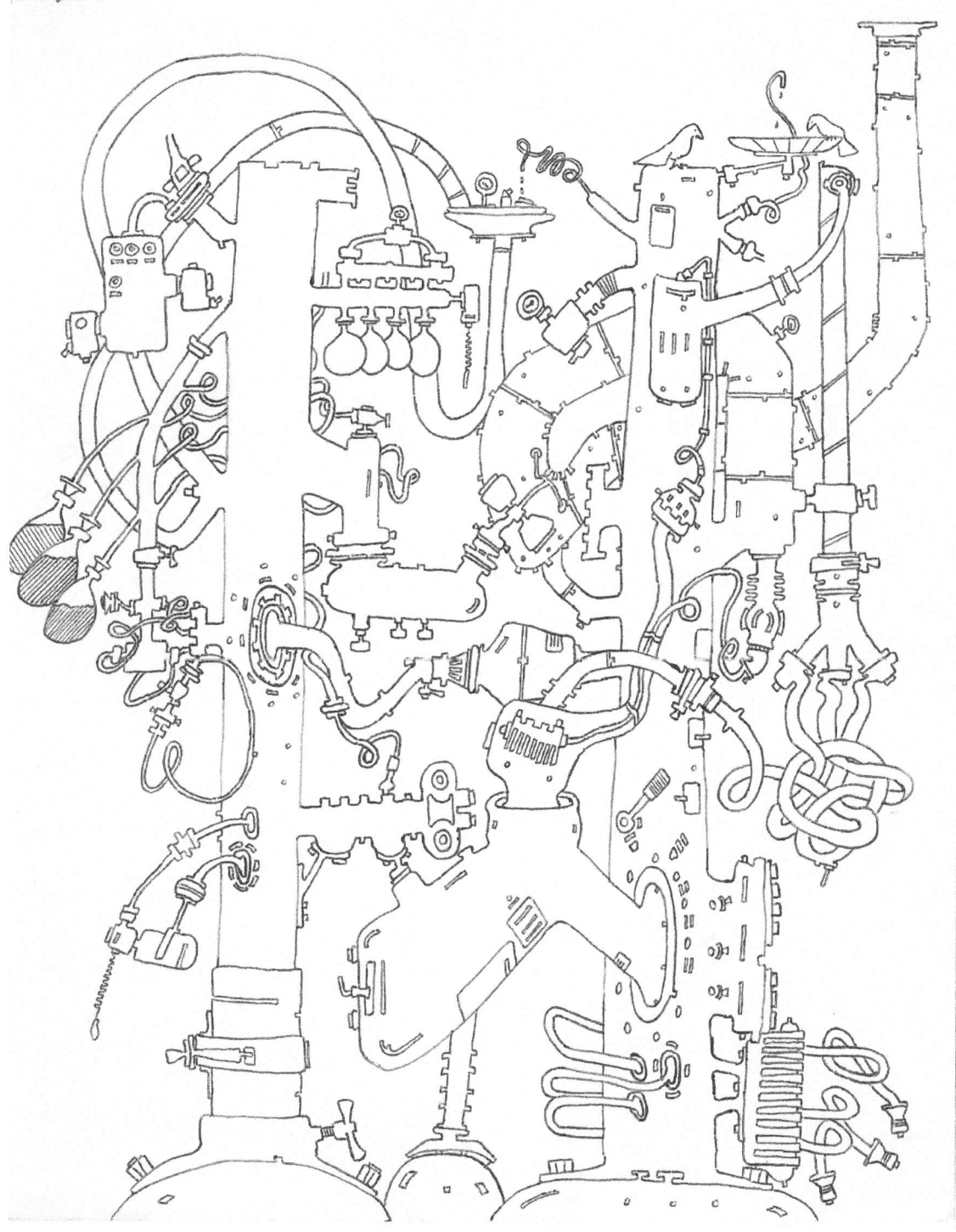

N°54

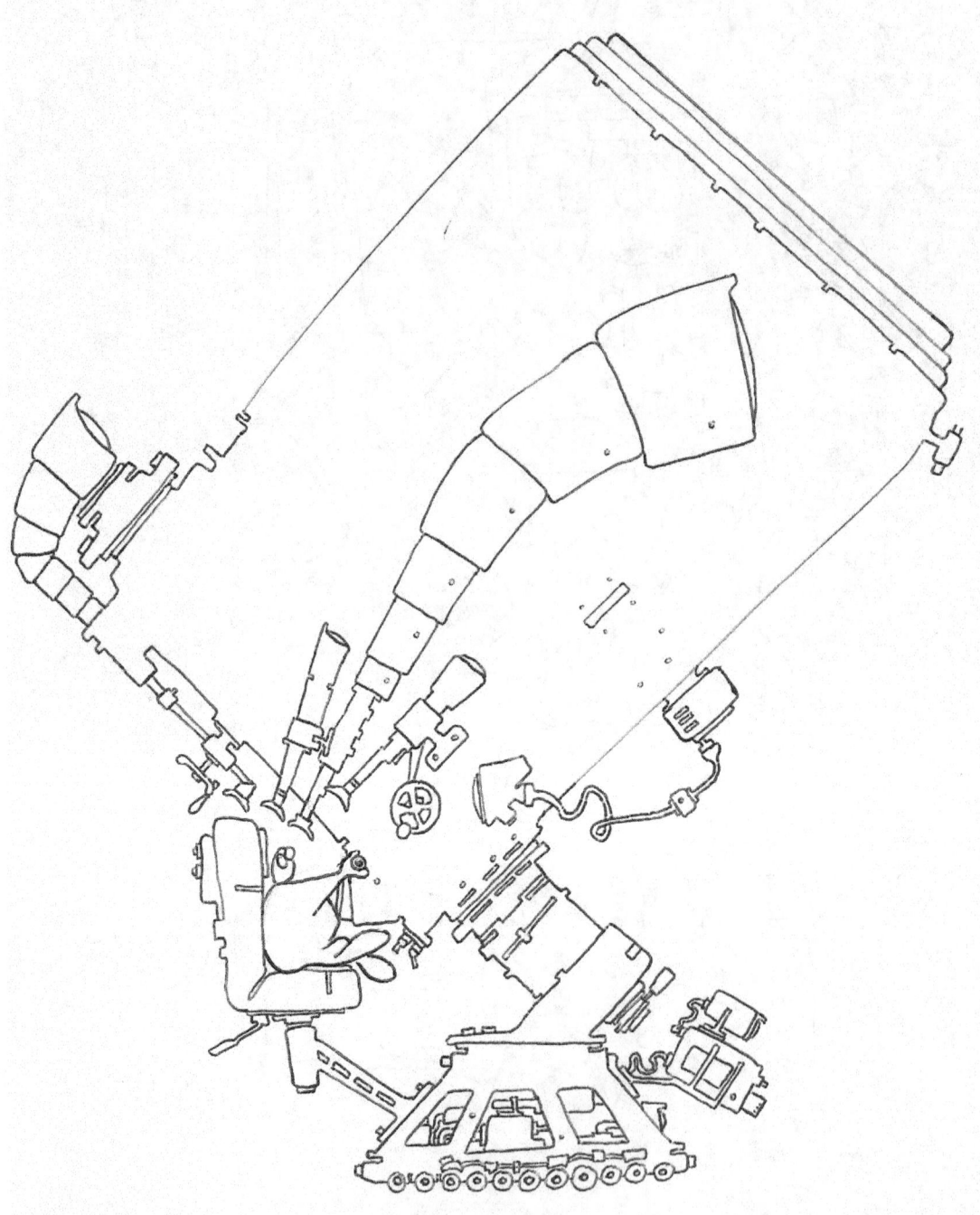

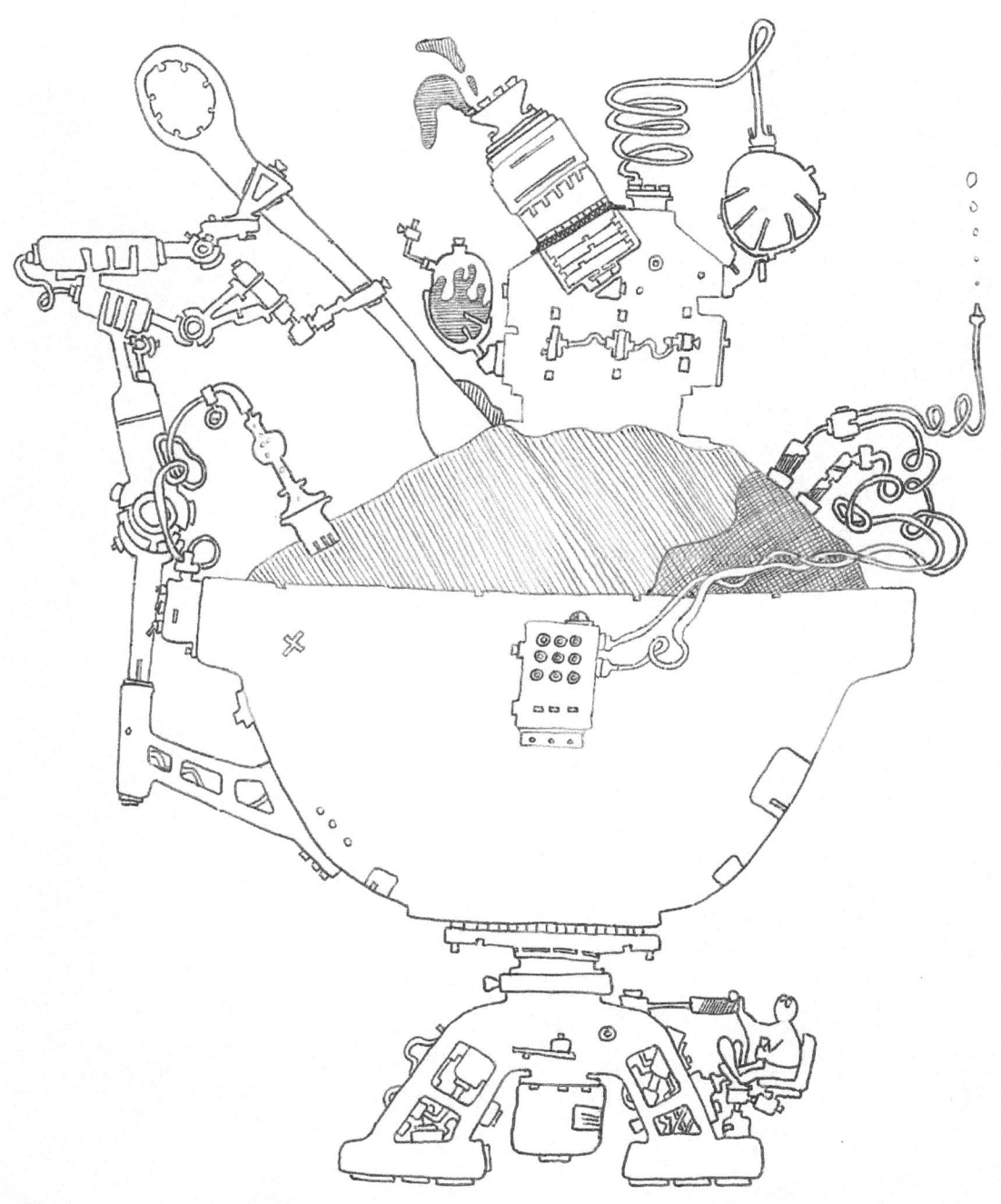

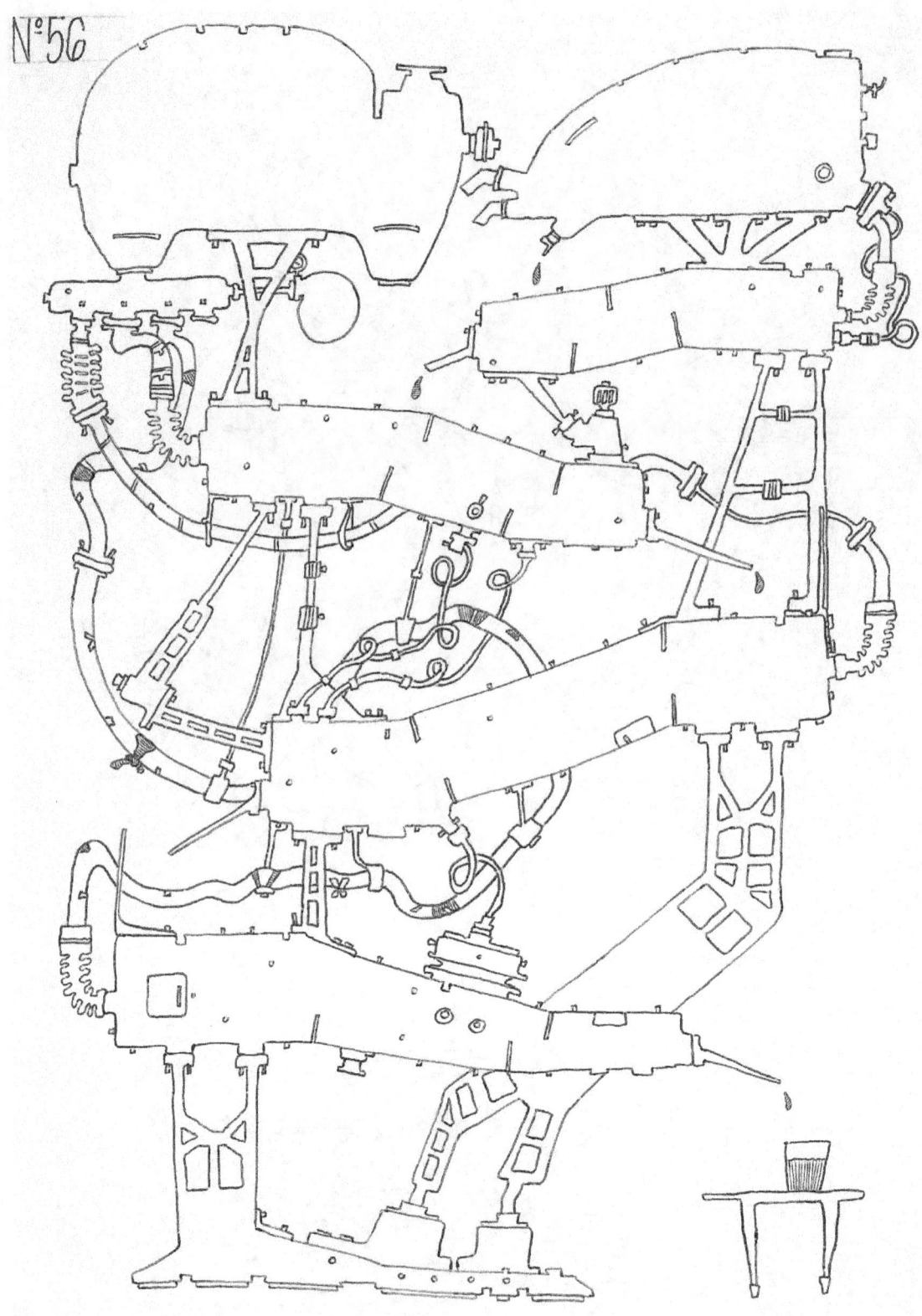

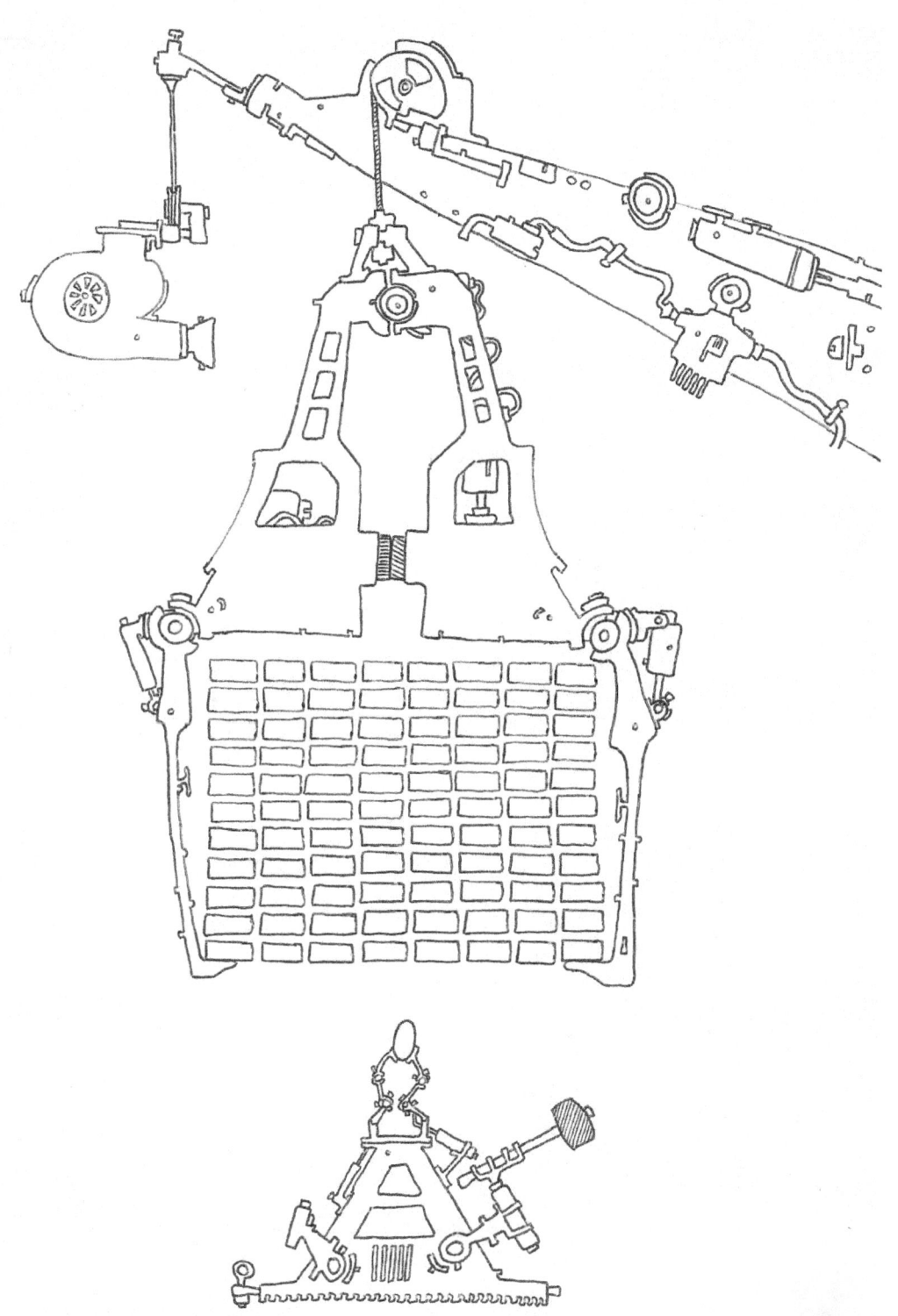

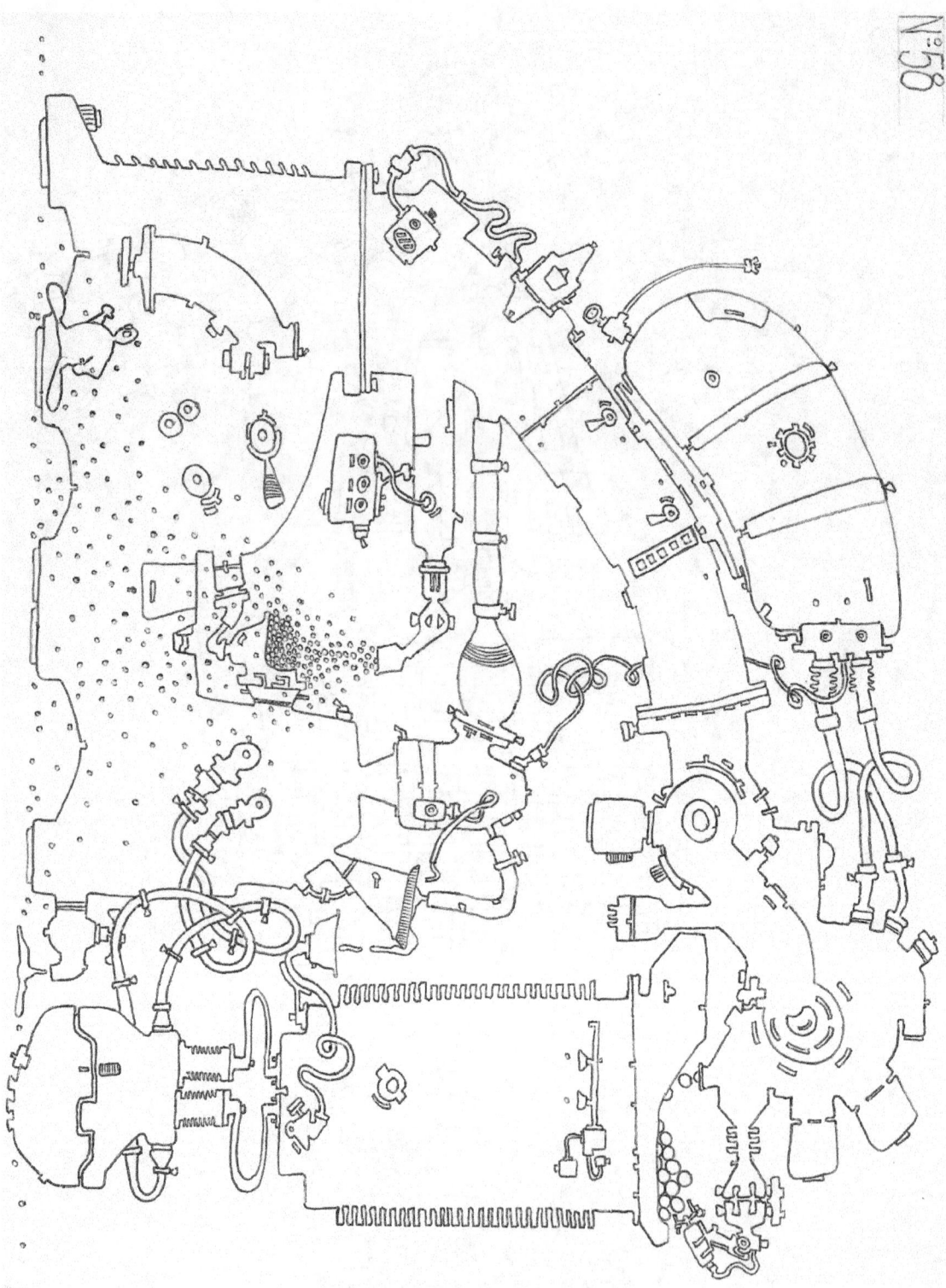

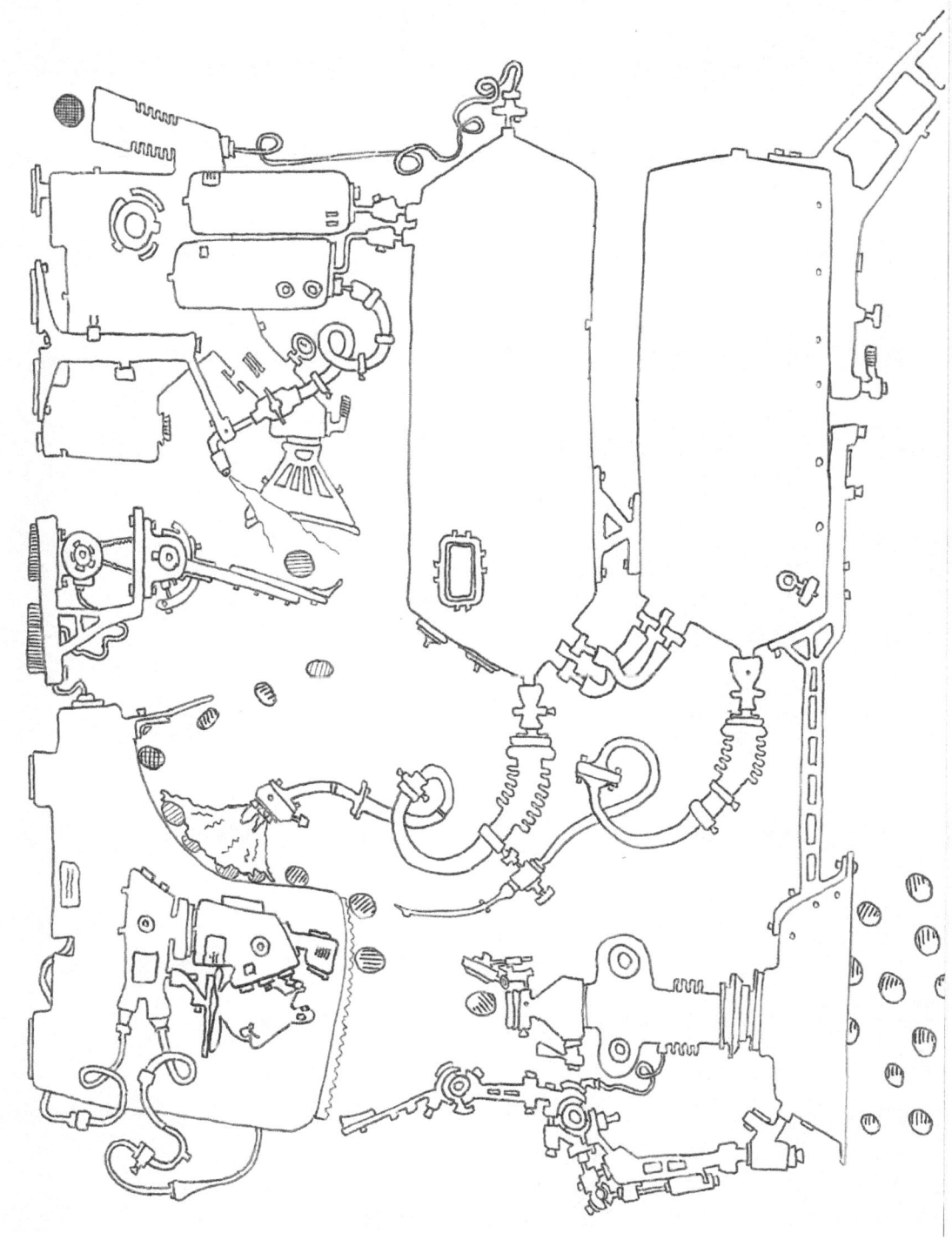

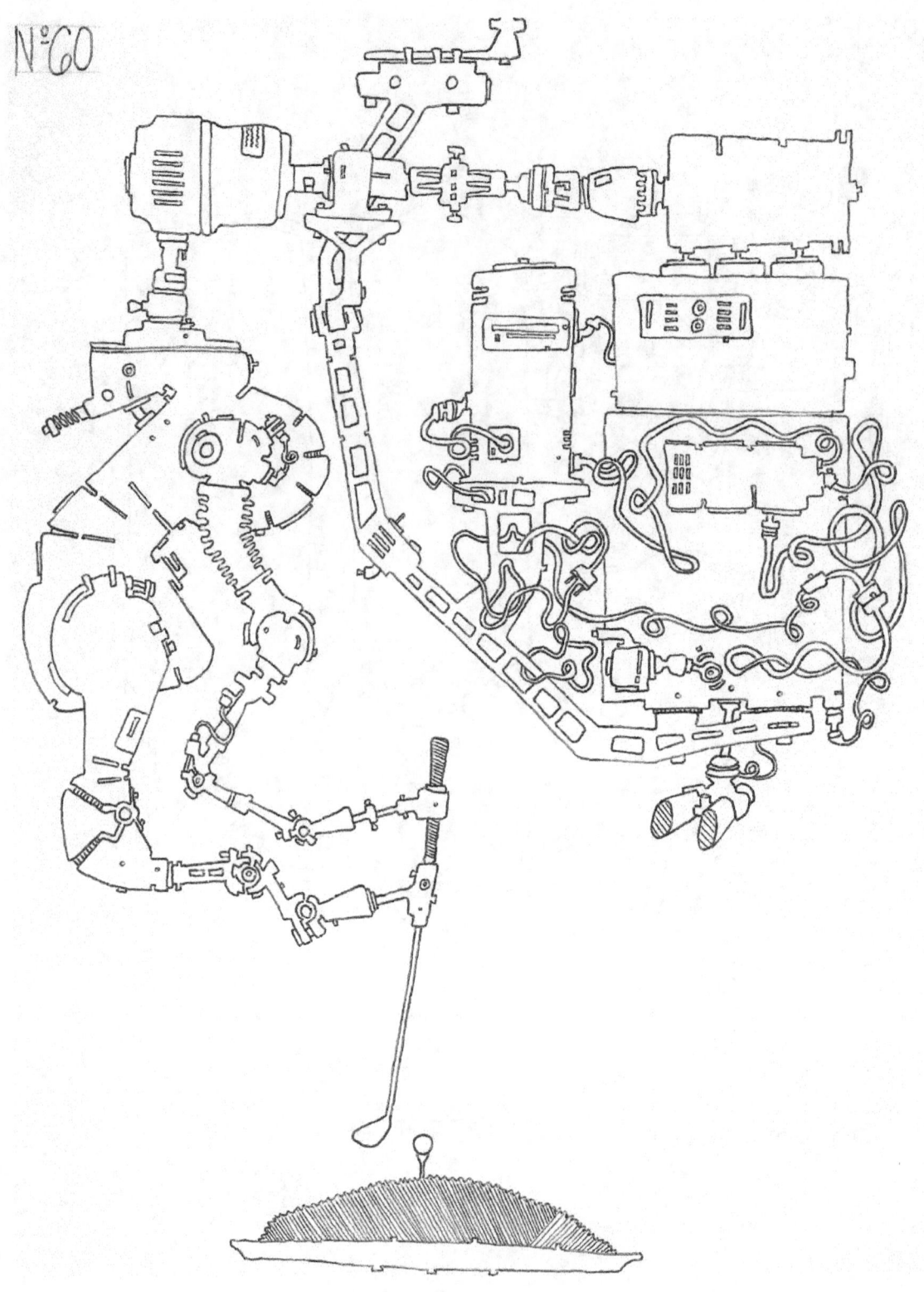

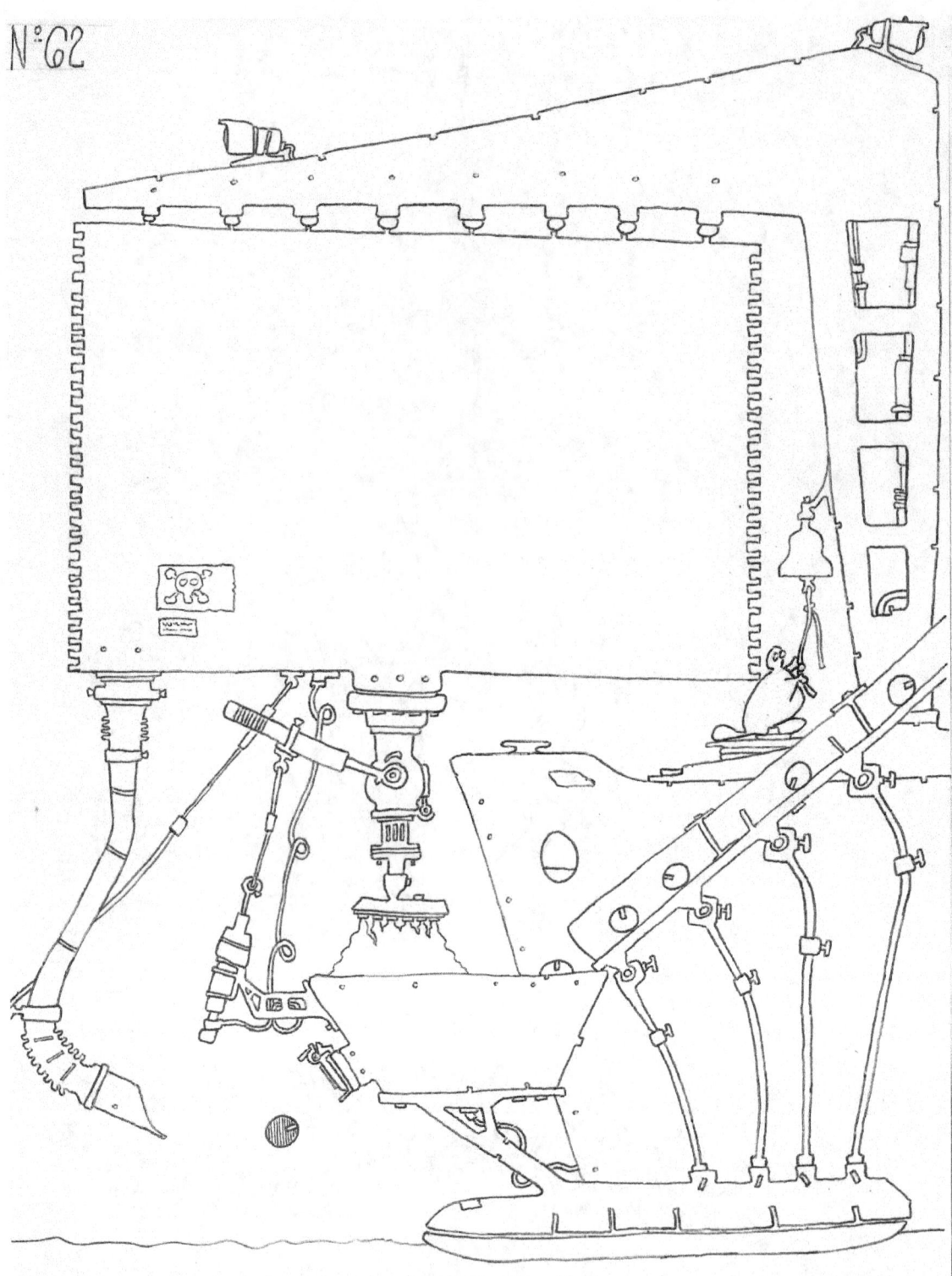

N°63

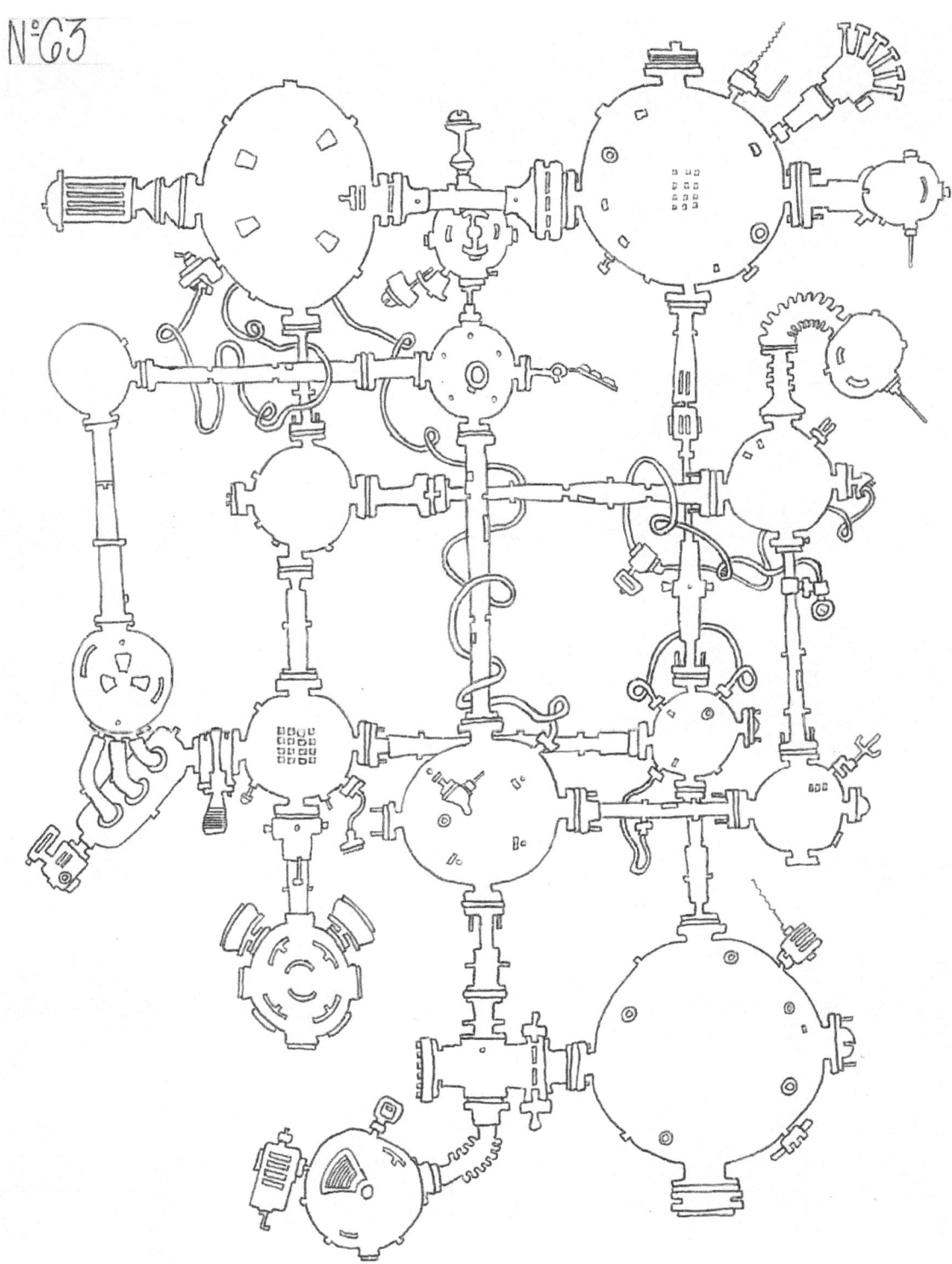

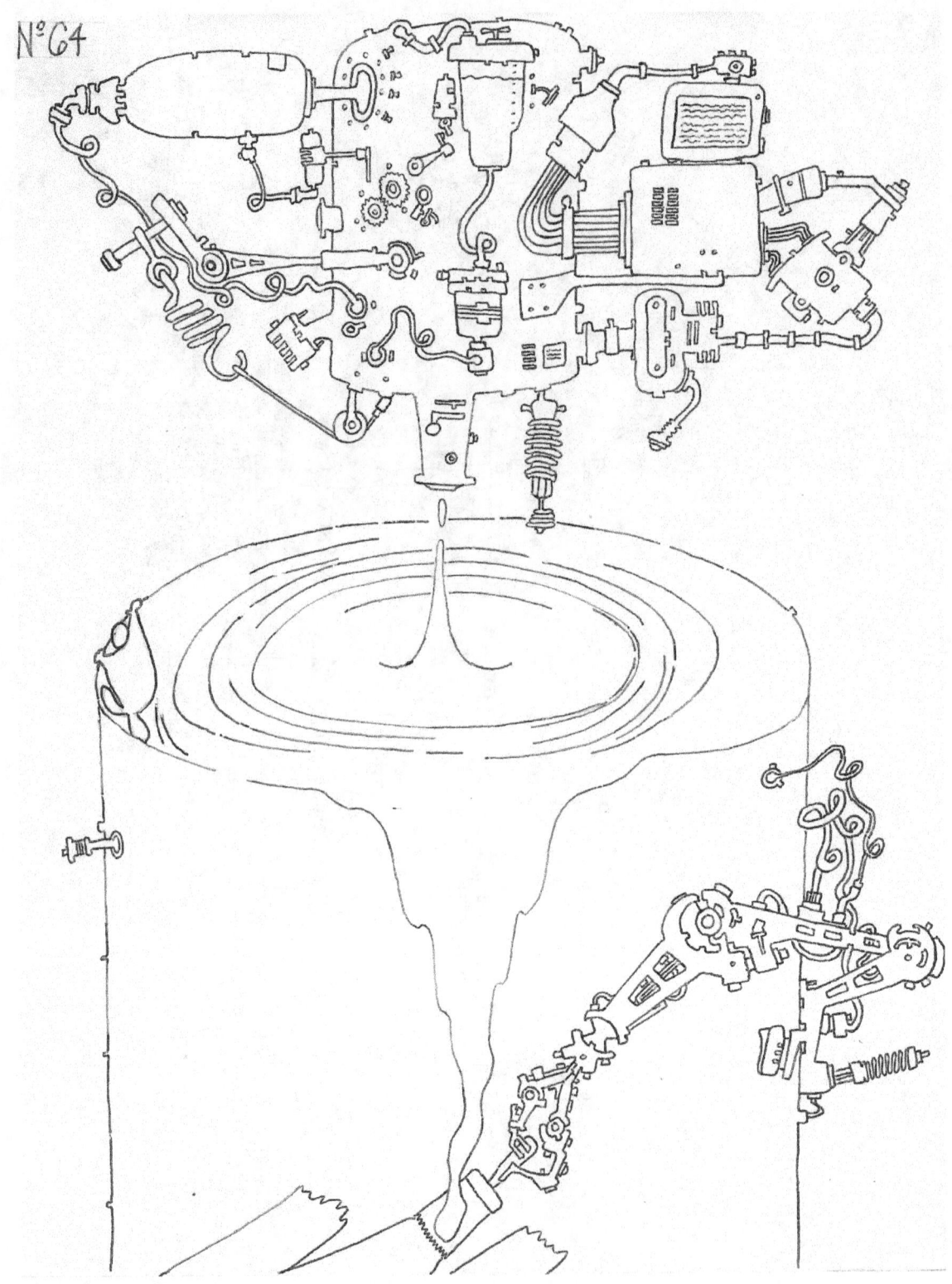

N°65

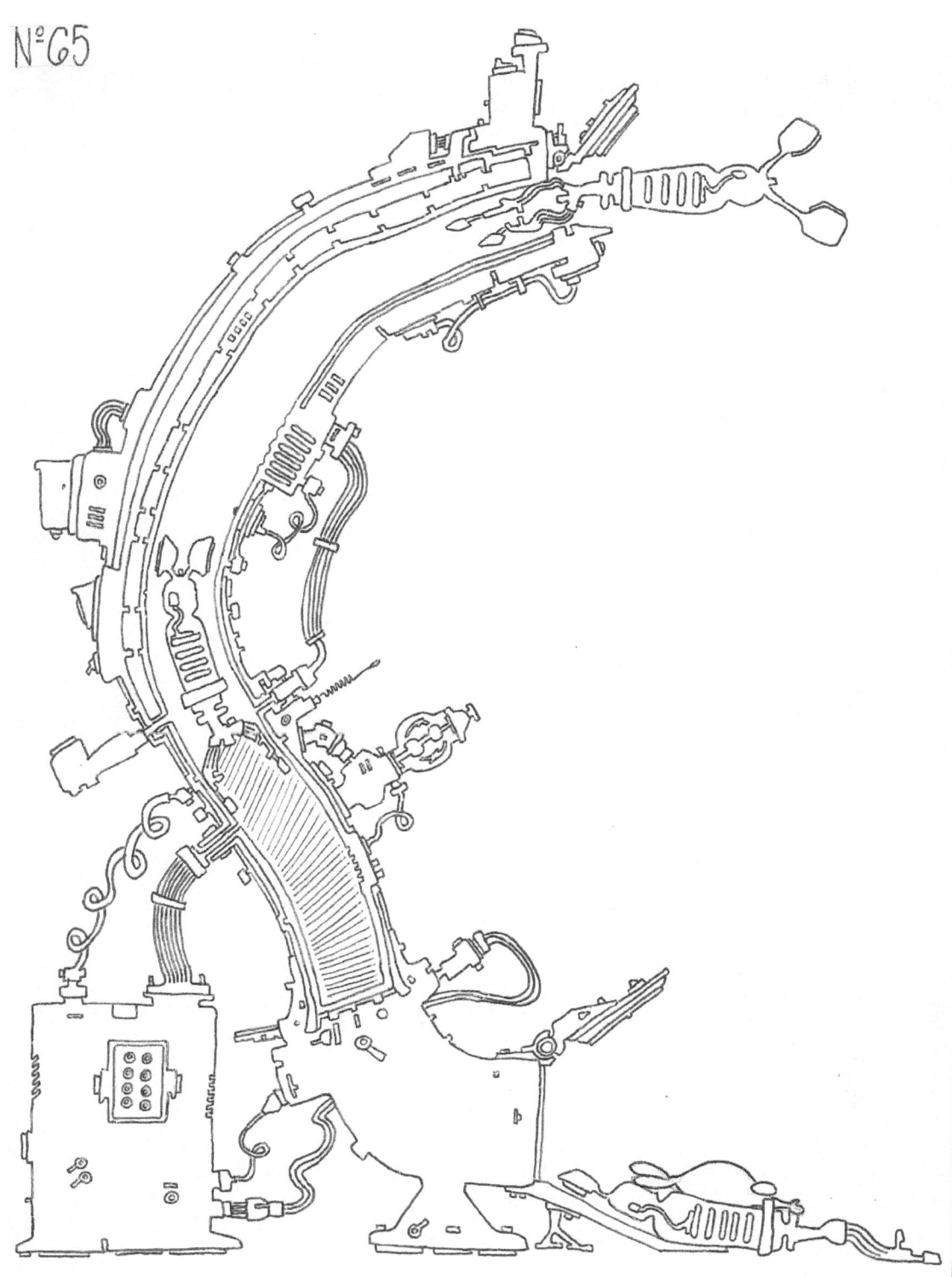

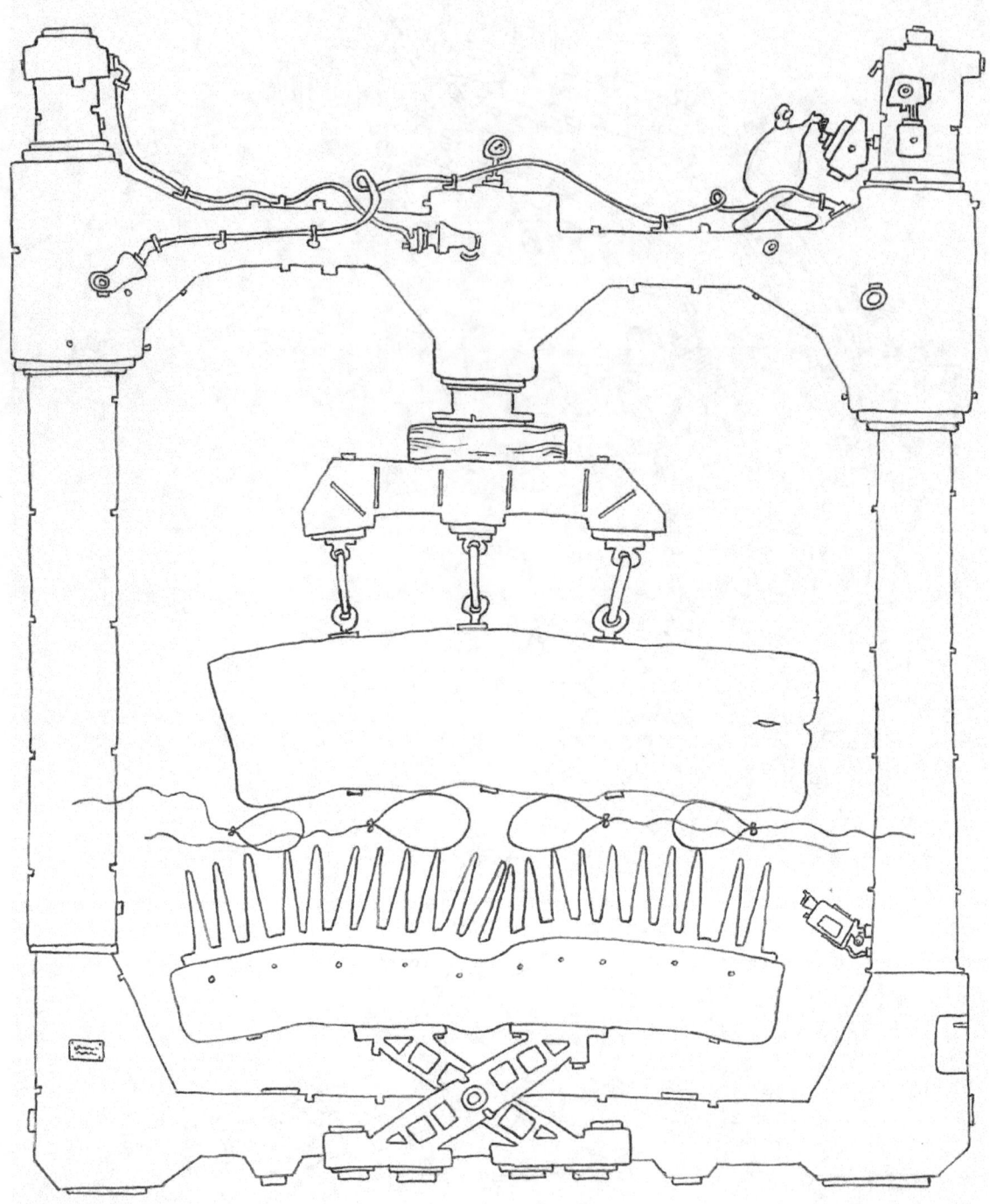

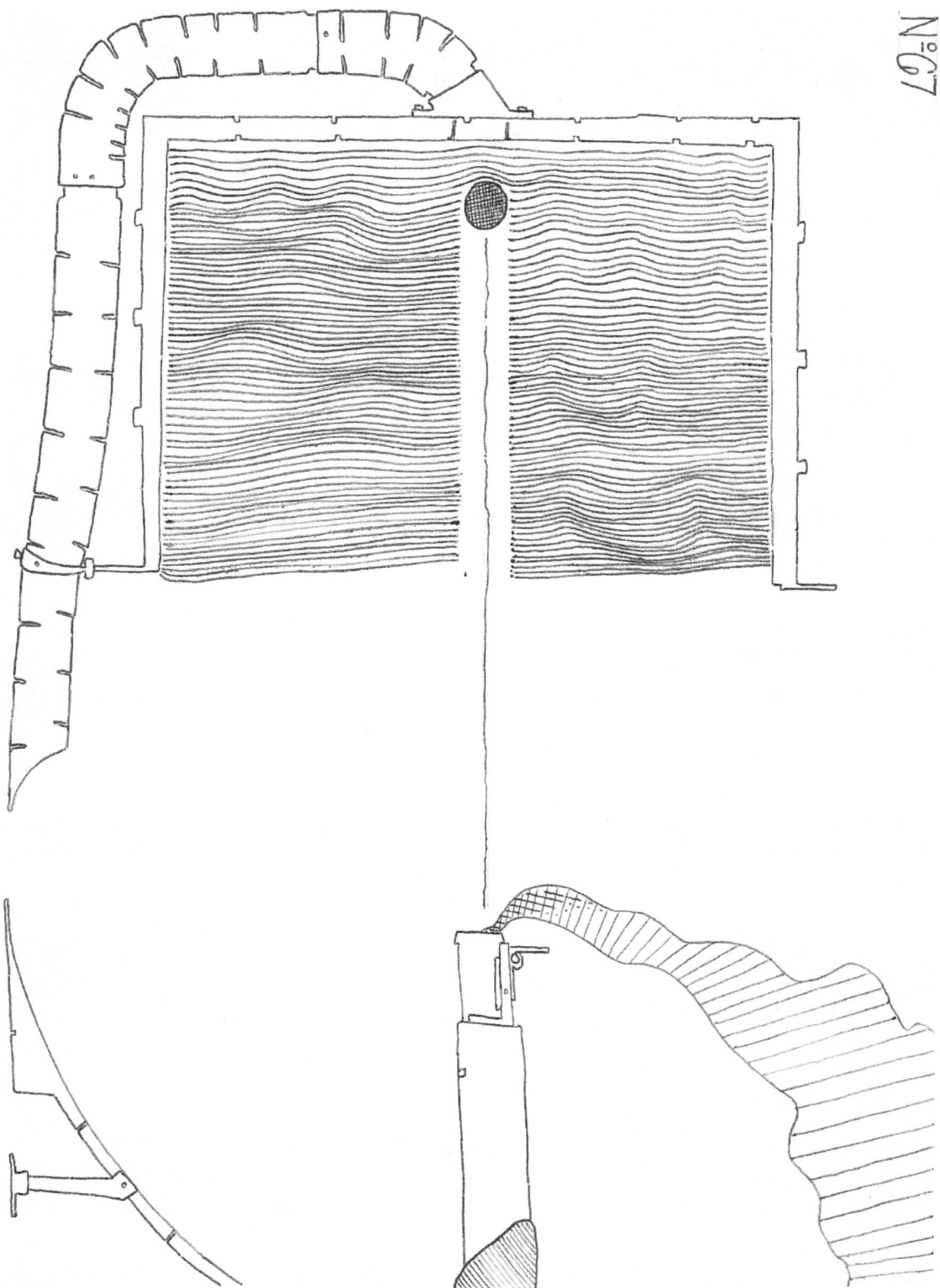

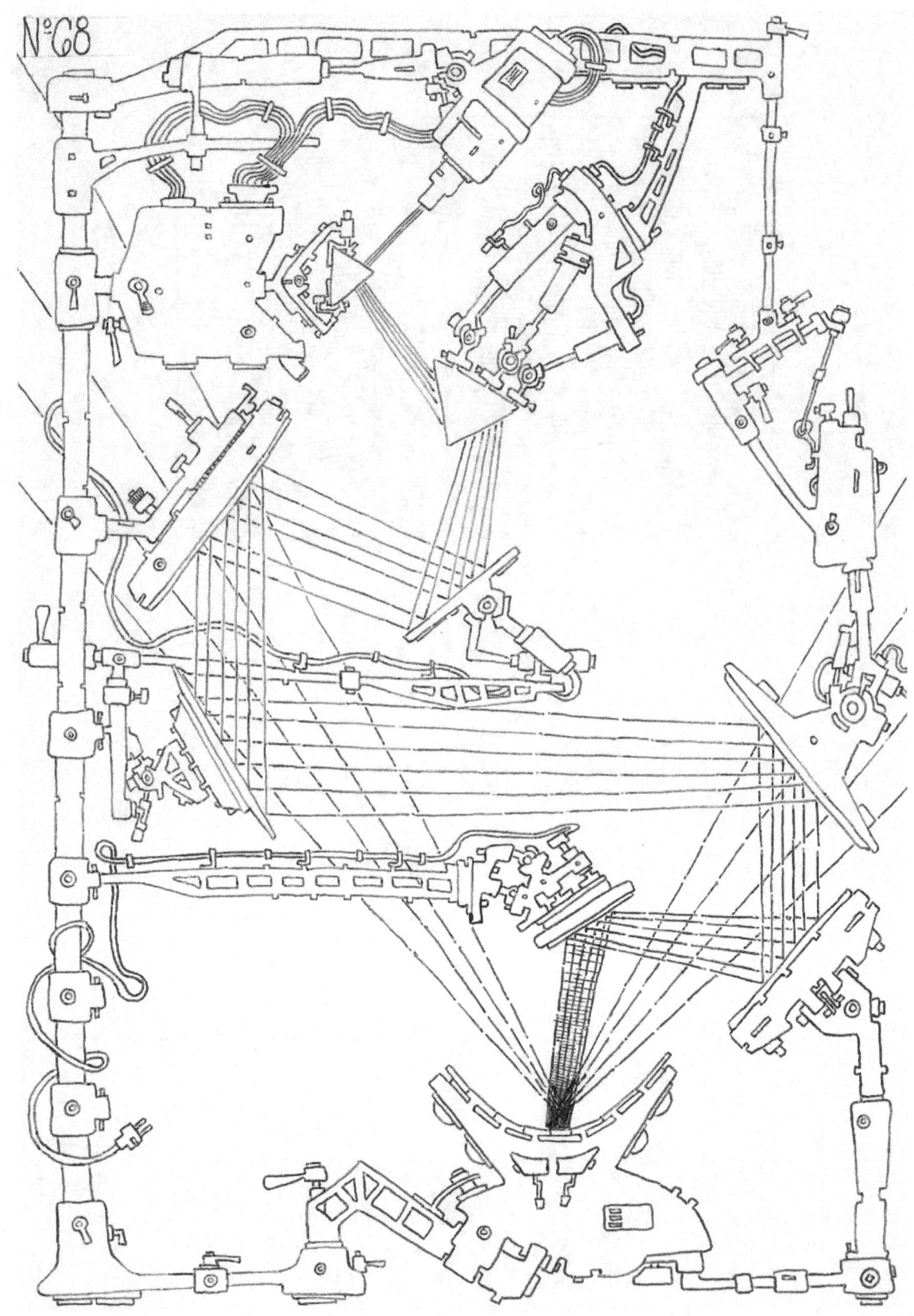

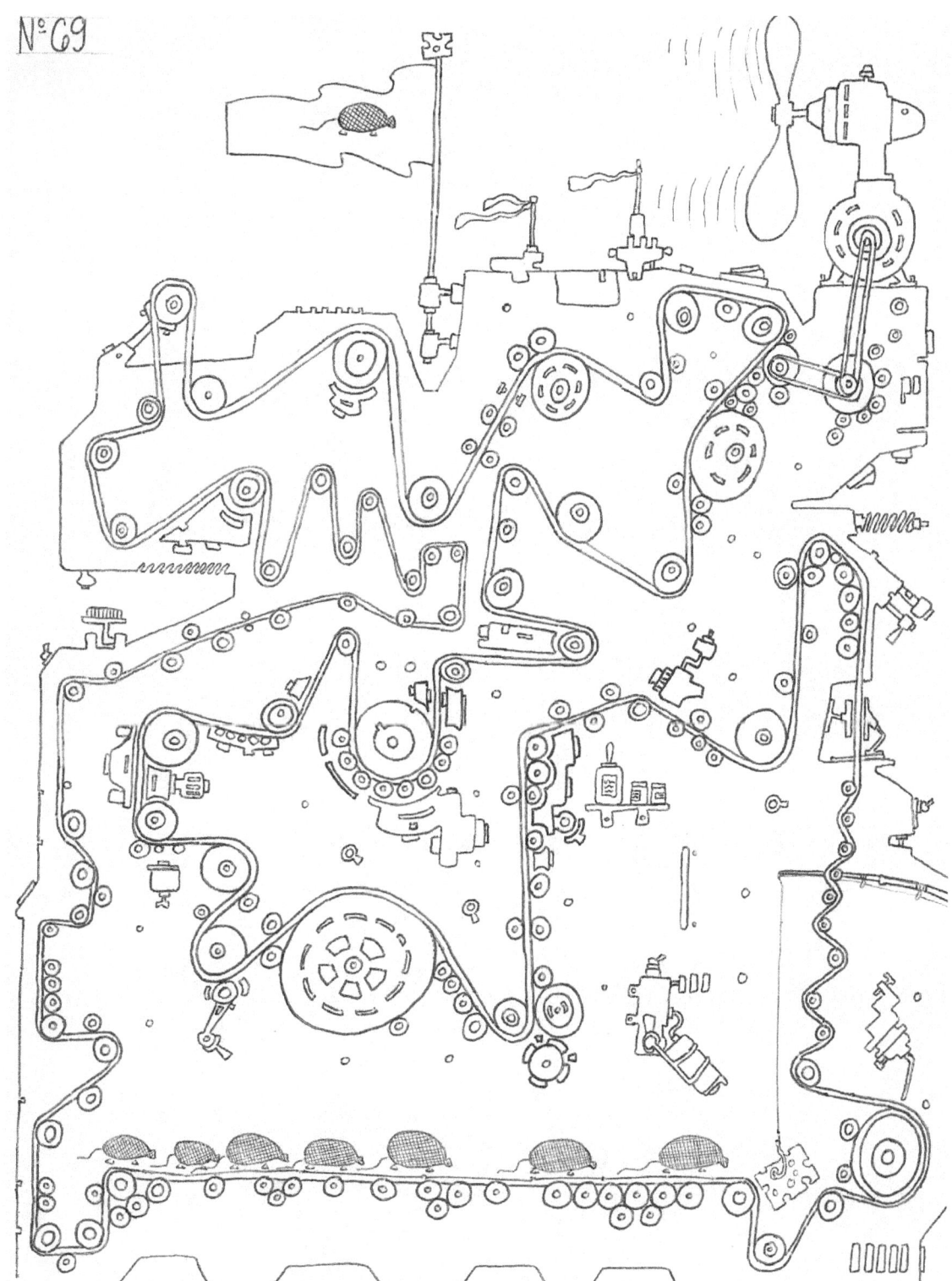

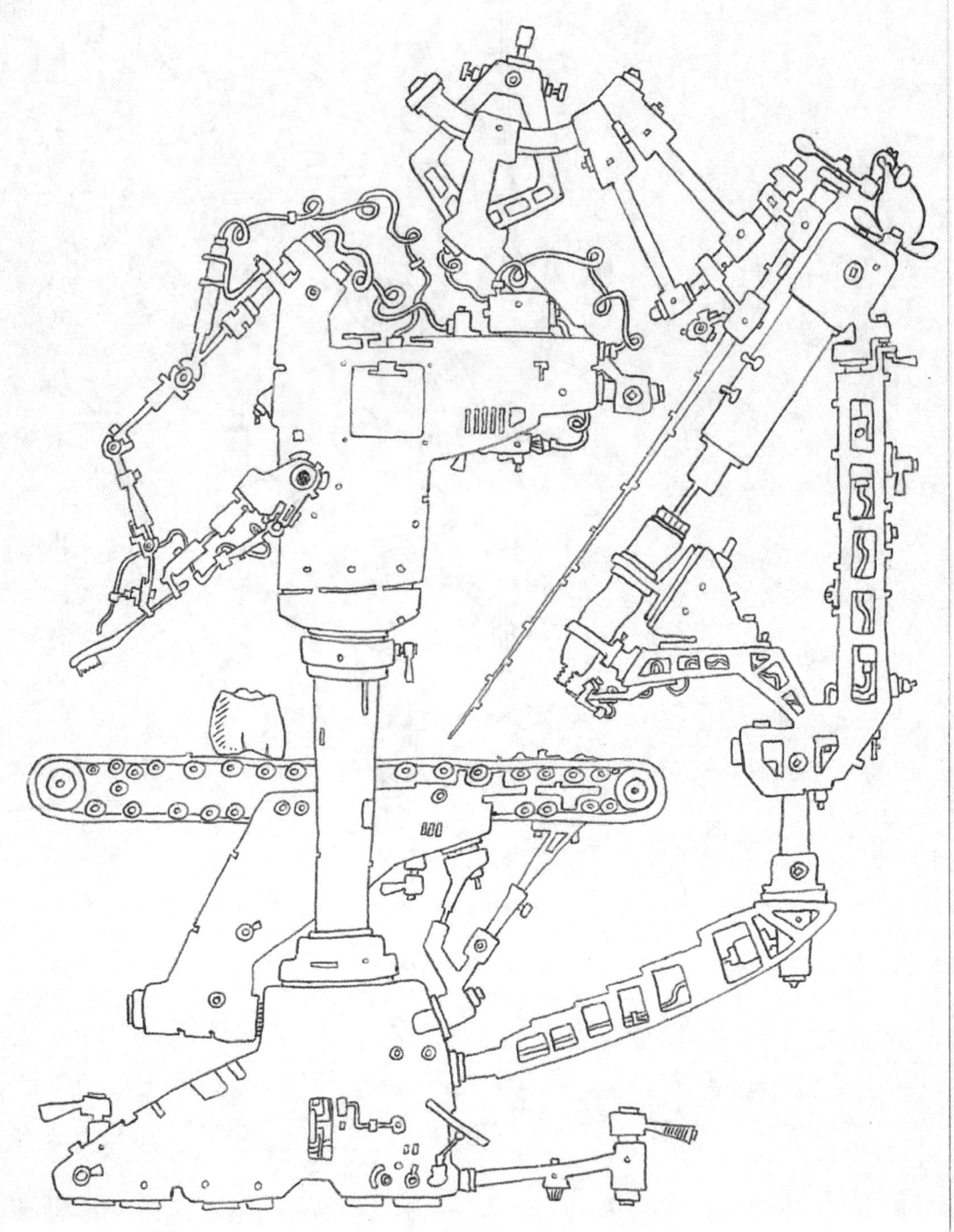

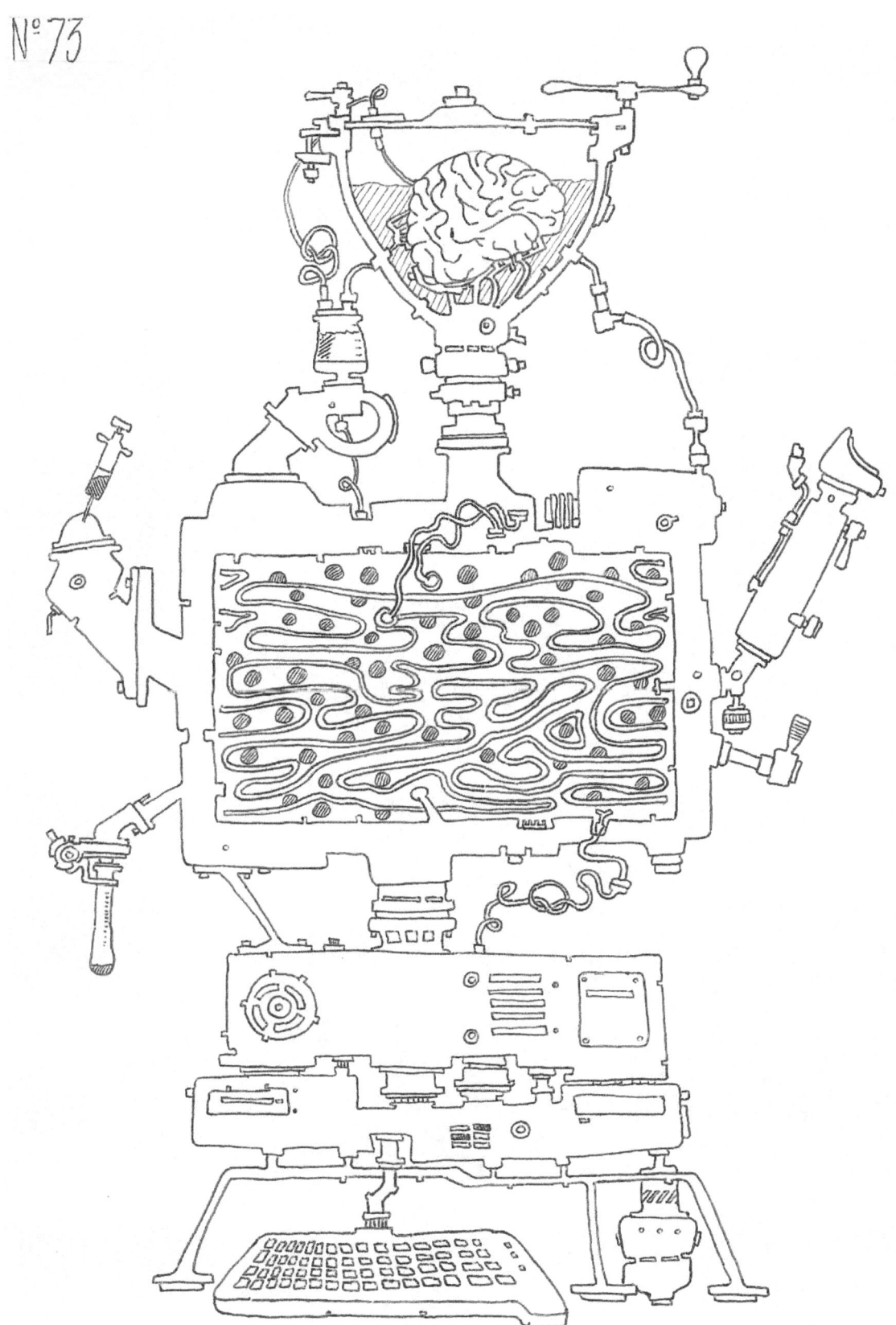

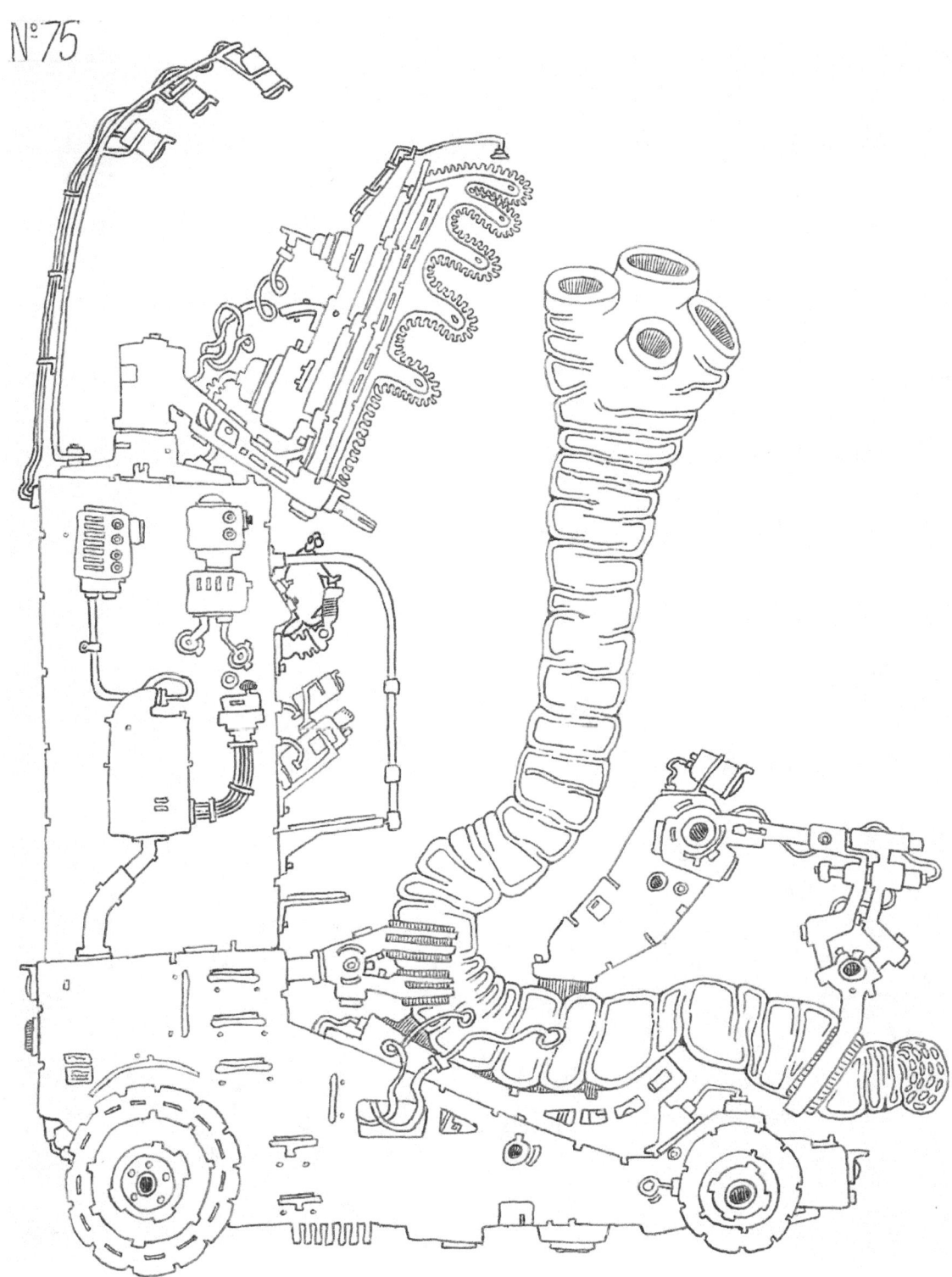

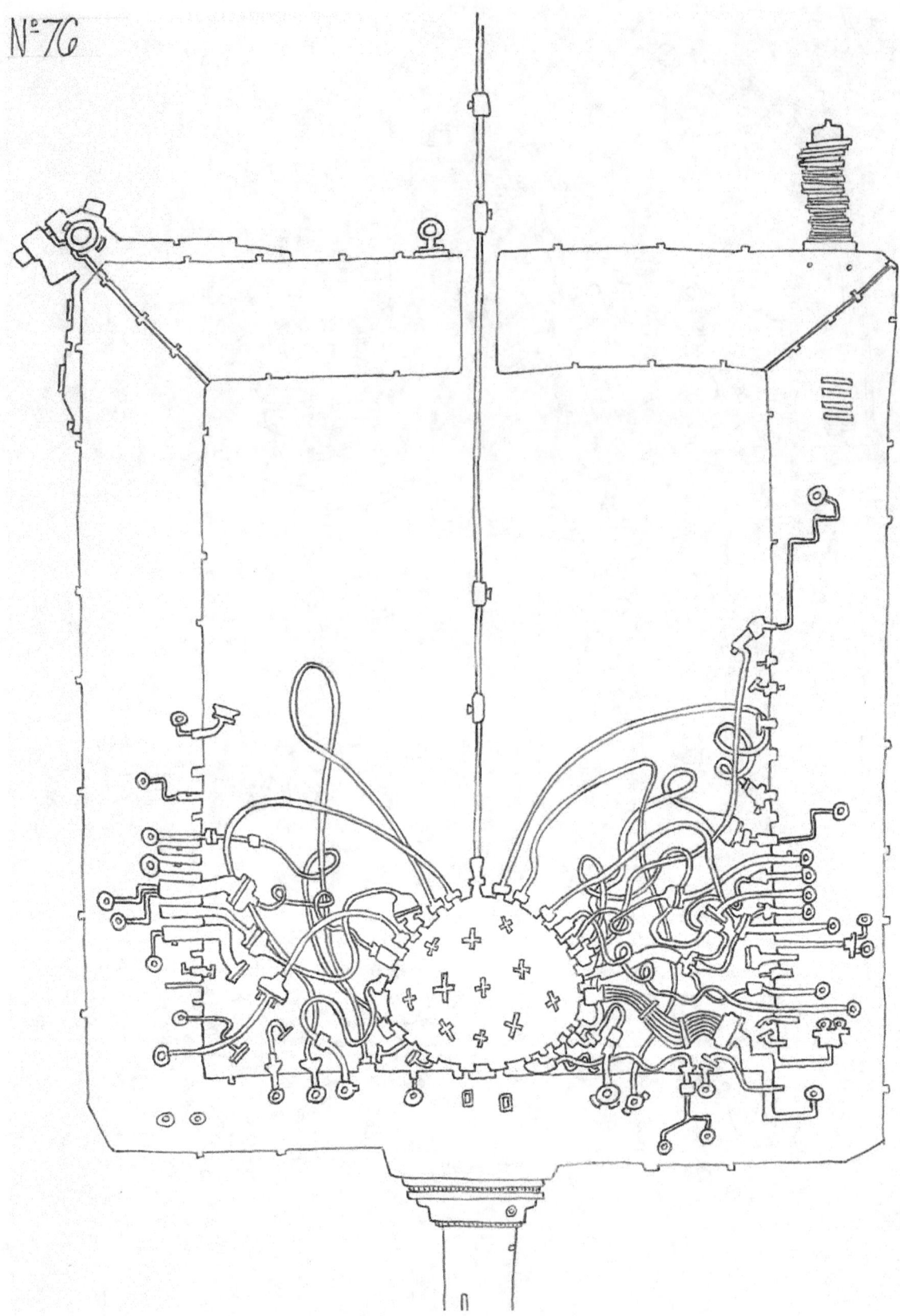

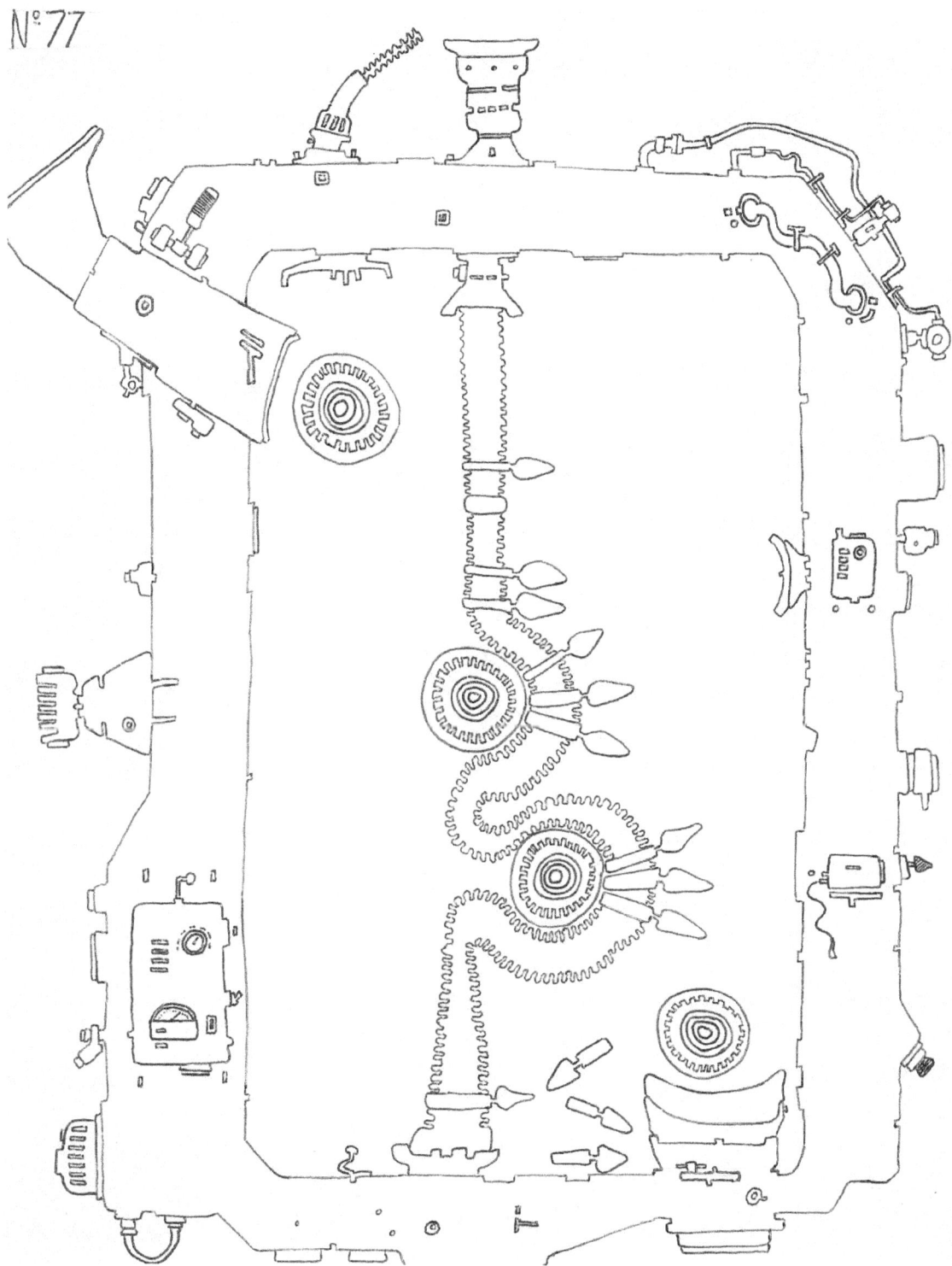

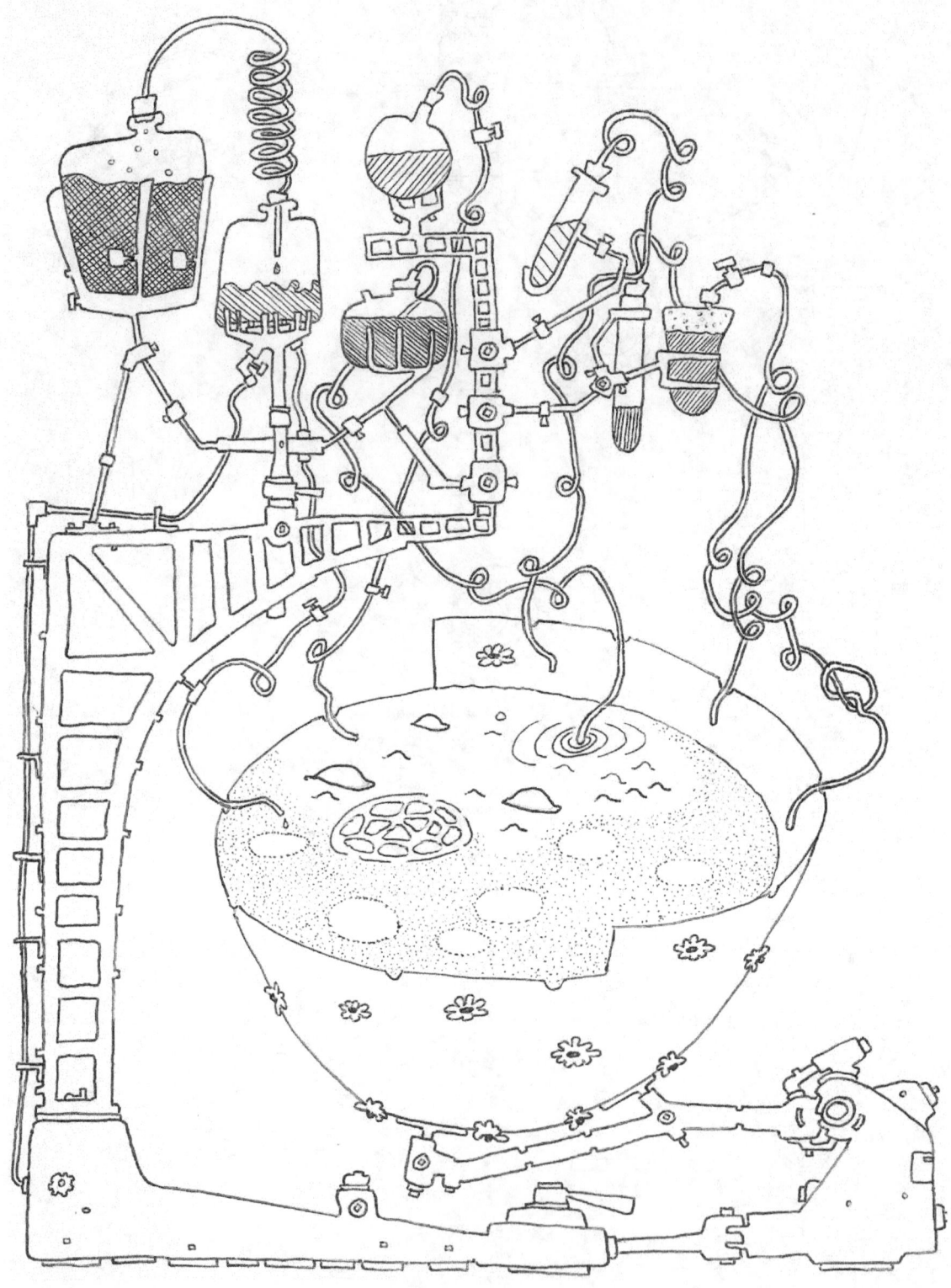

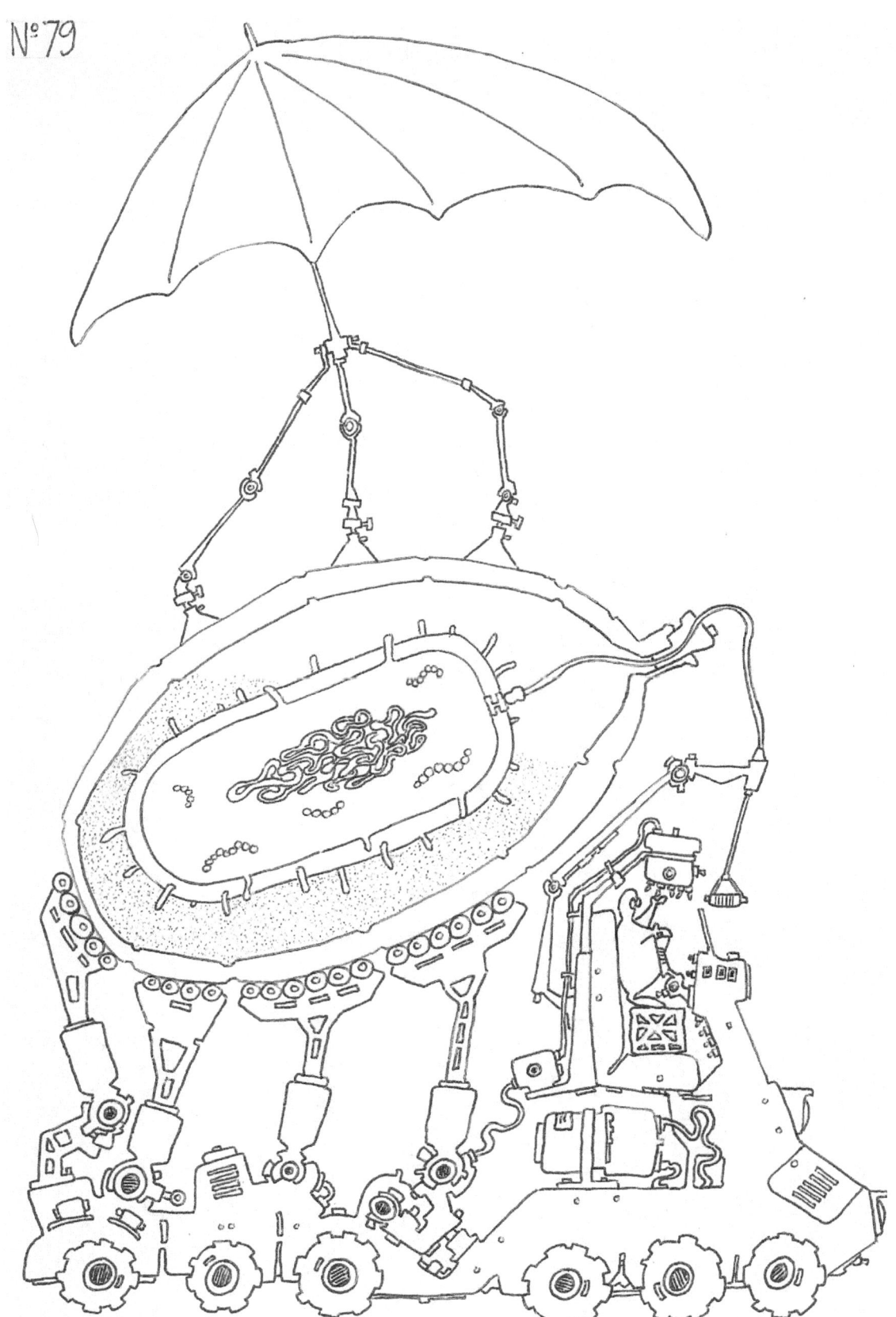

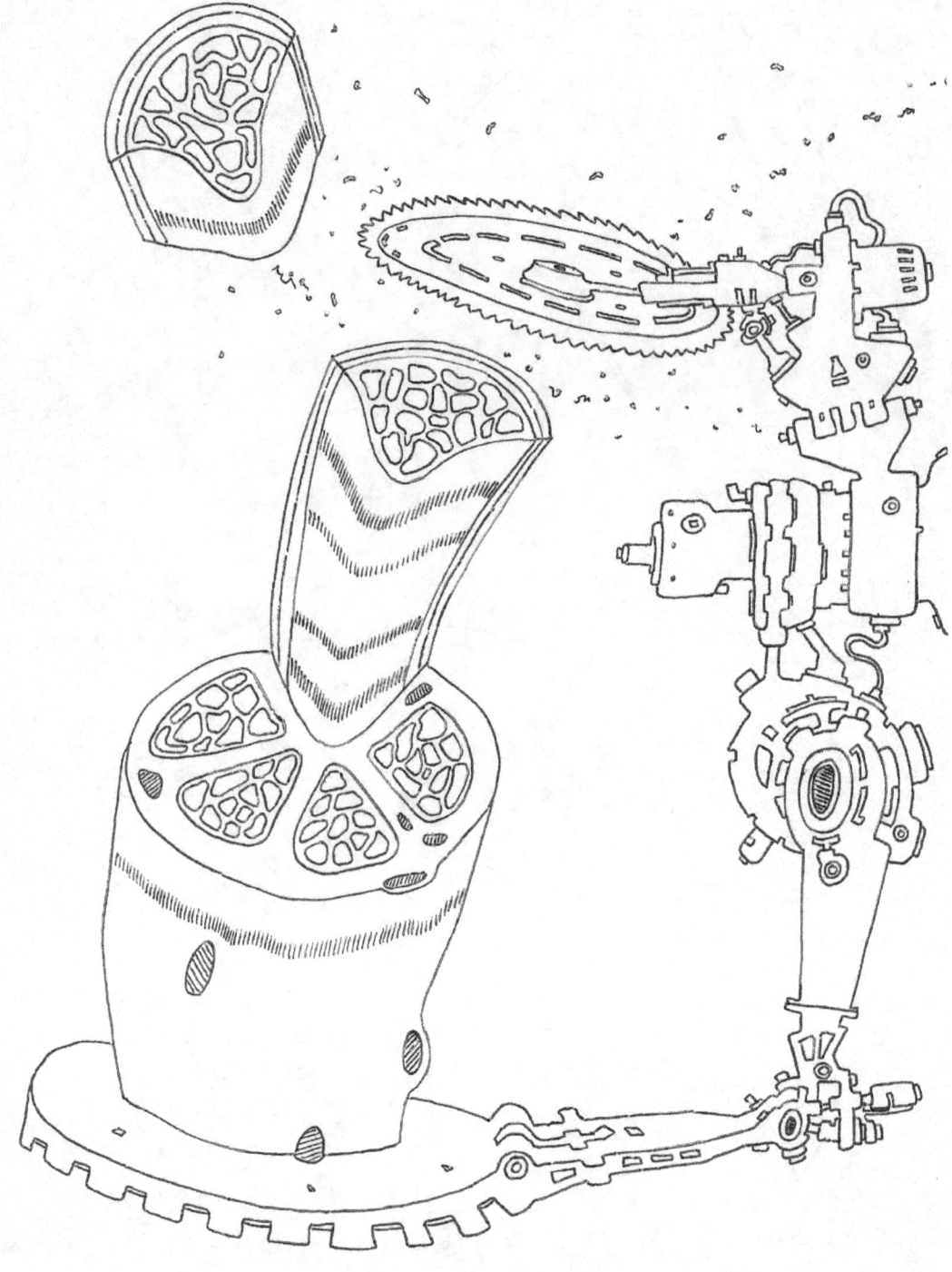

N°81

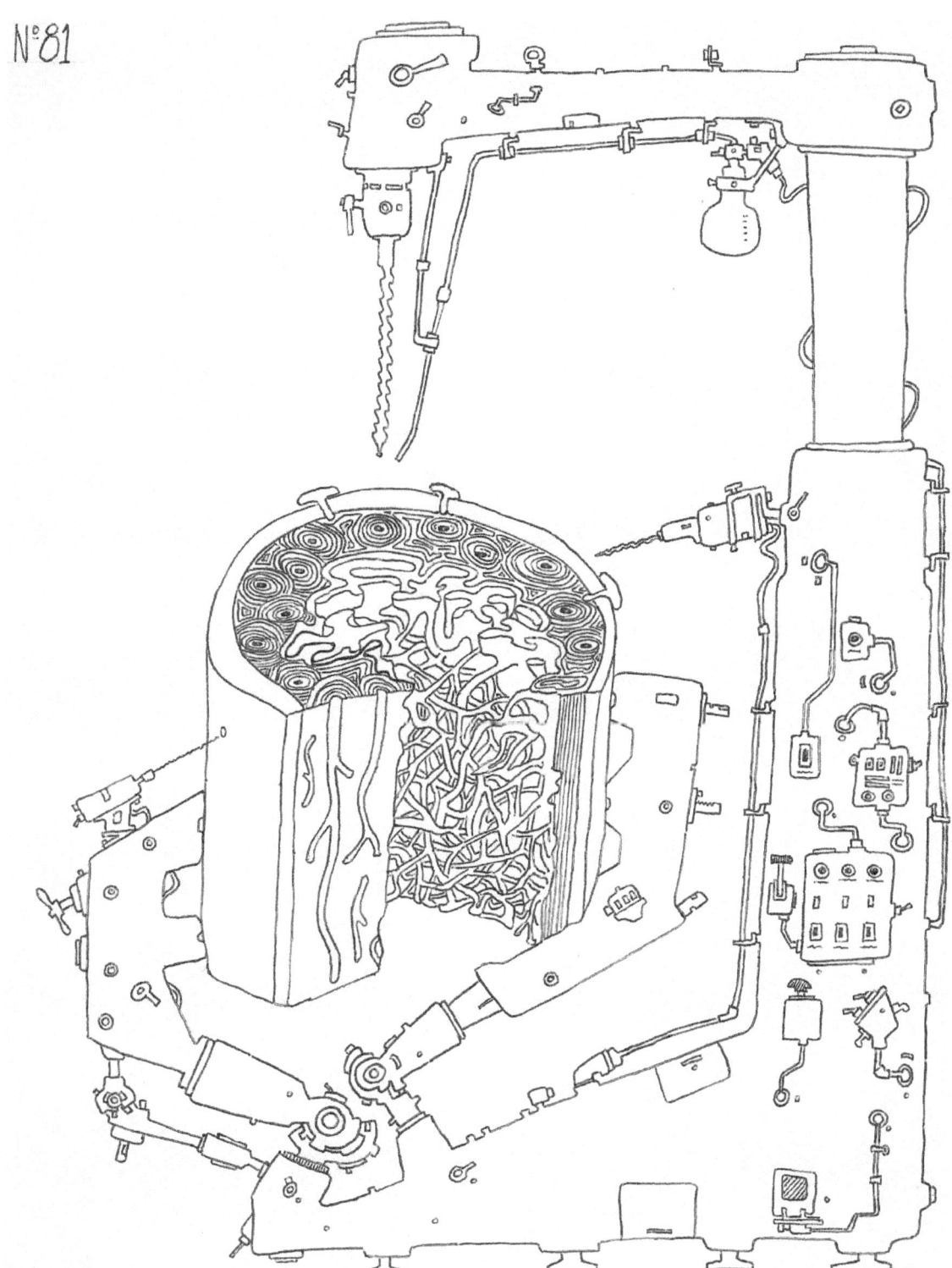

N° 83

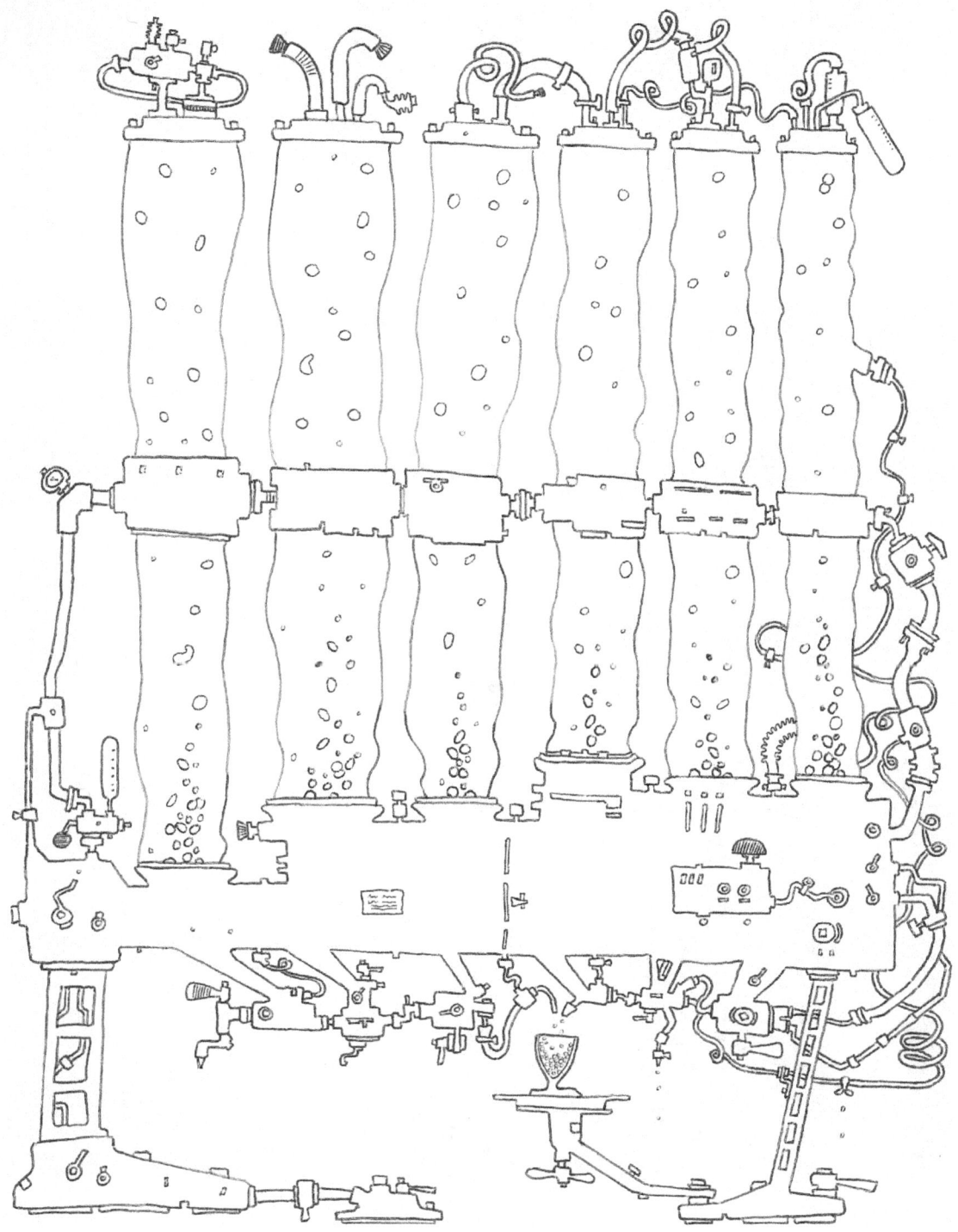

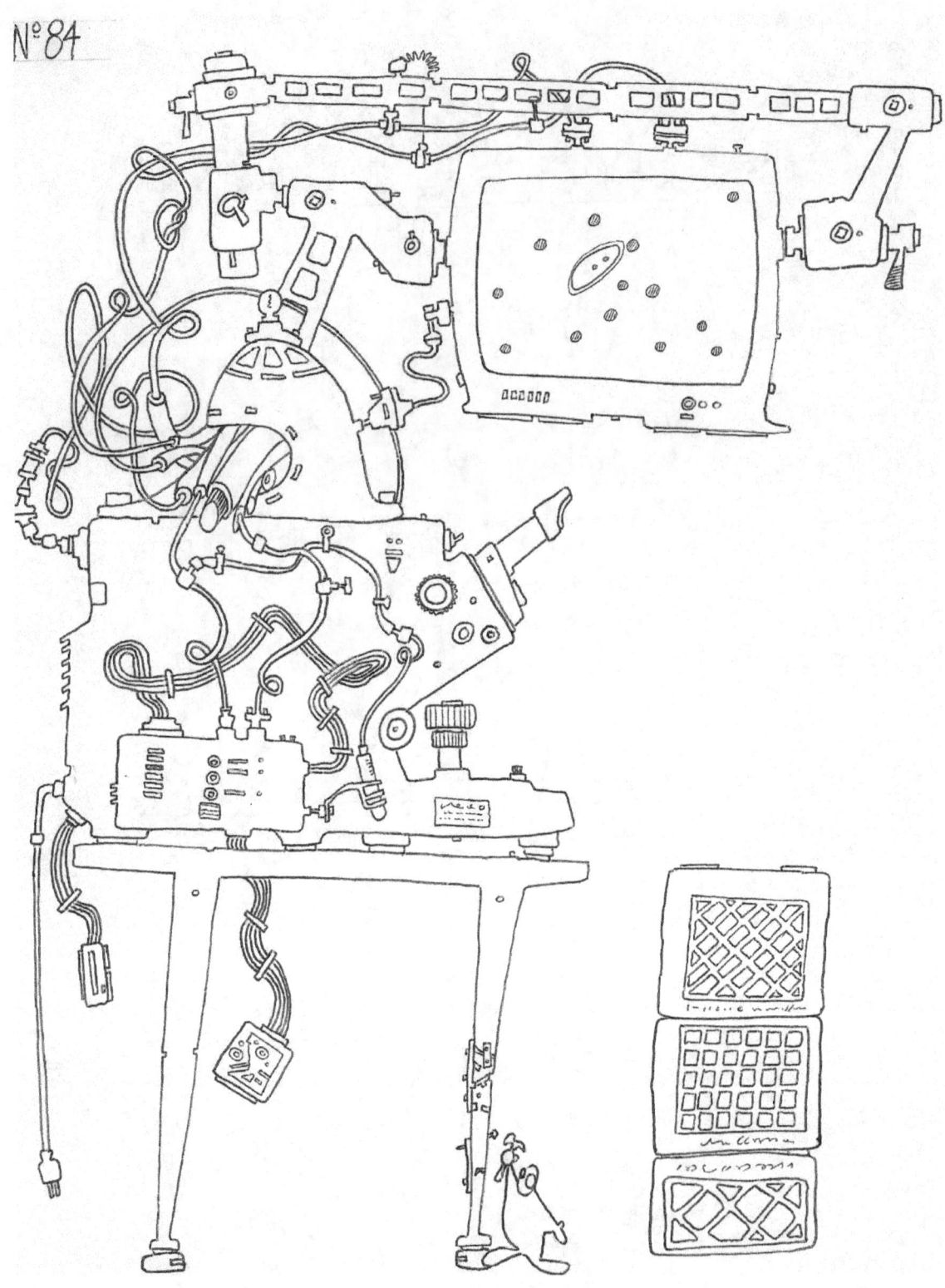

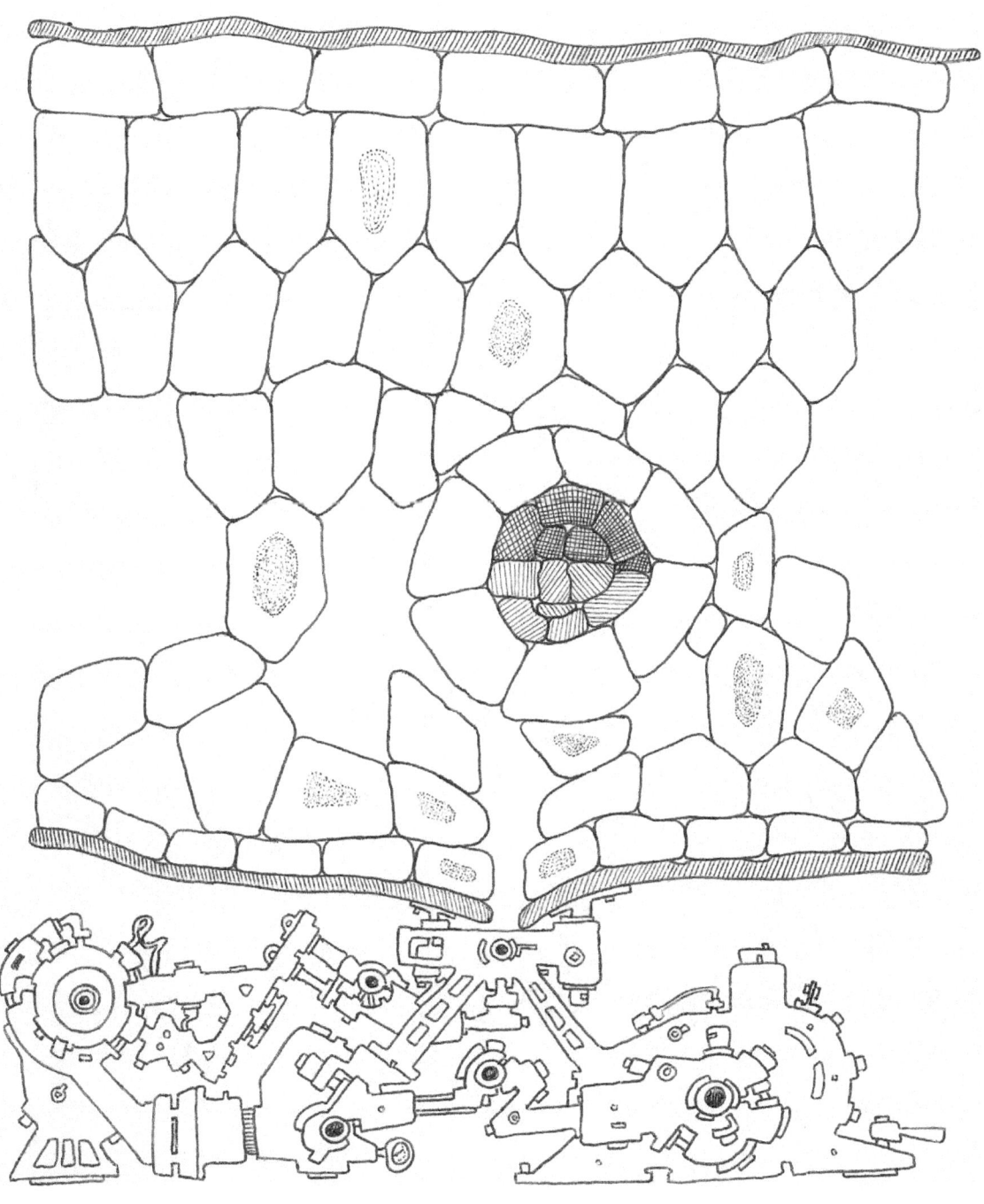

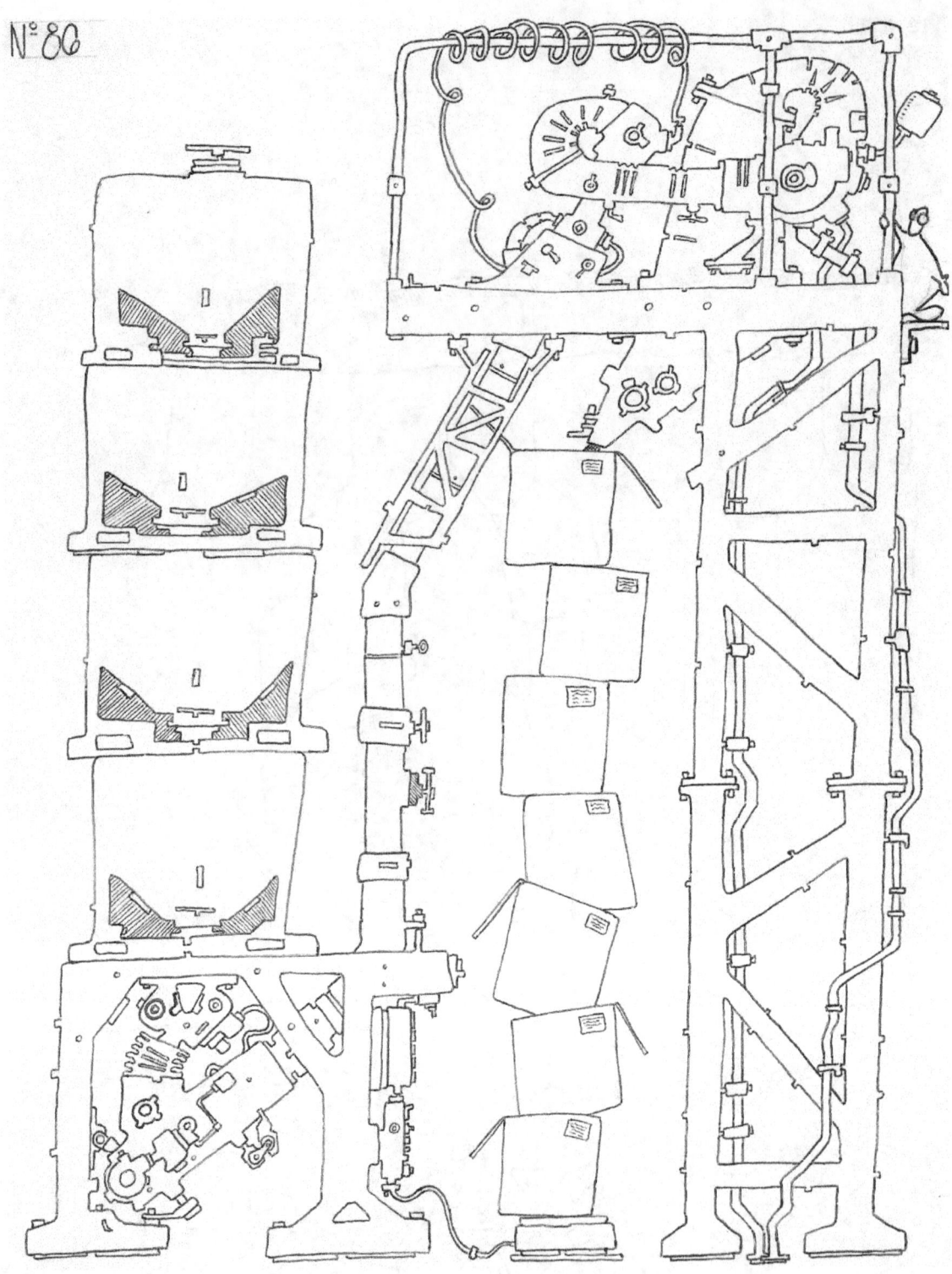

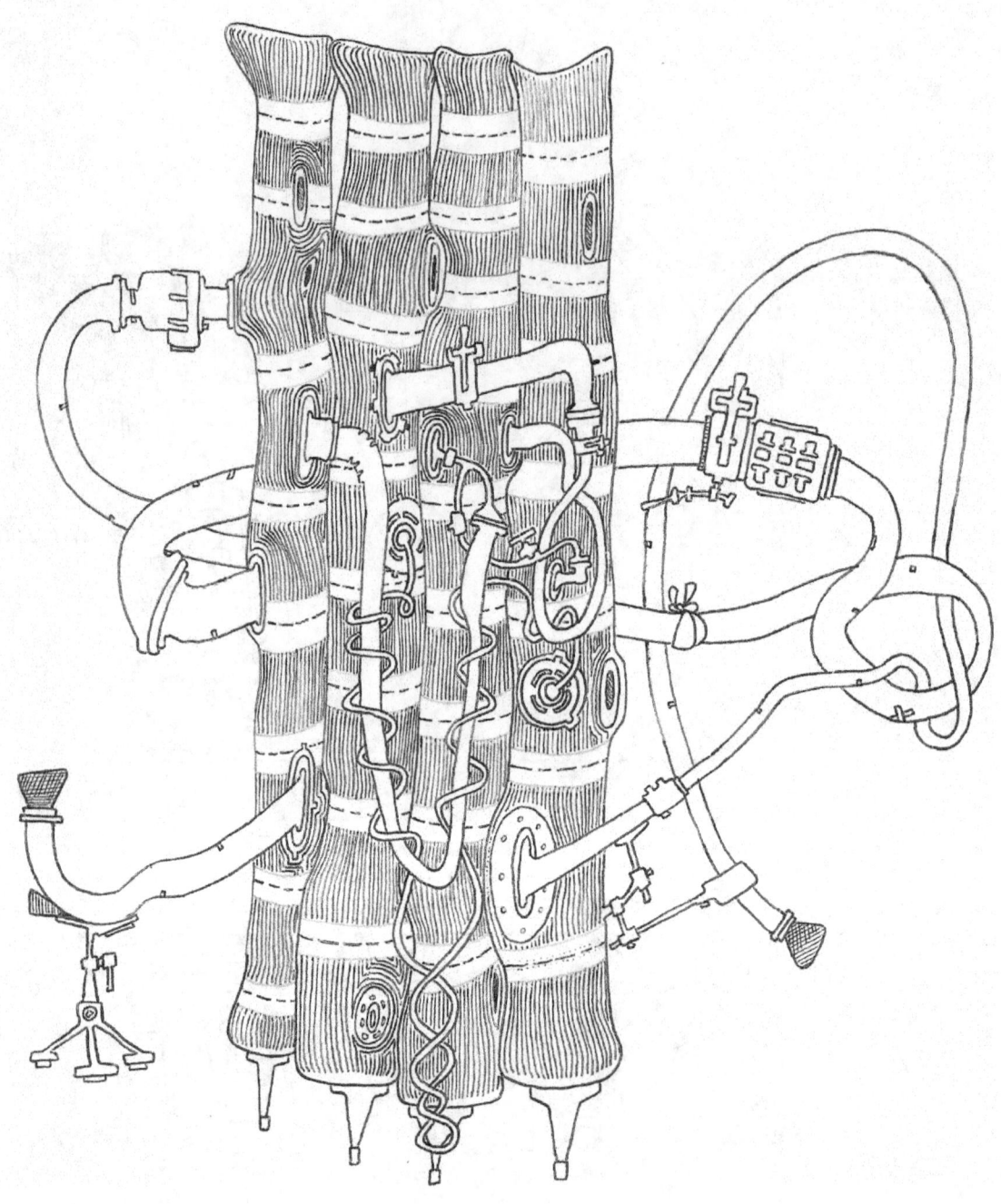

N°89

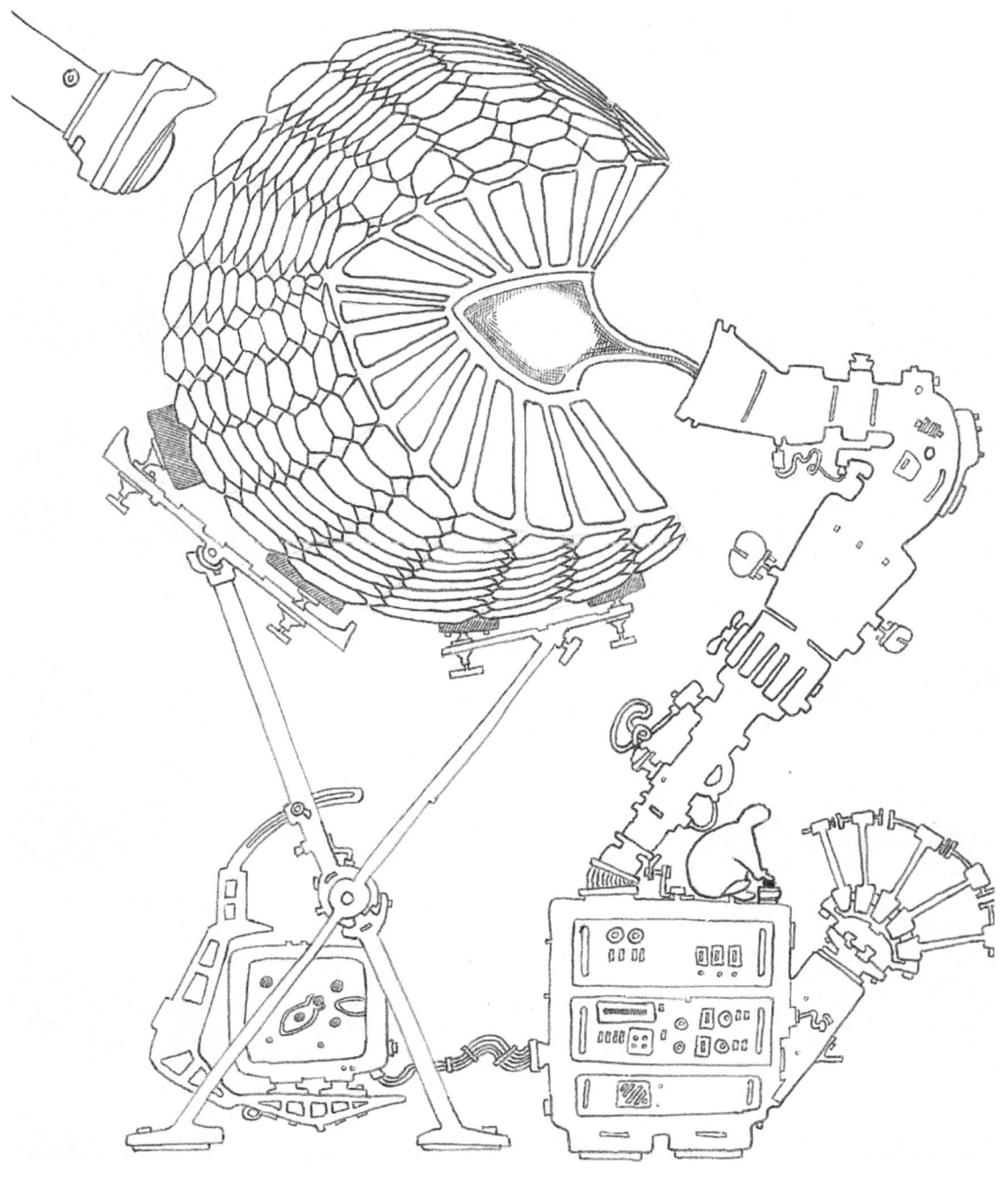

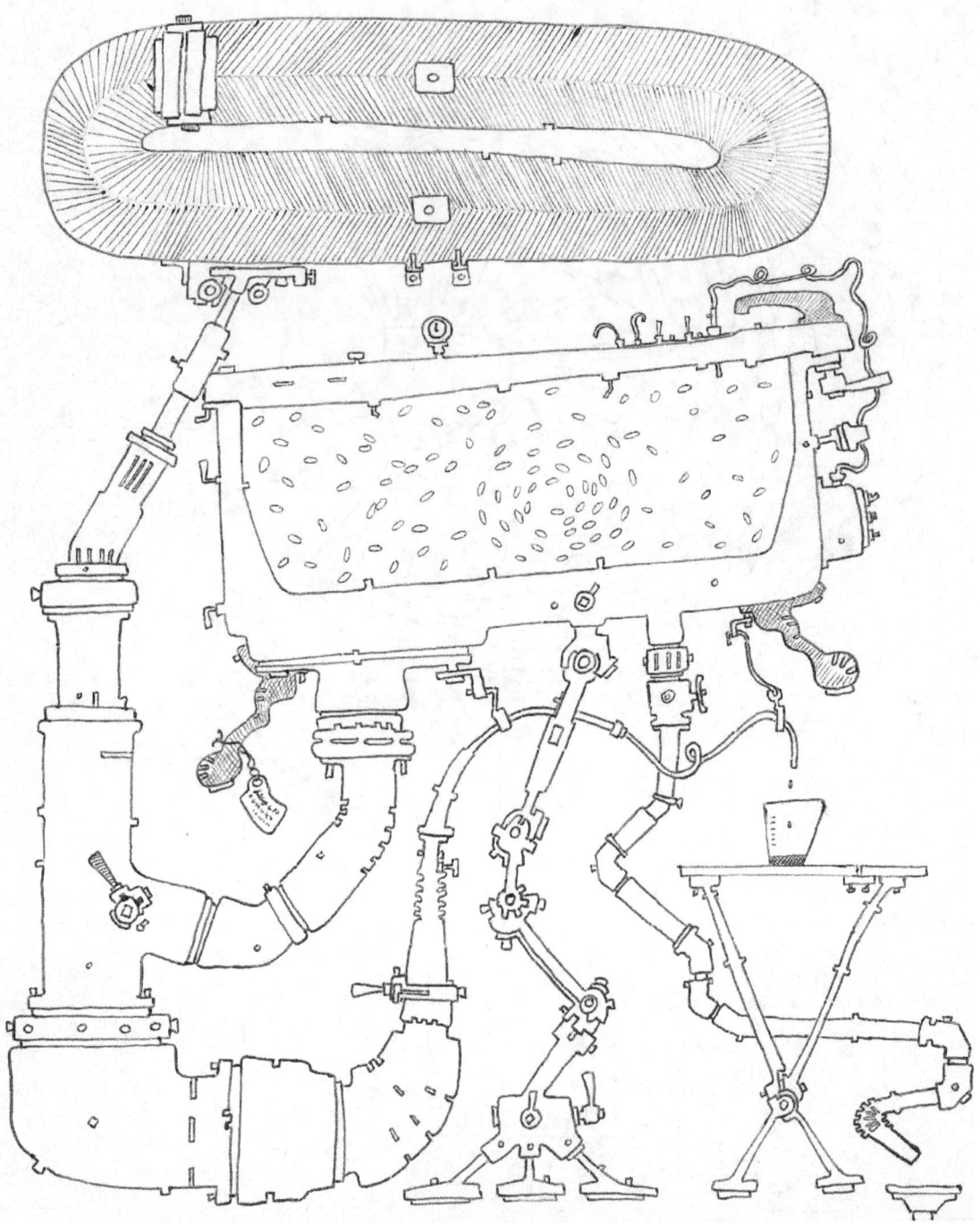

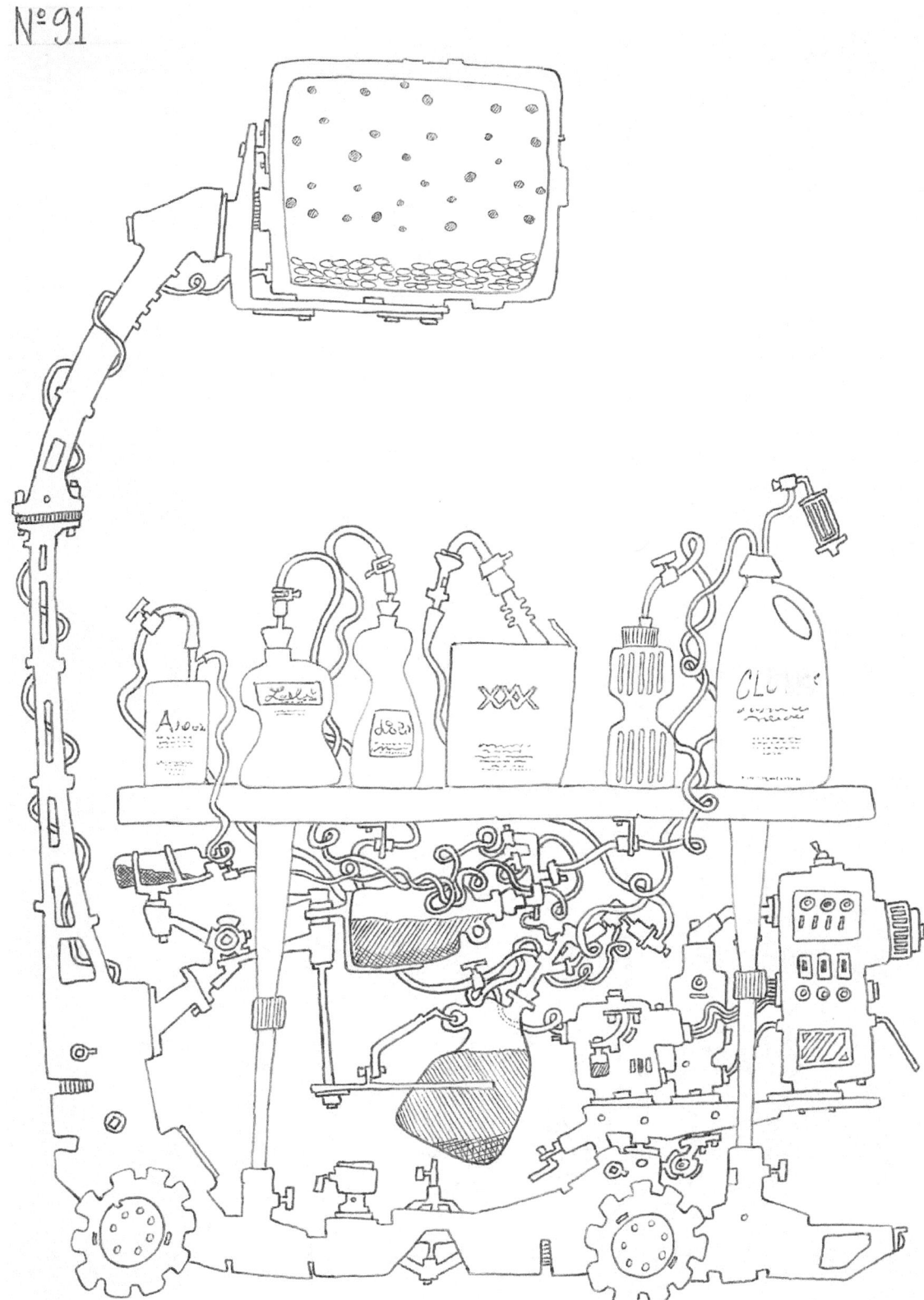

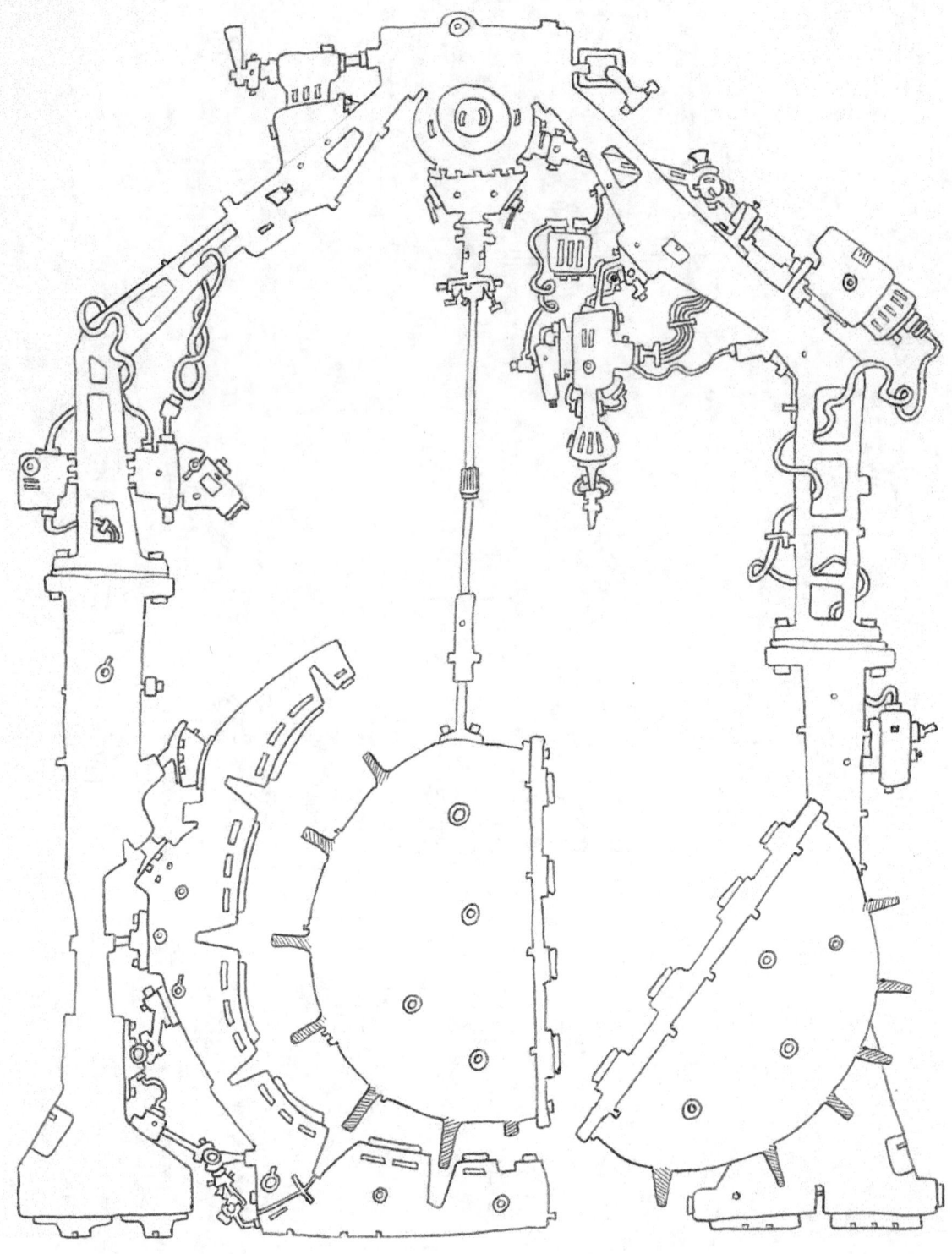

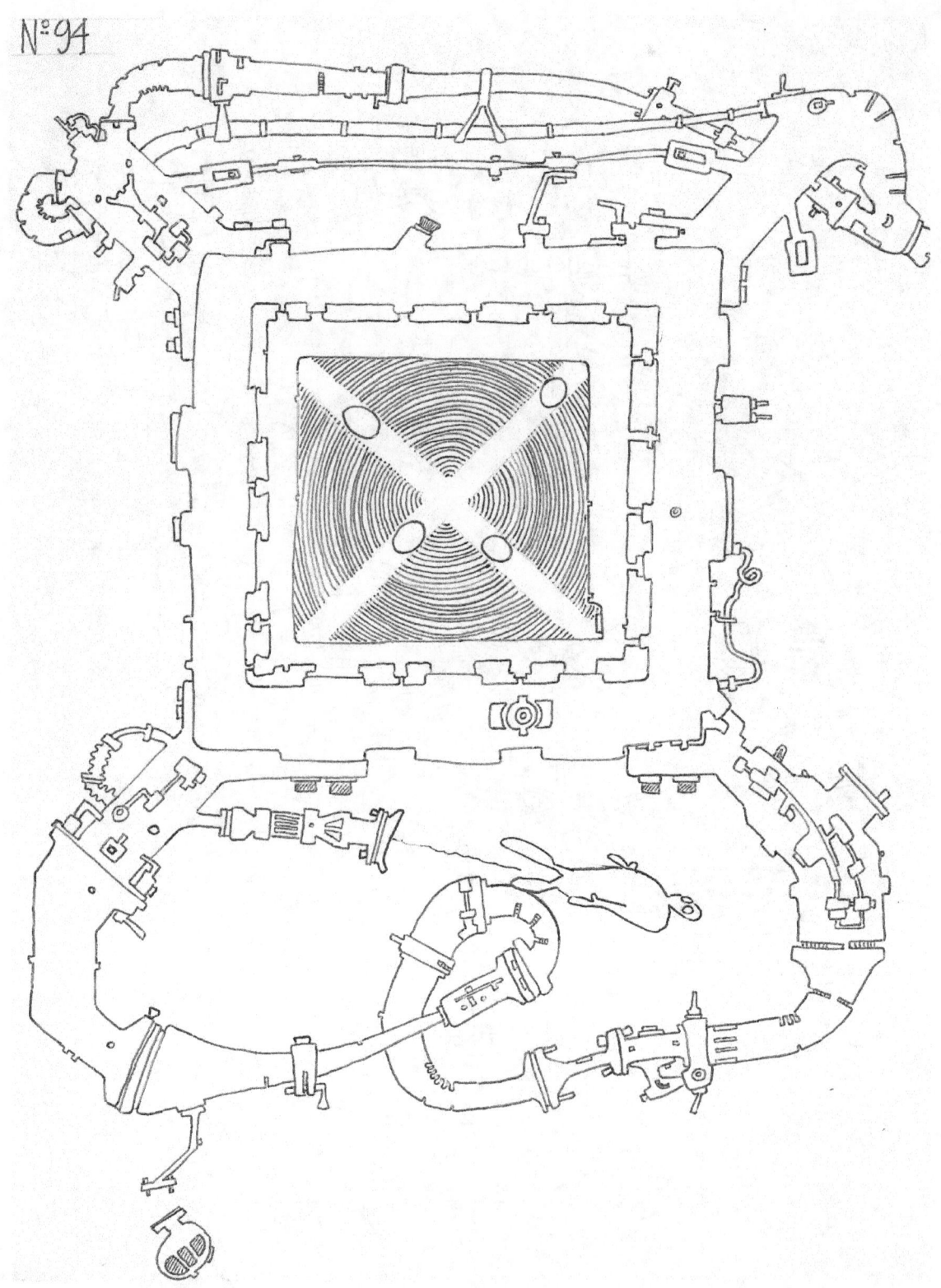

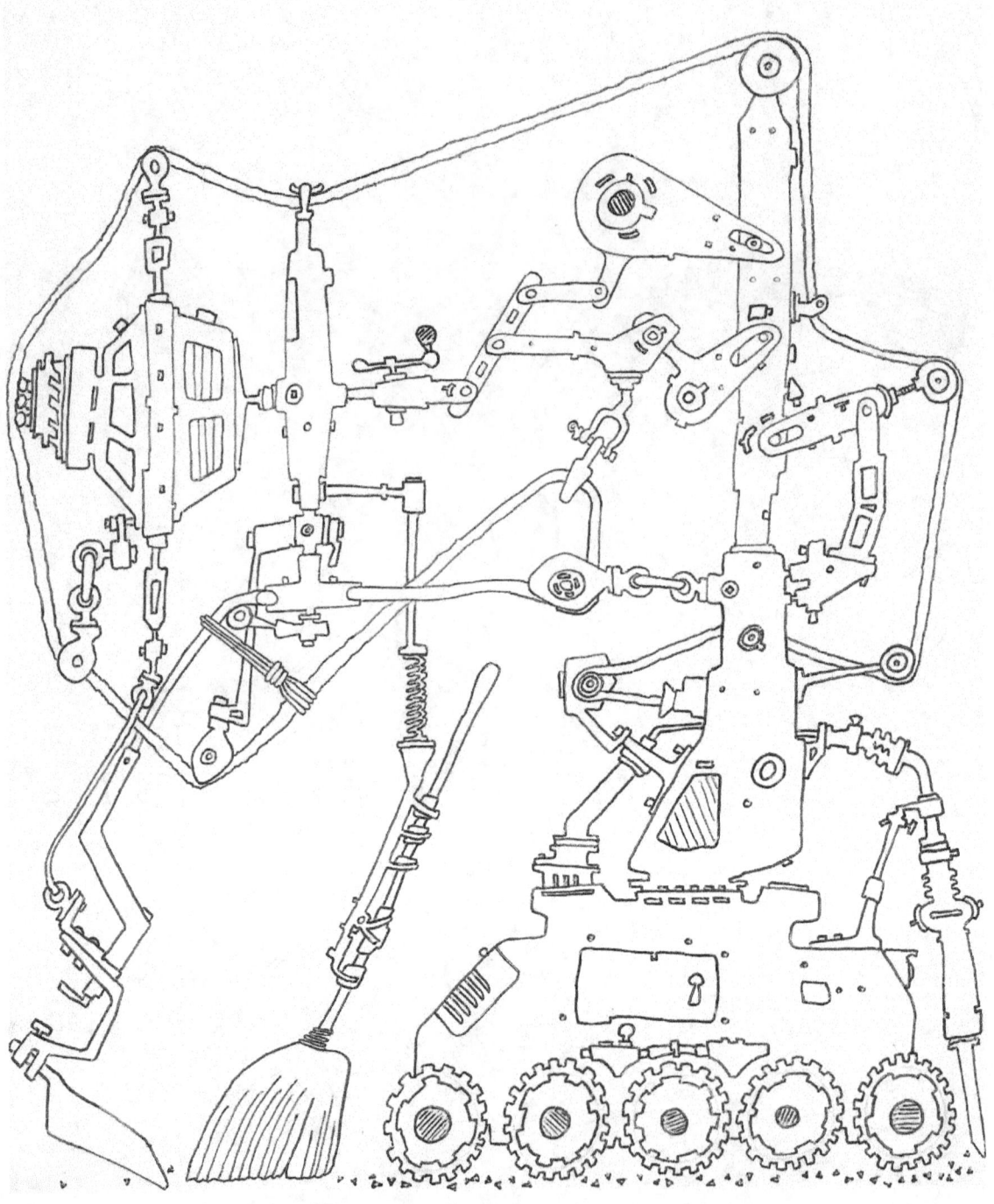

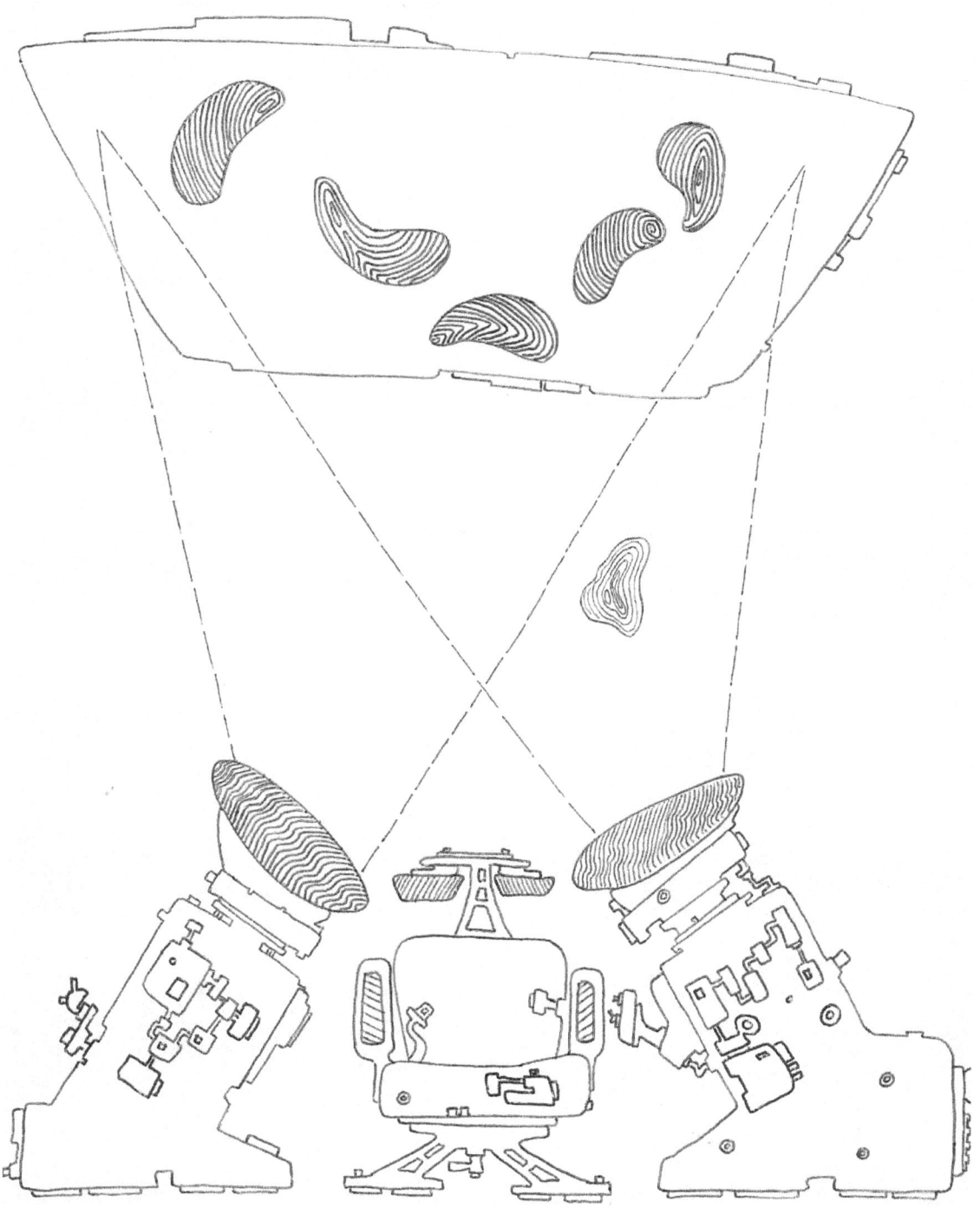

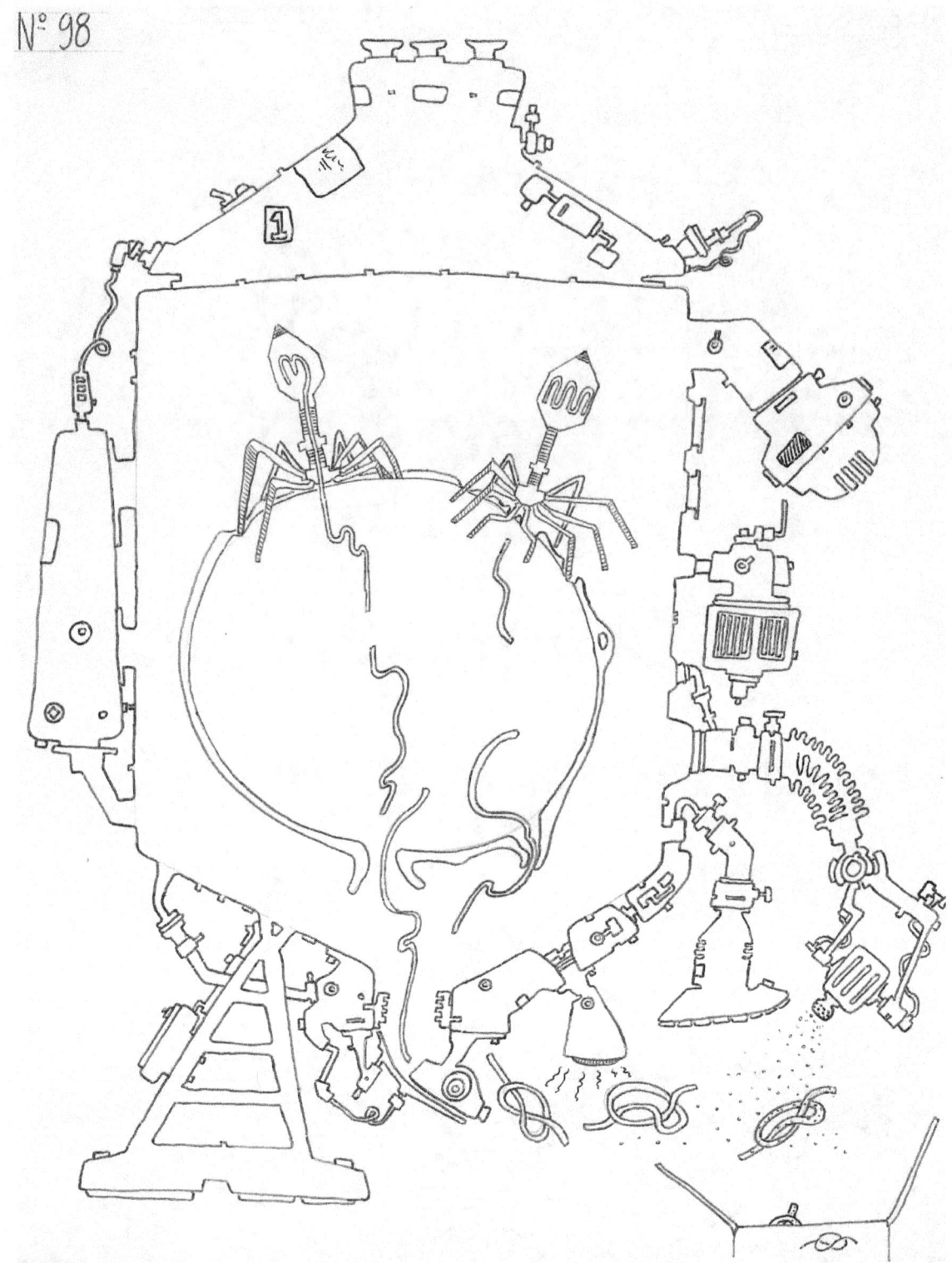

Nº 99

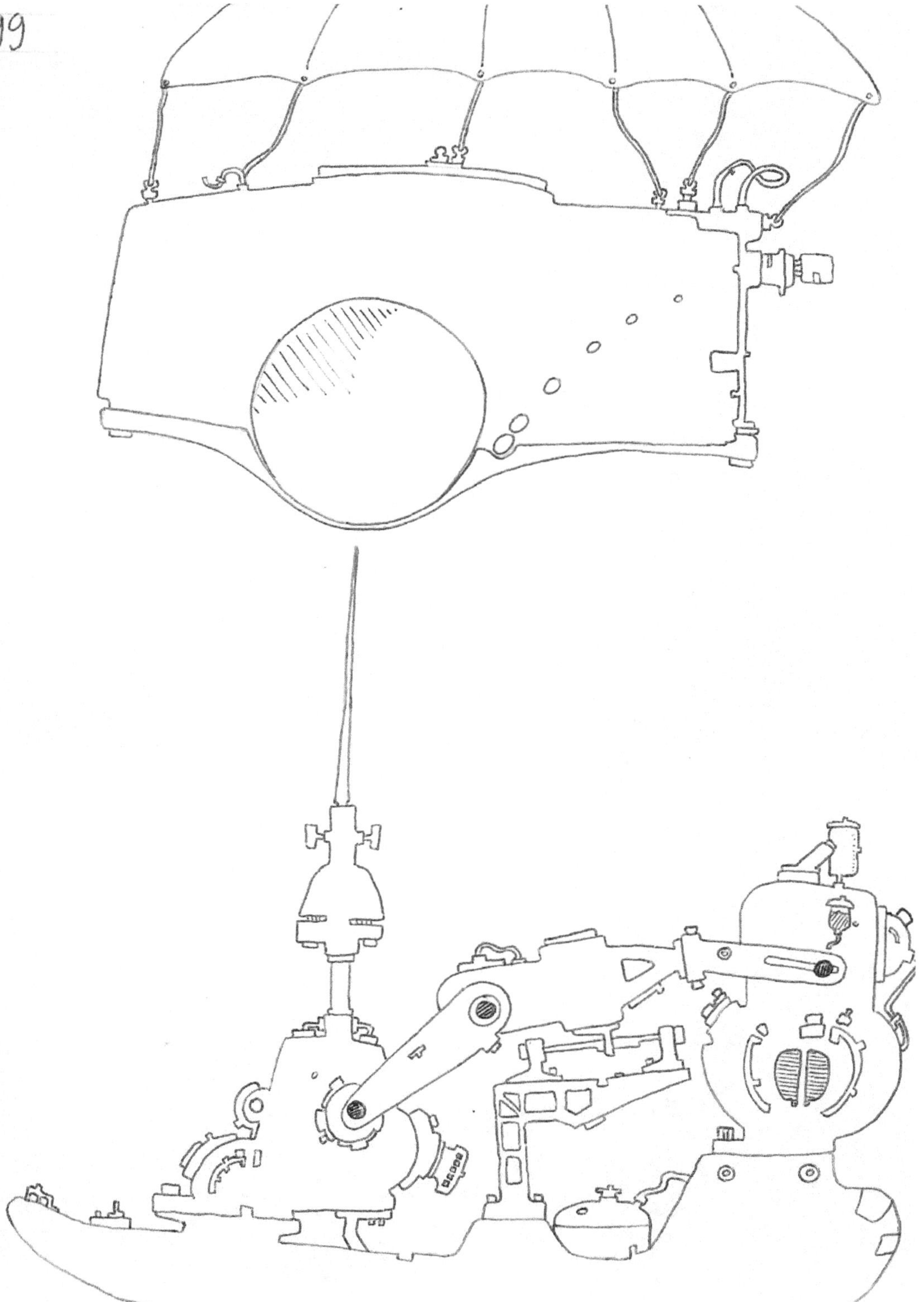

10,000 lbs.

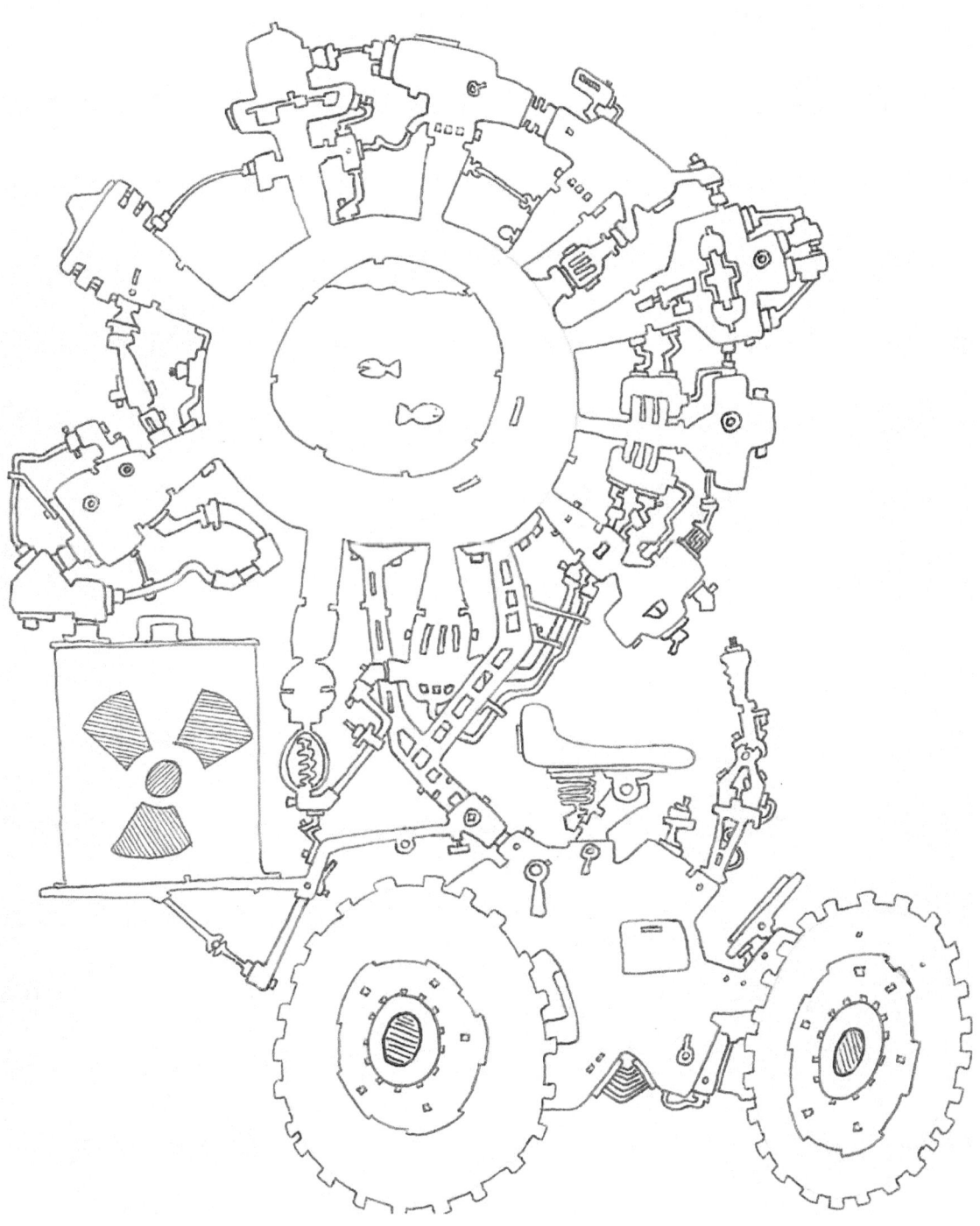

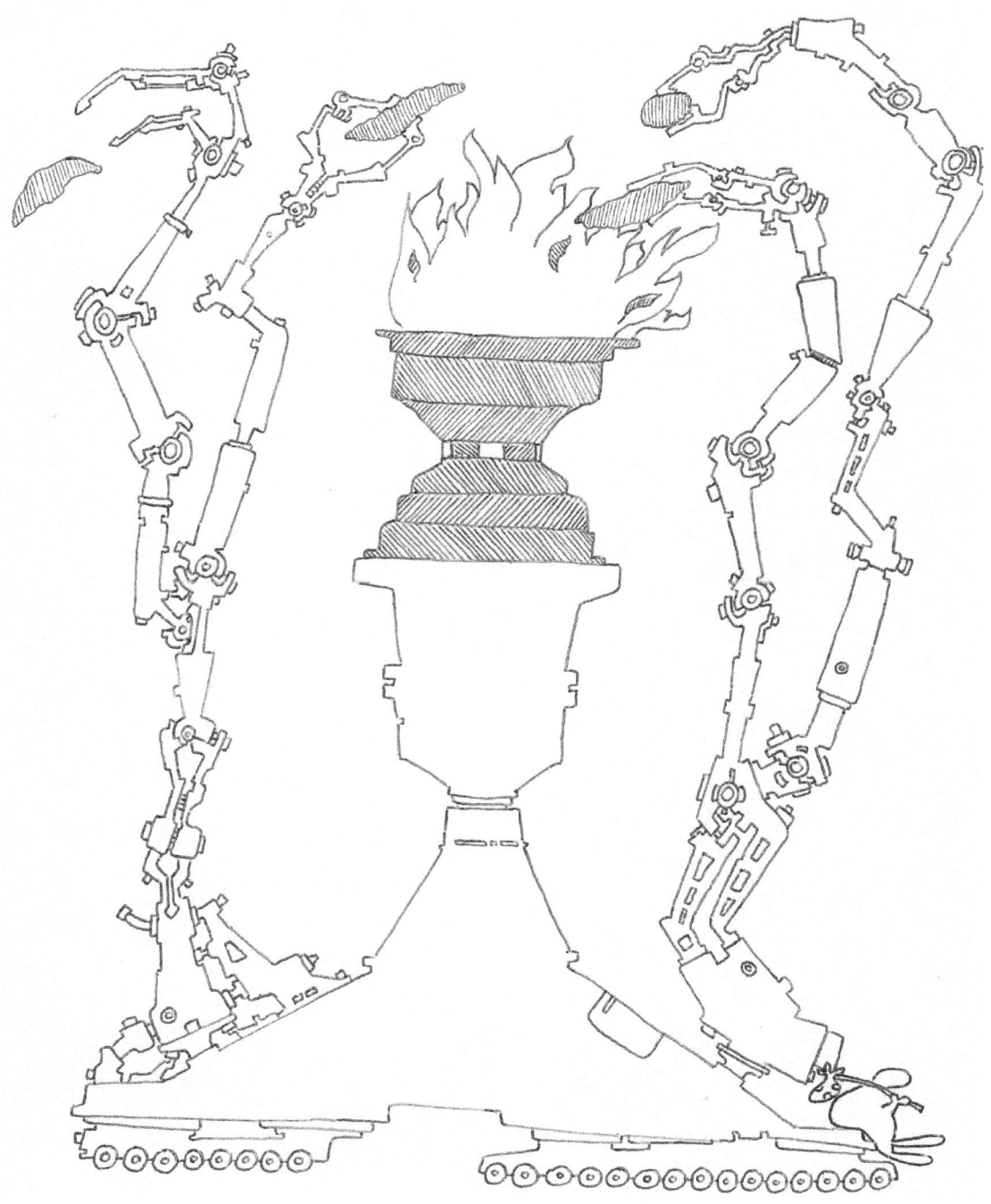

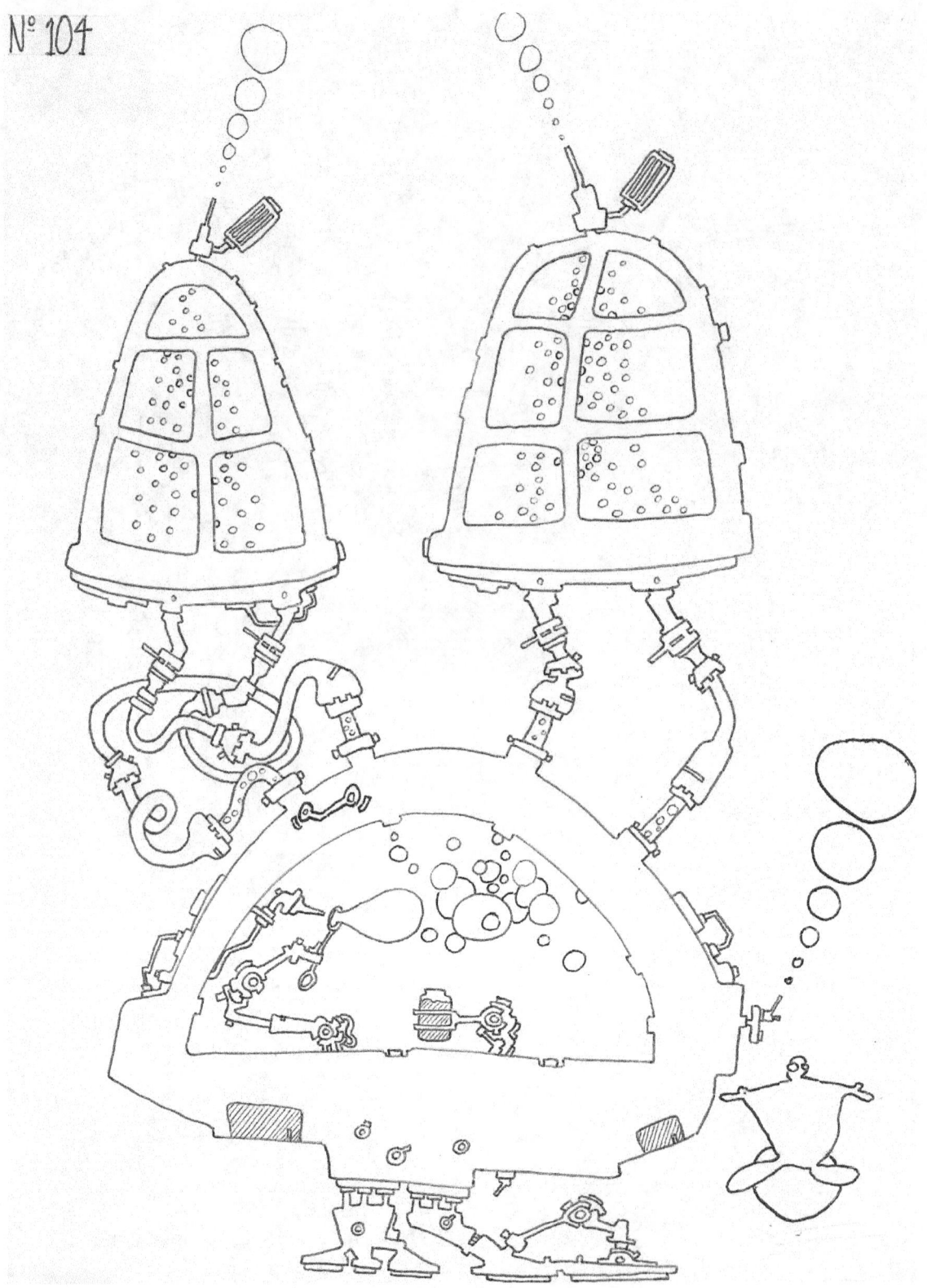

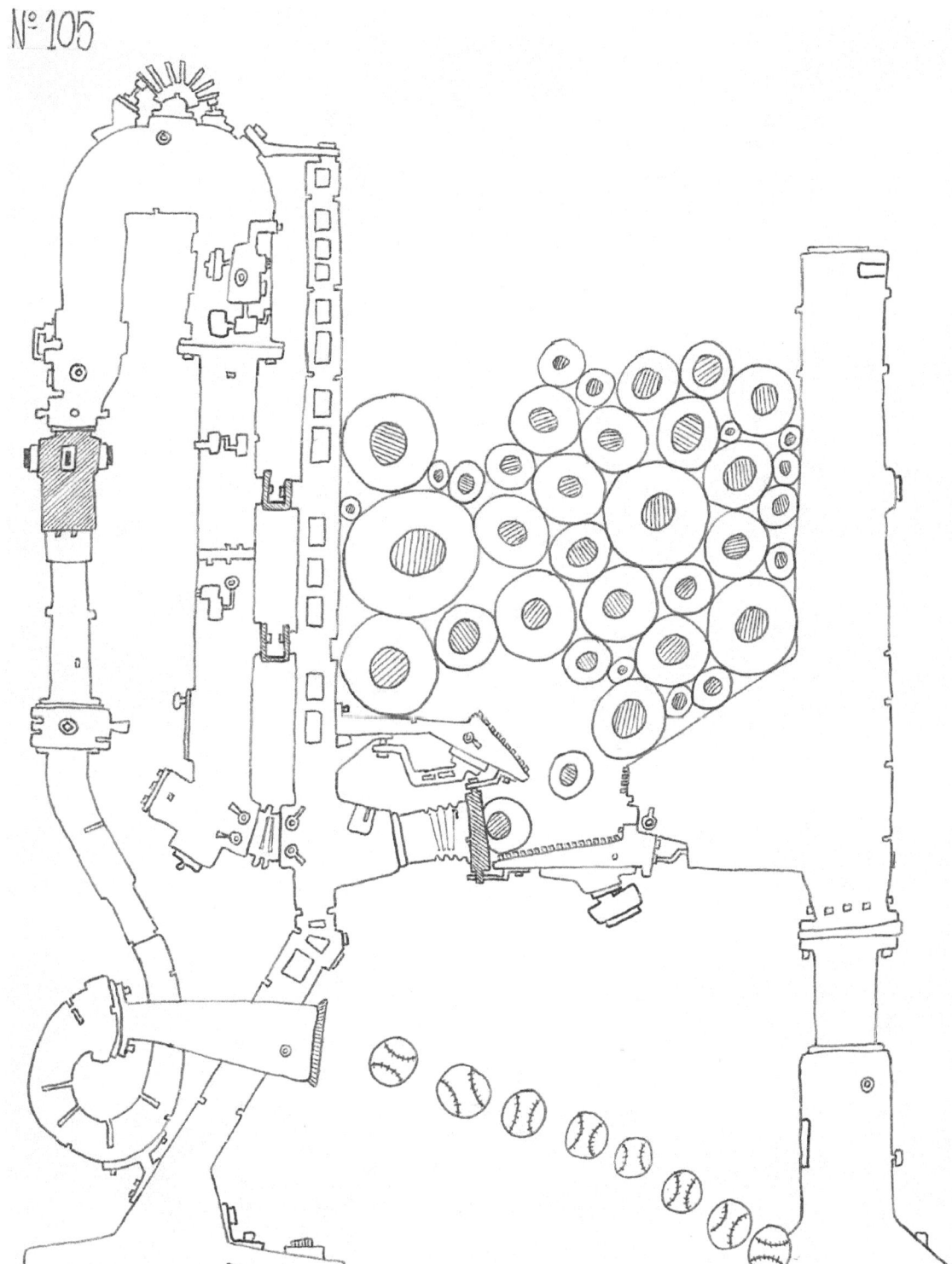

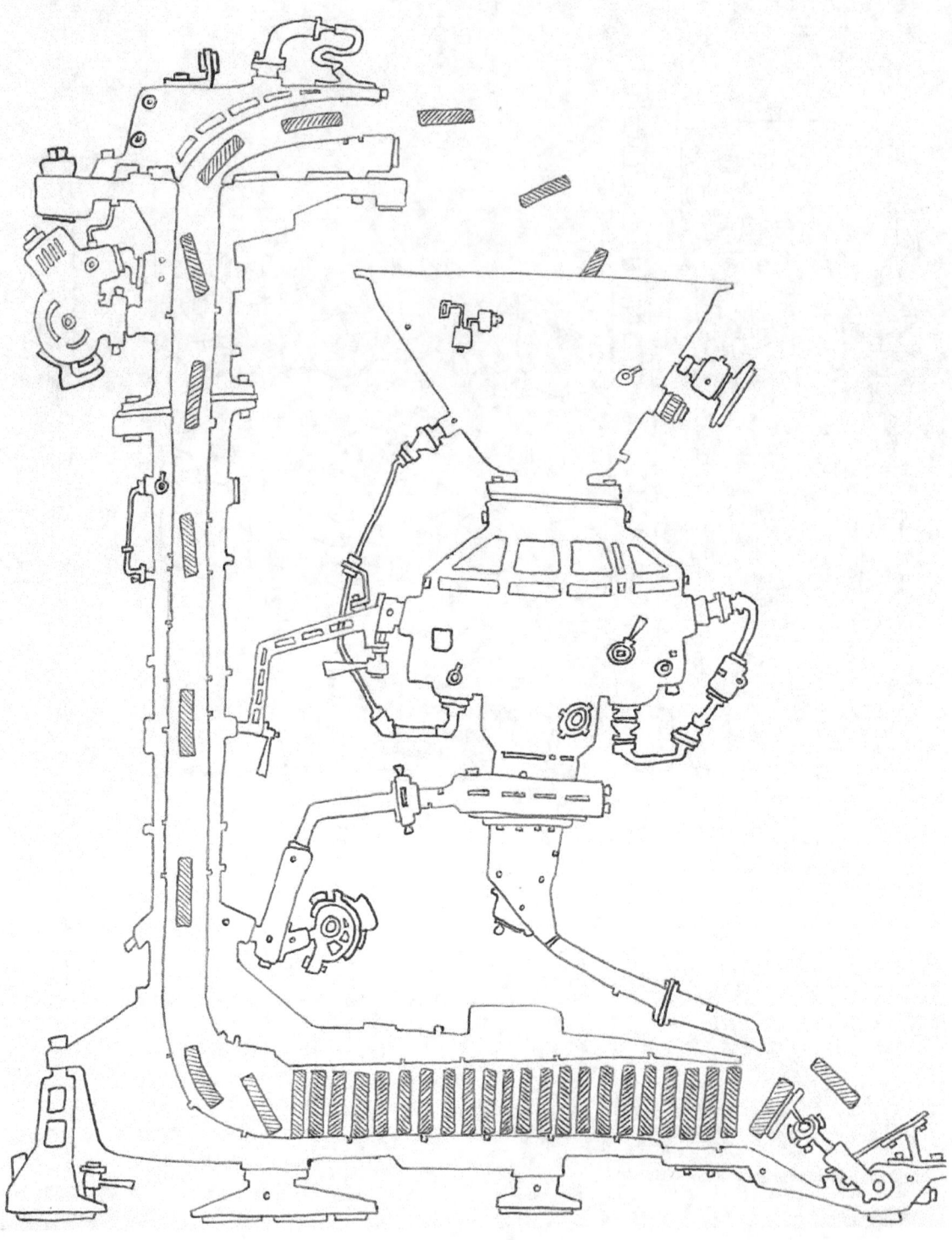

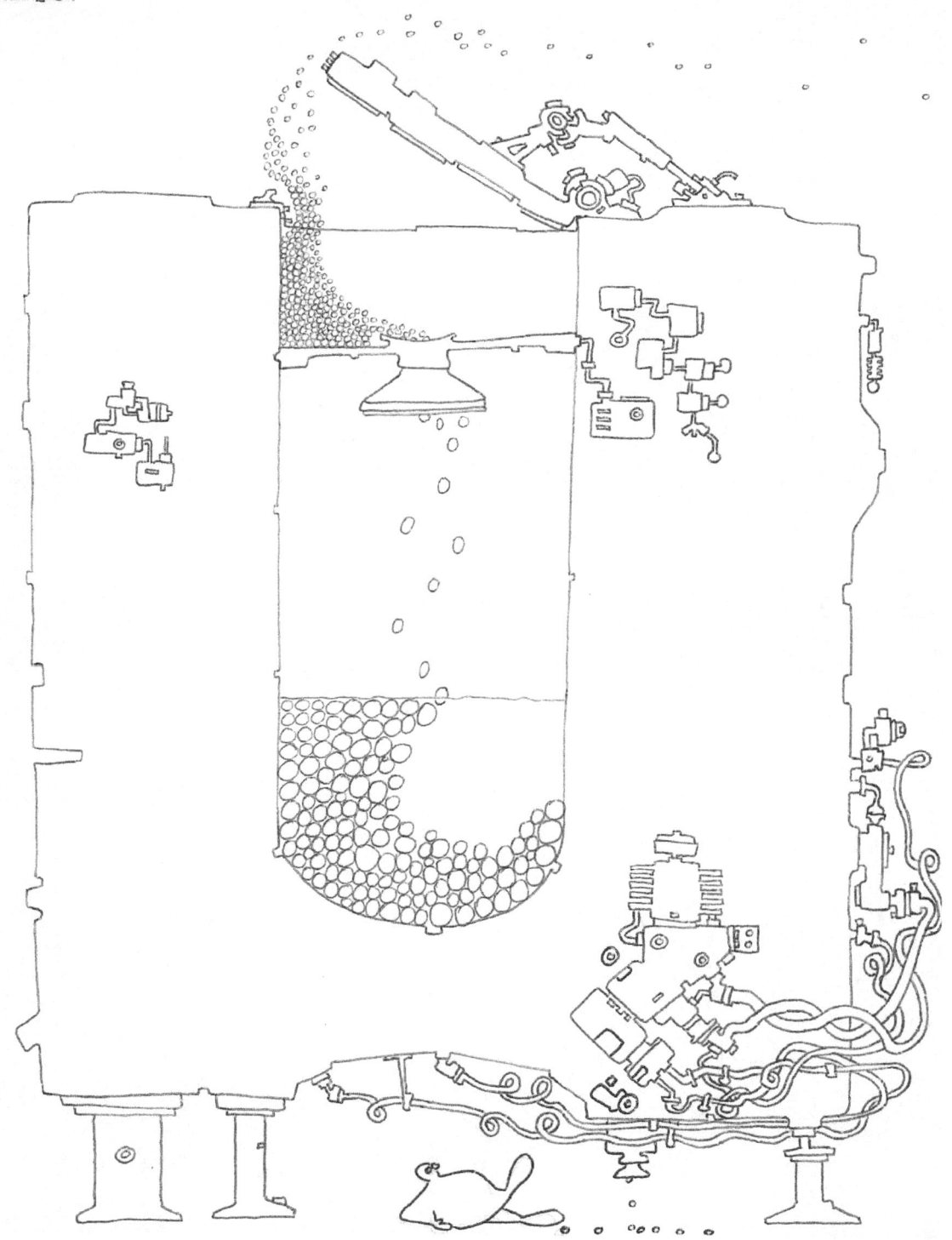

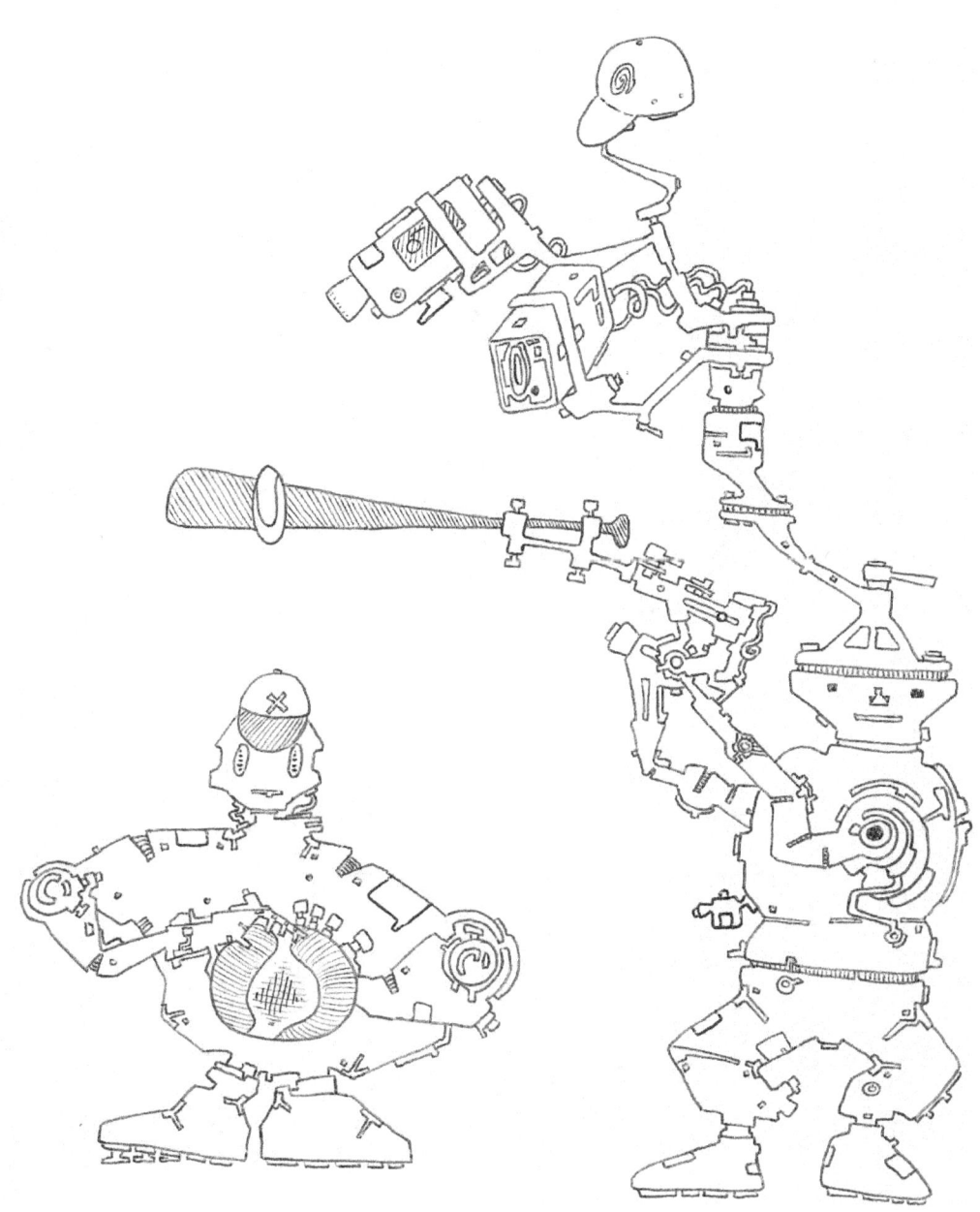

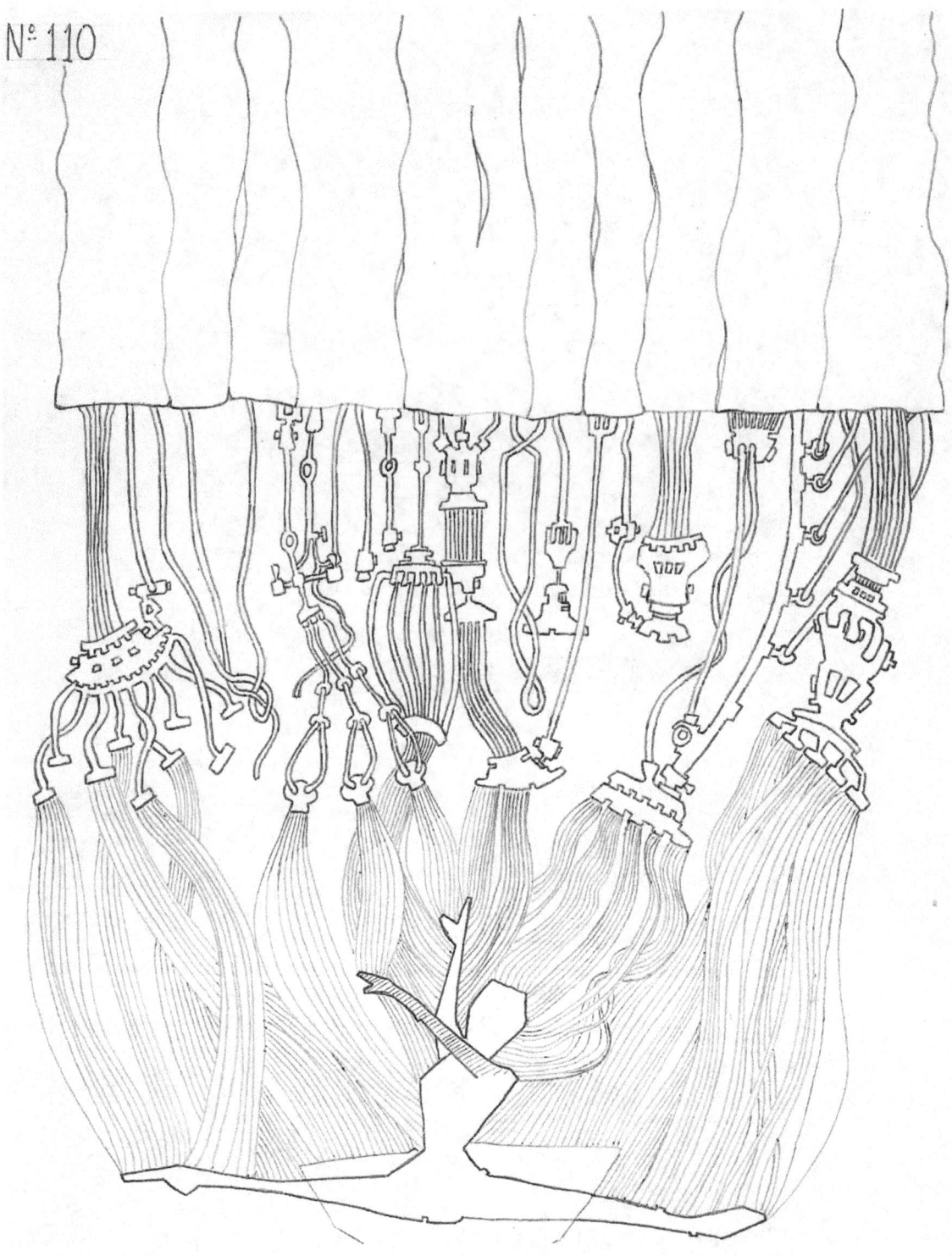

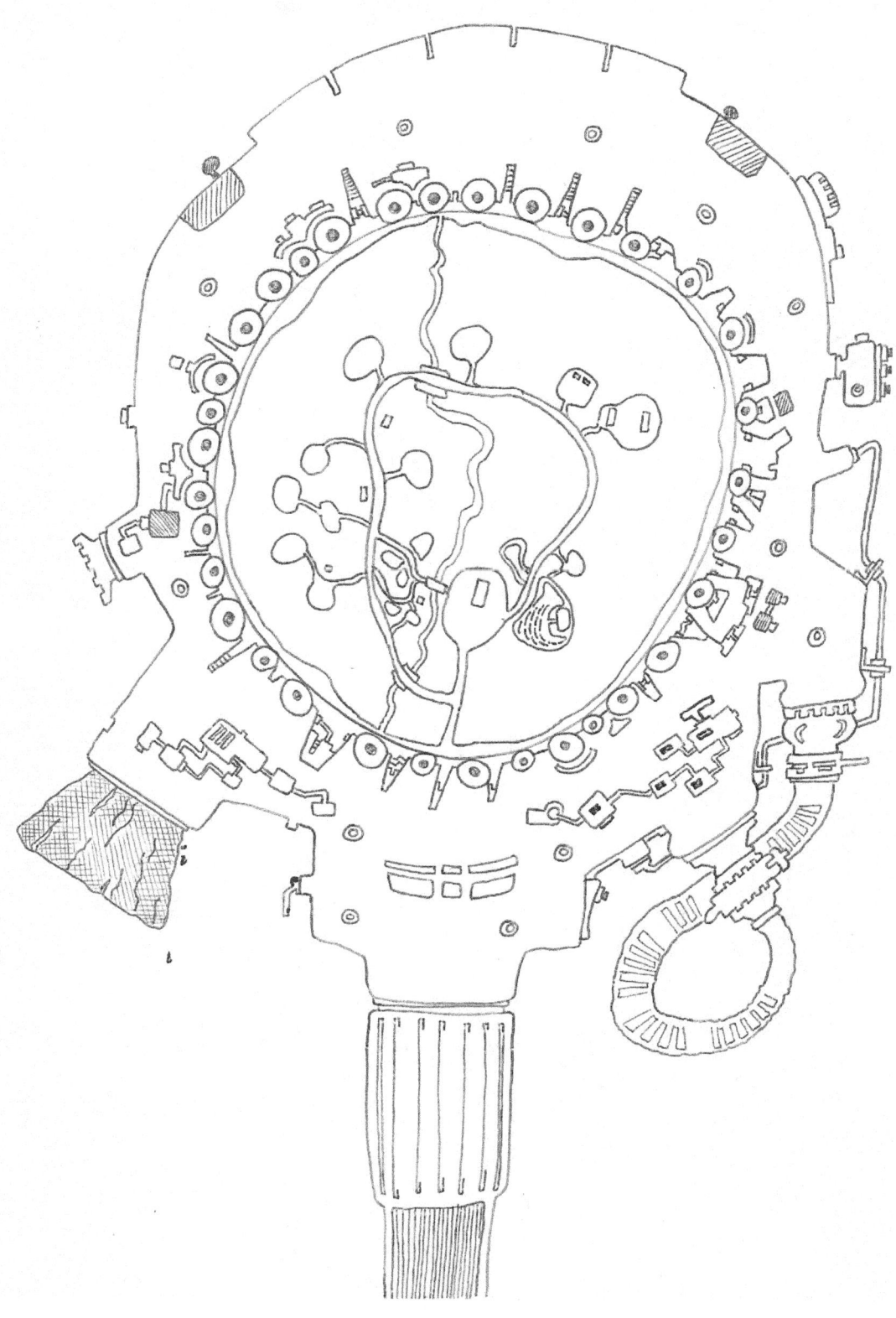

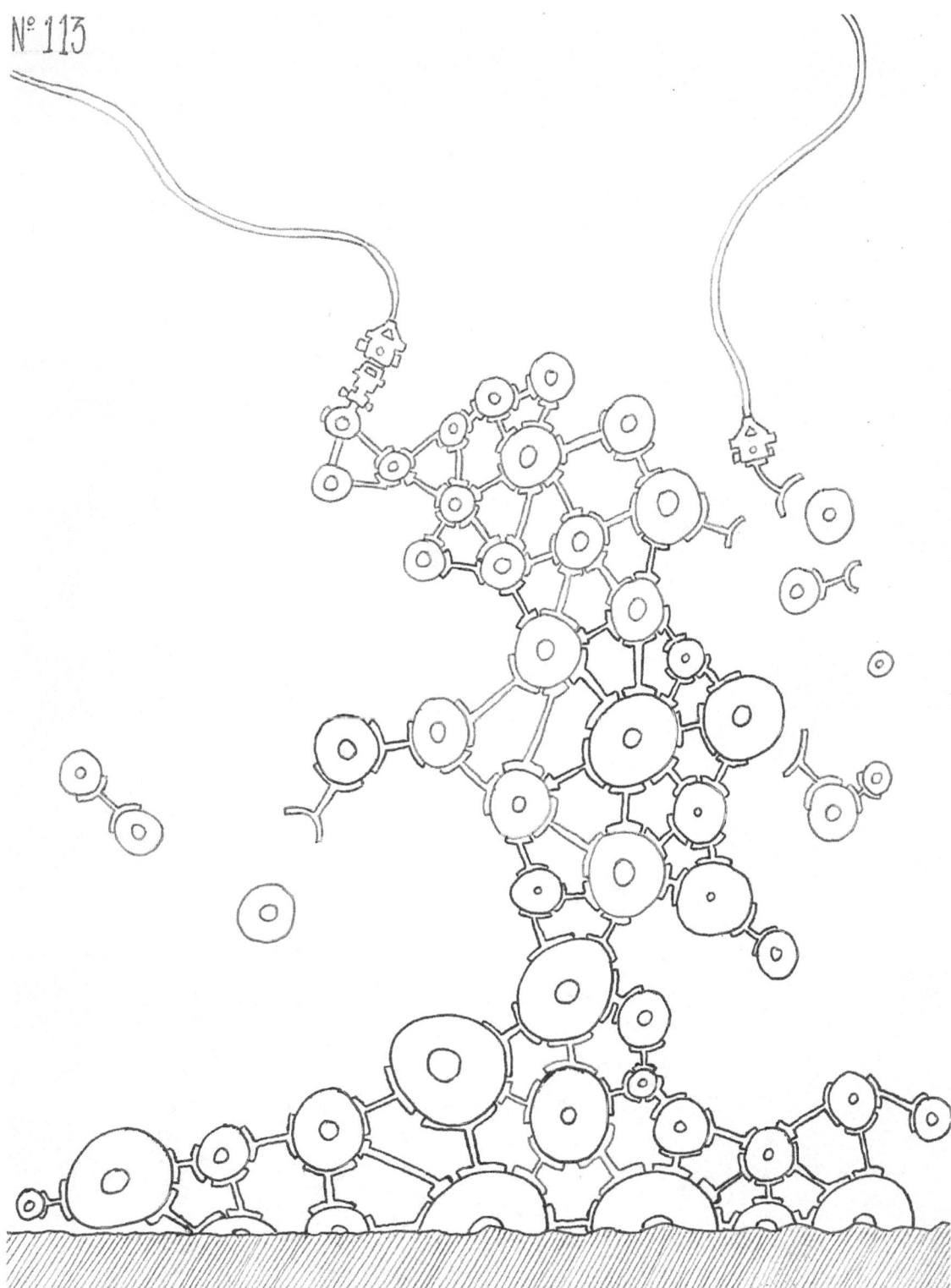

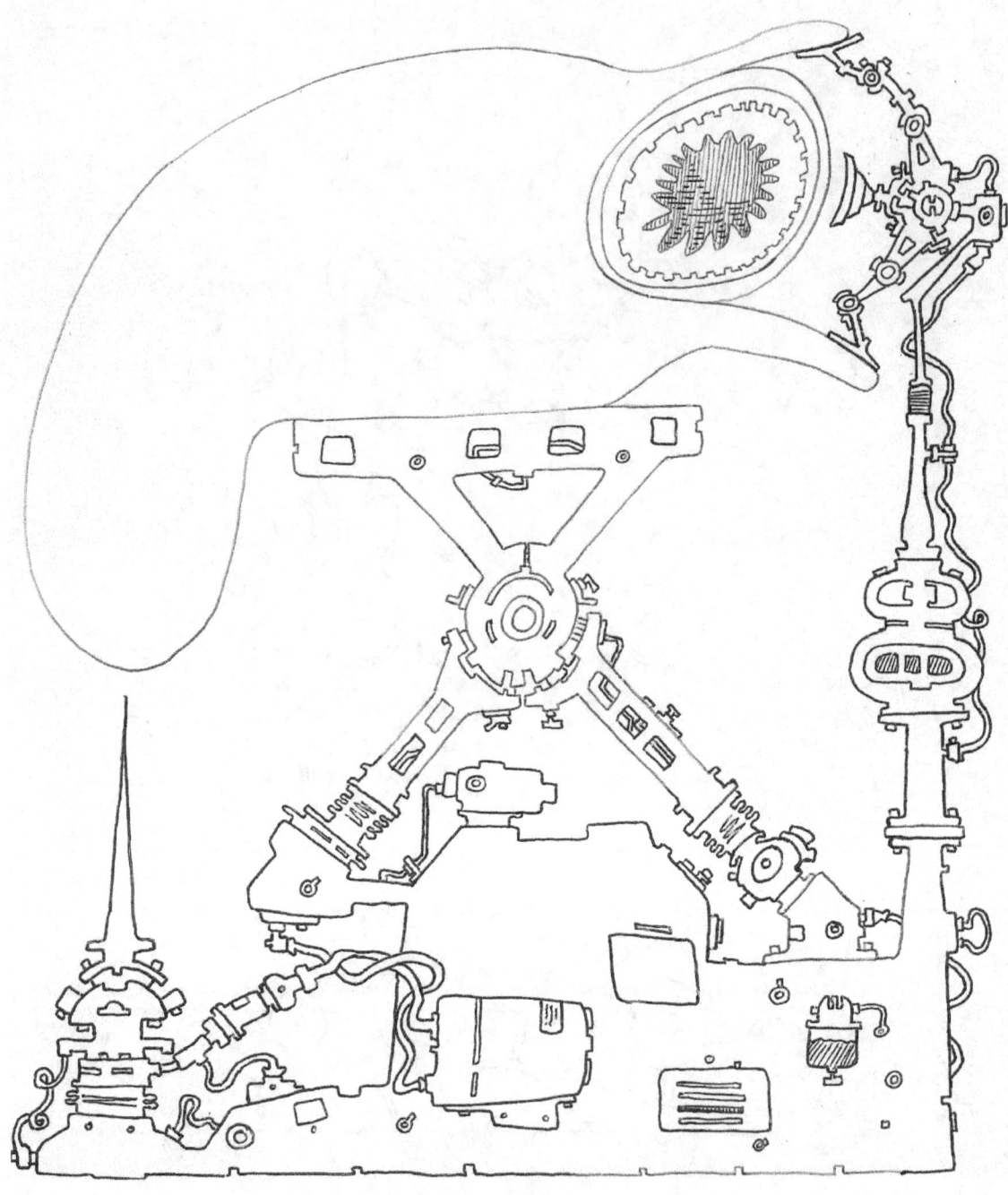

№ 115

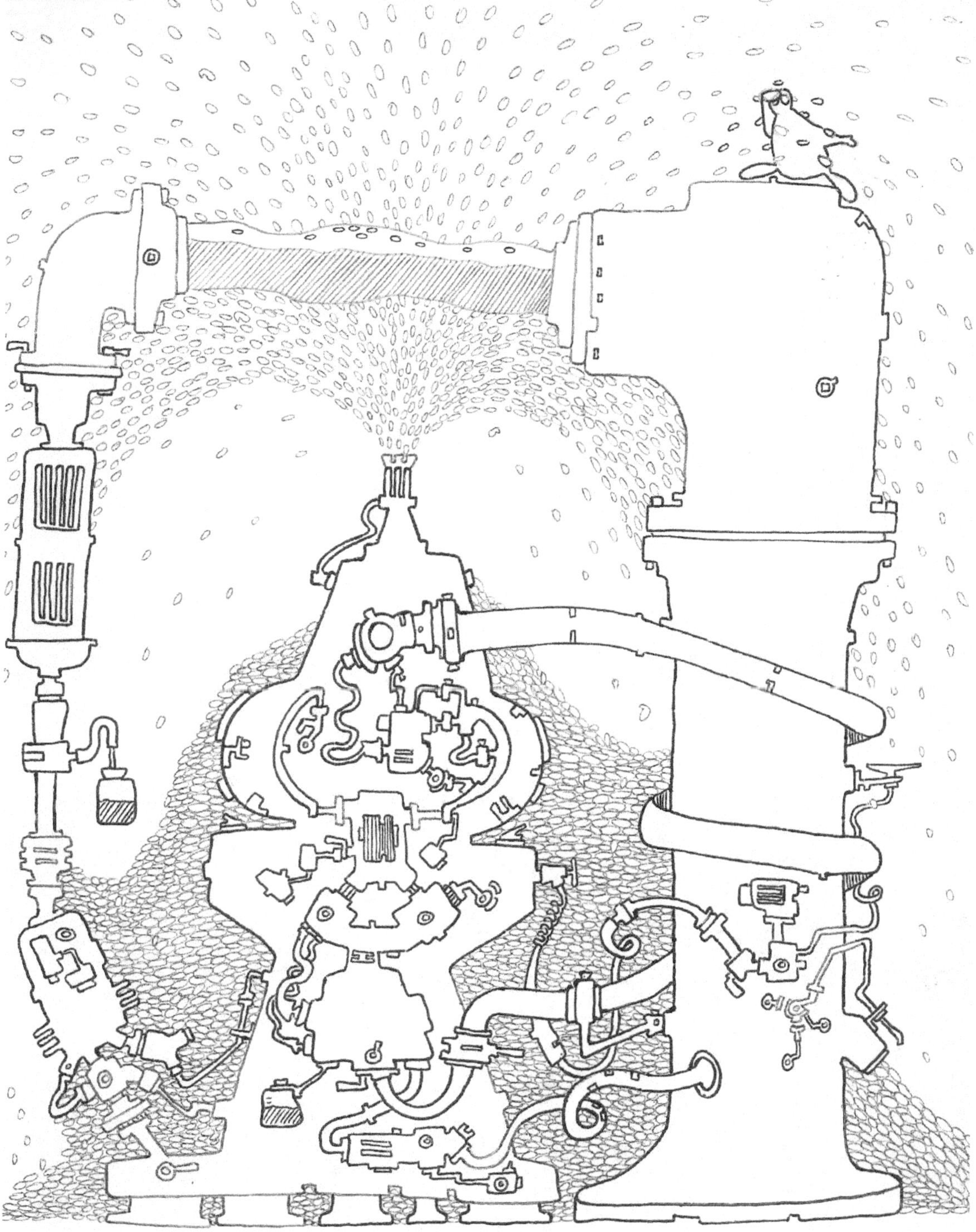

№ 116

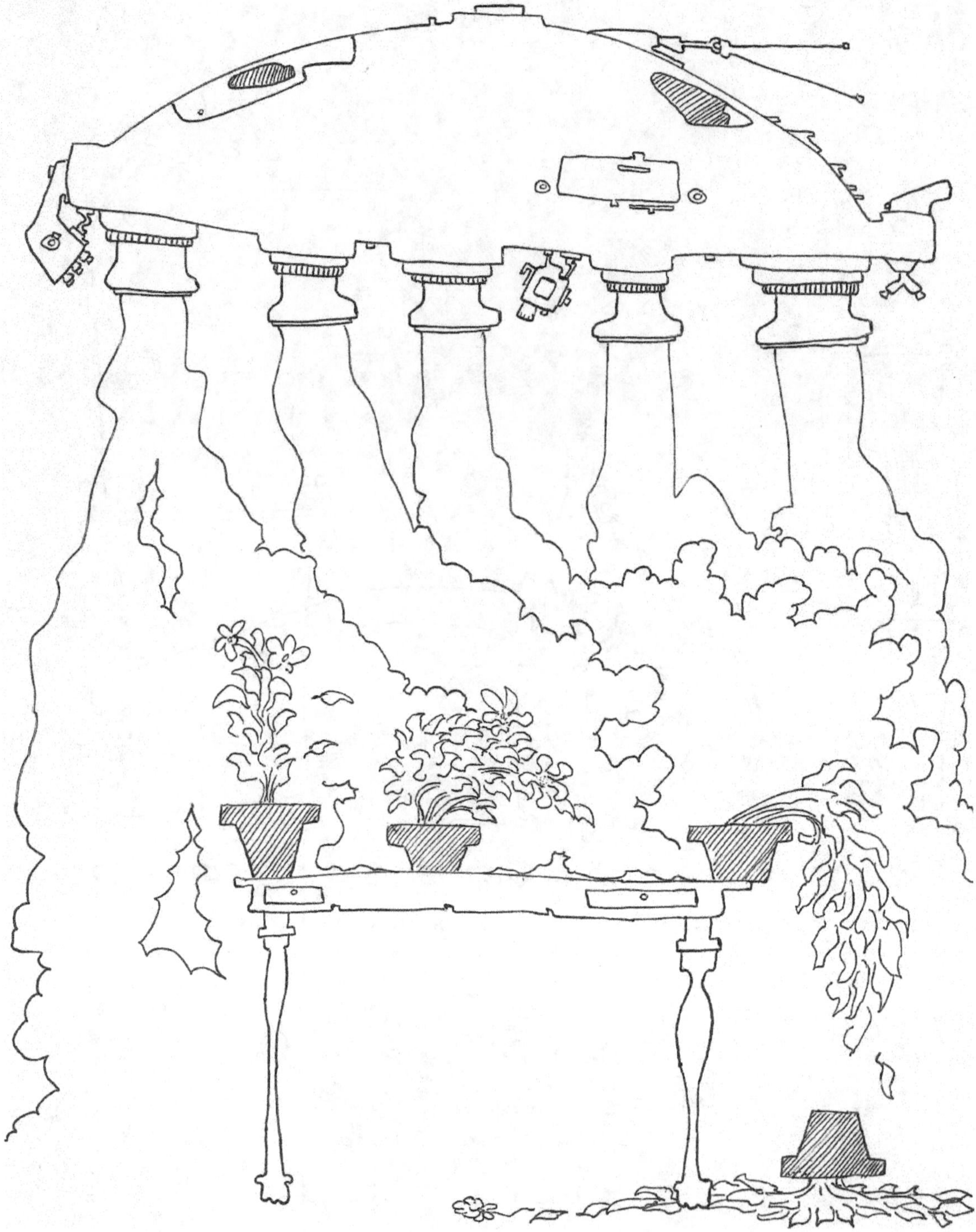

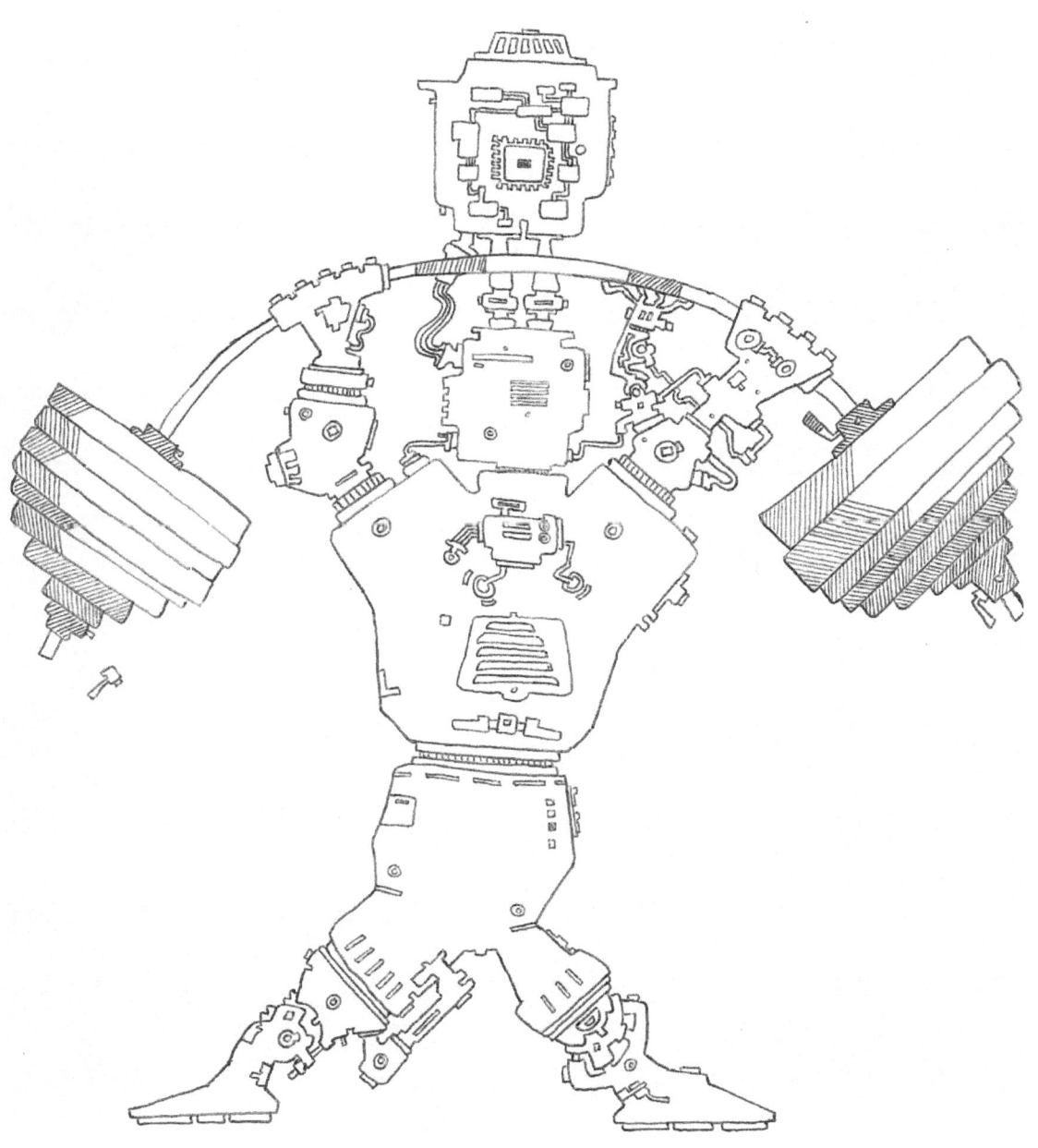

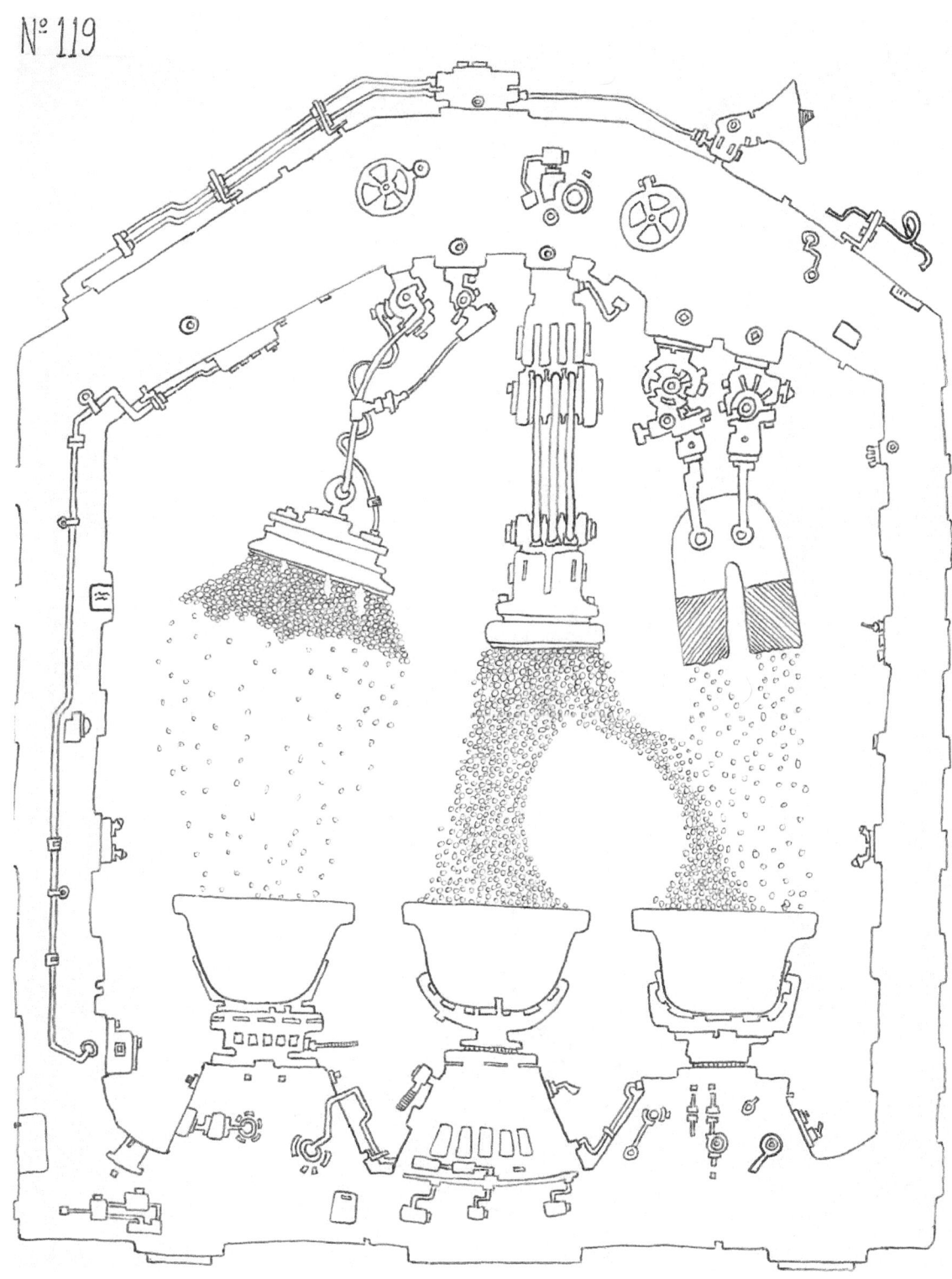

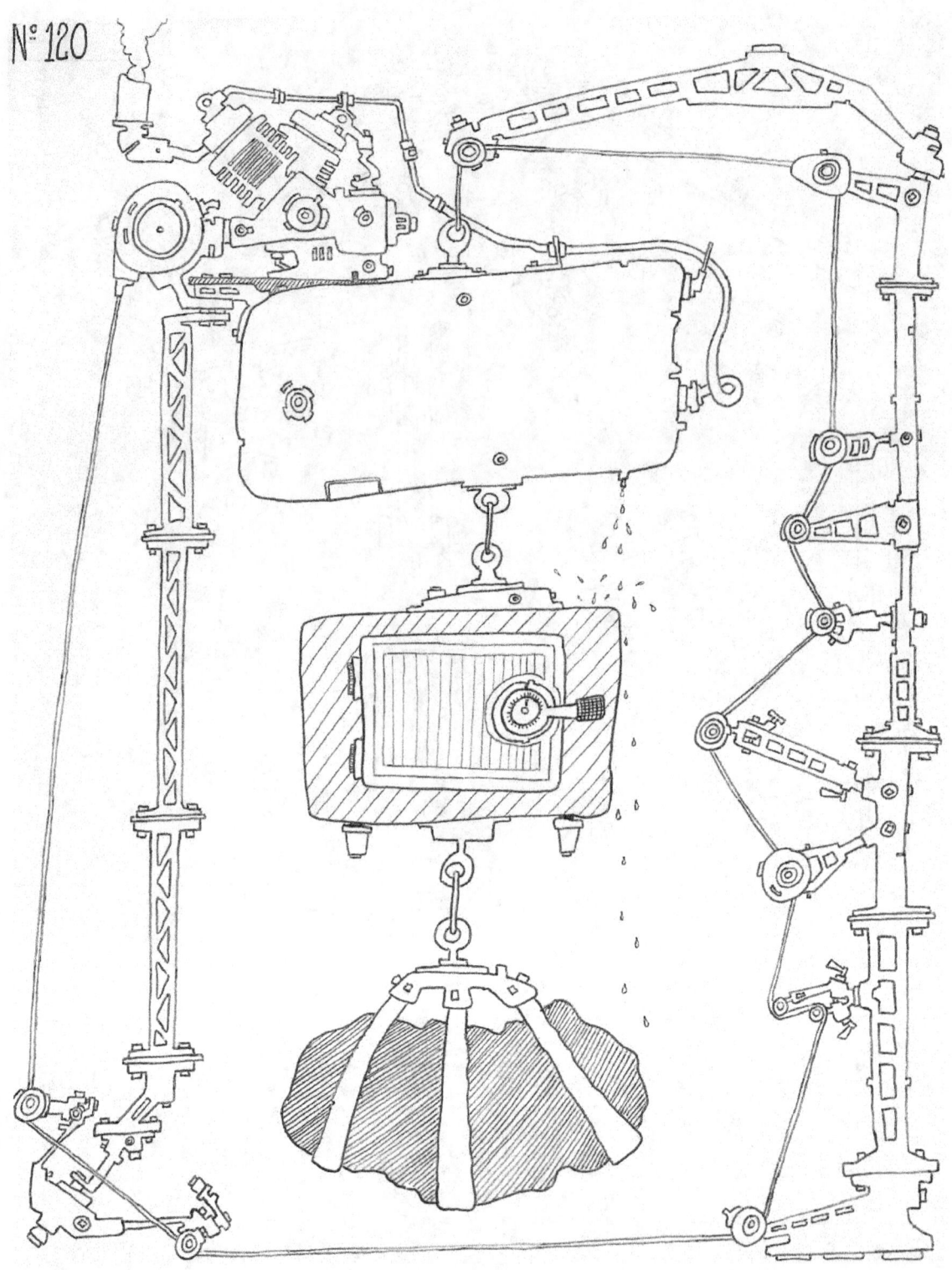

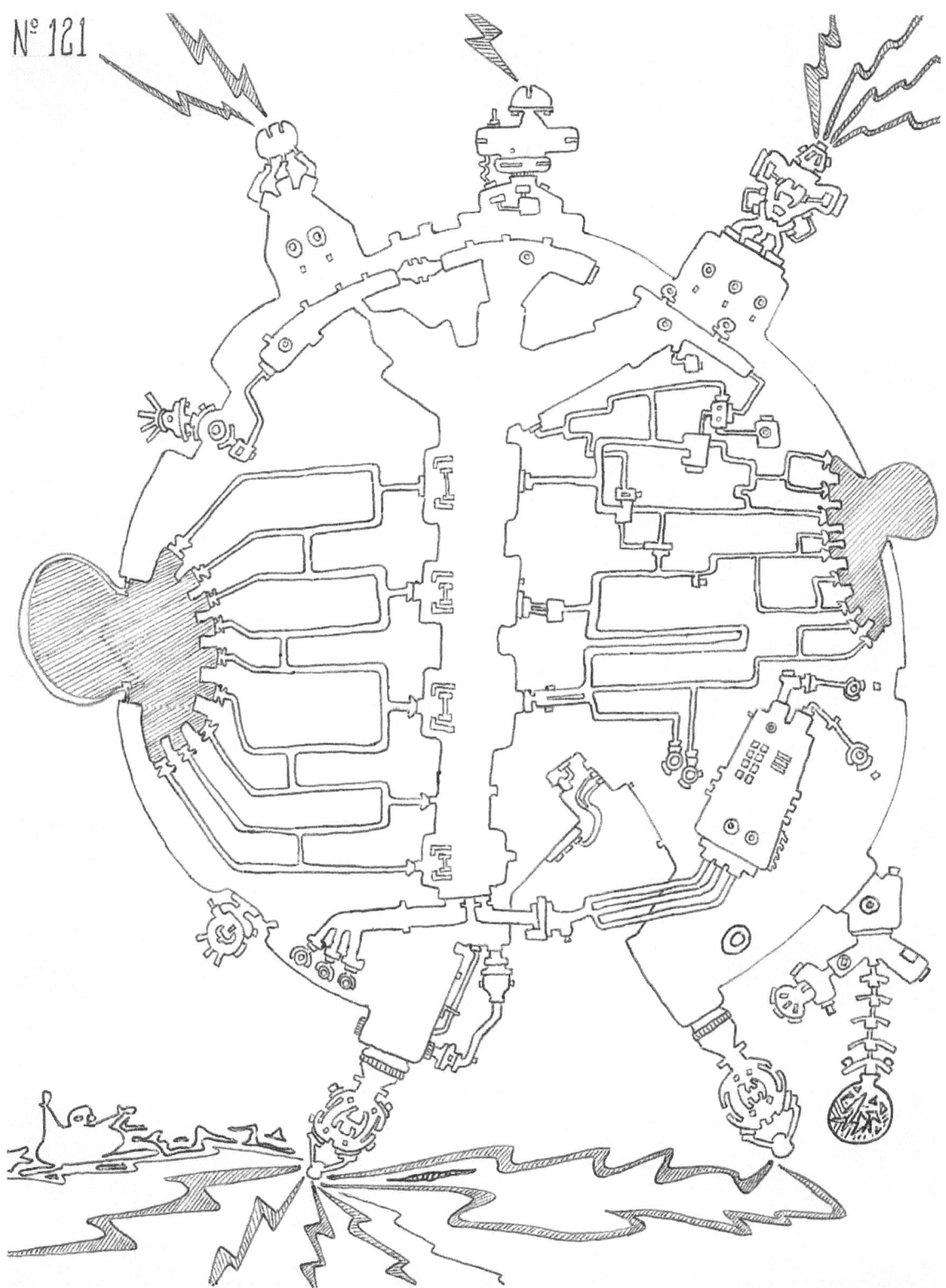

N° 122

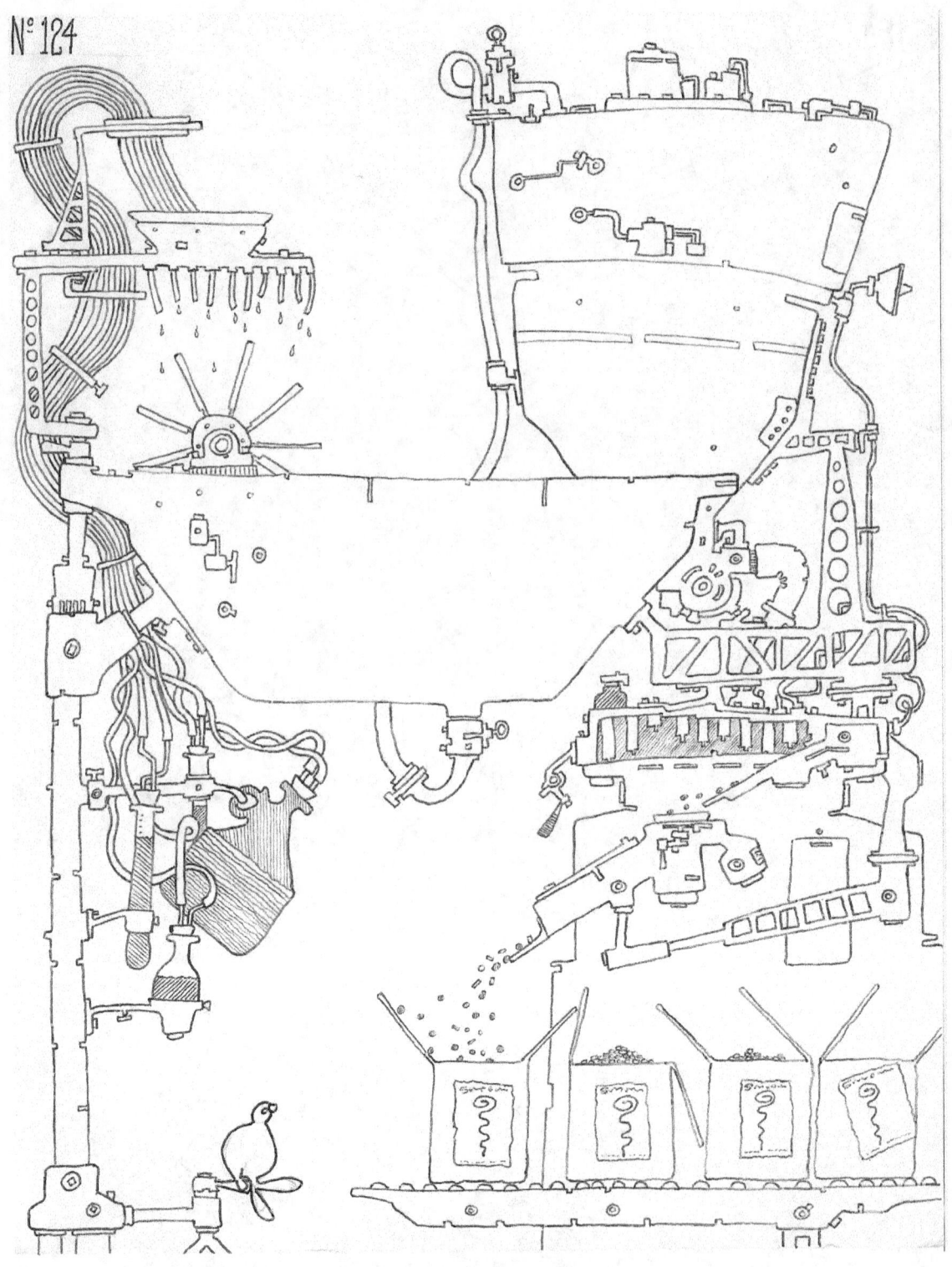

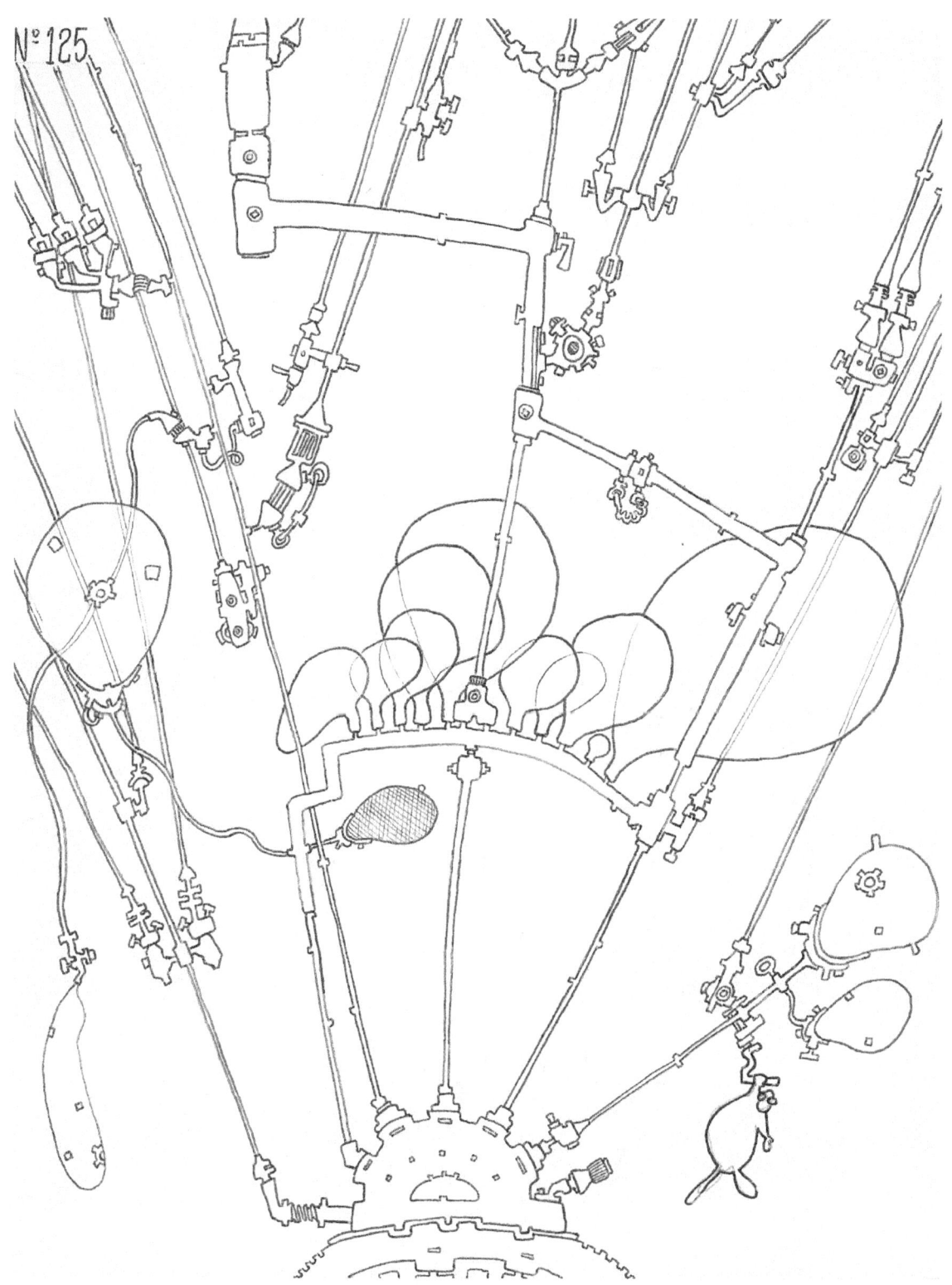

N° 126

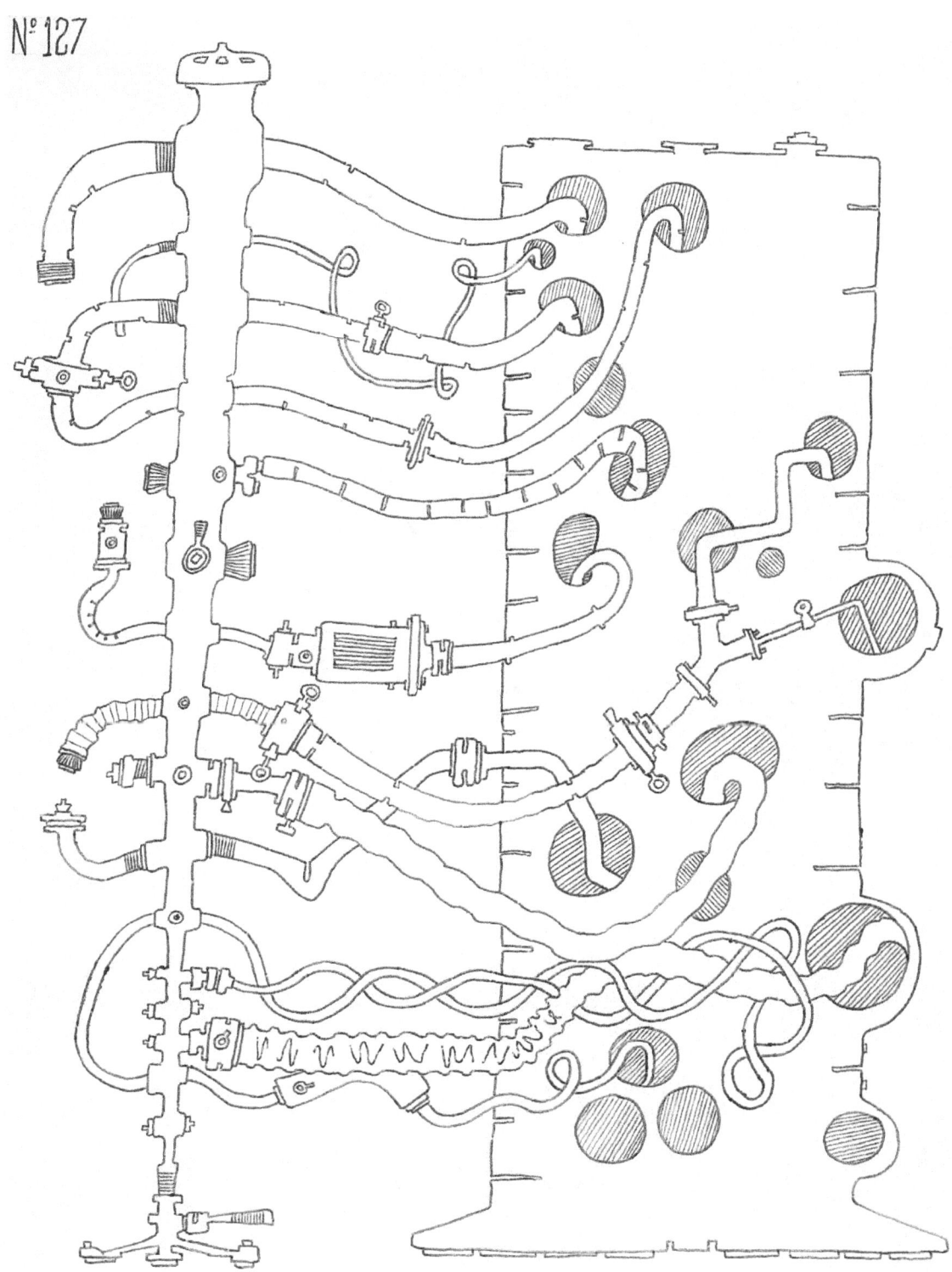

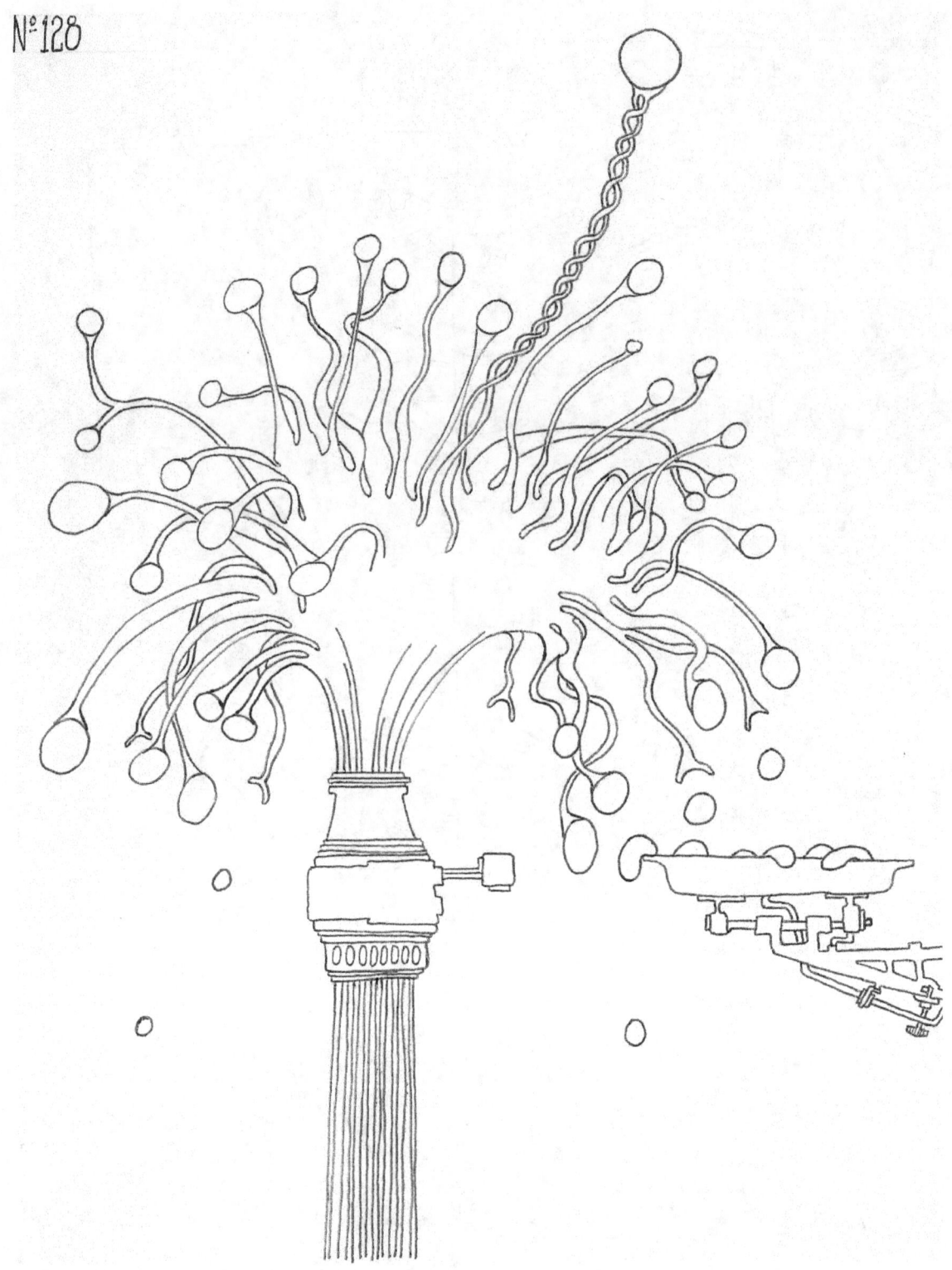

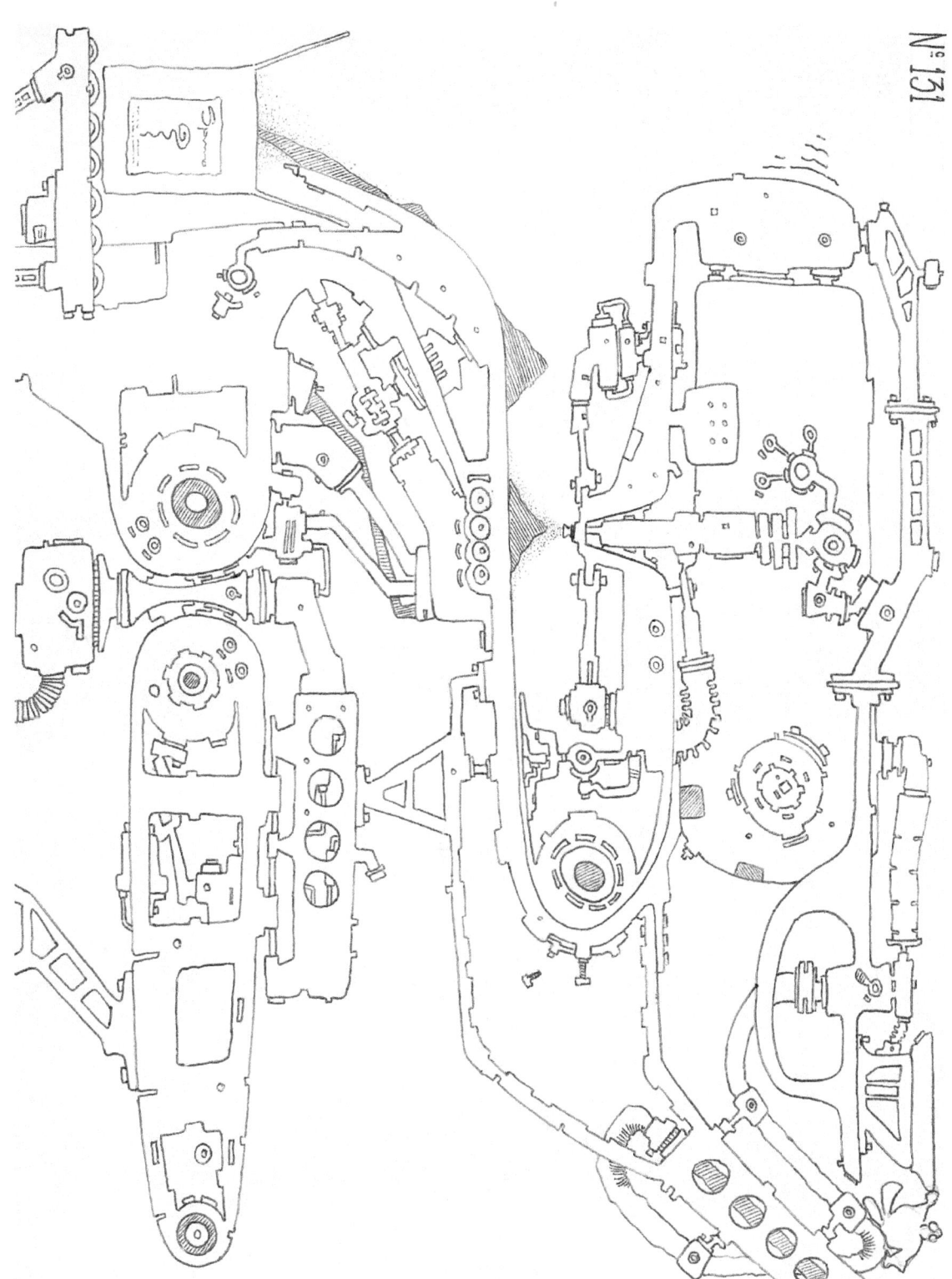

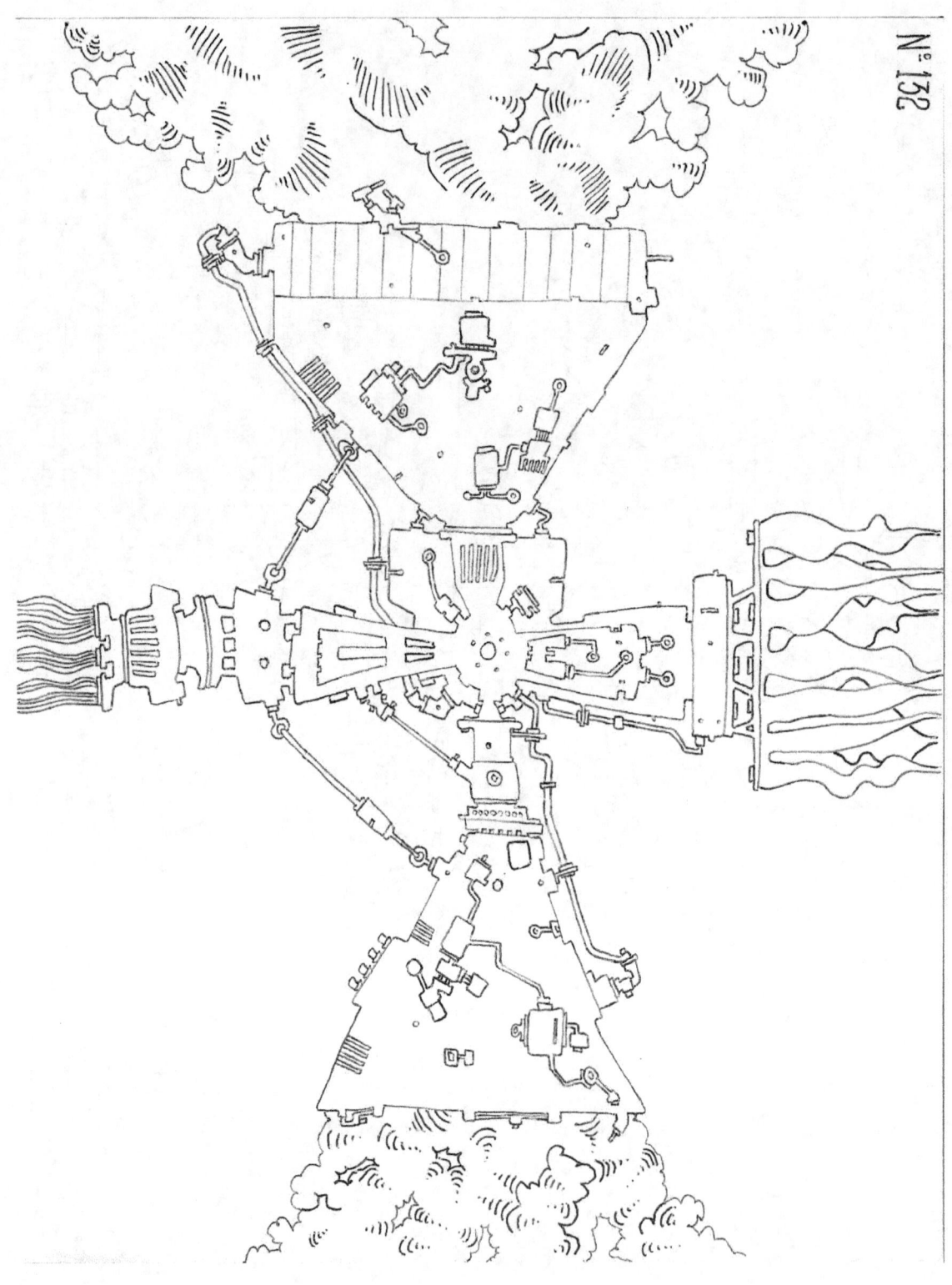

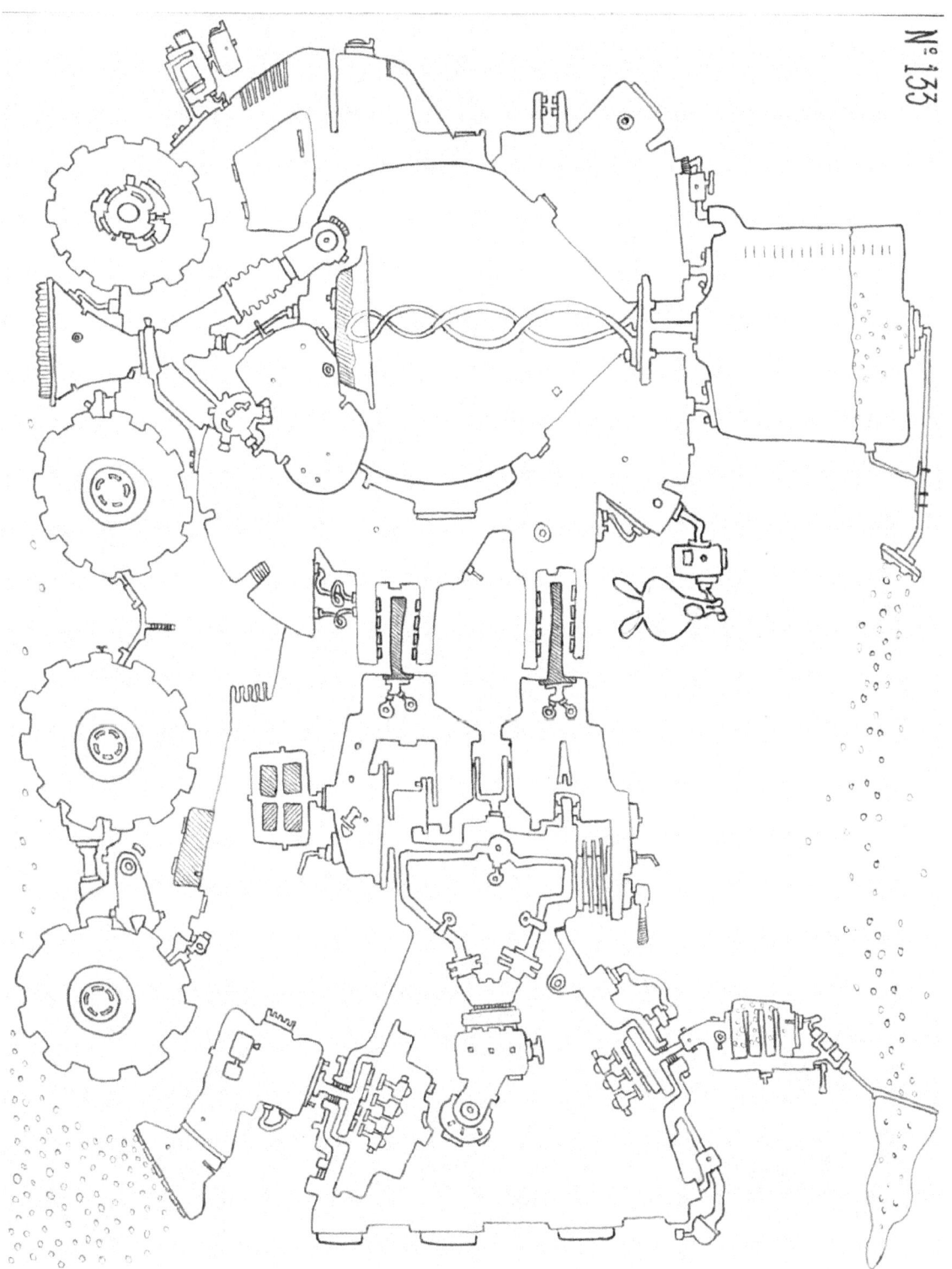

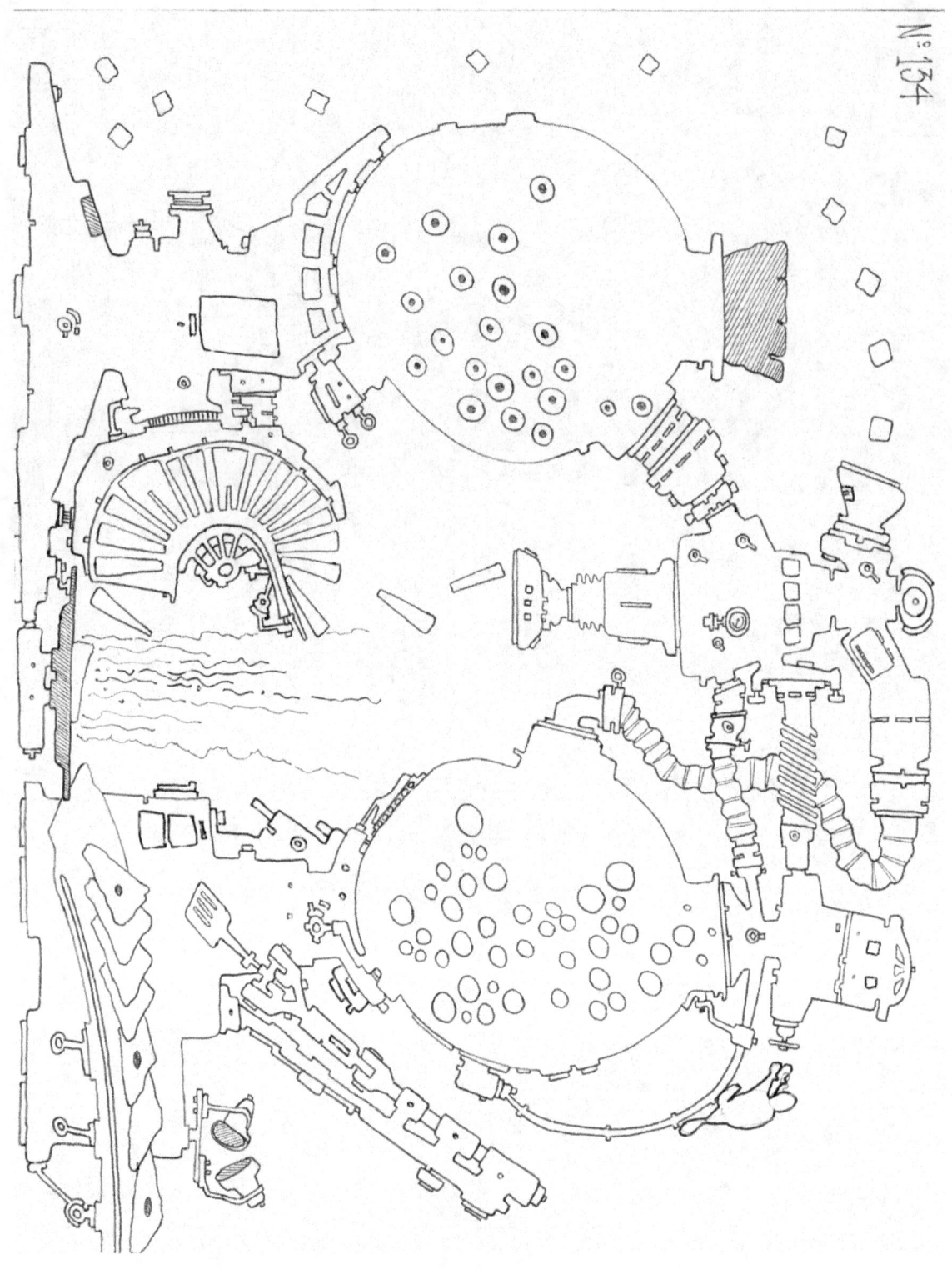

Nº 135

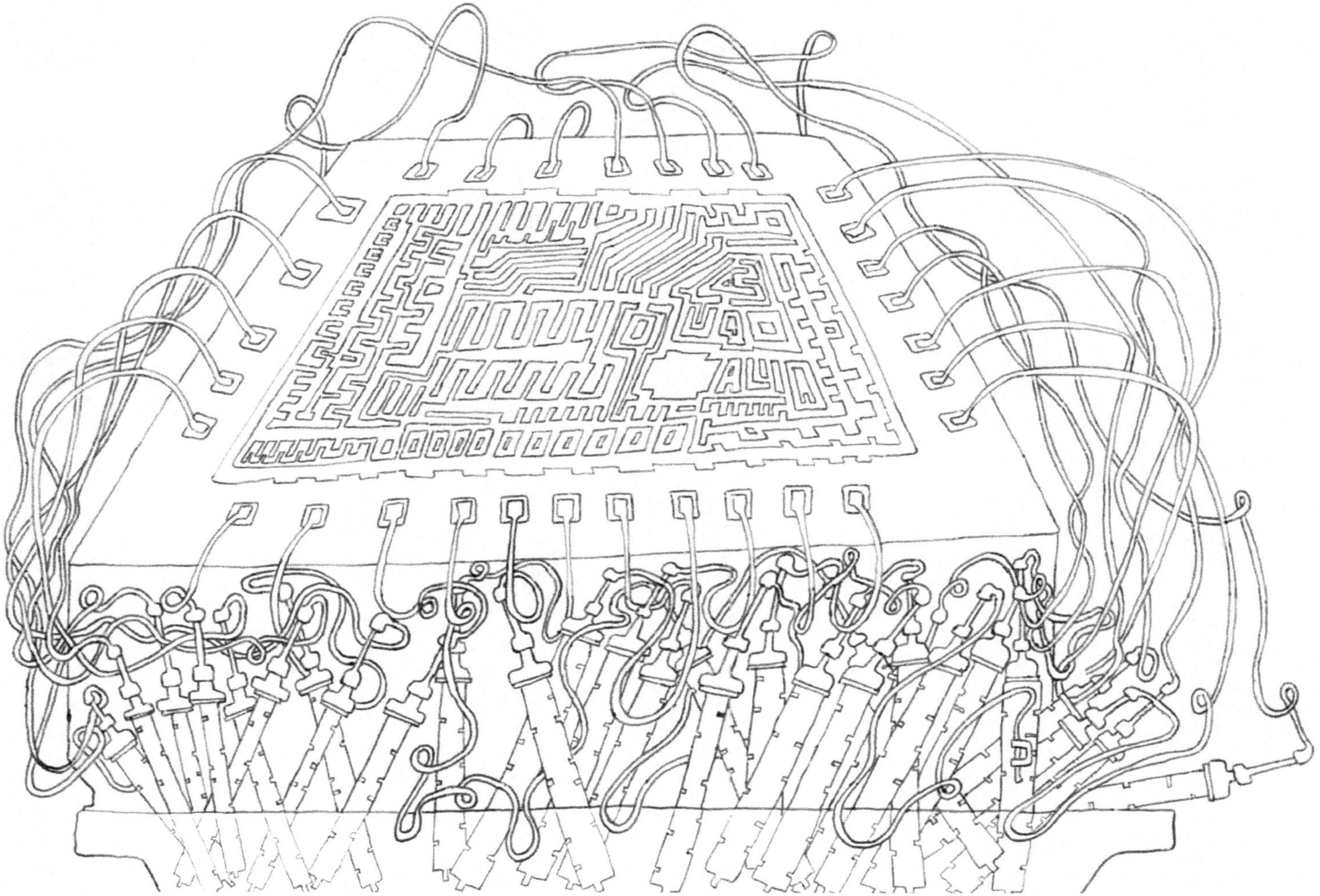

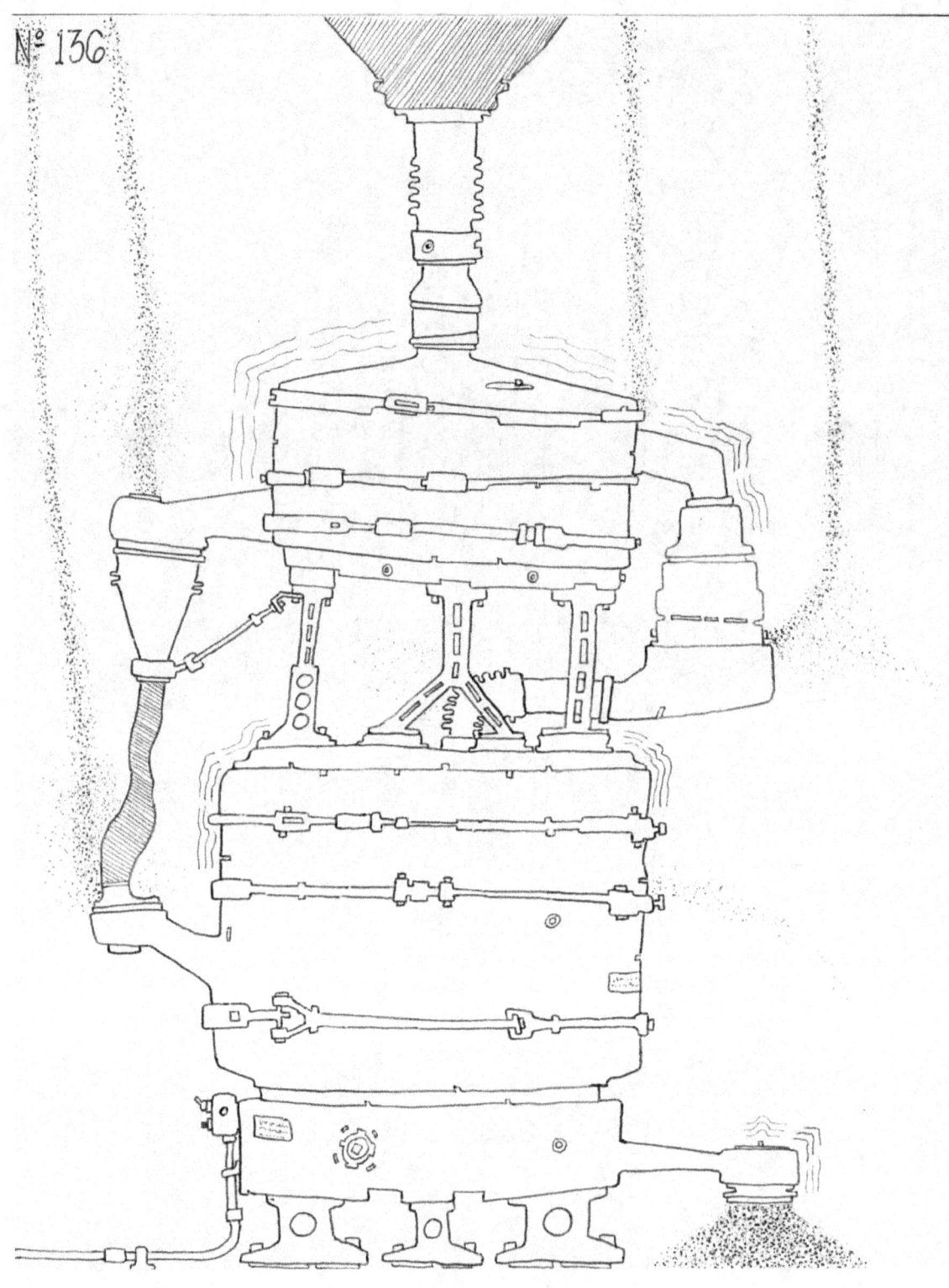

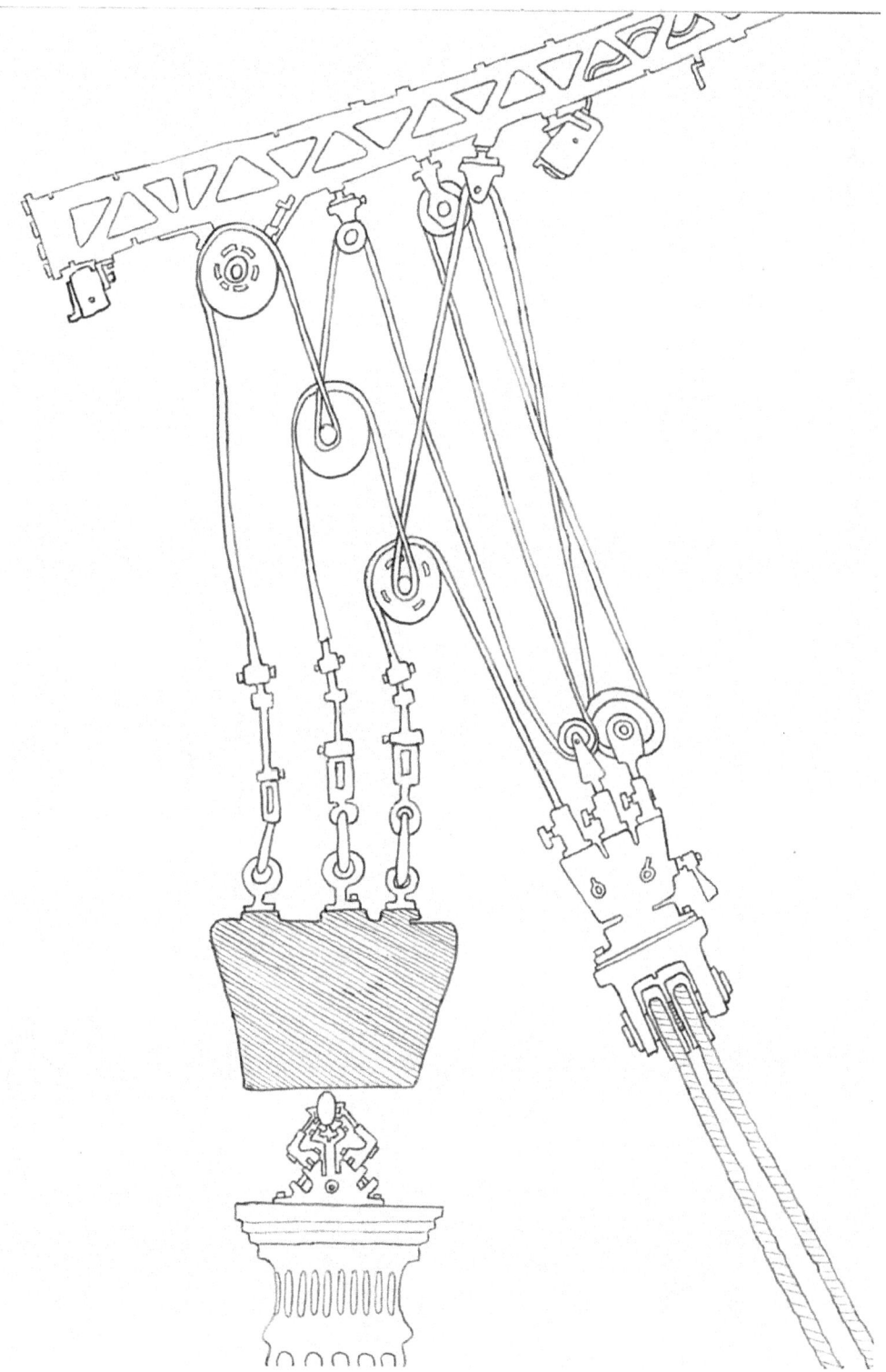

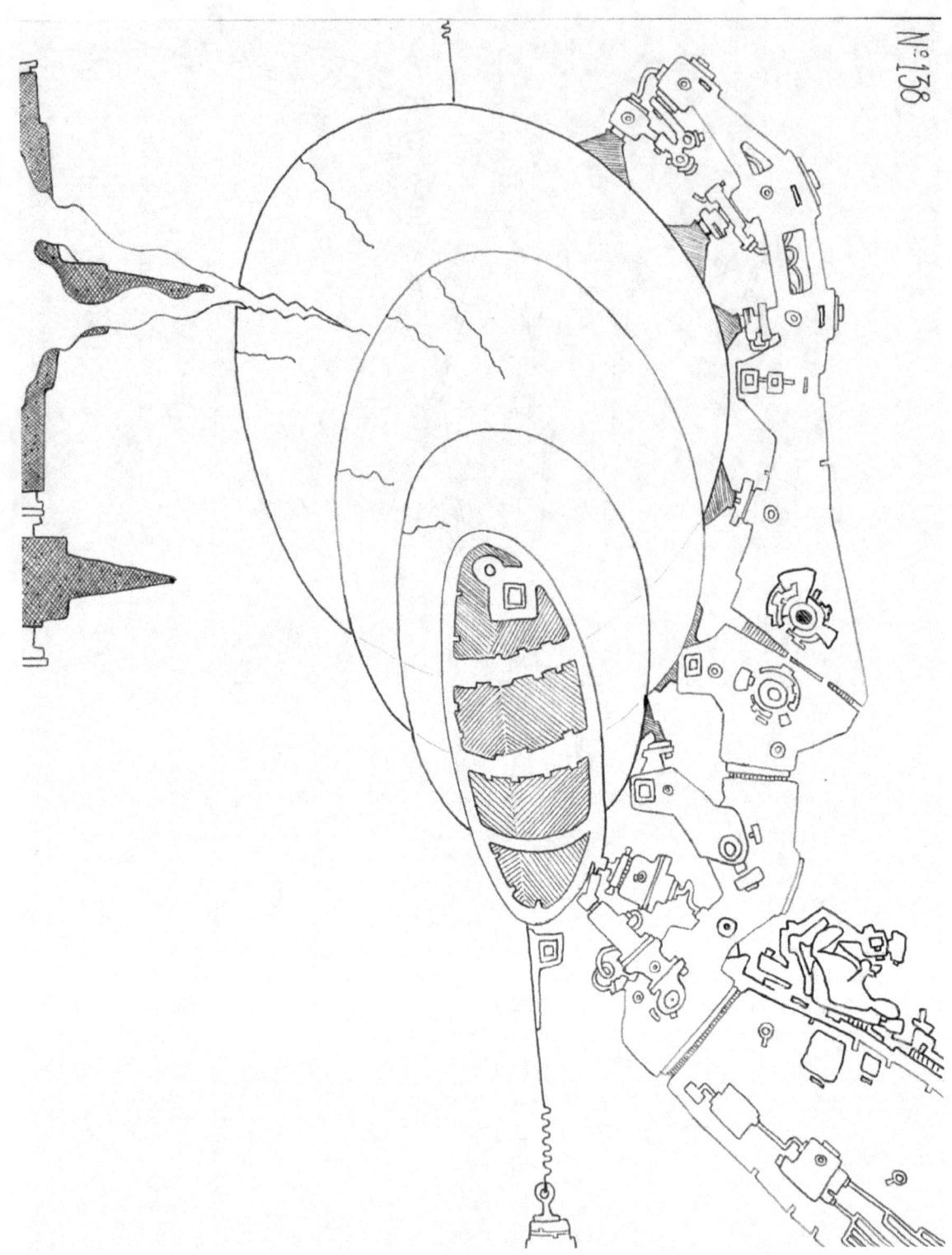

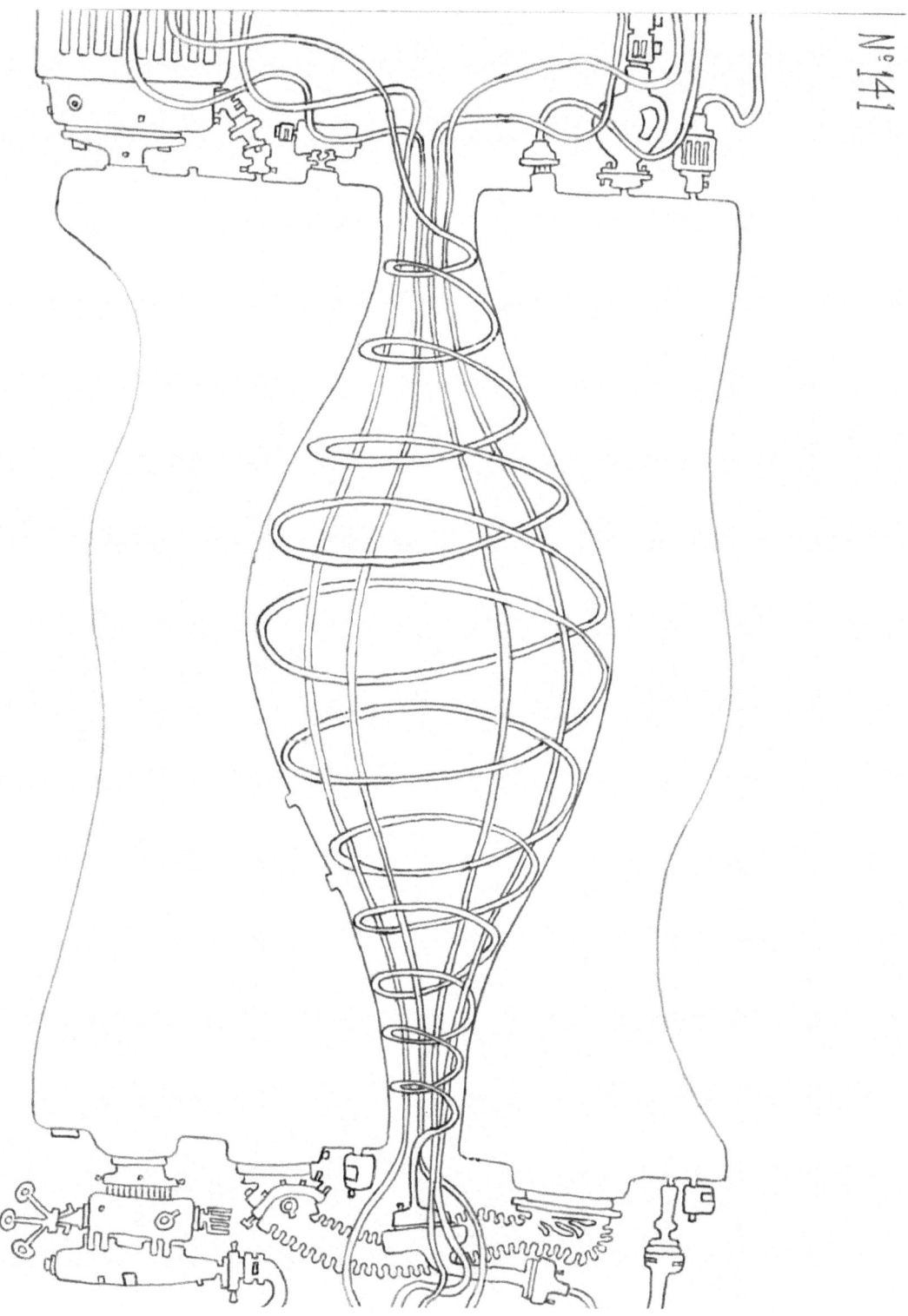

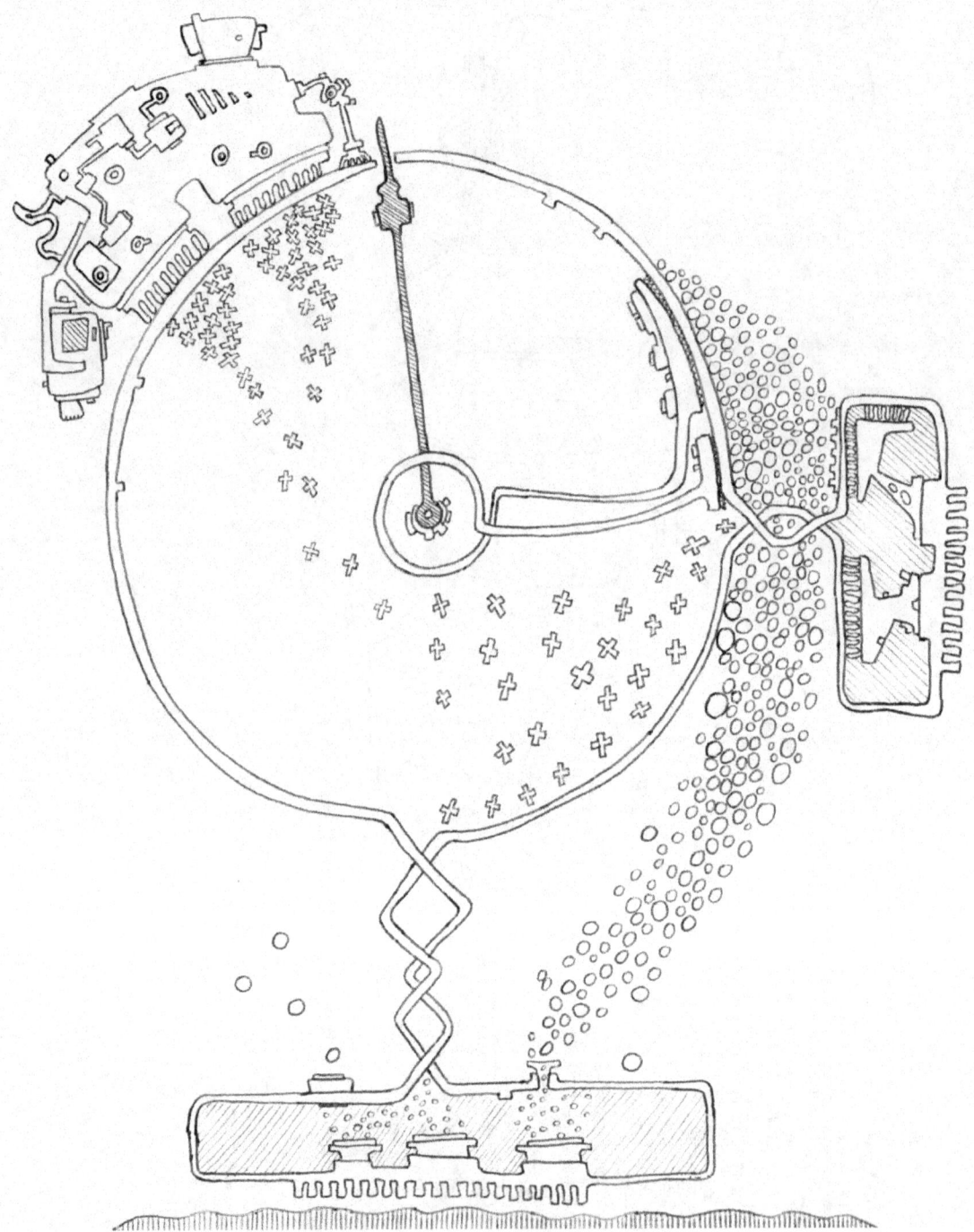

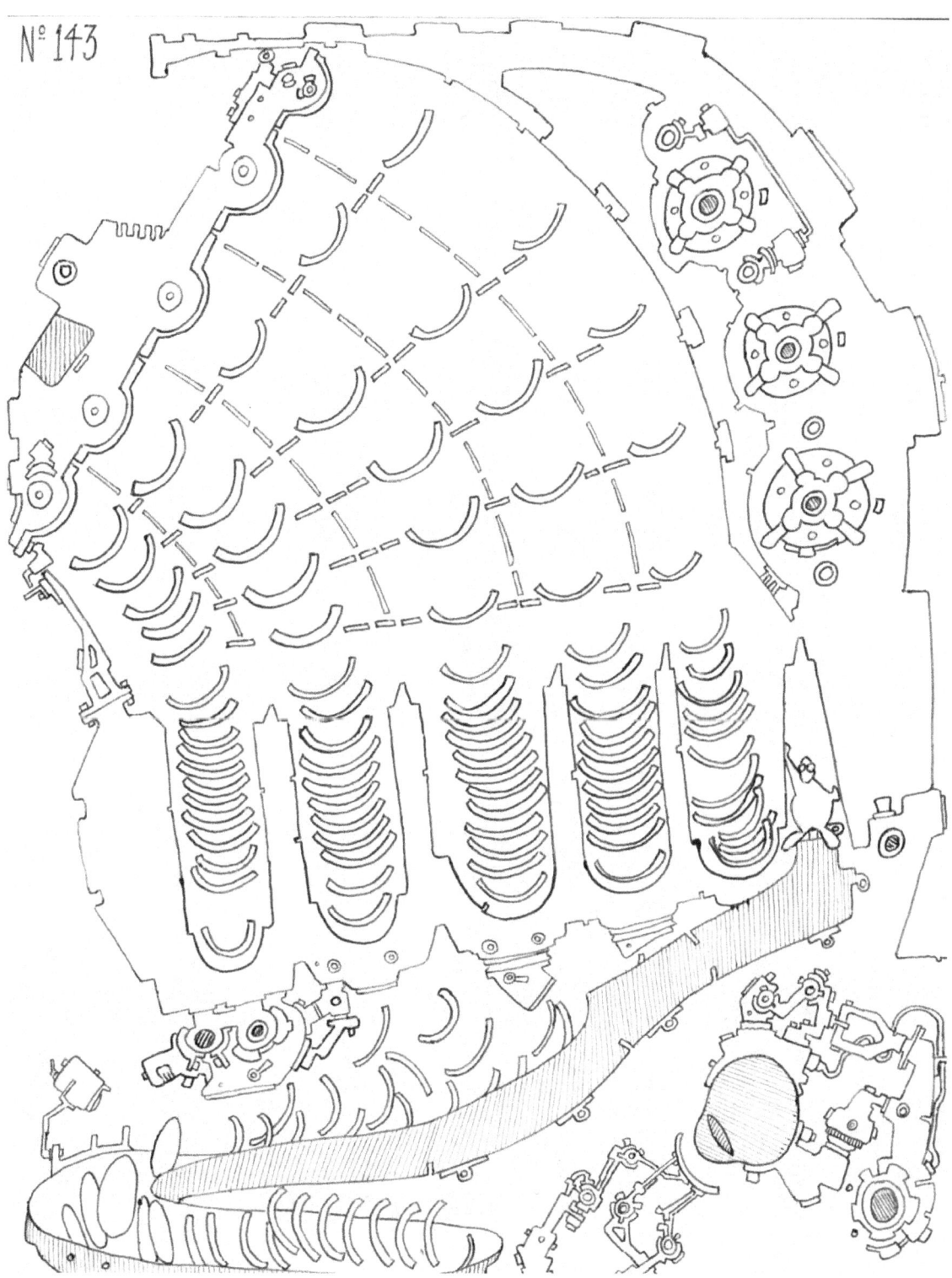

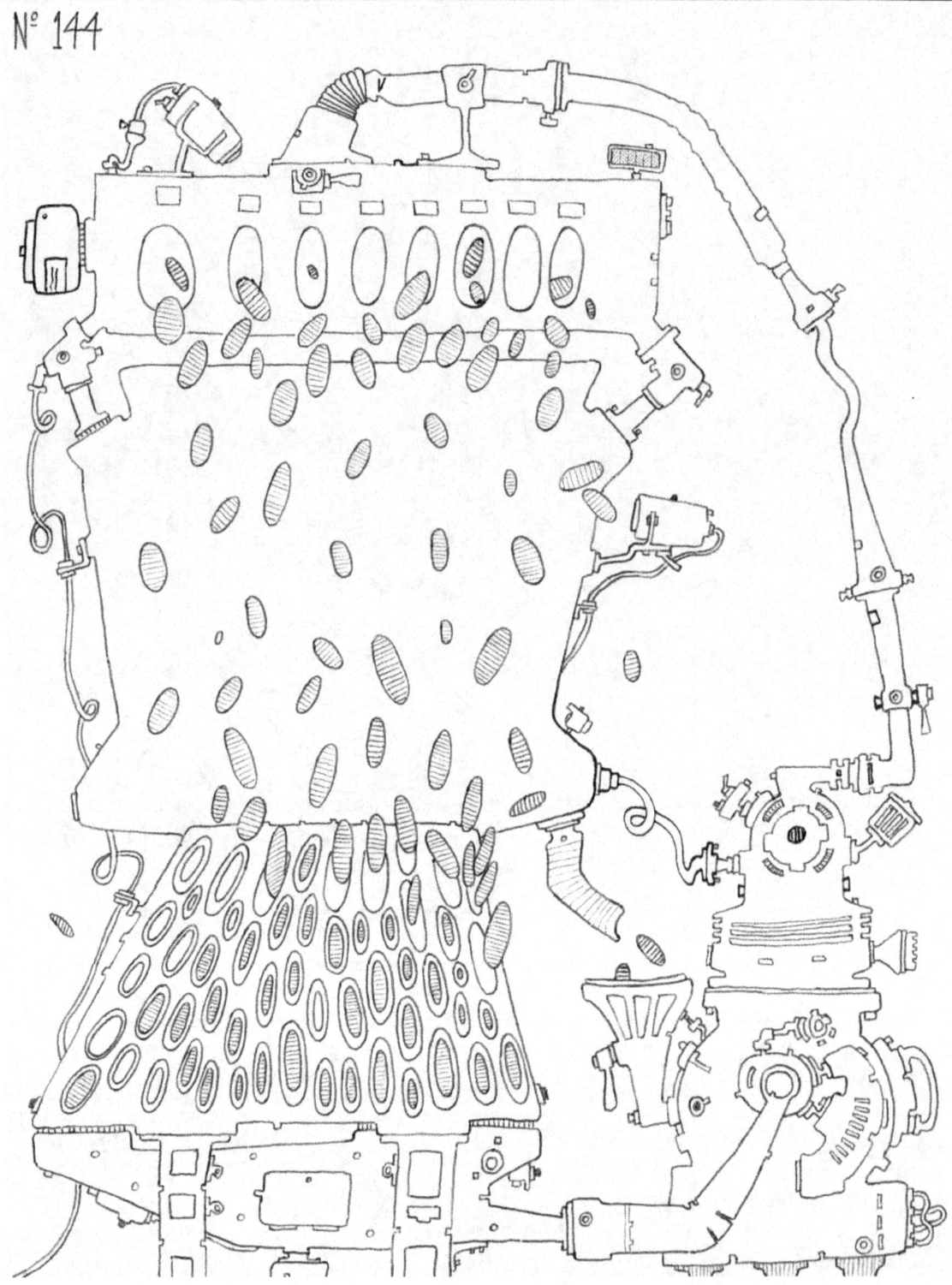

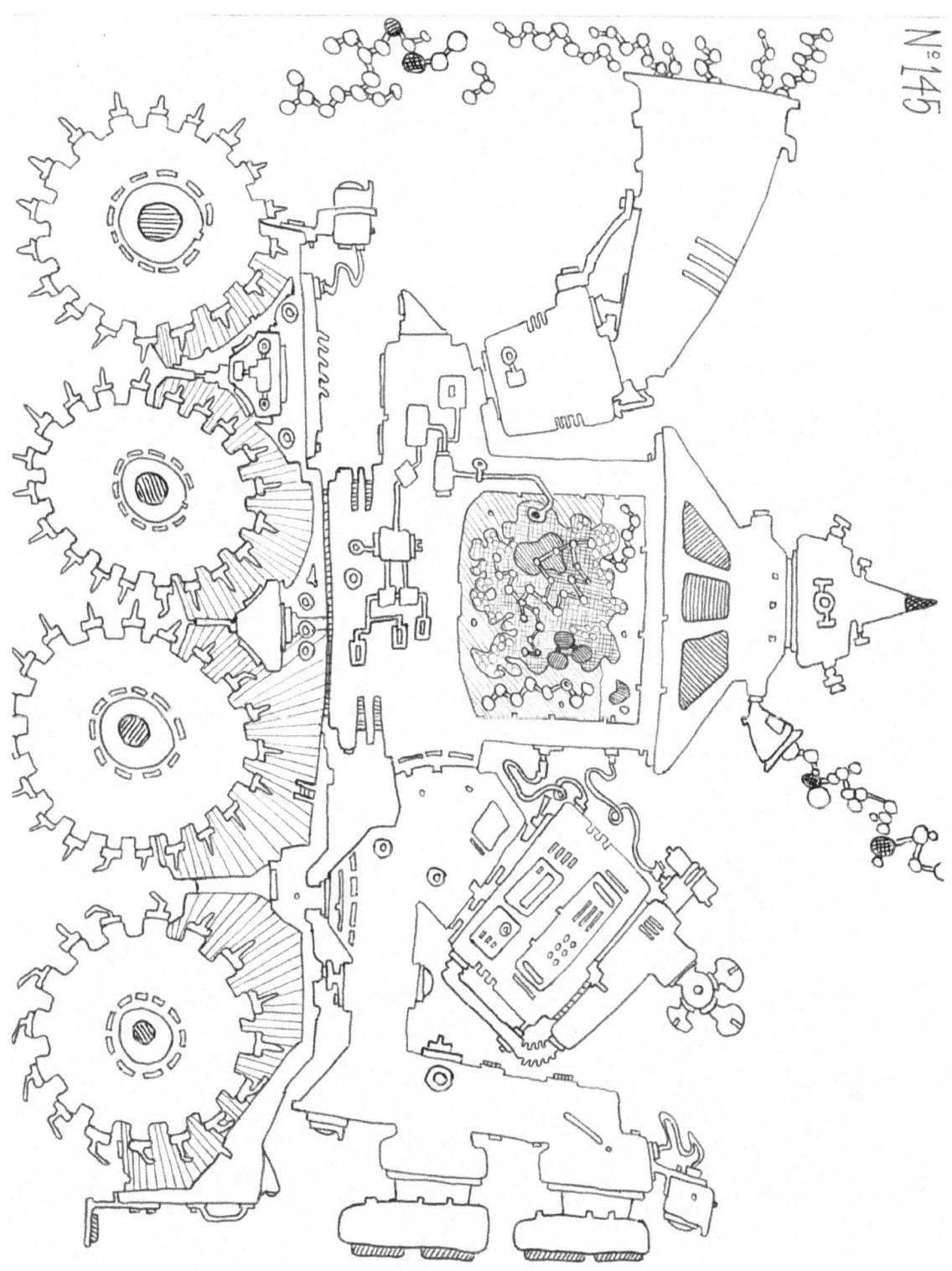

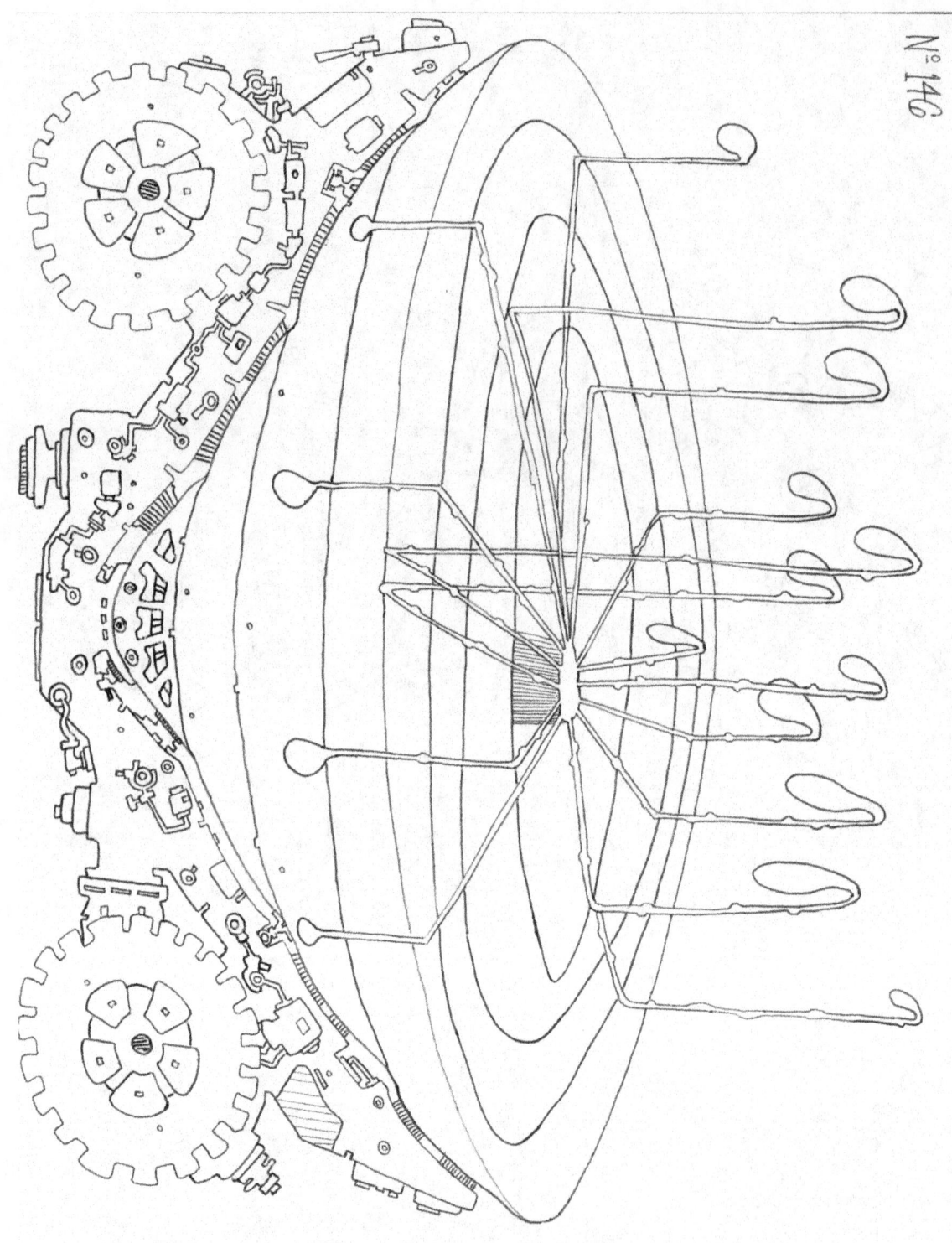

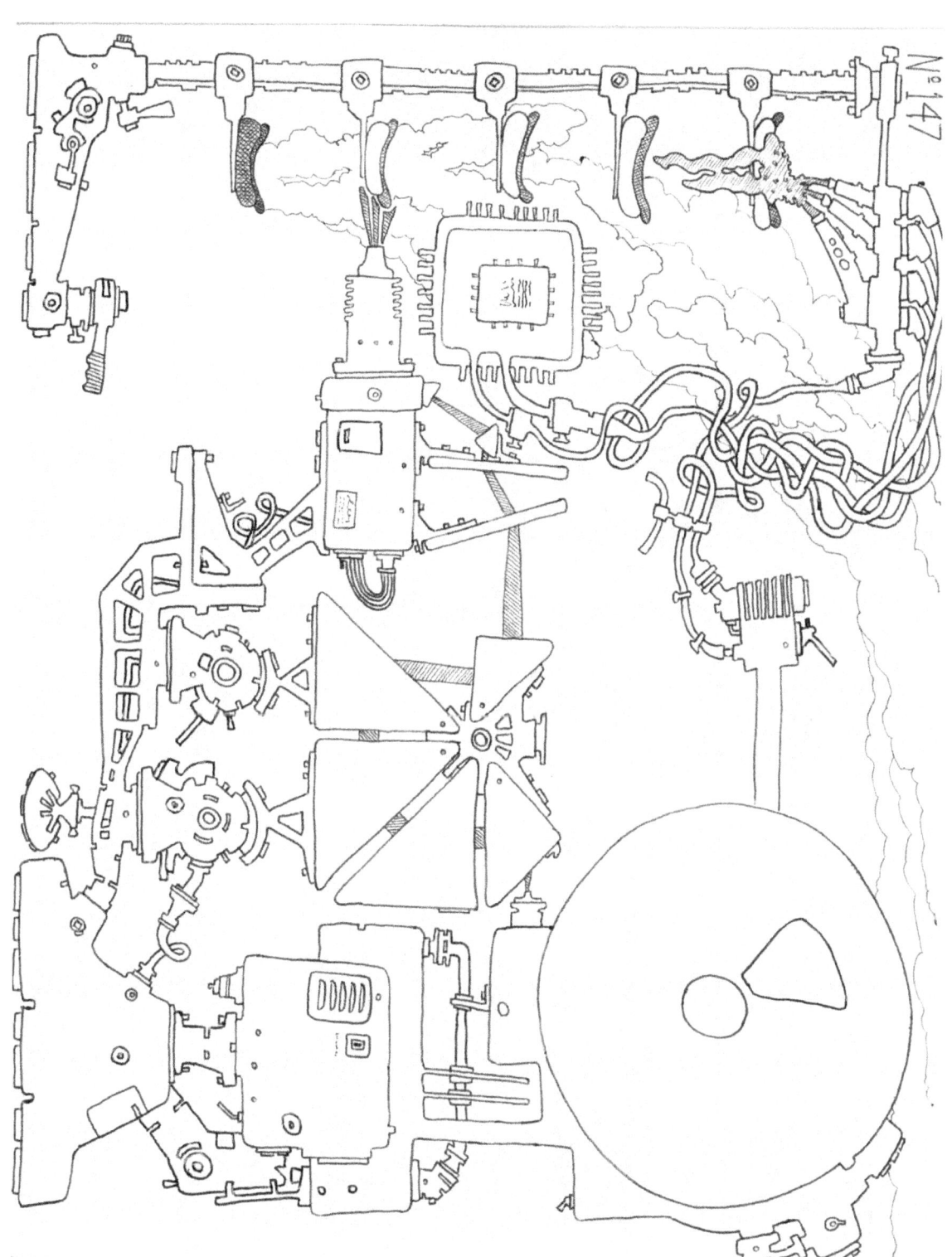

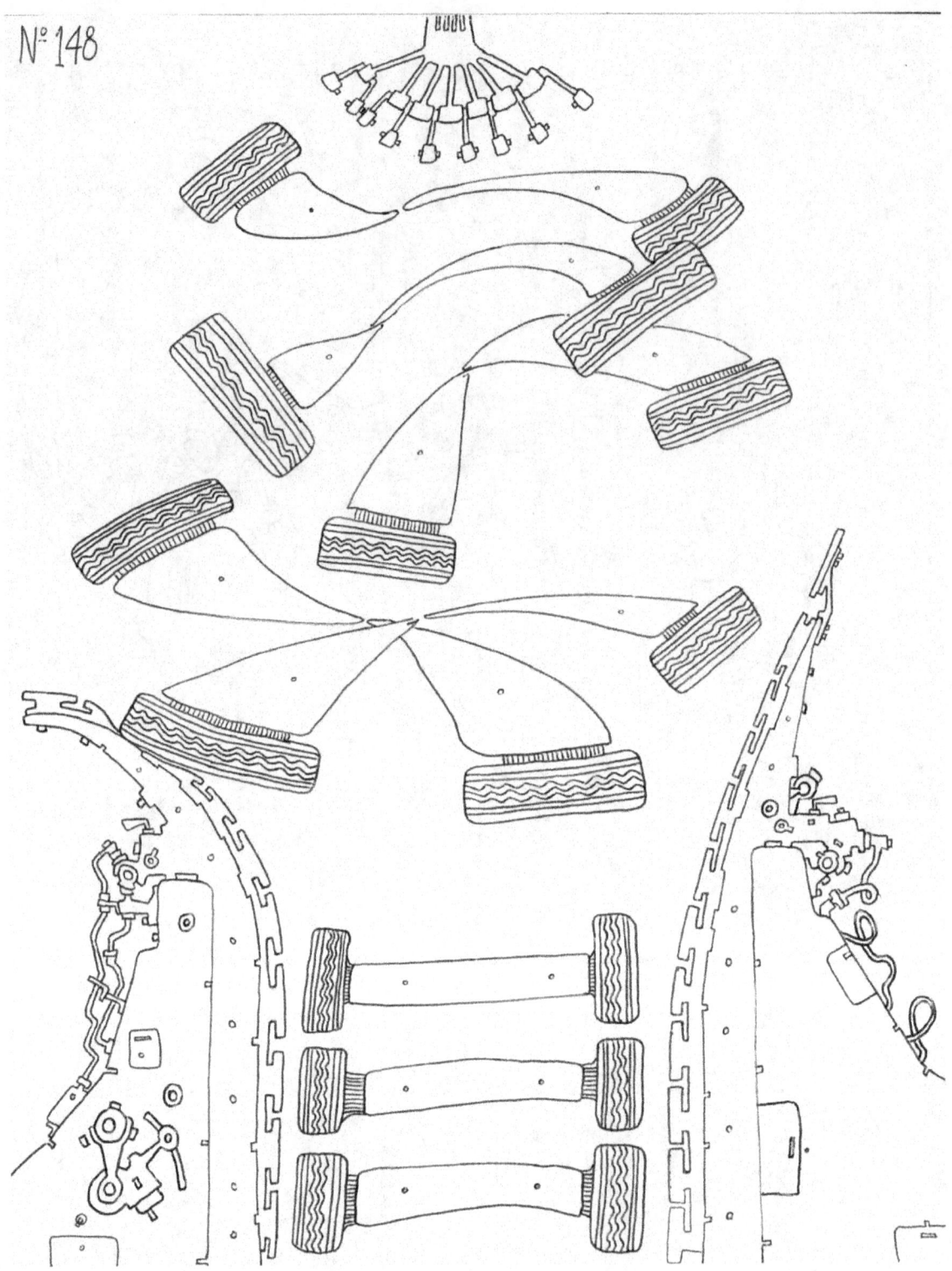

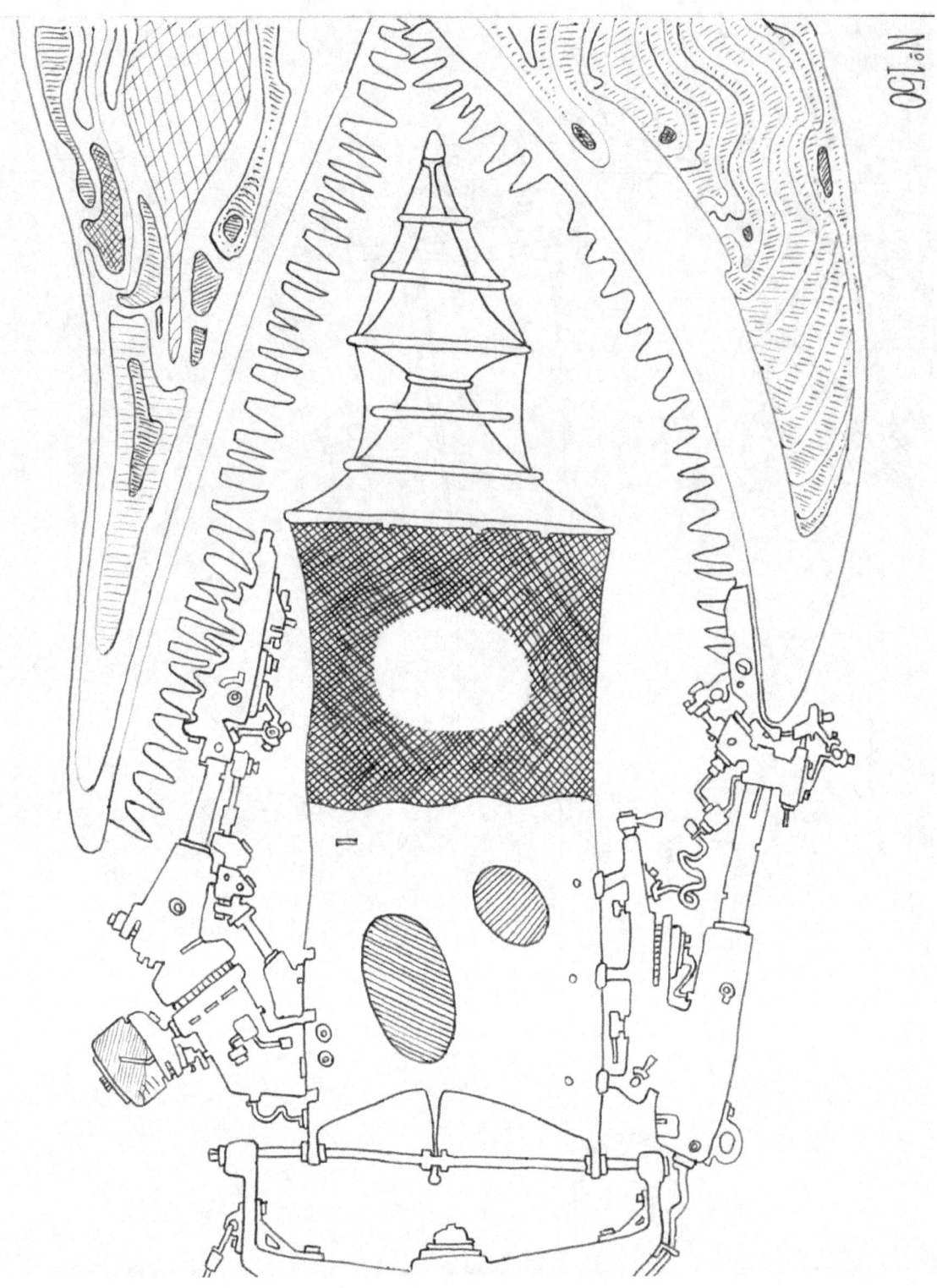

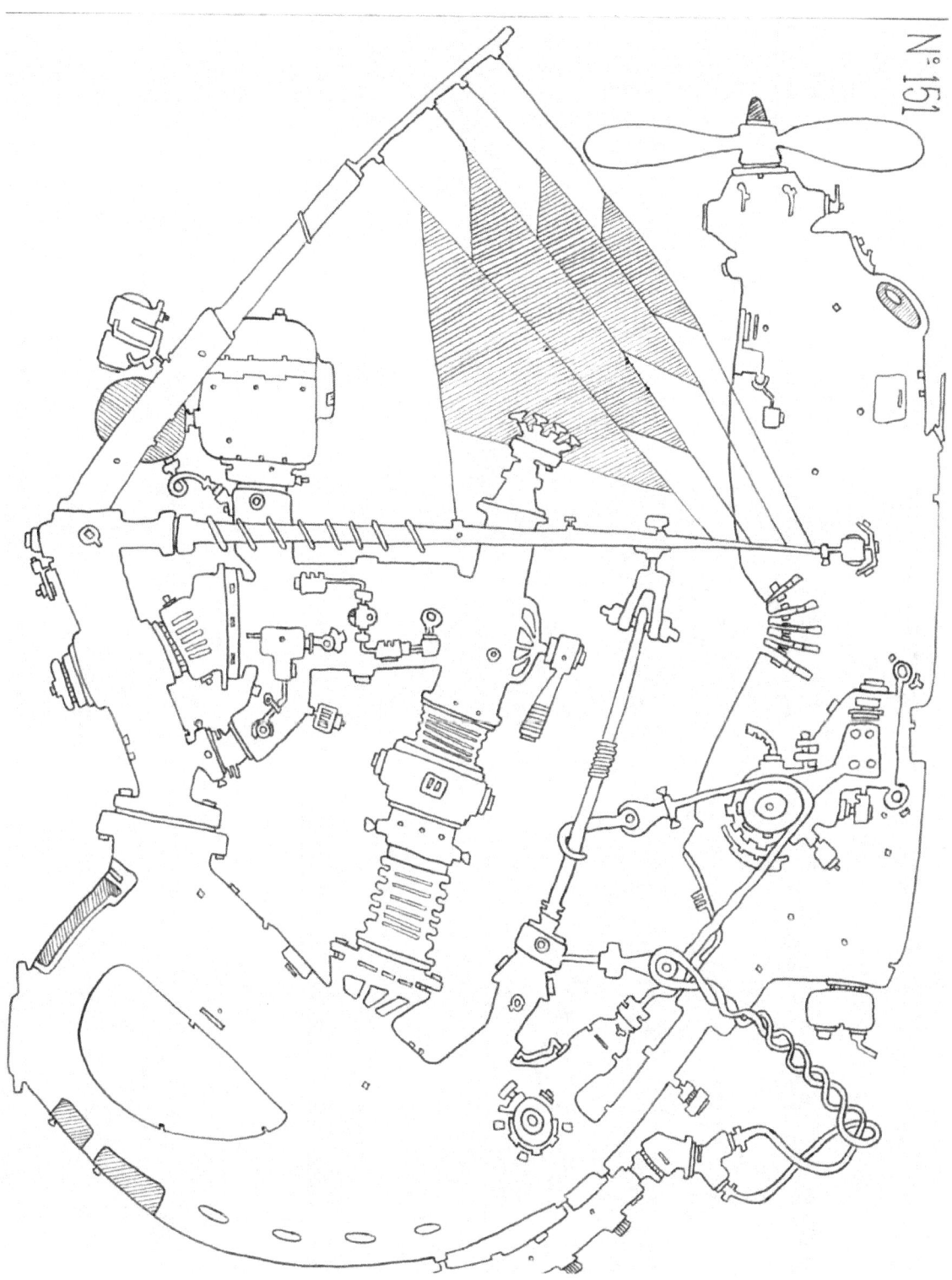

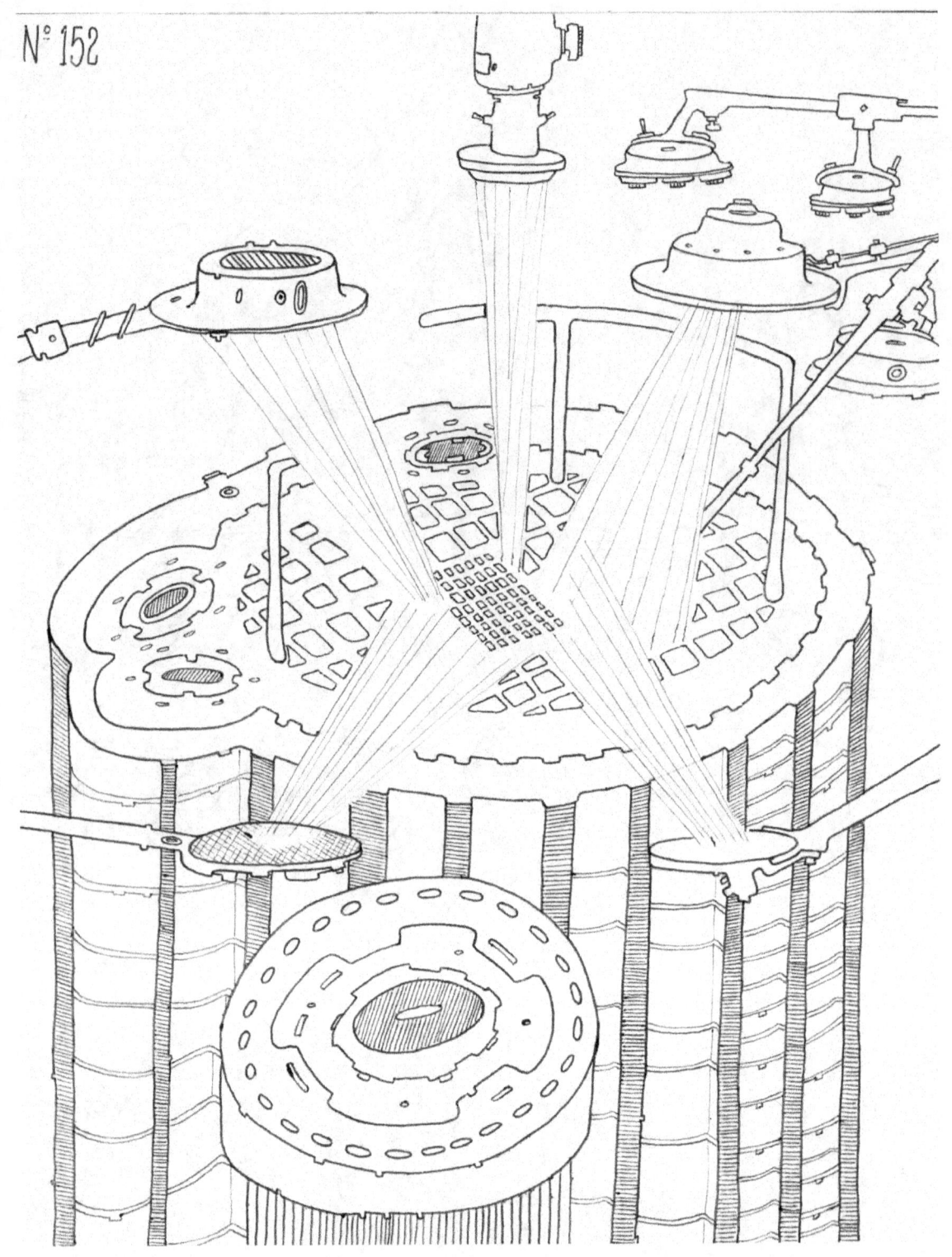

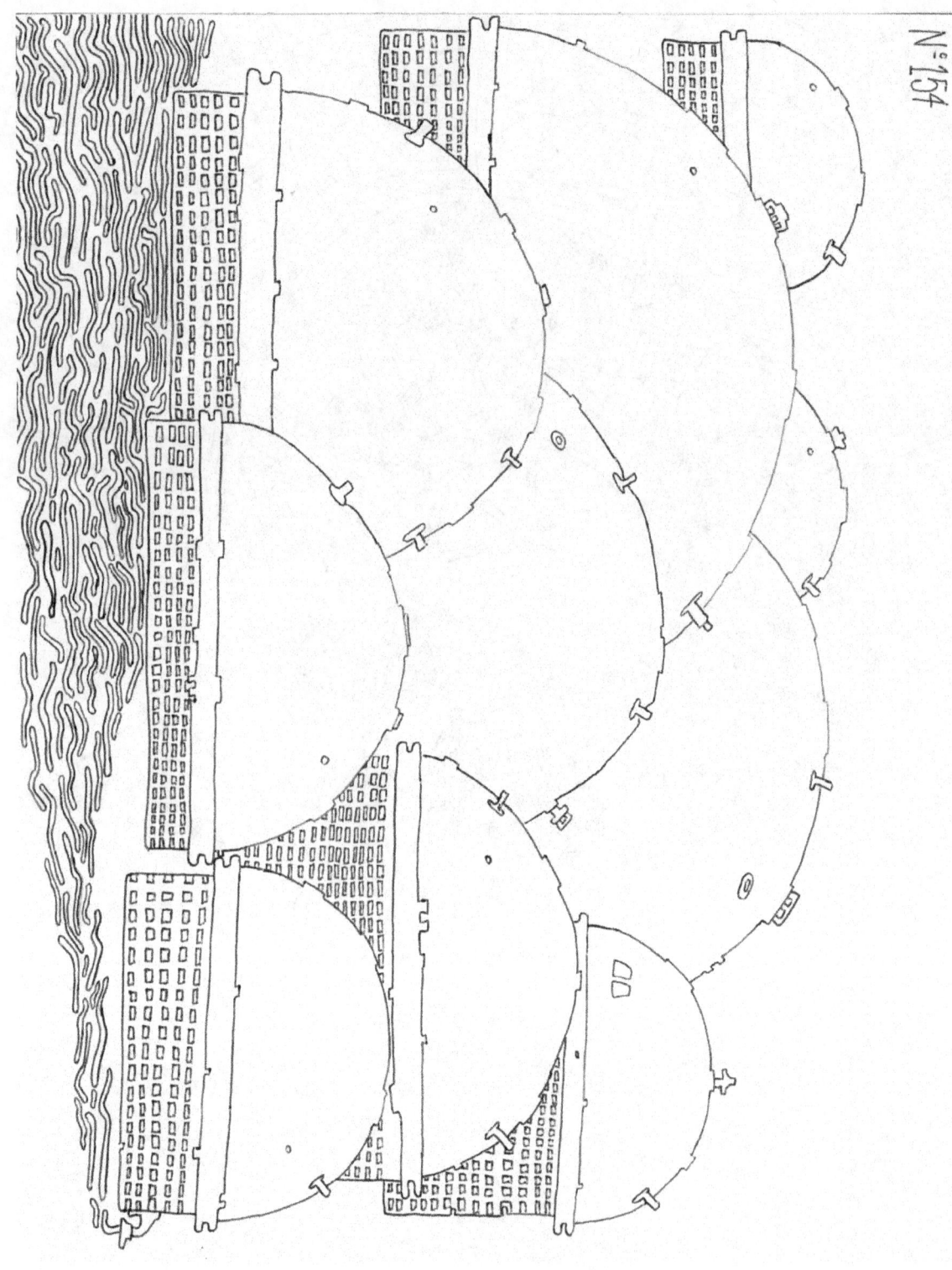

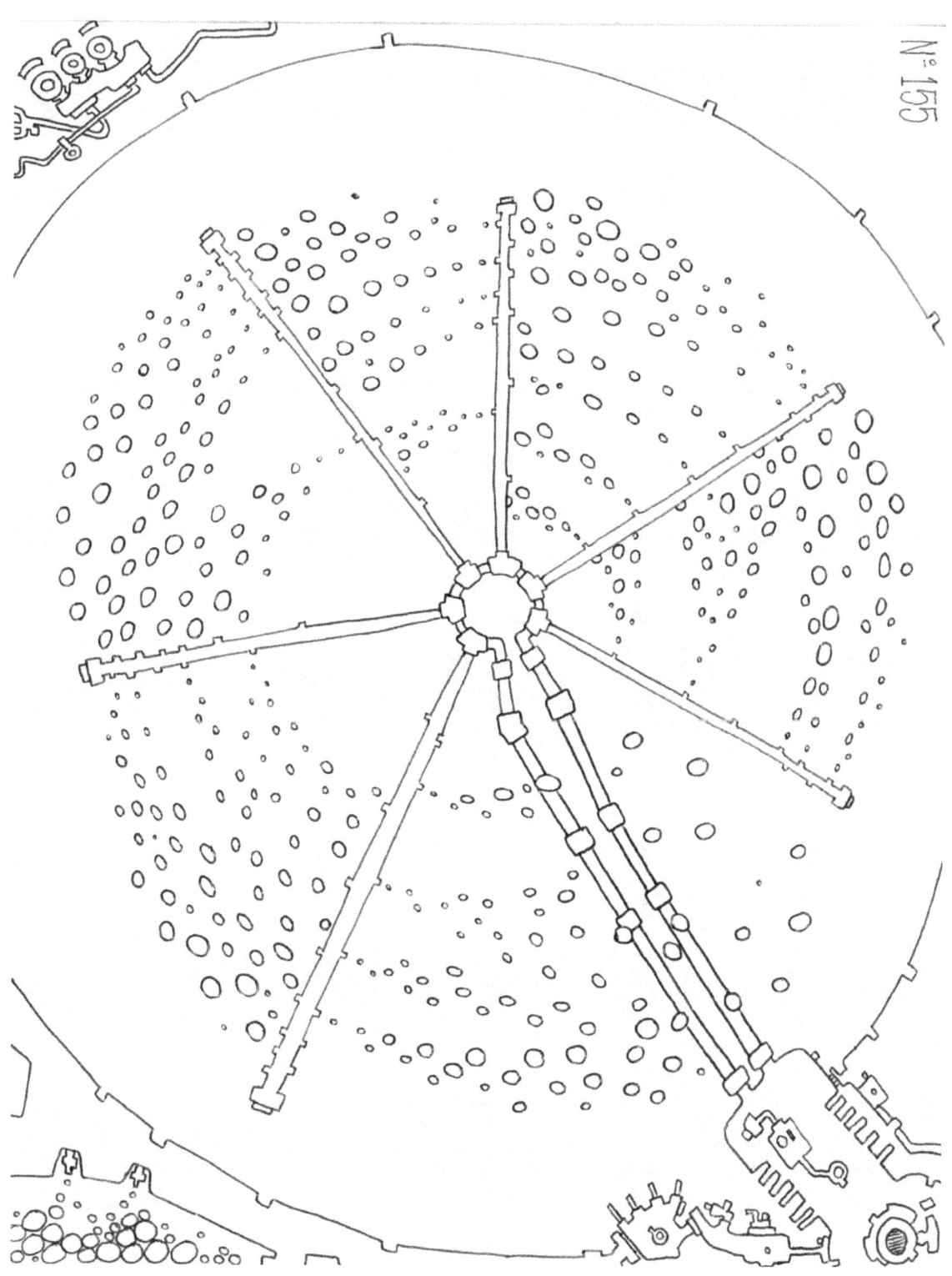

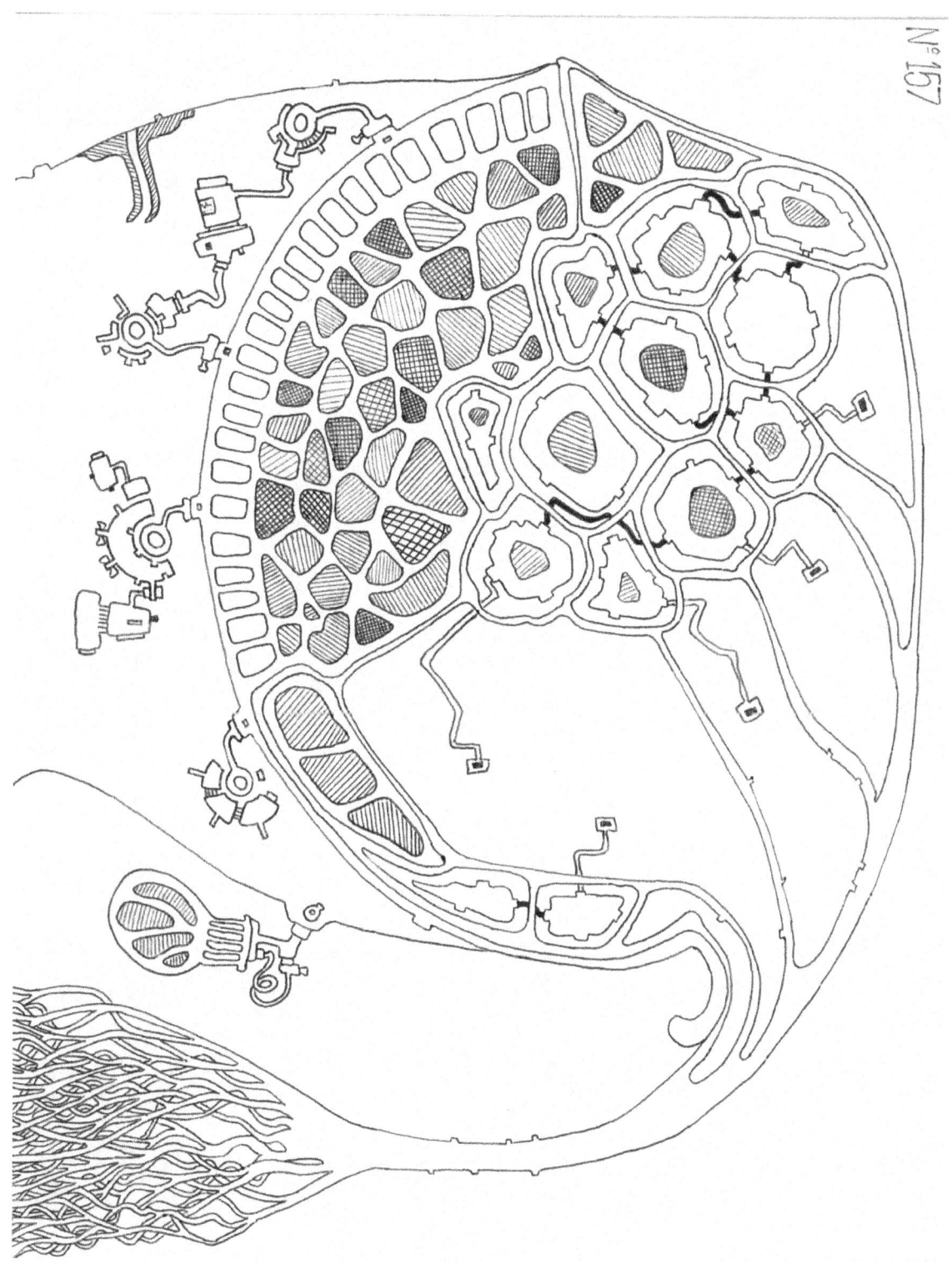

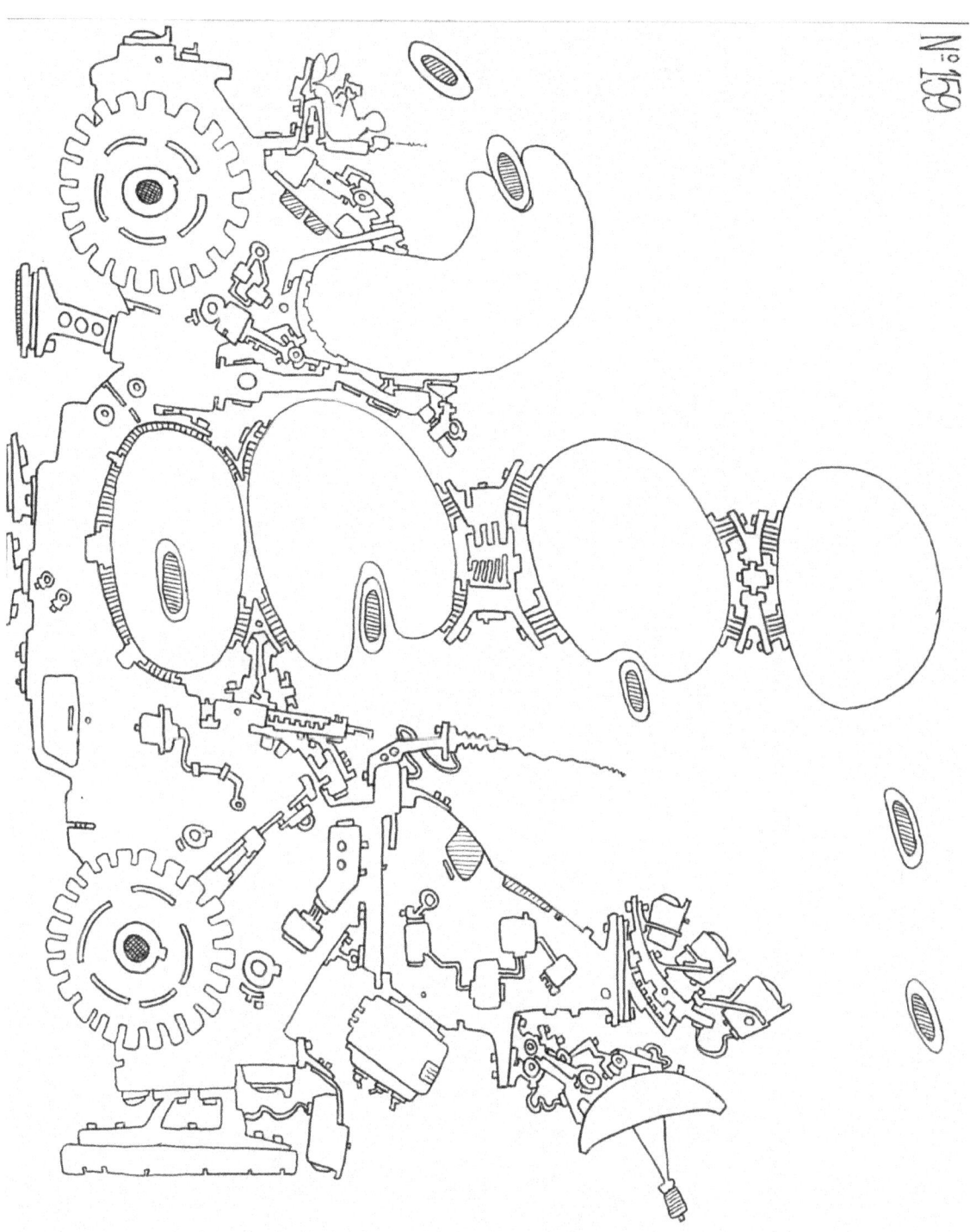

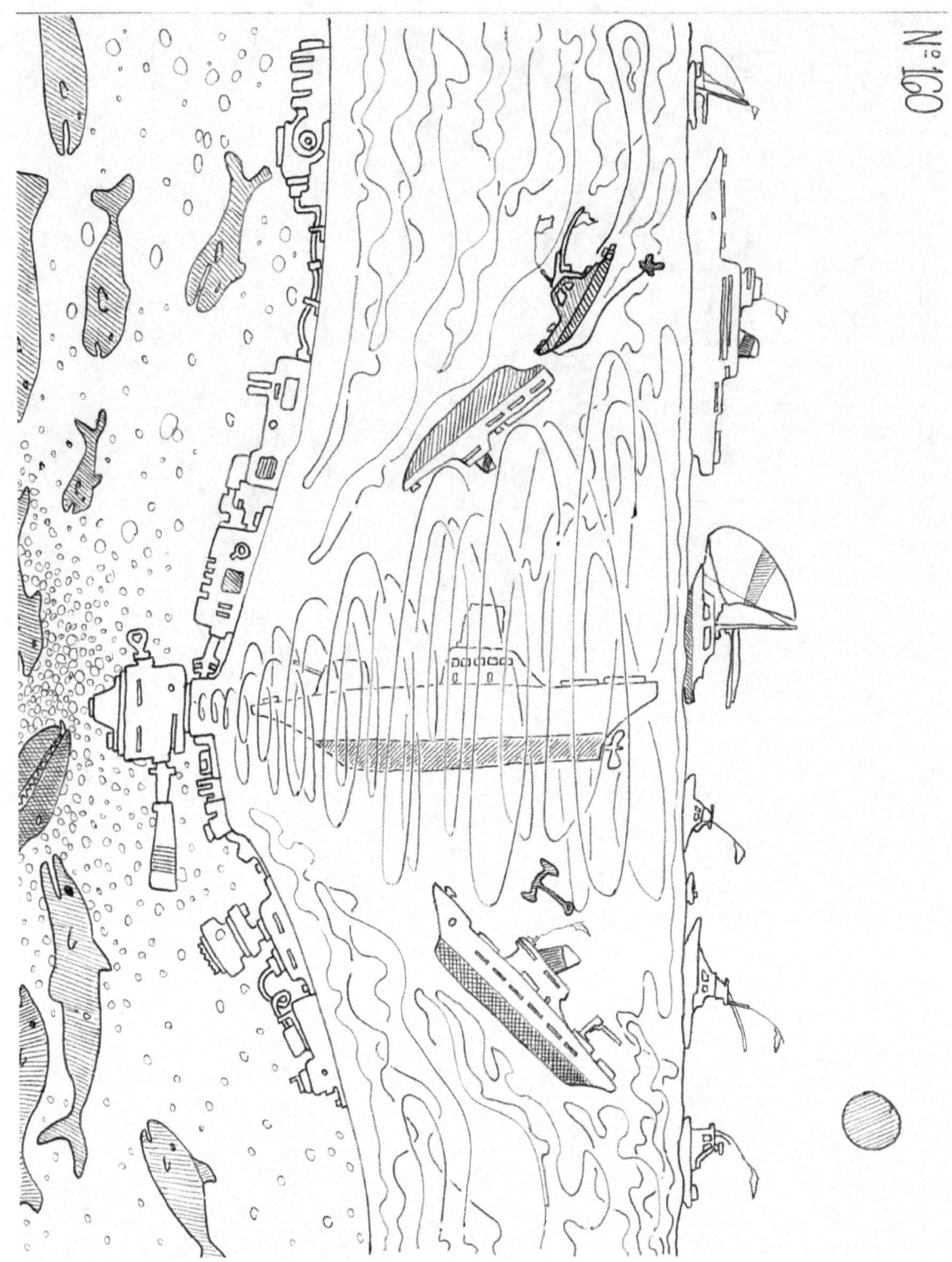

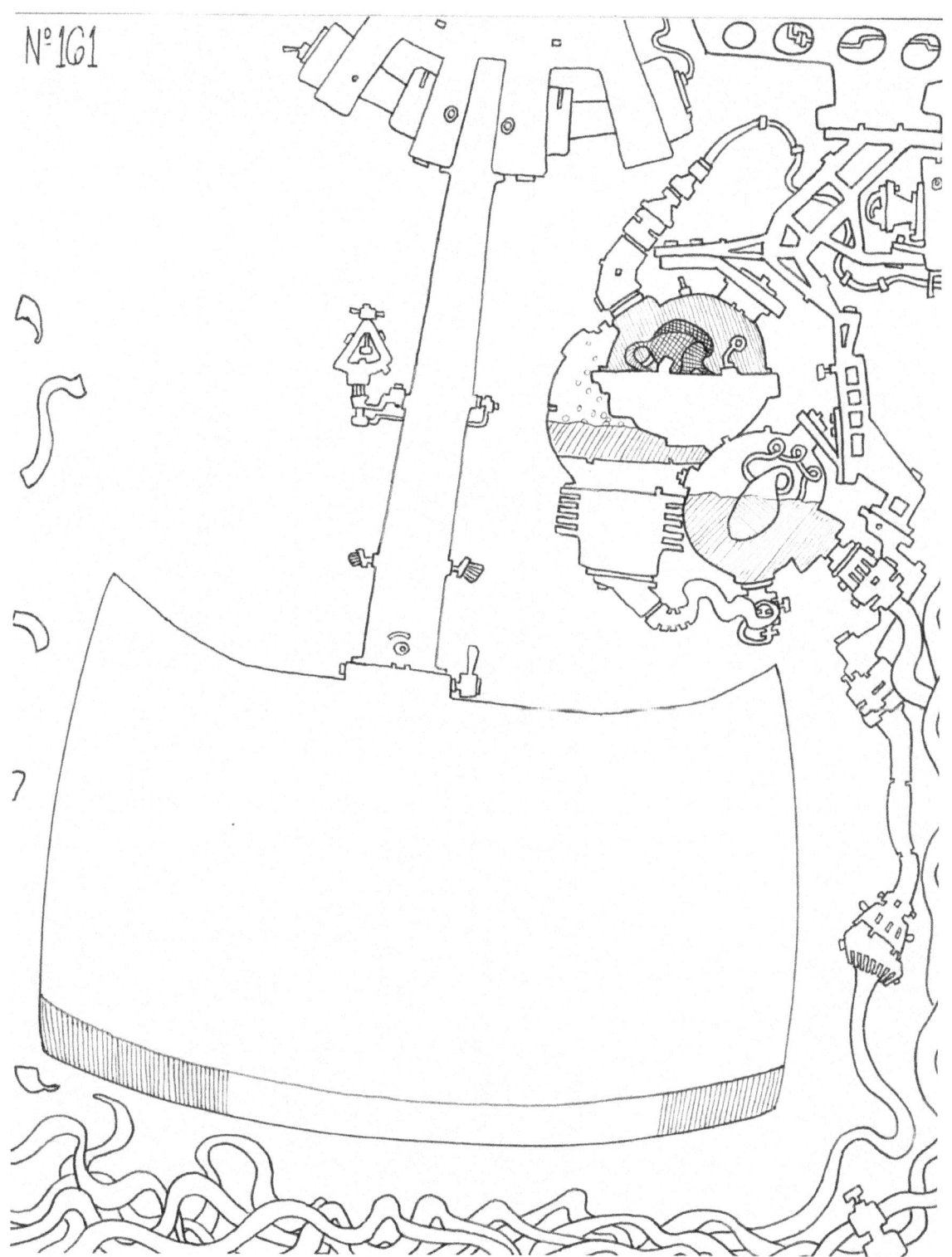

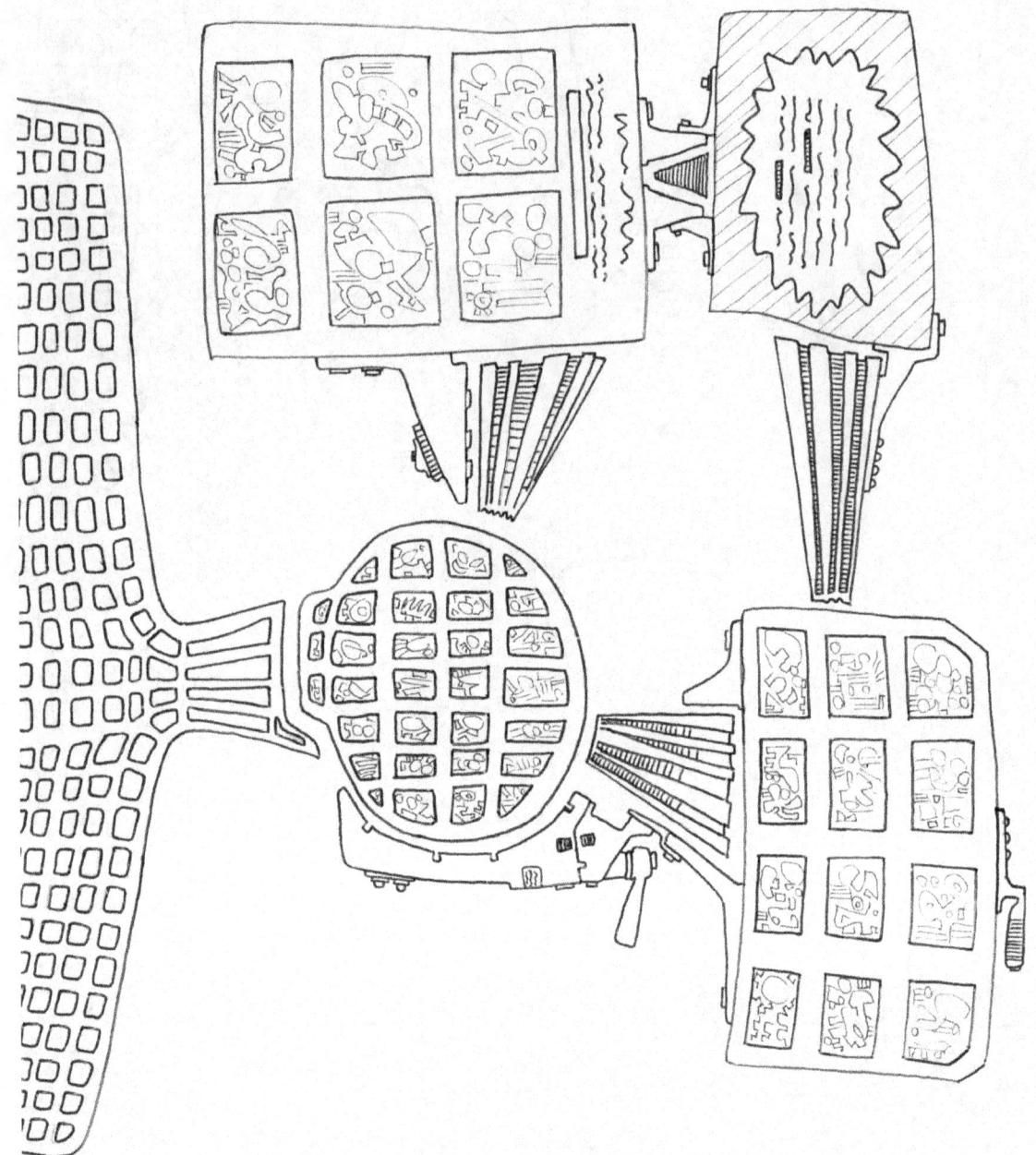

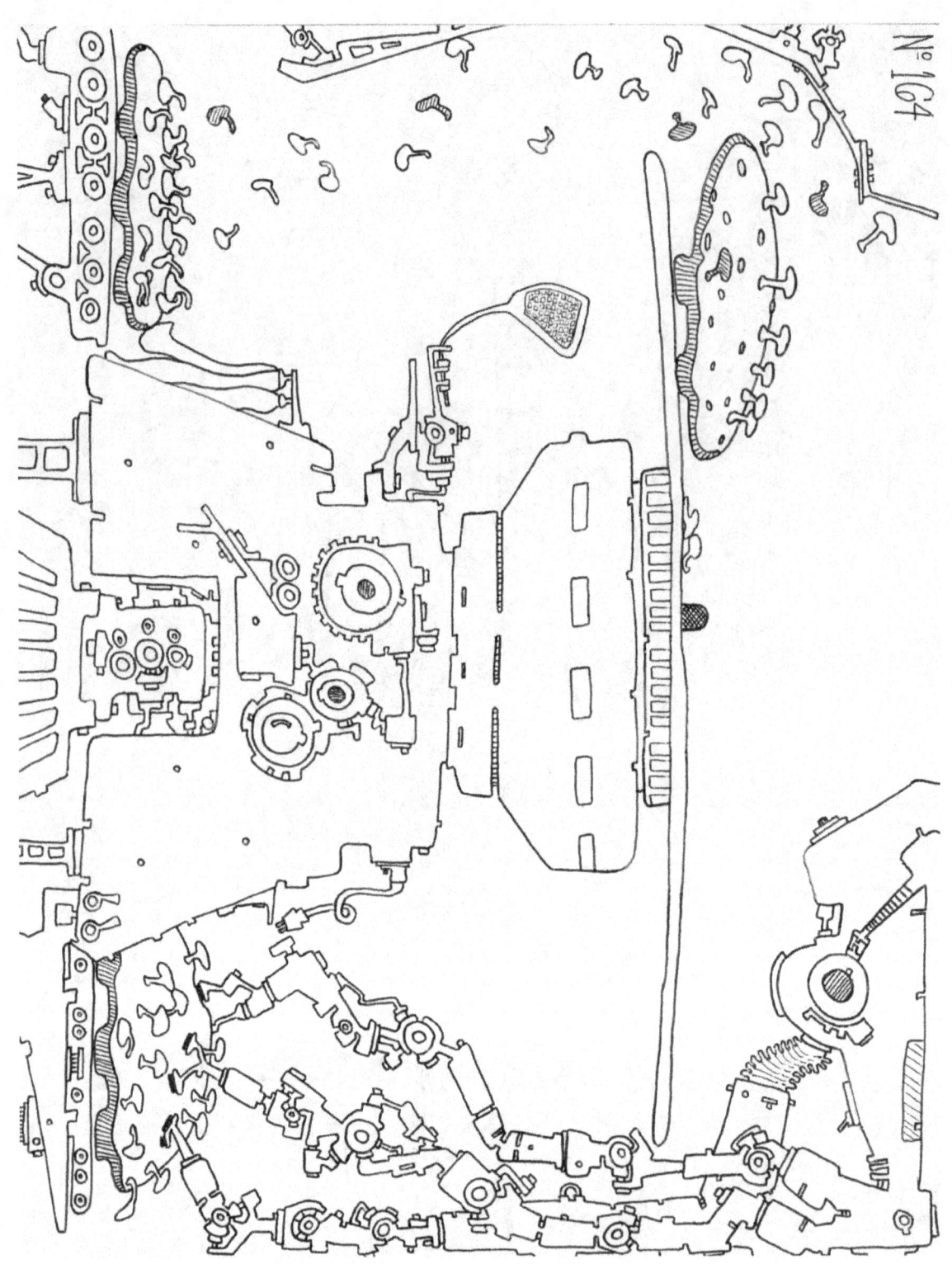

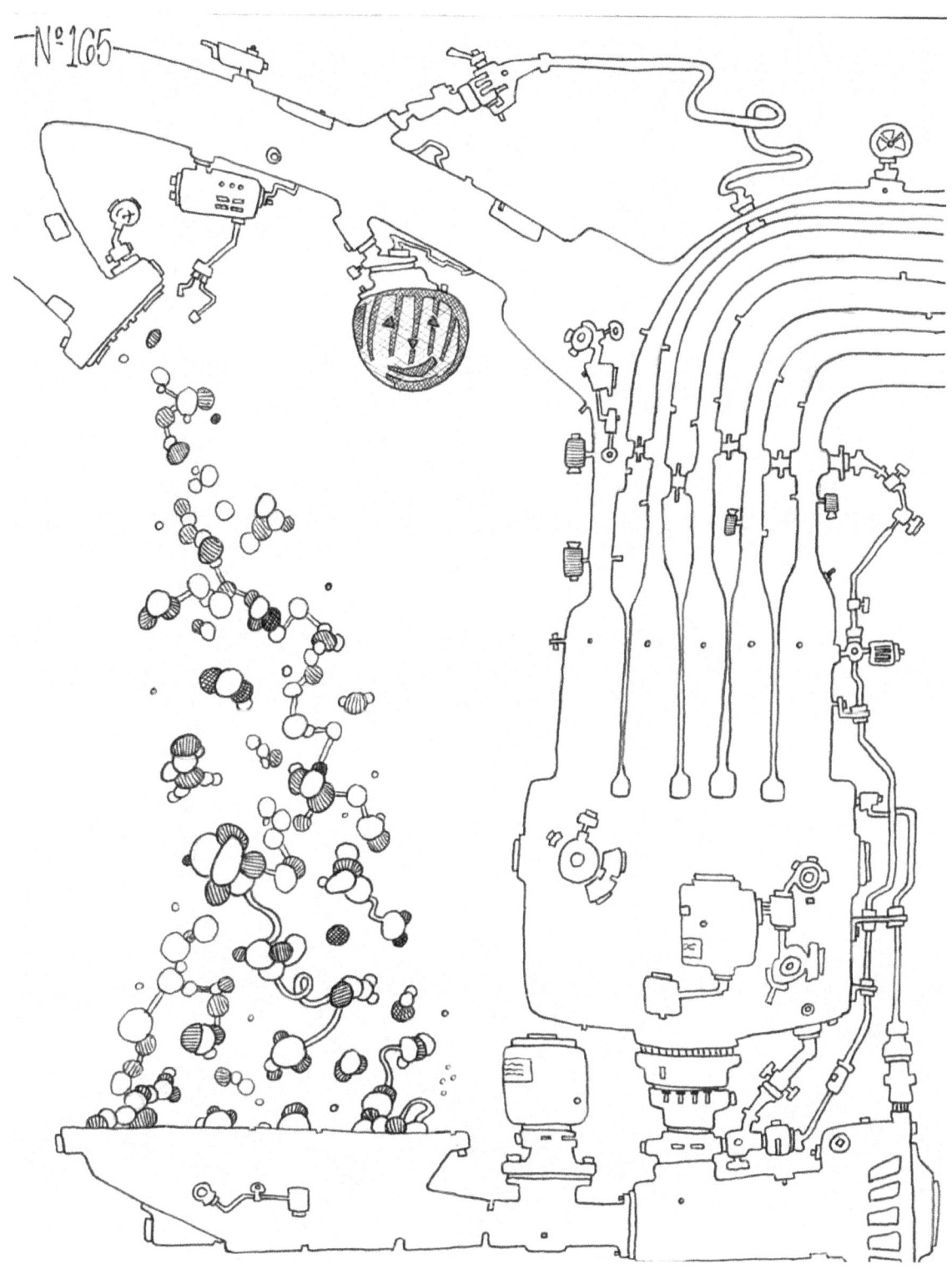

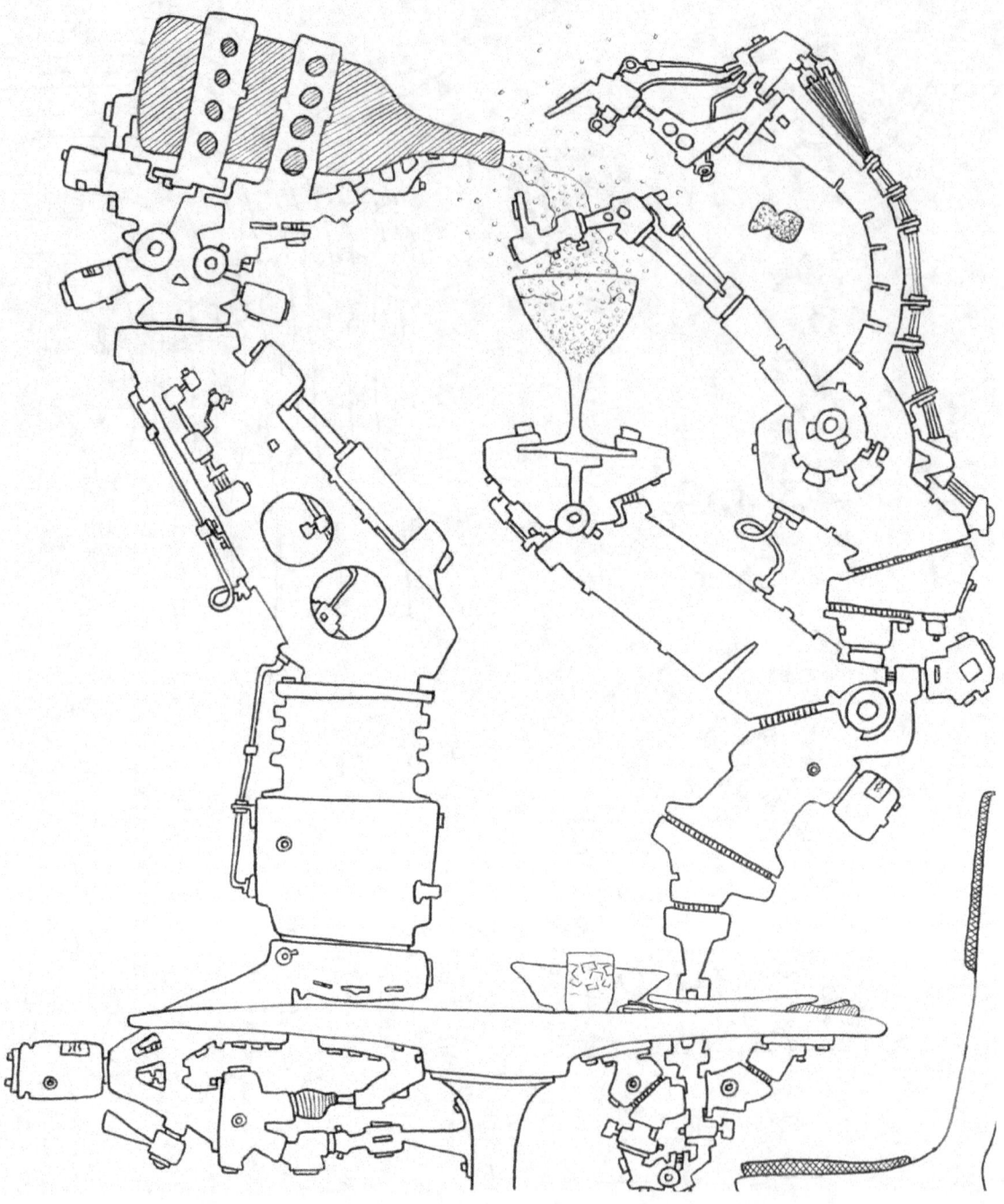

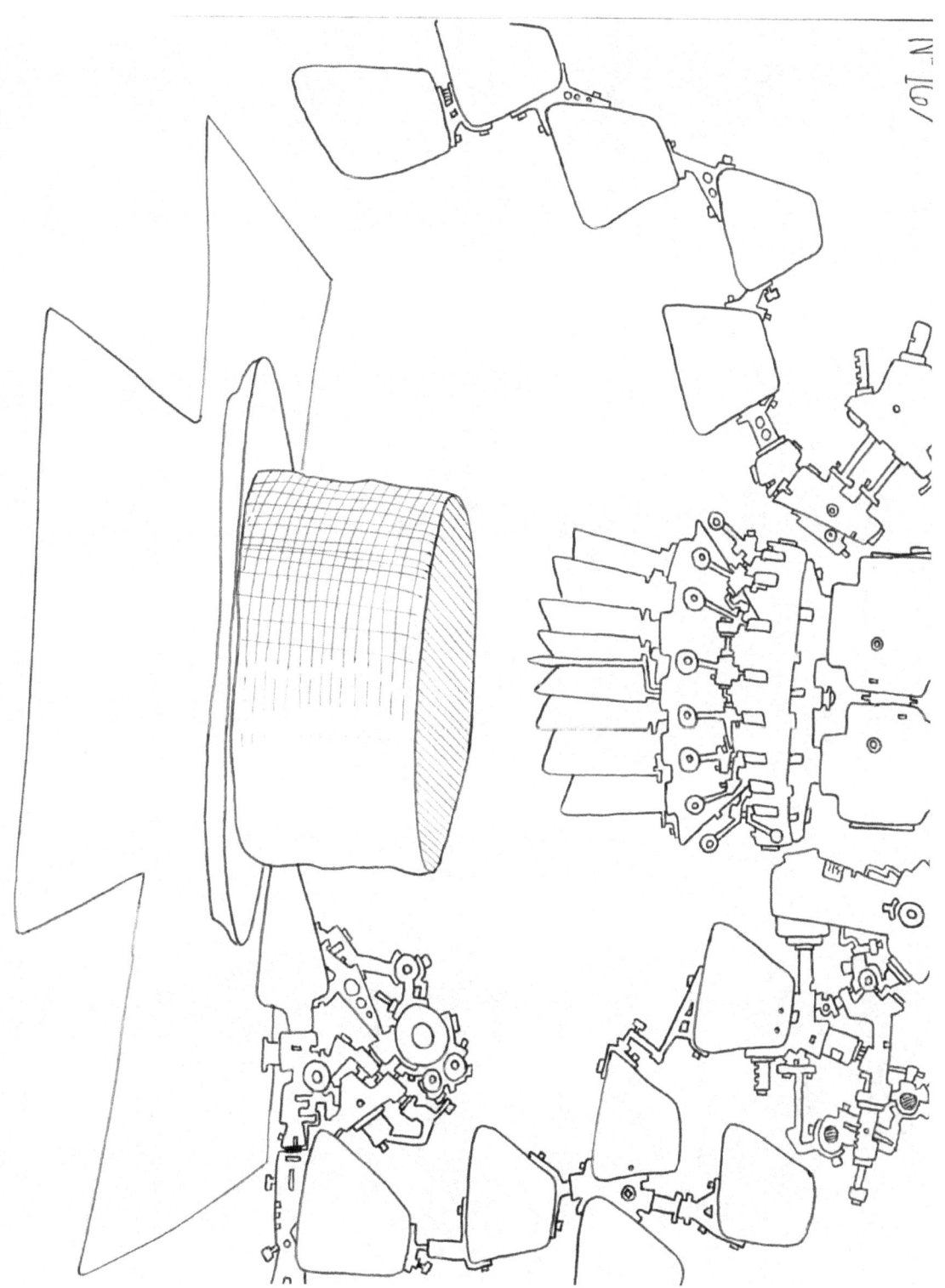

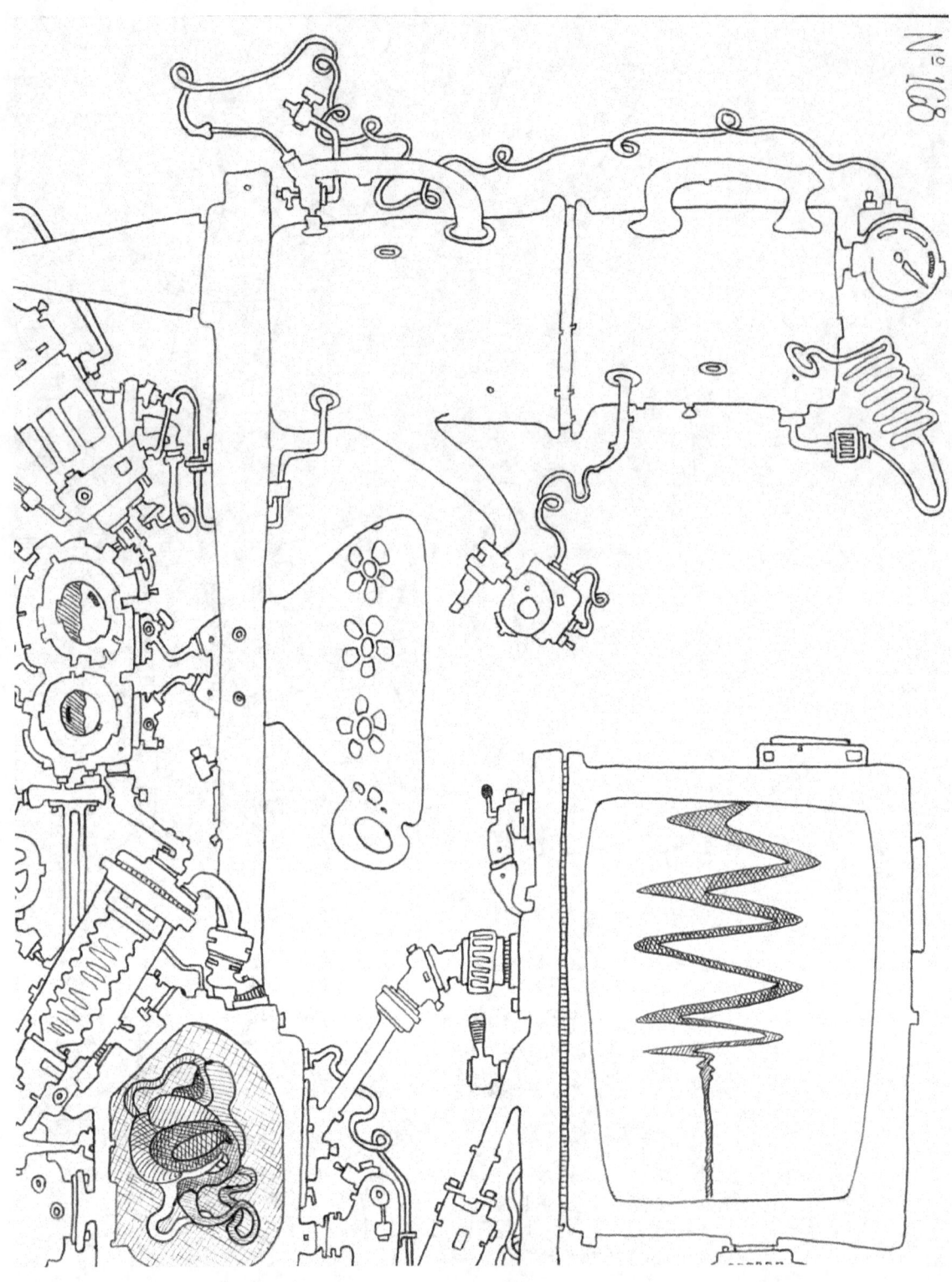

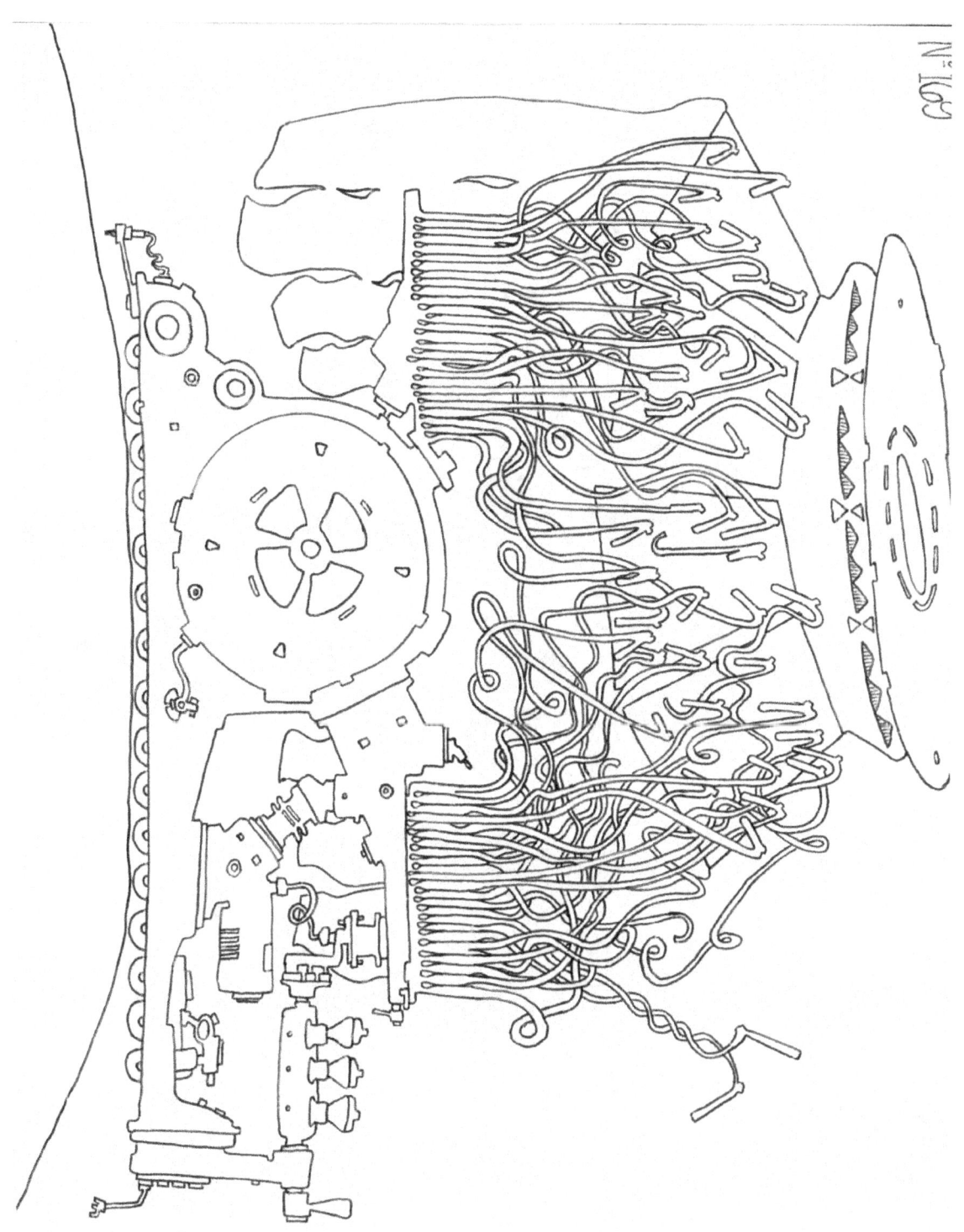

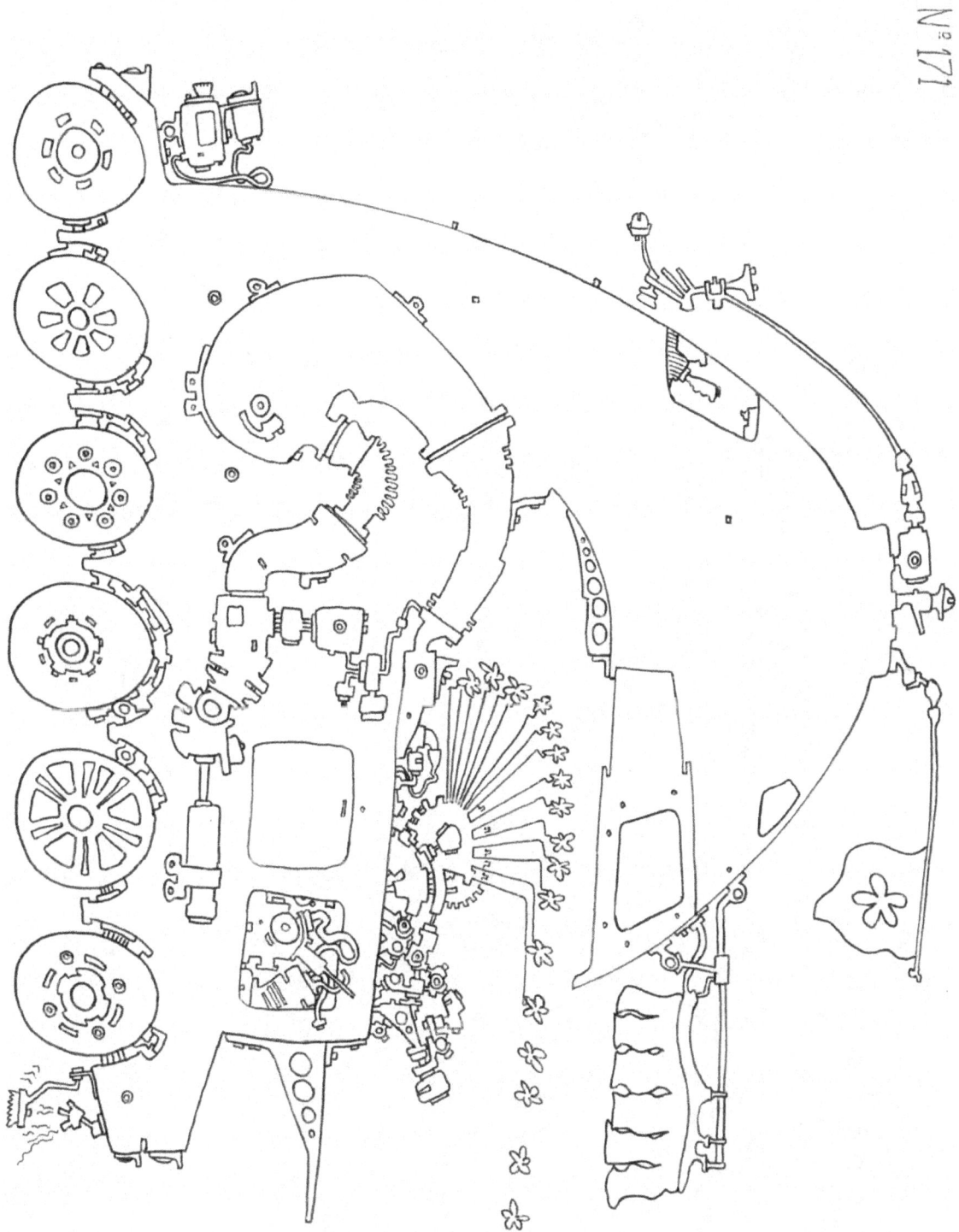

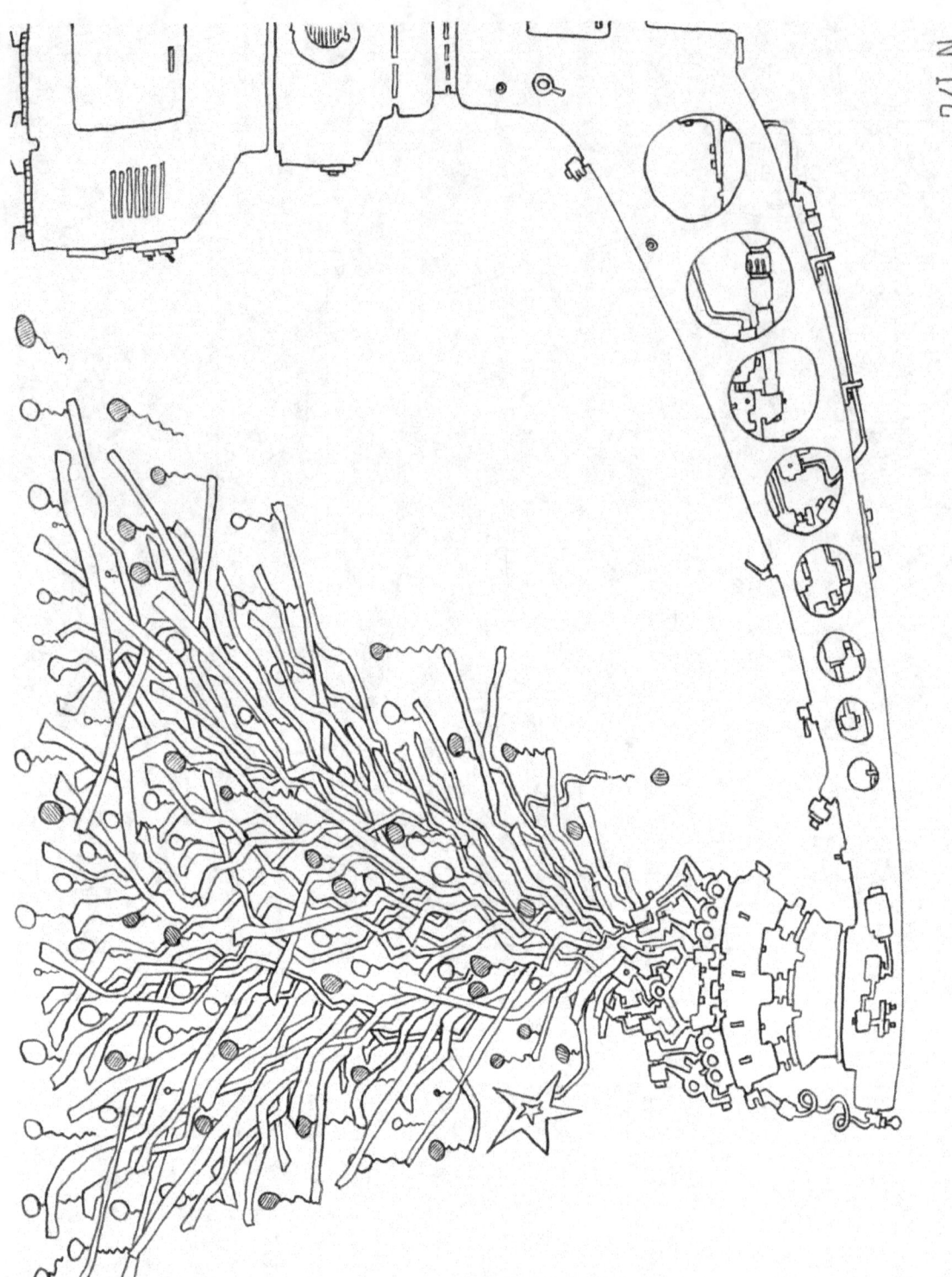

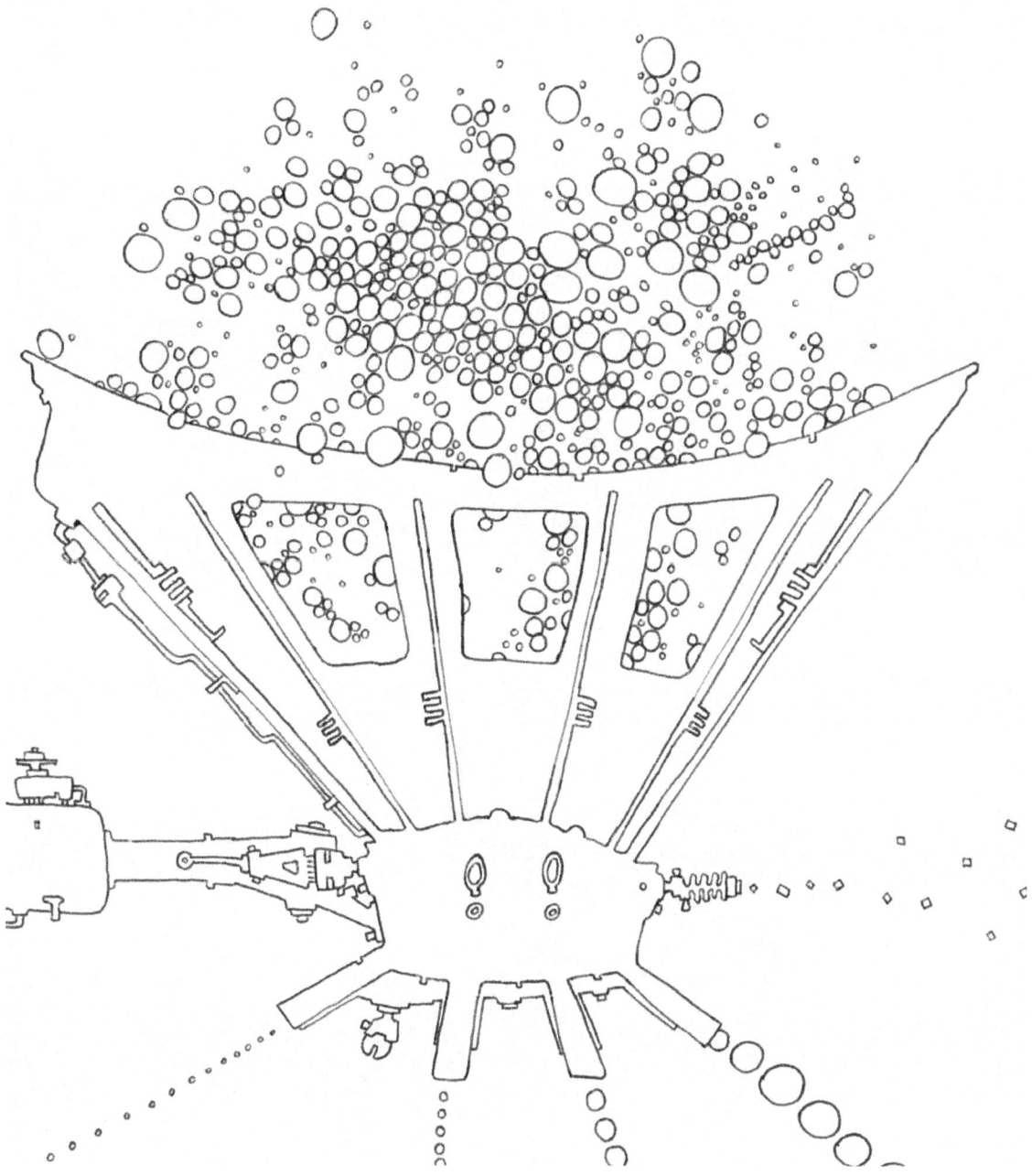

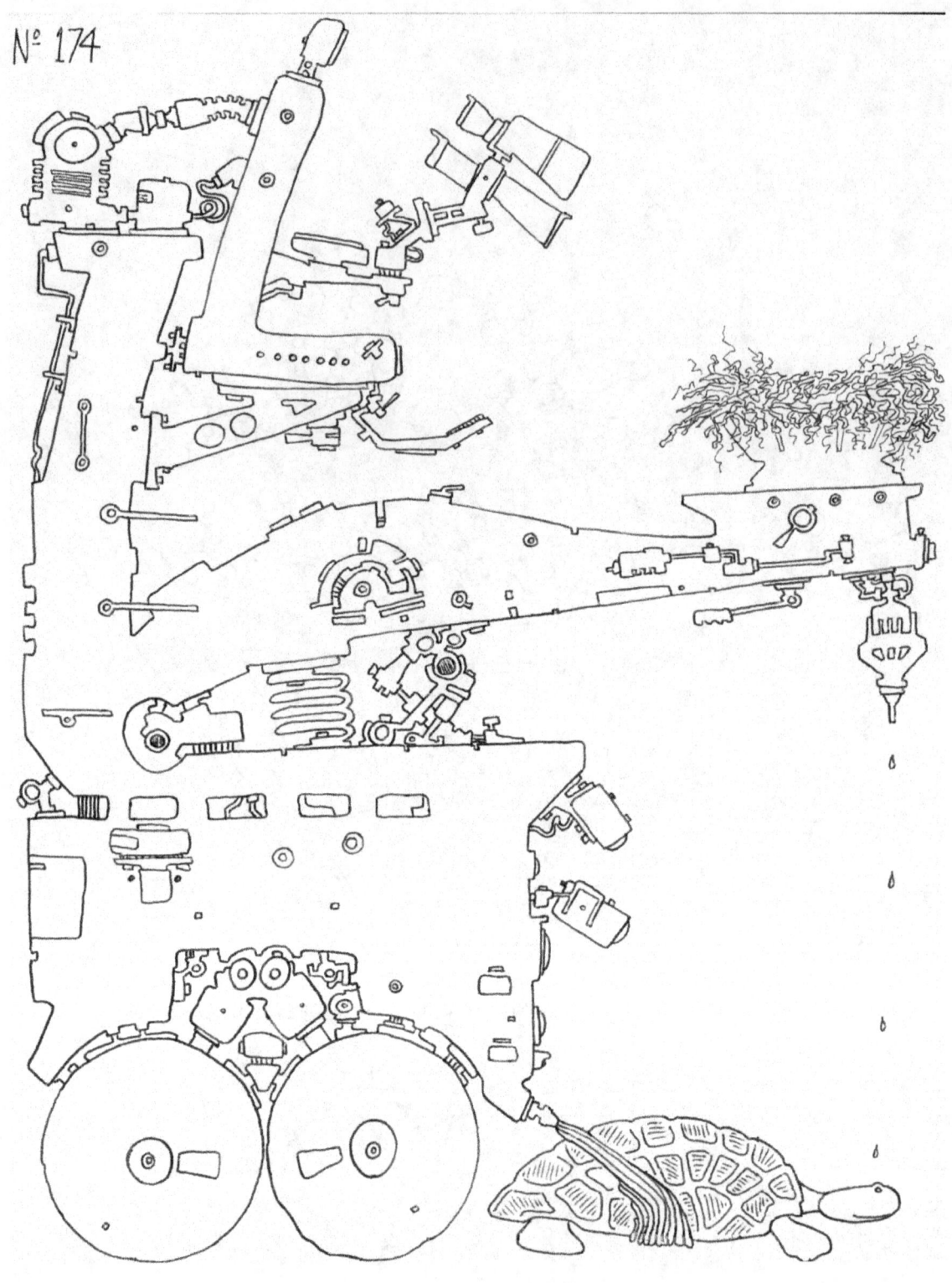

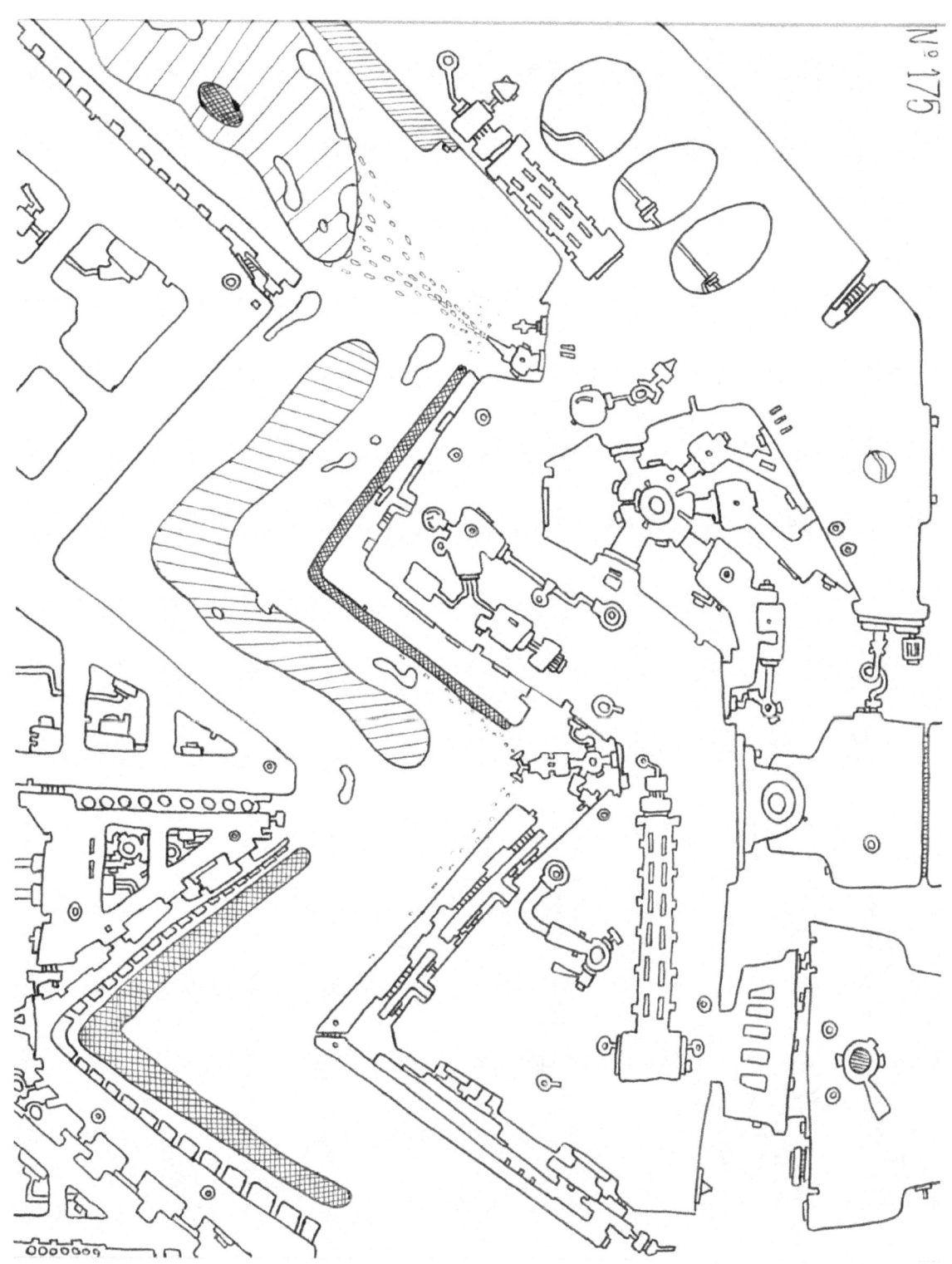

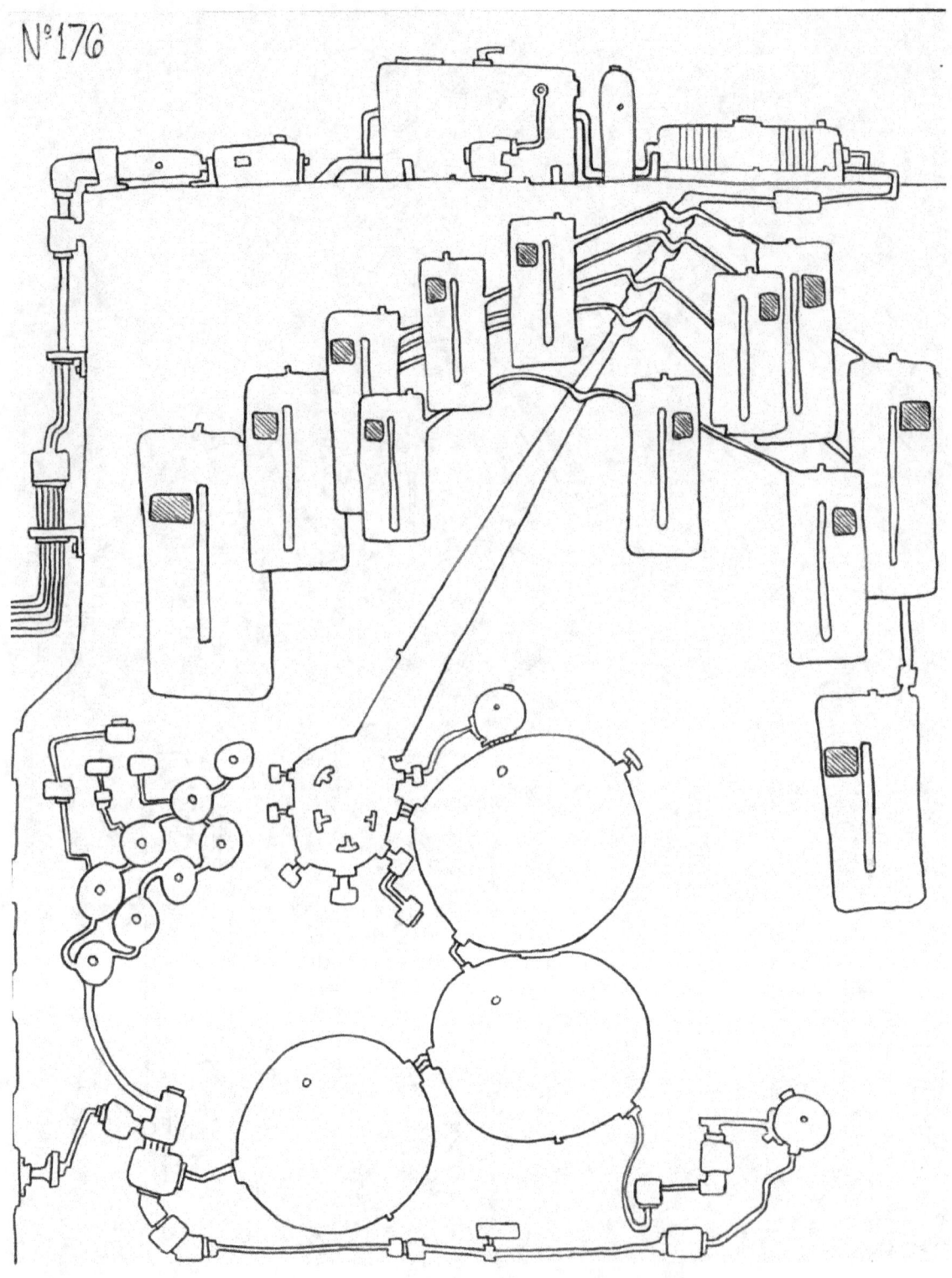

№177

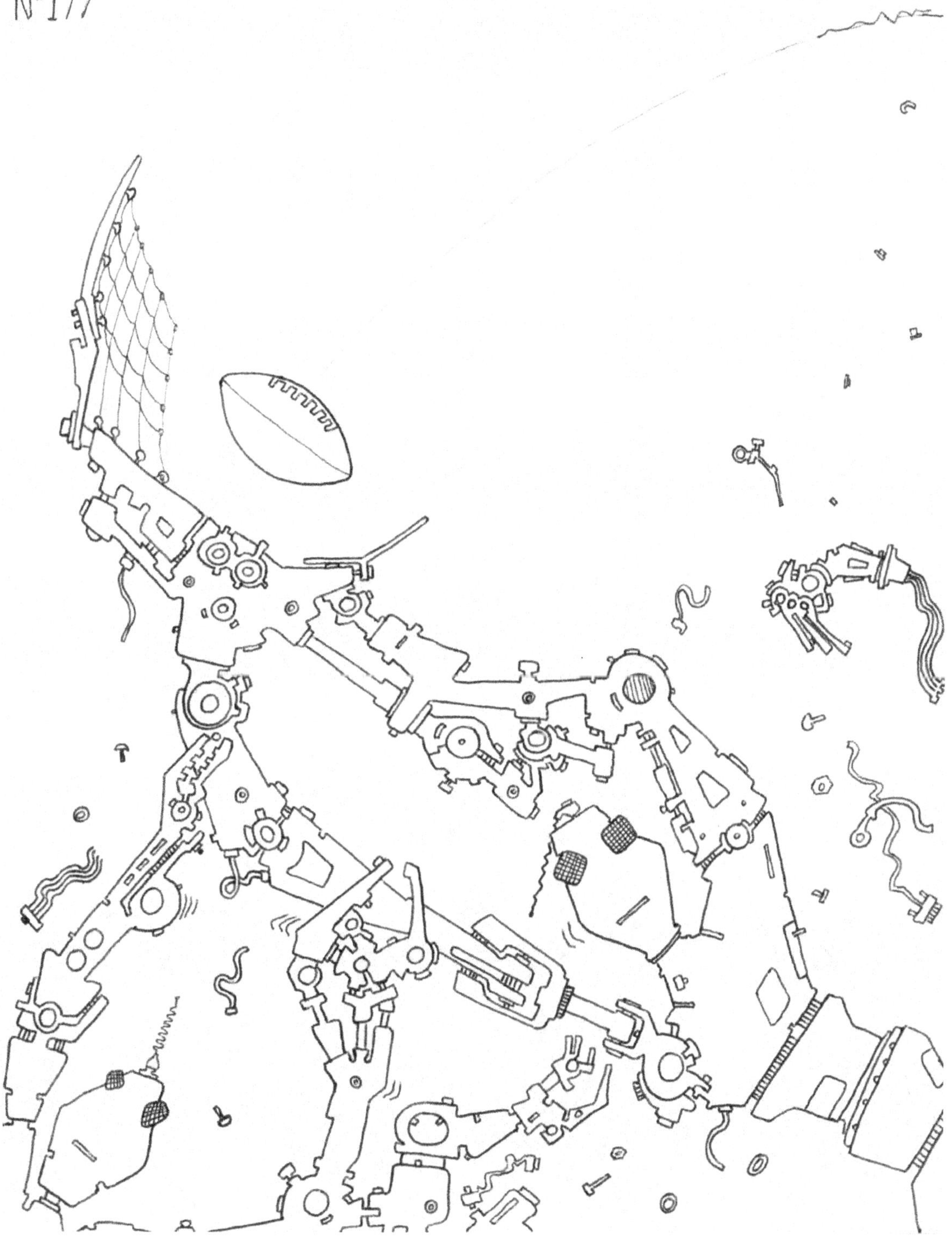

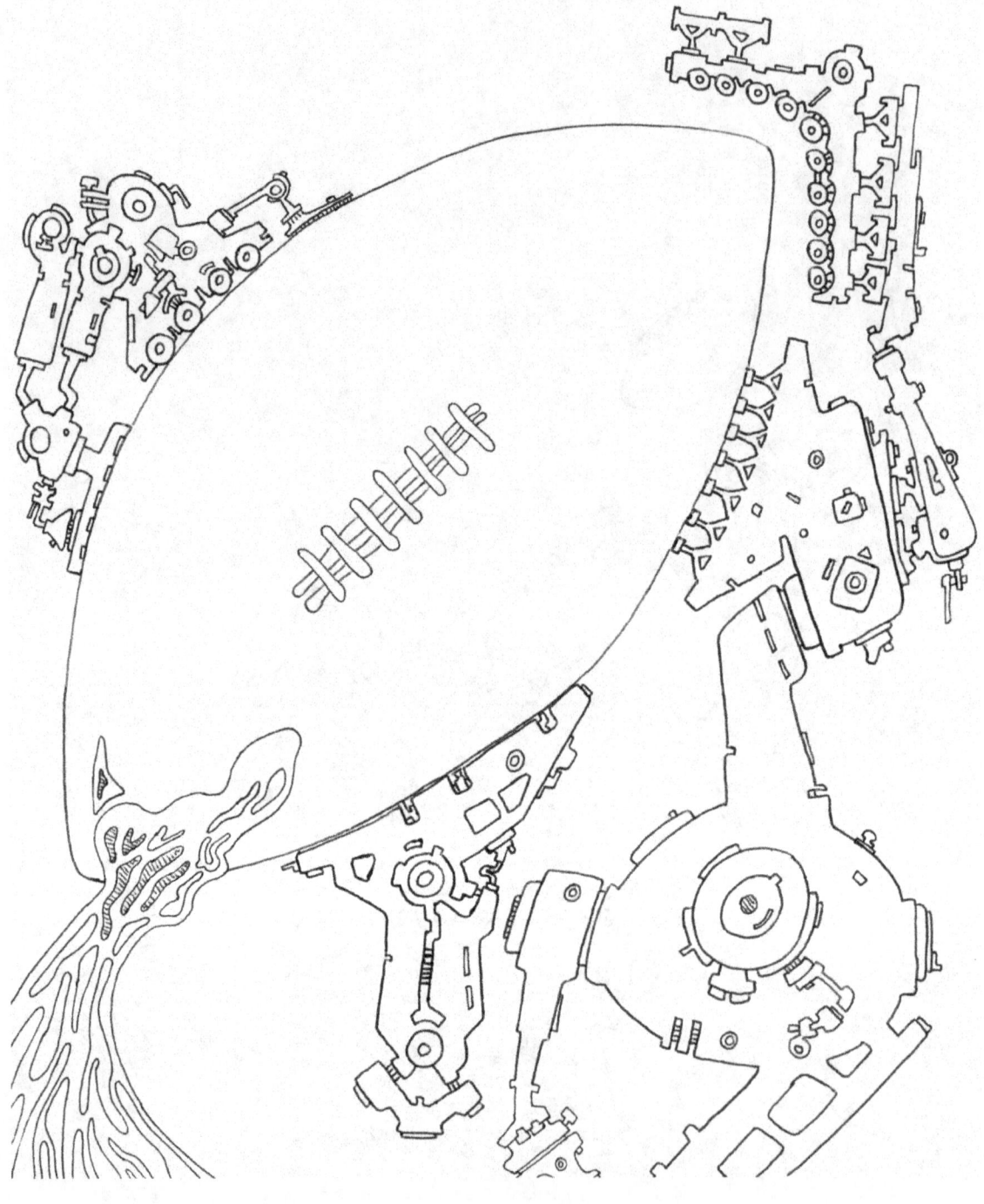

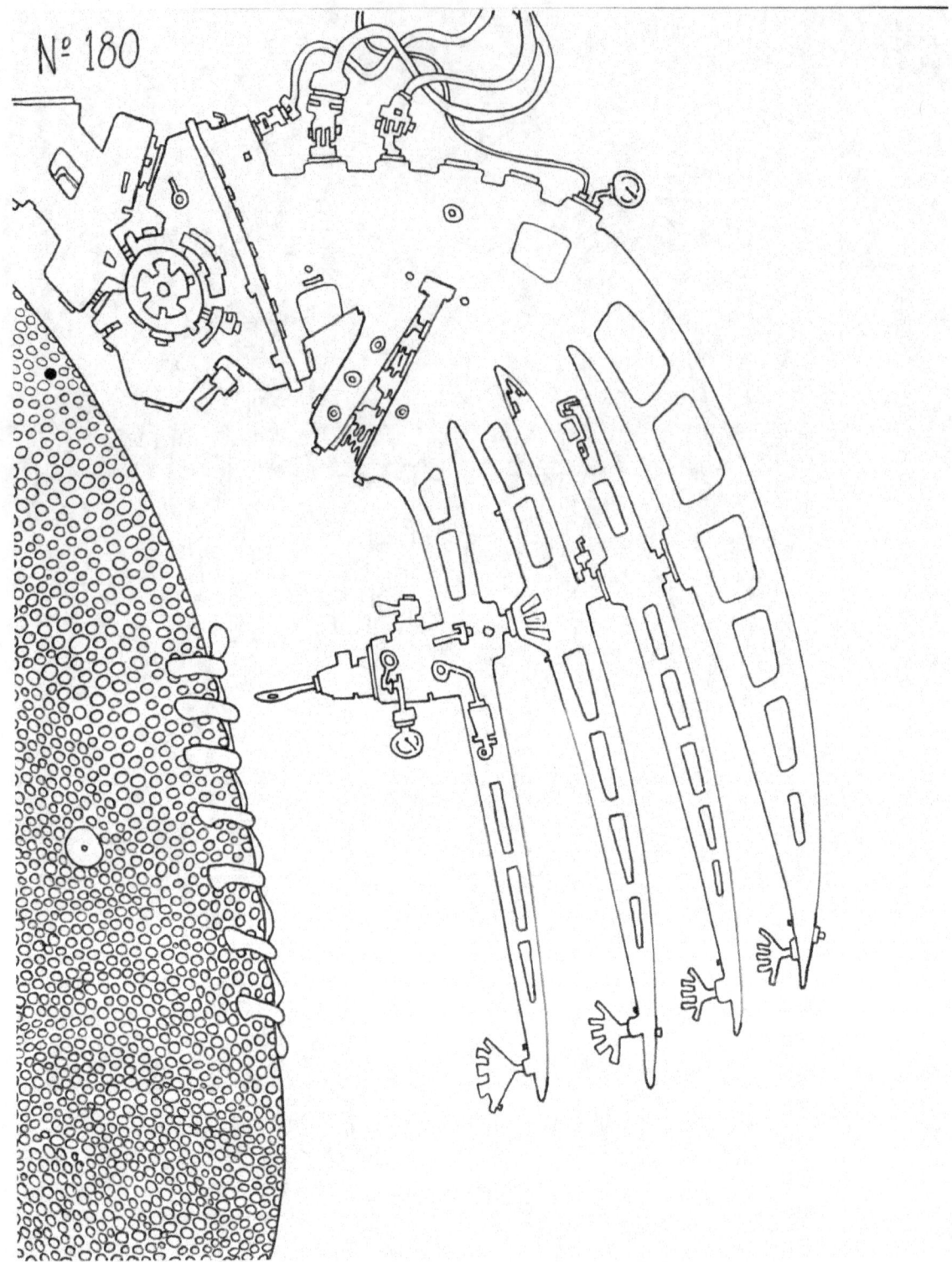

Nº 181

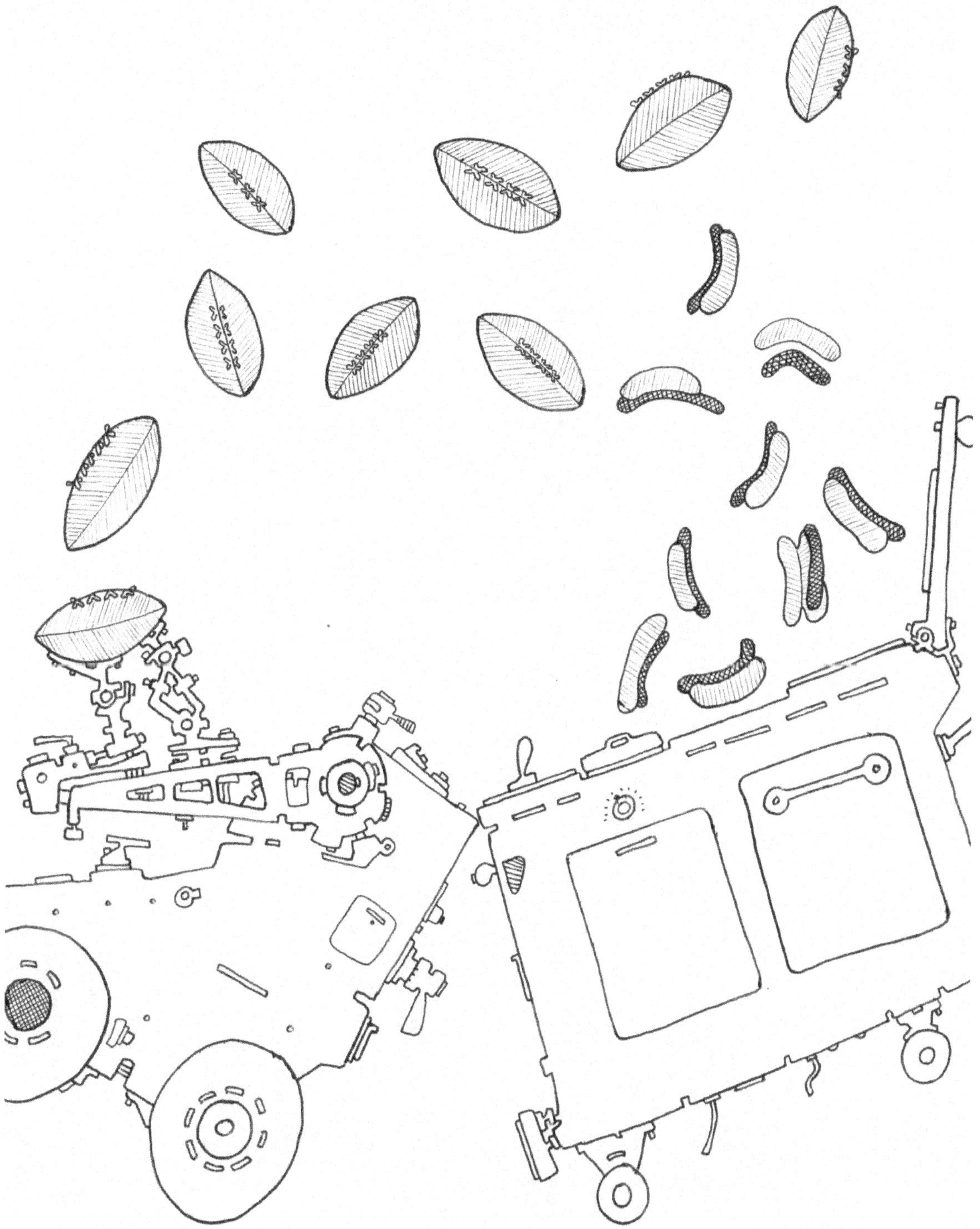

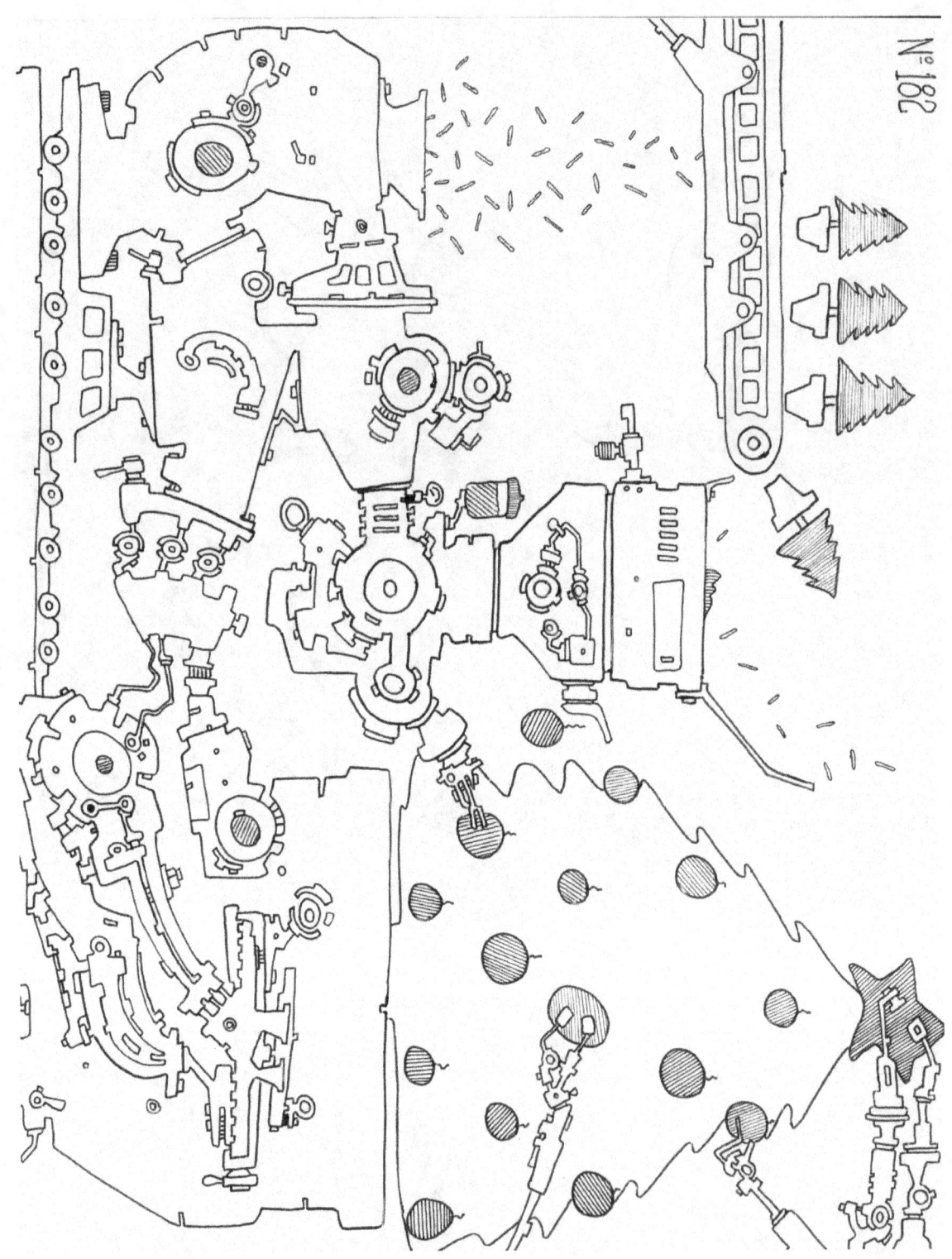

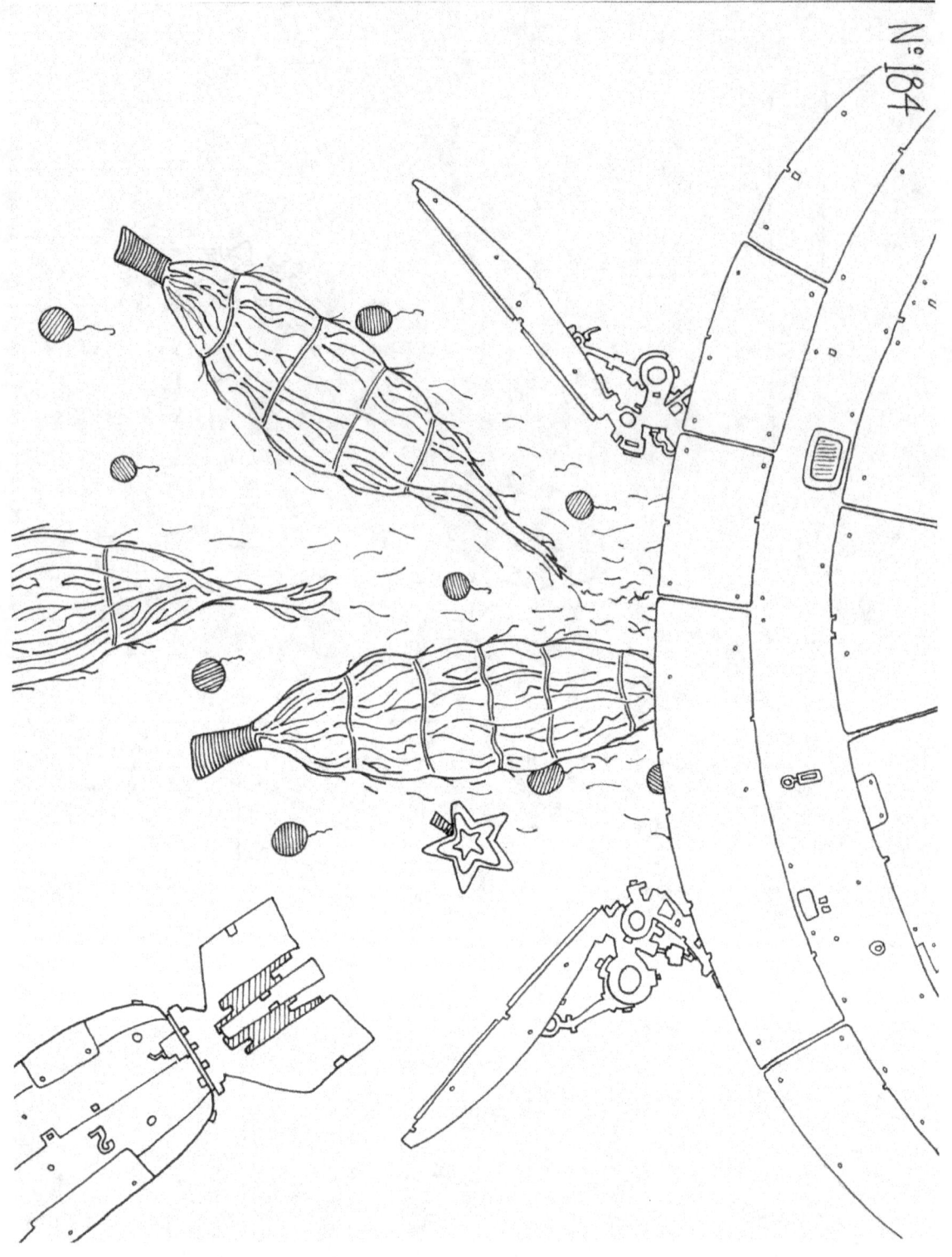

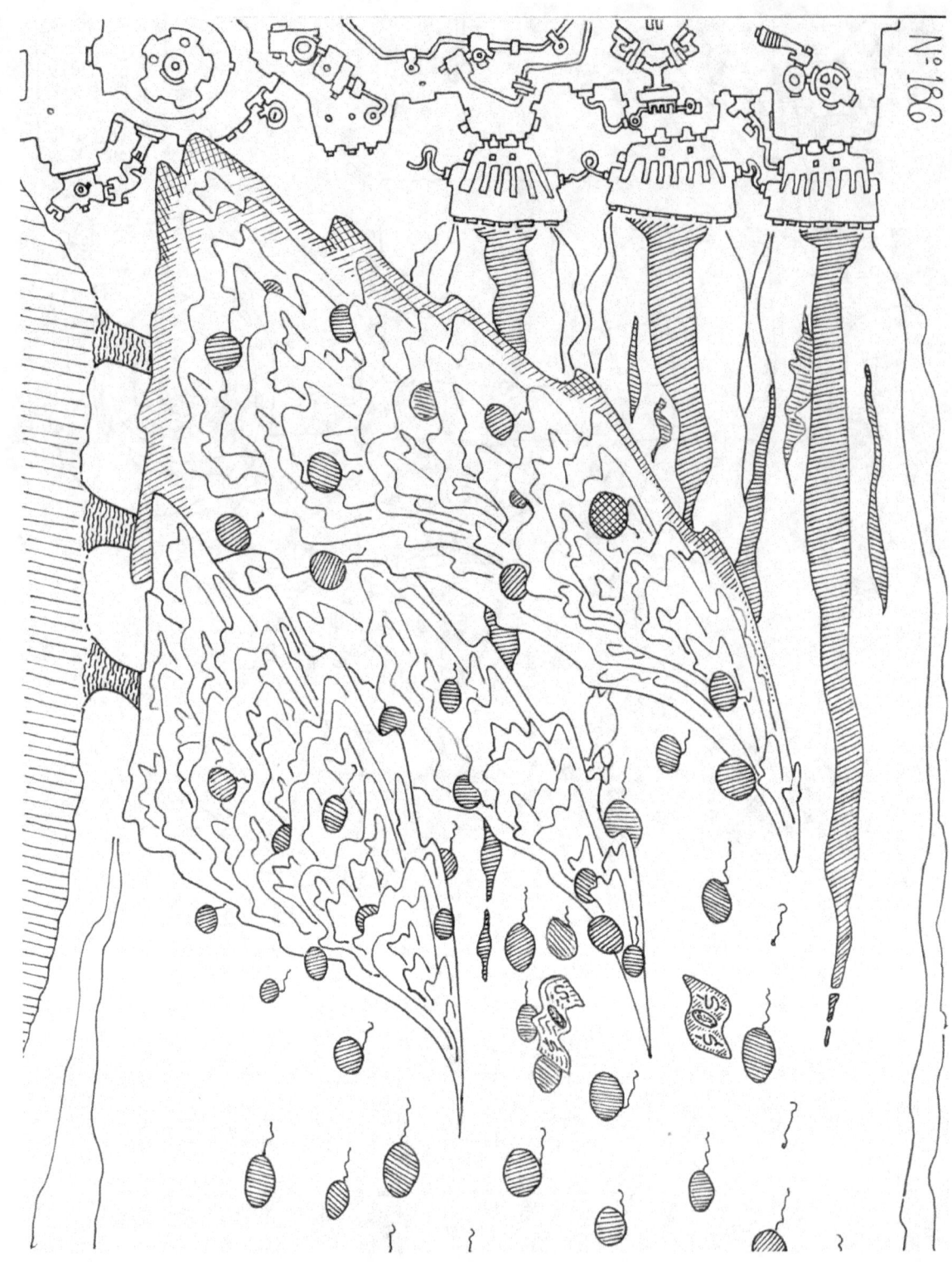

N° 187

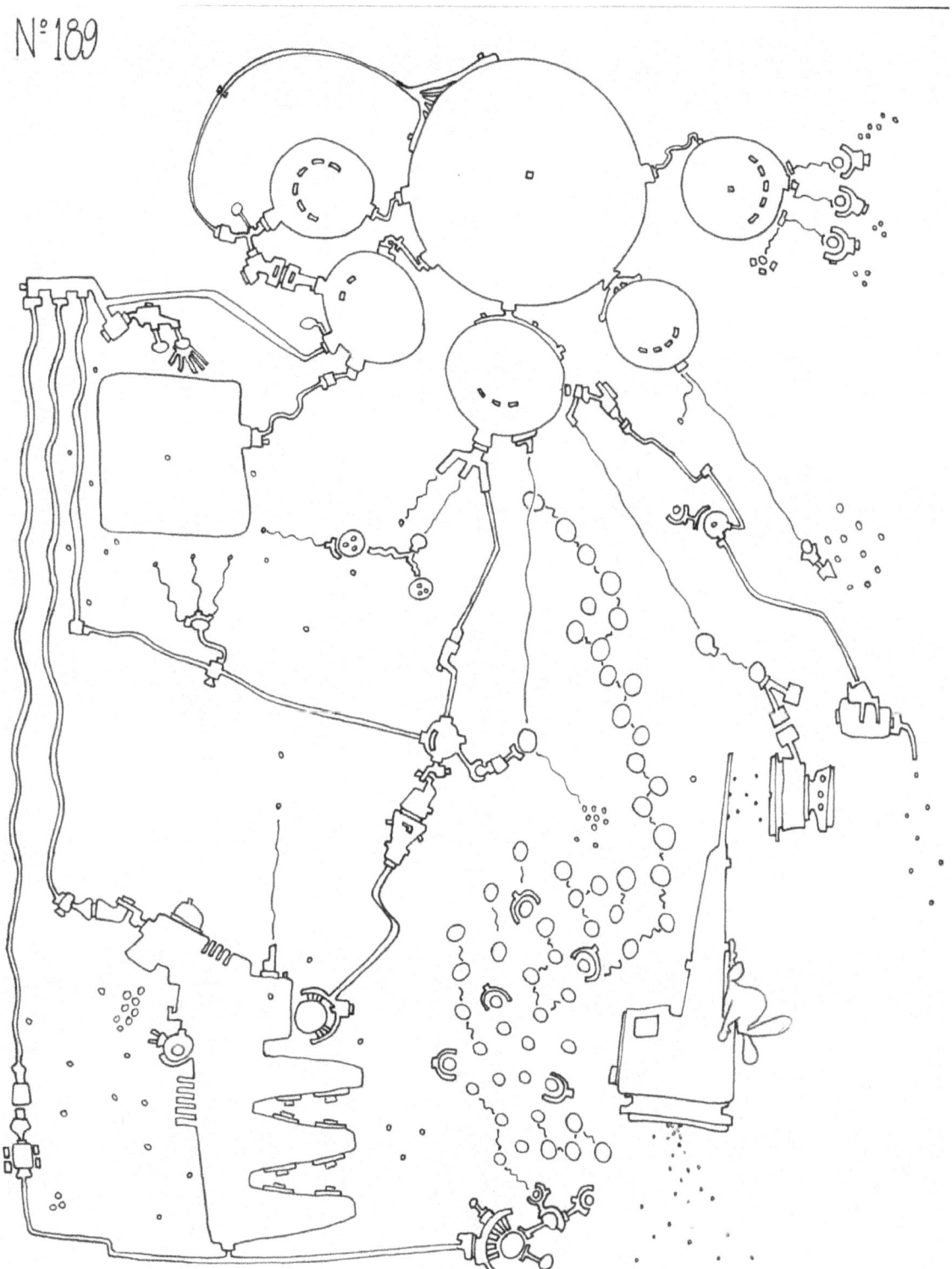

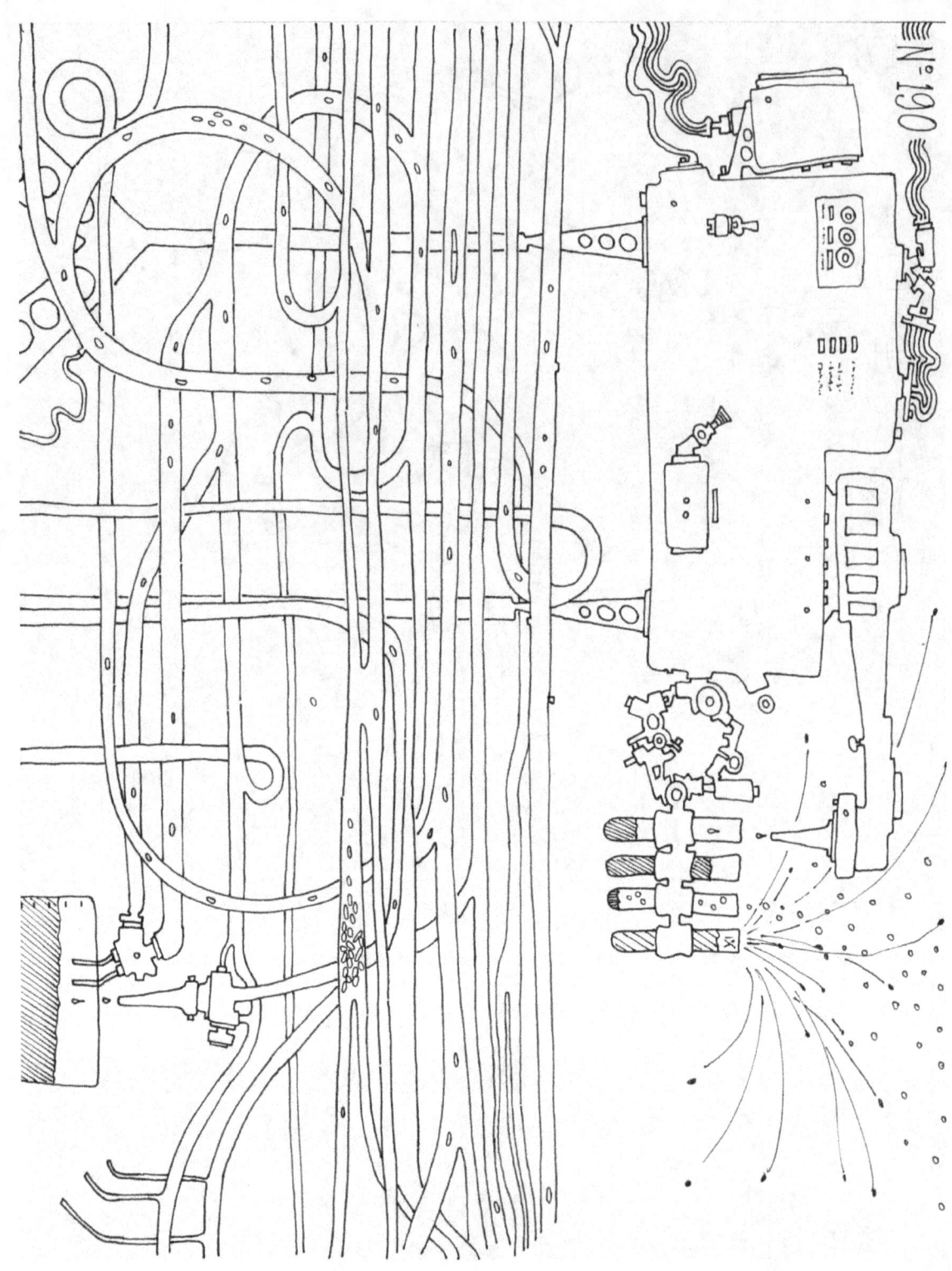

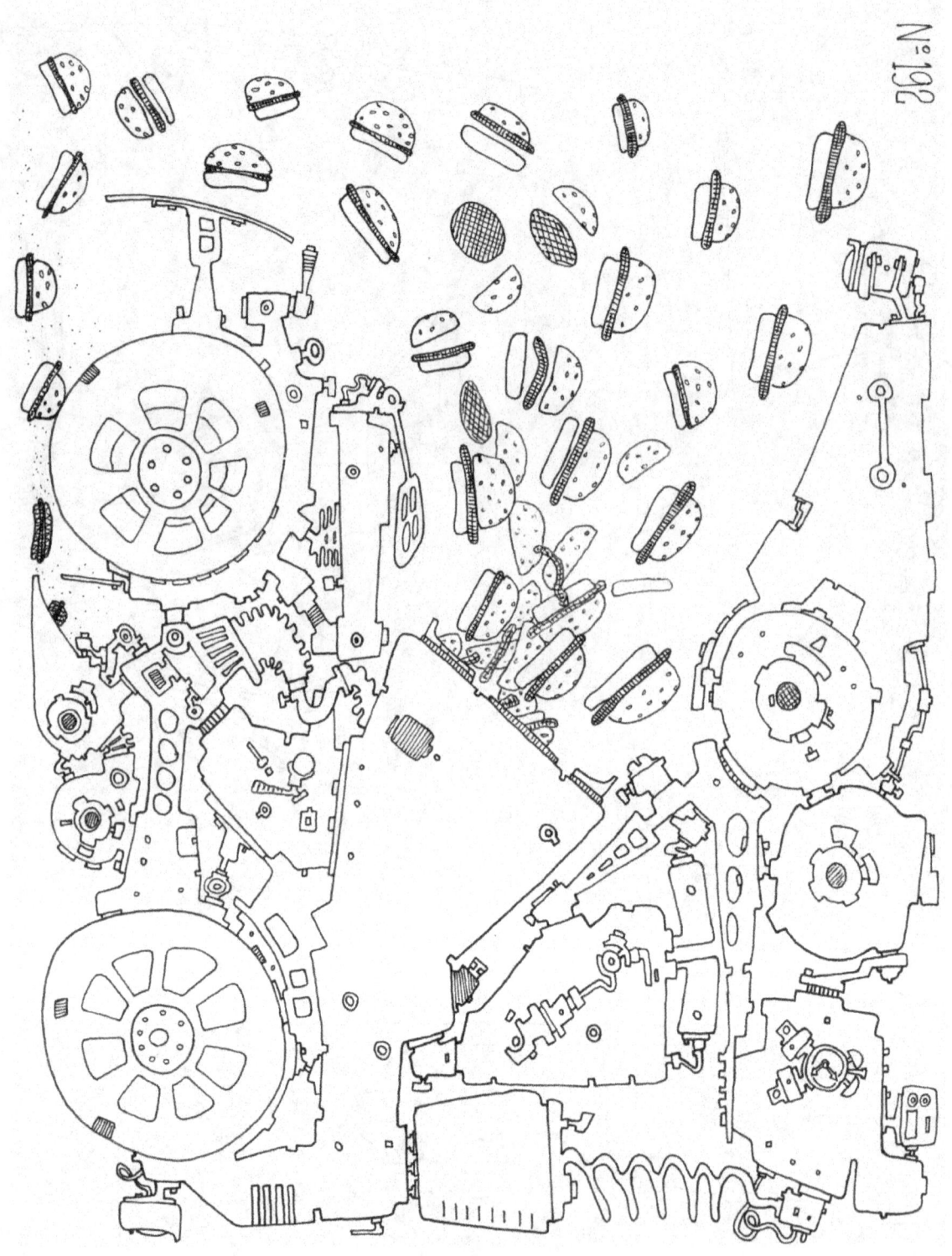

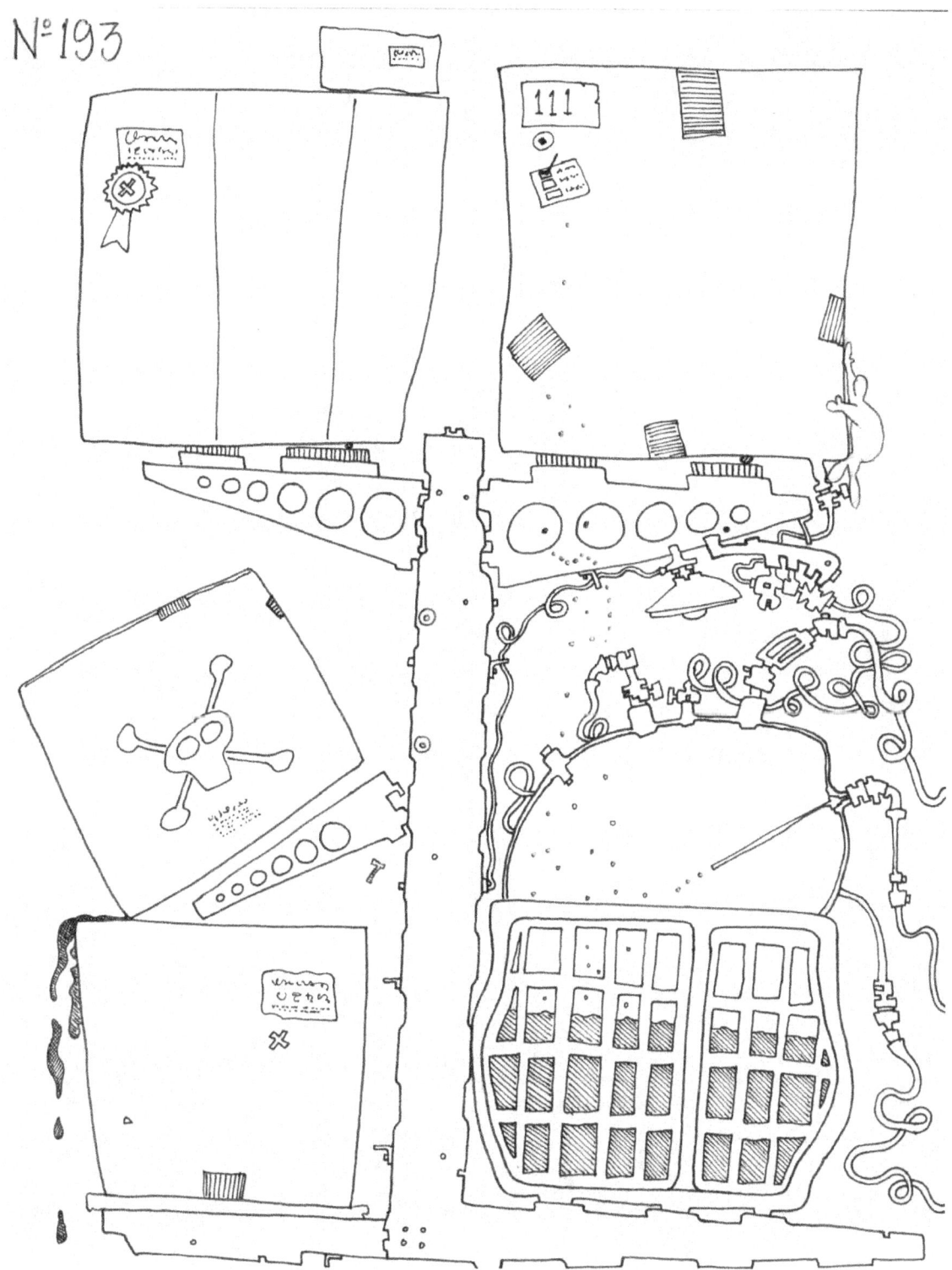

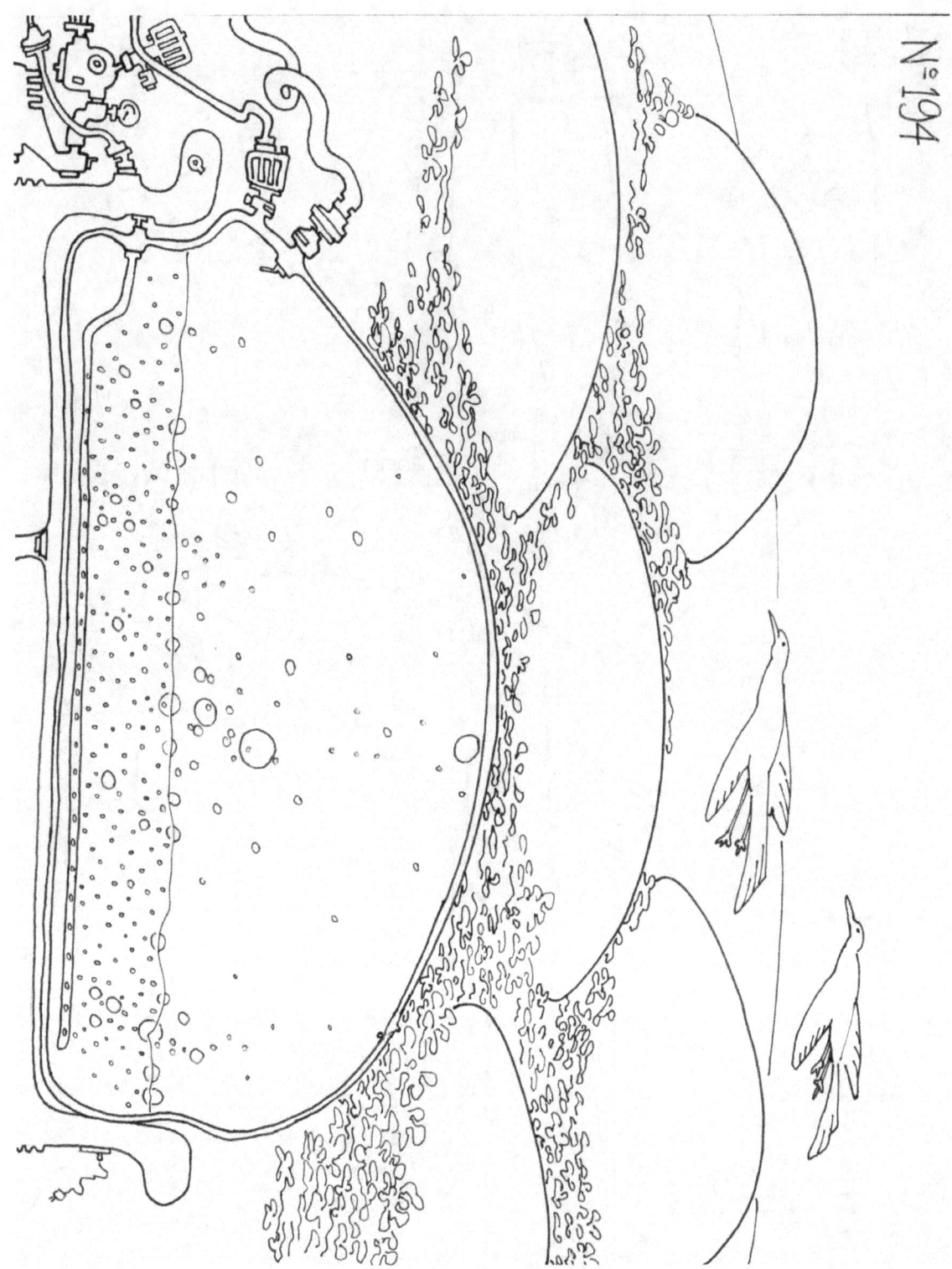

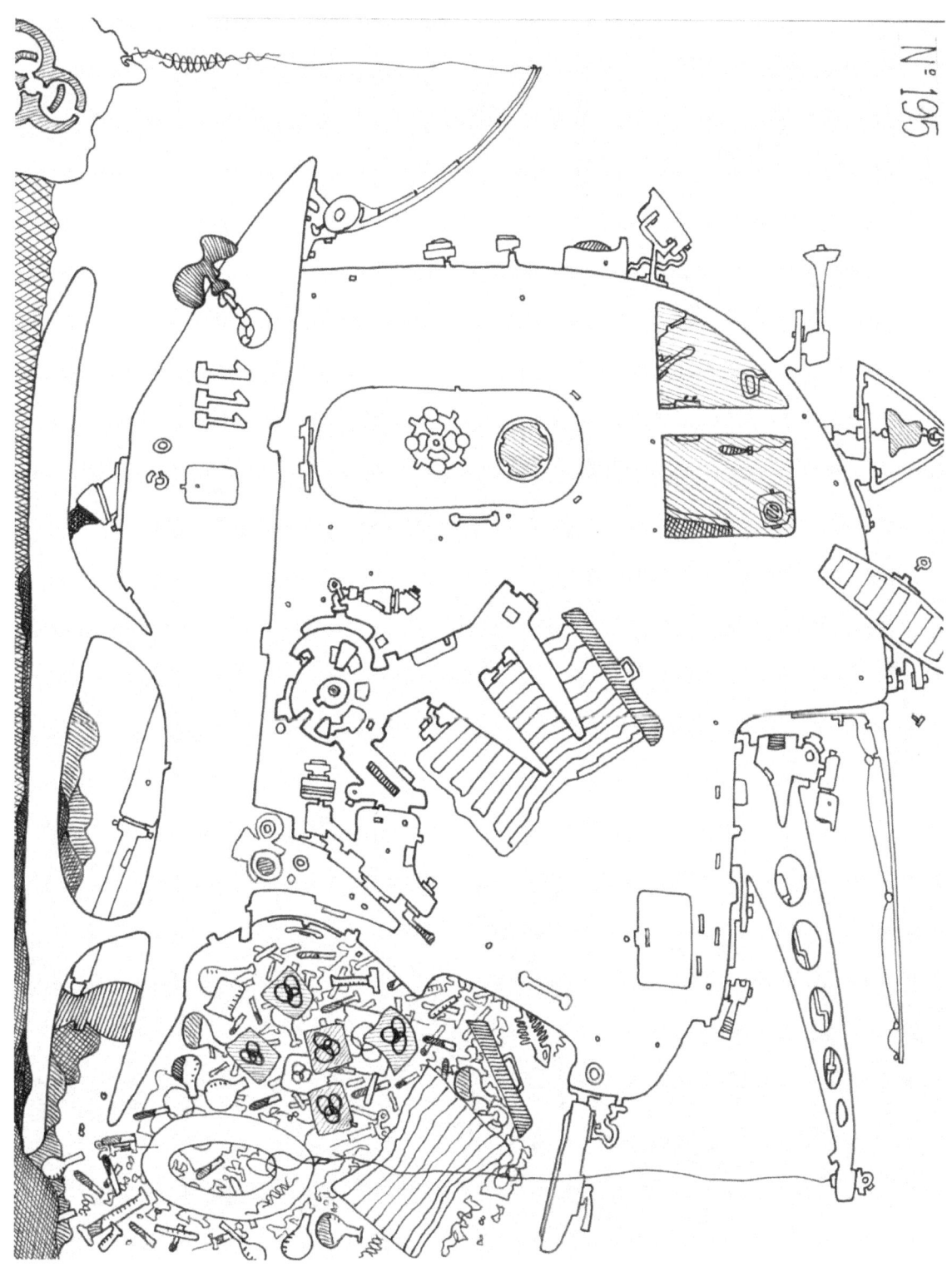

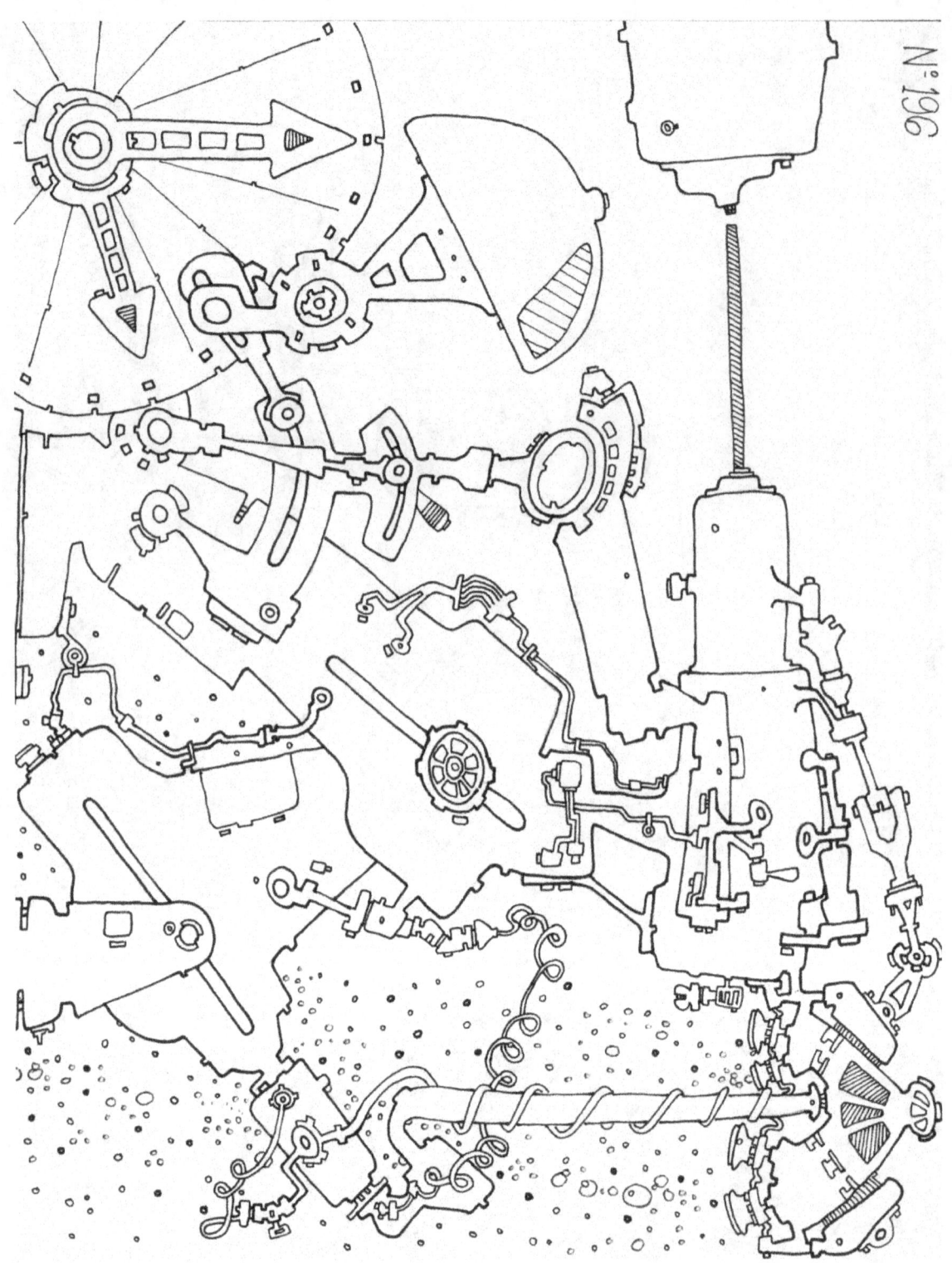

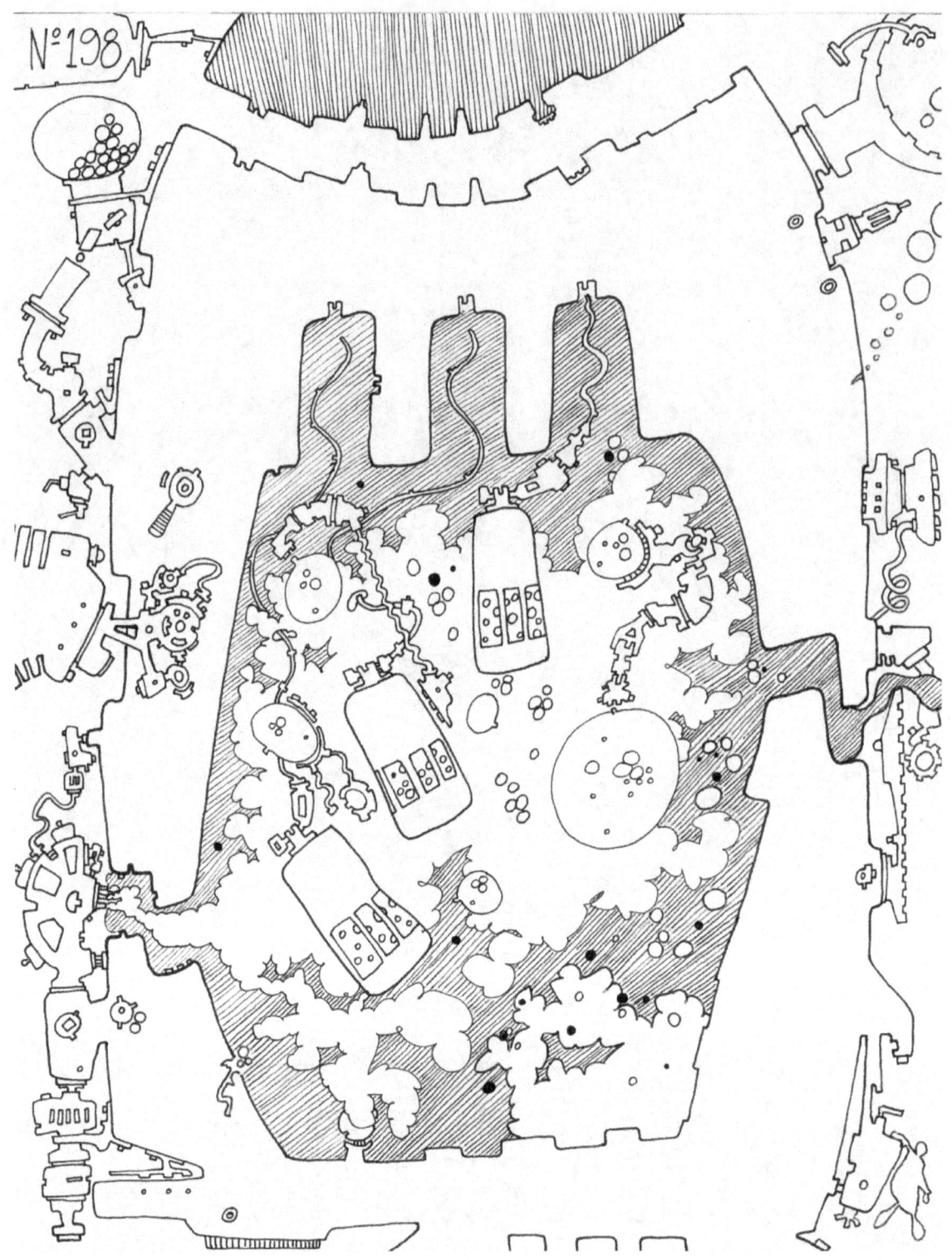

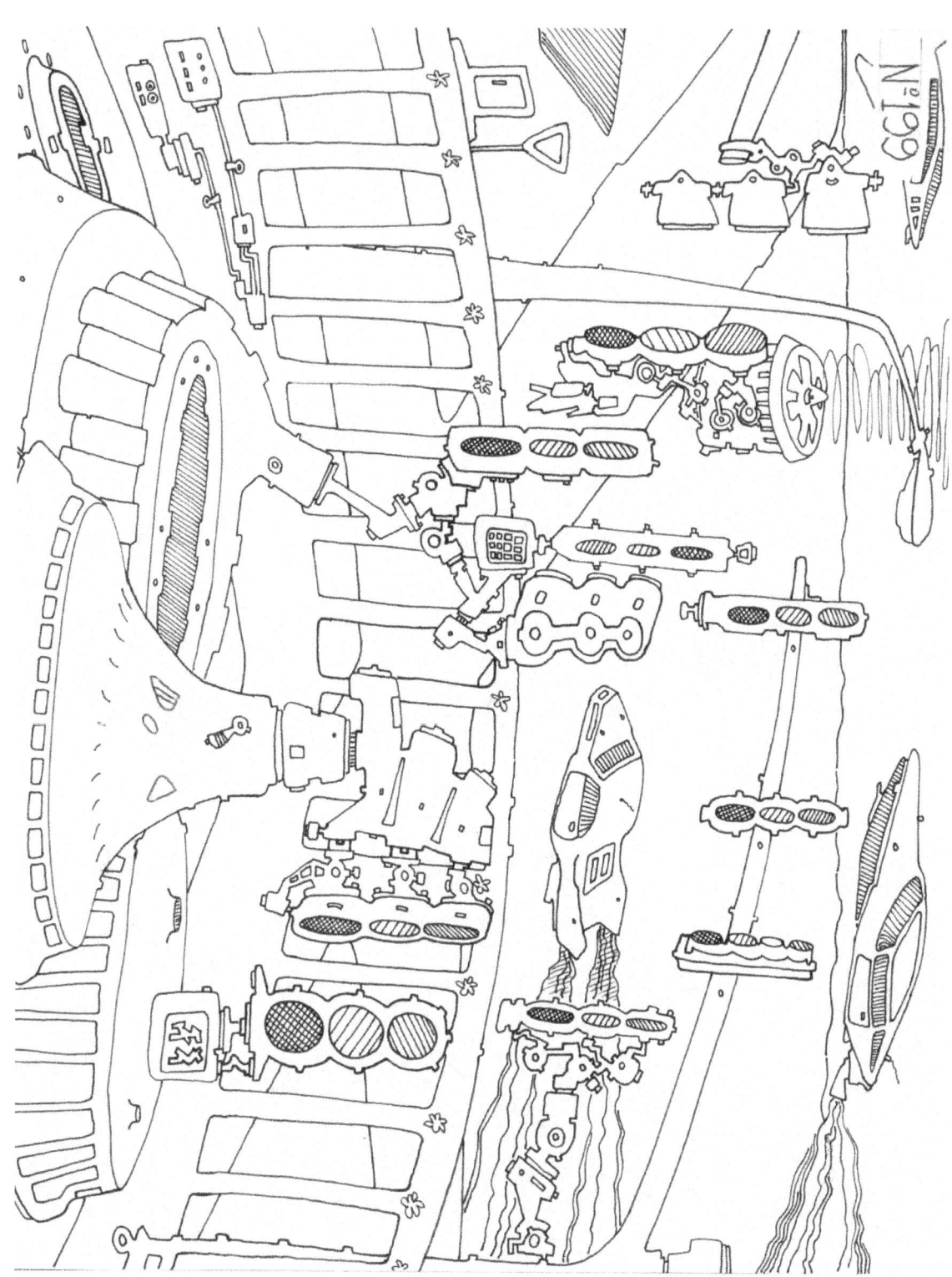

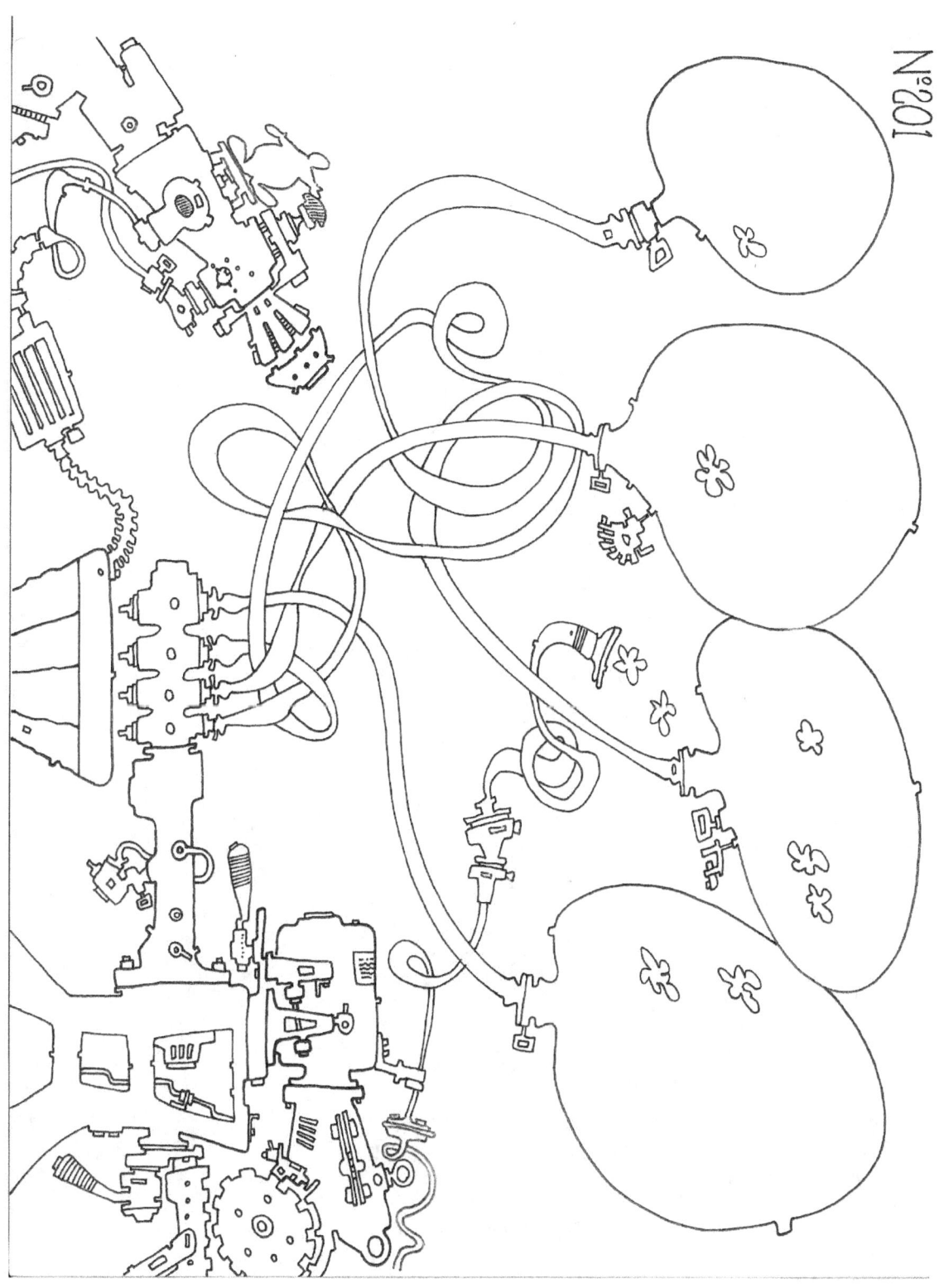

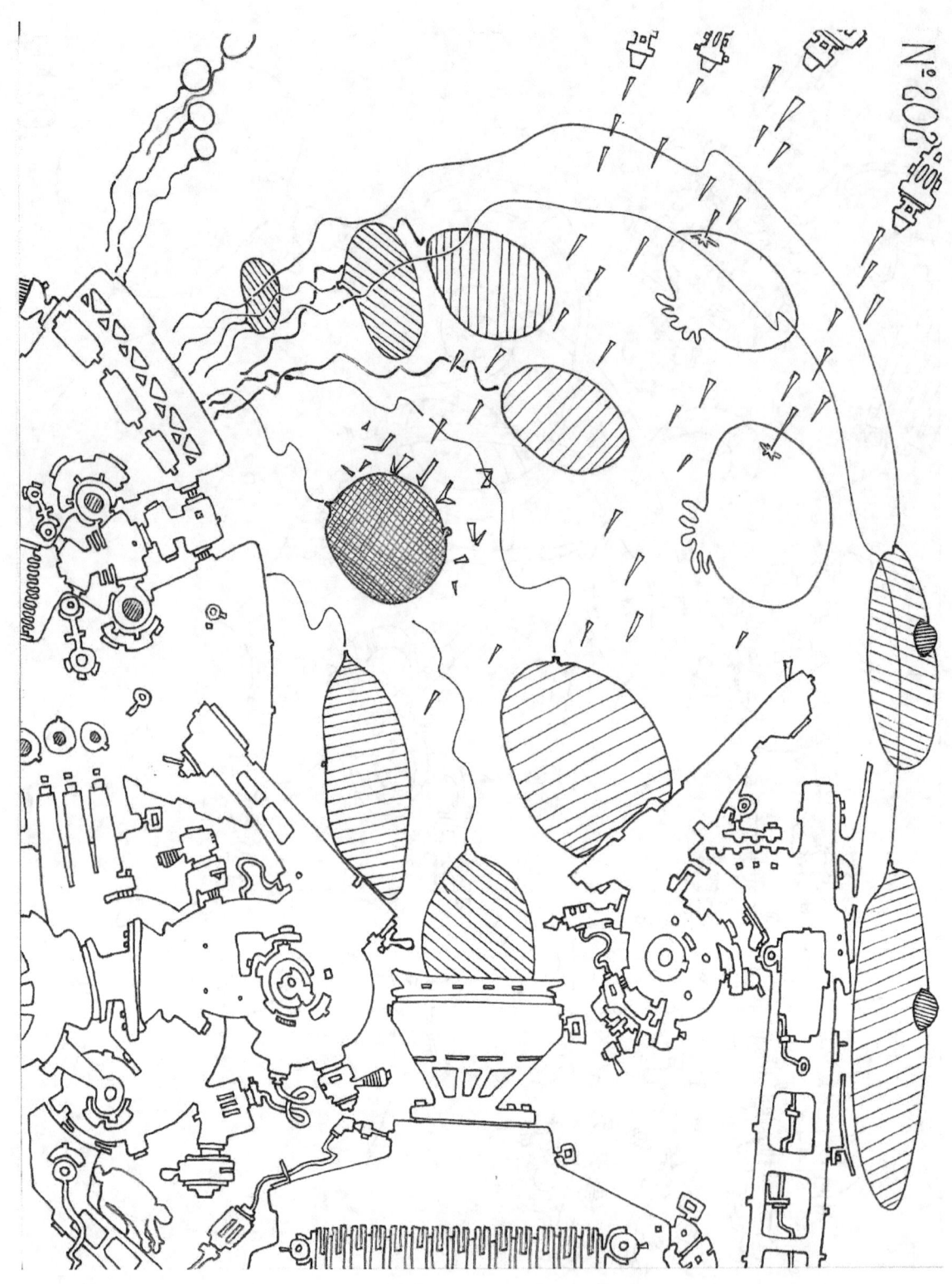

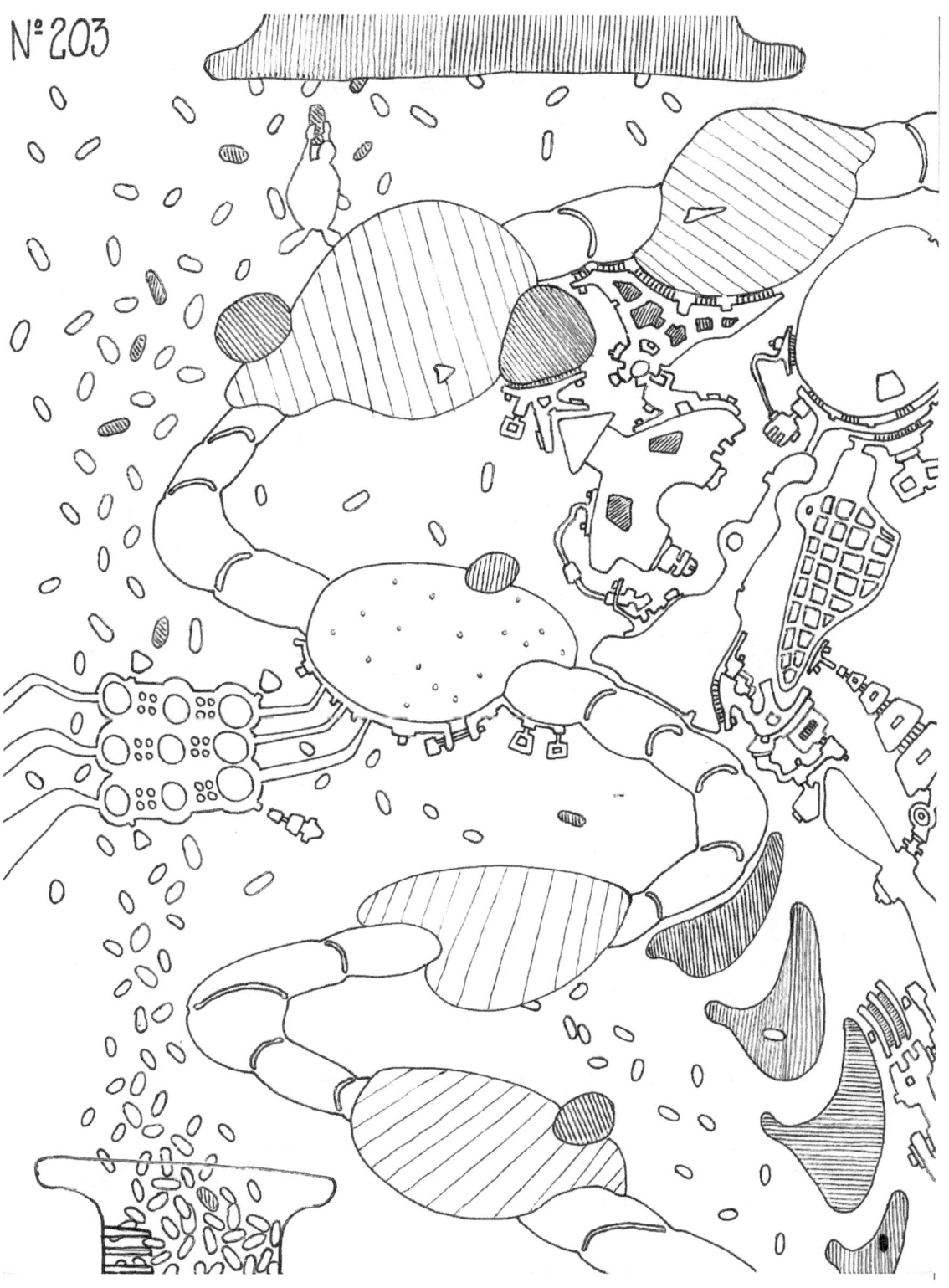

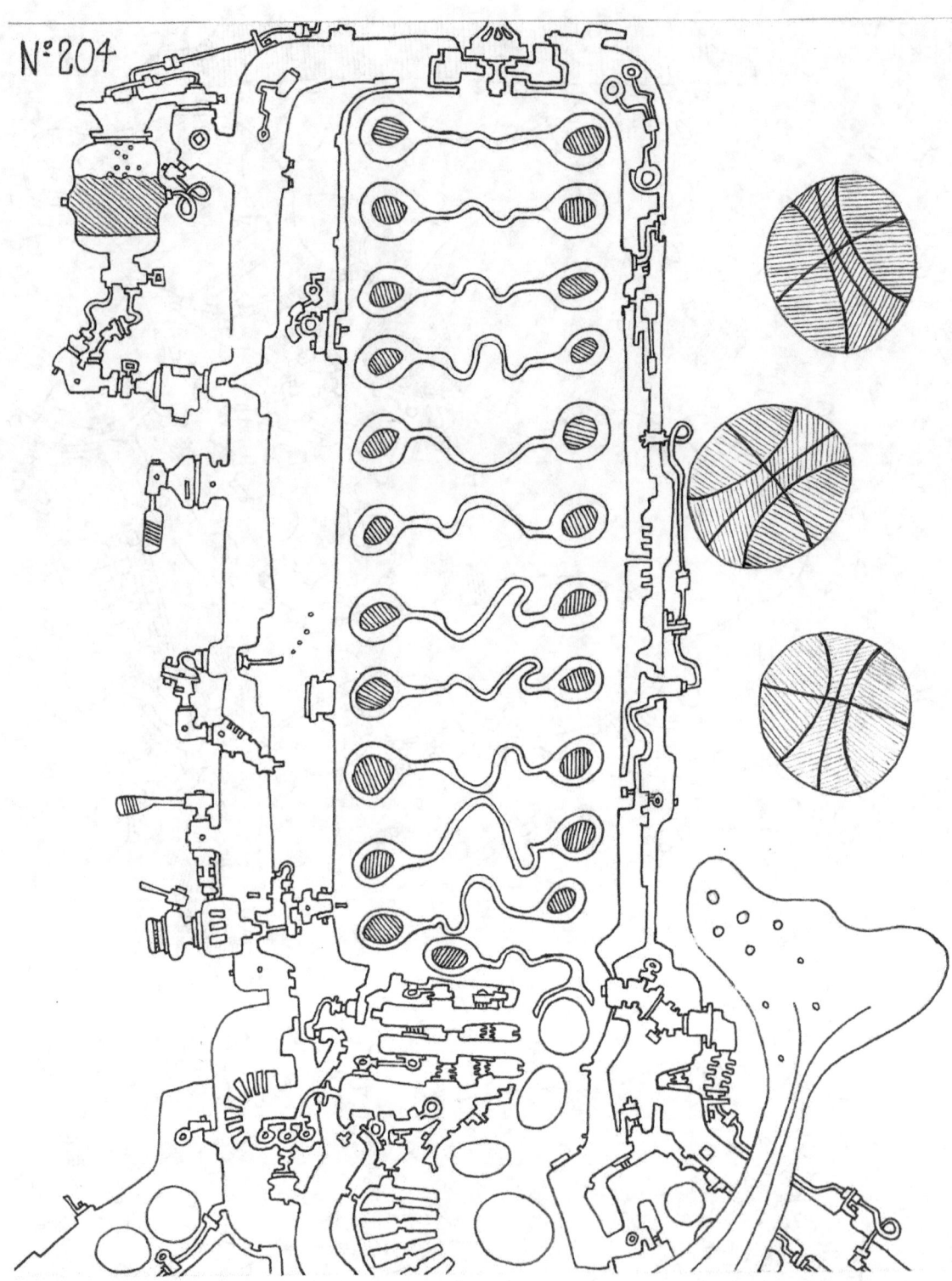

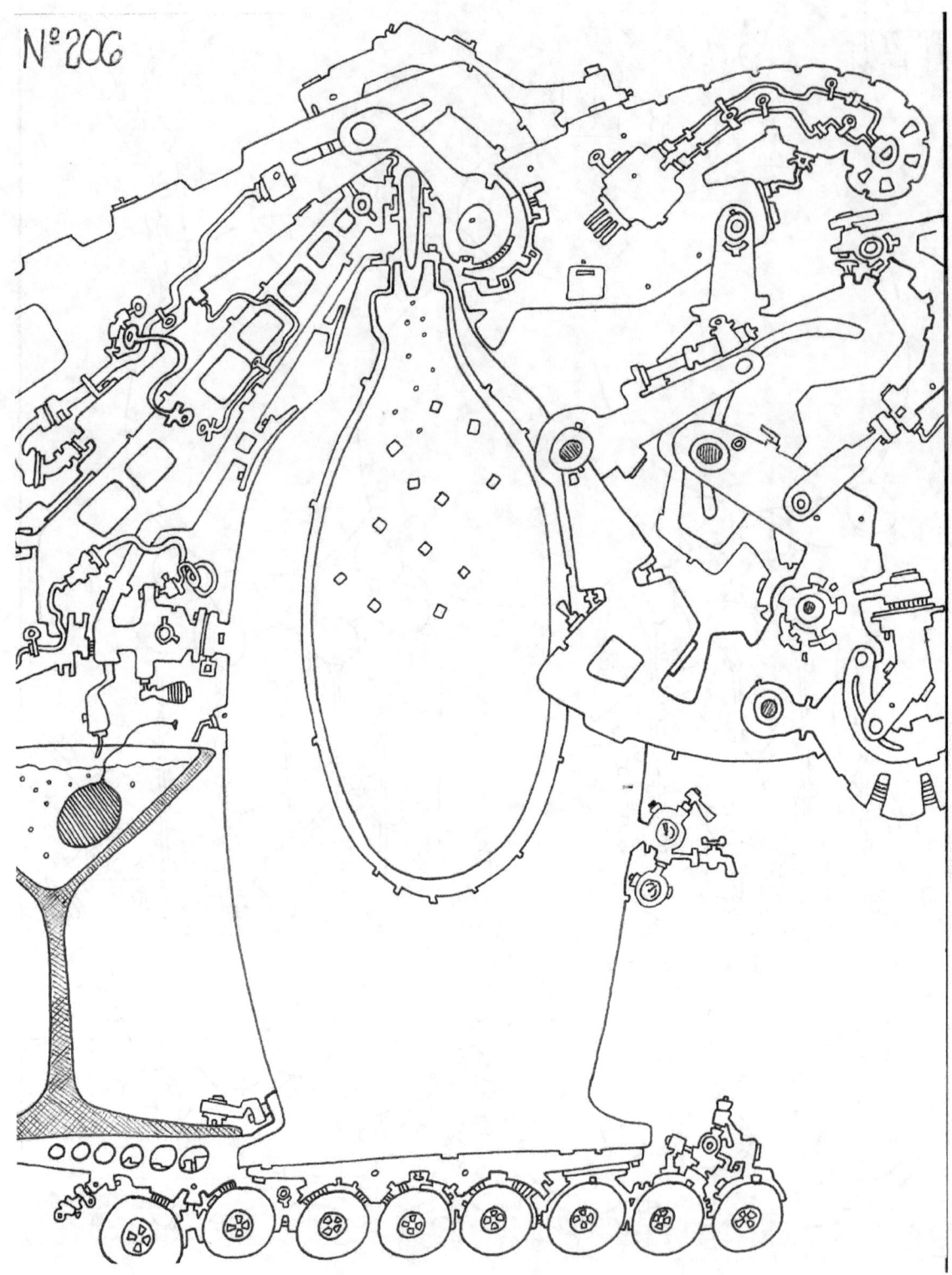

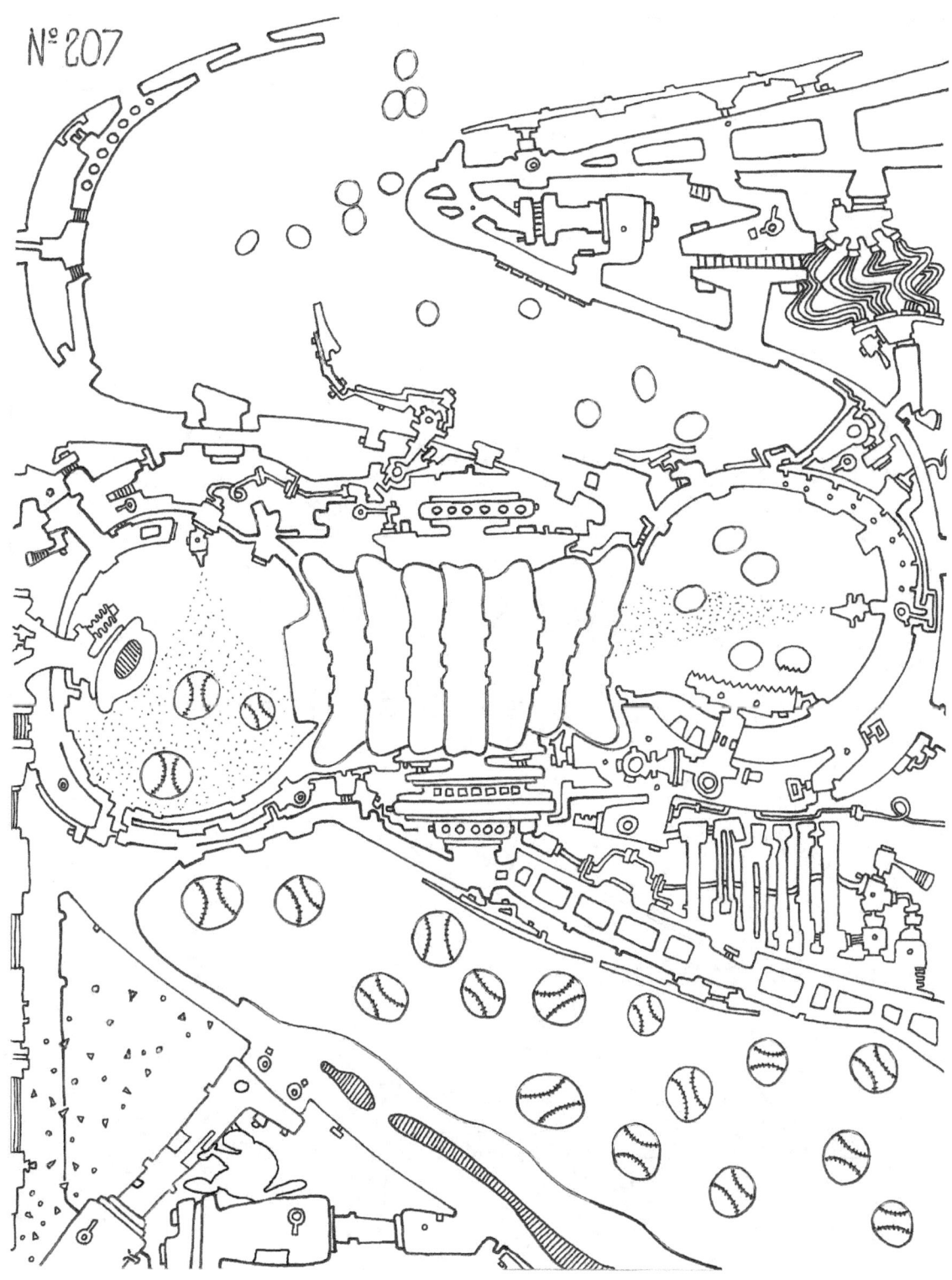

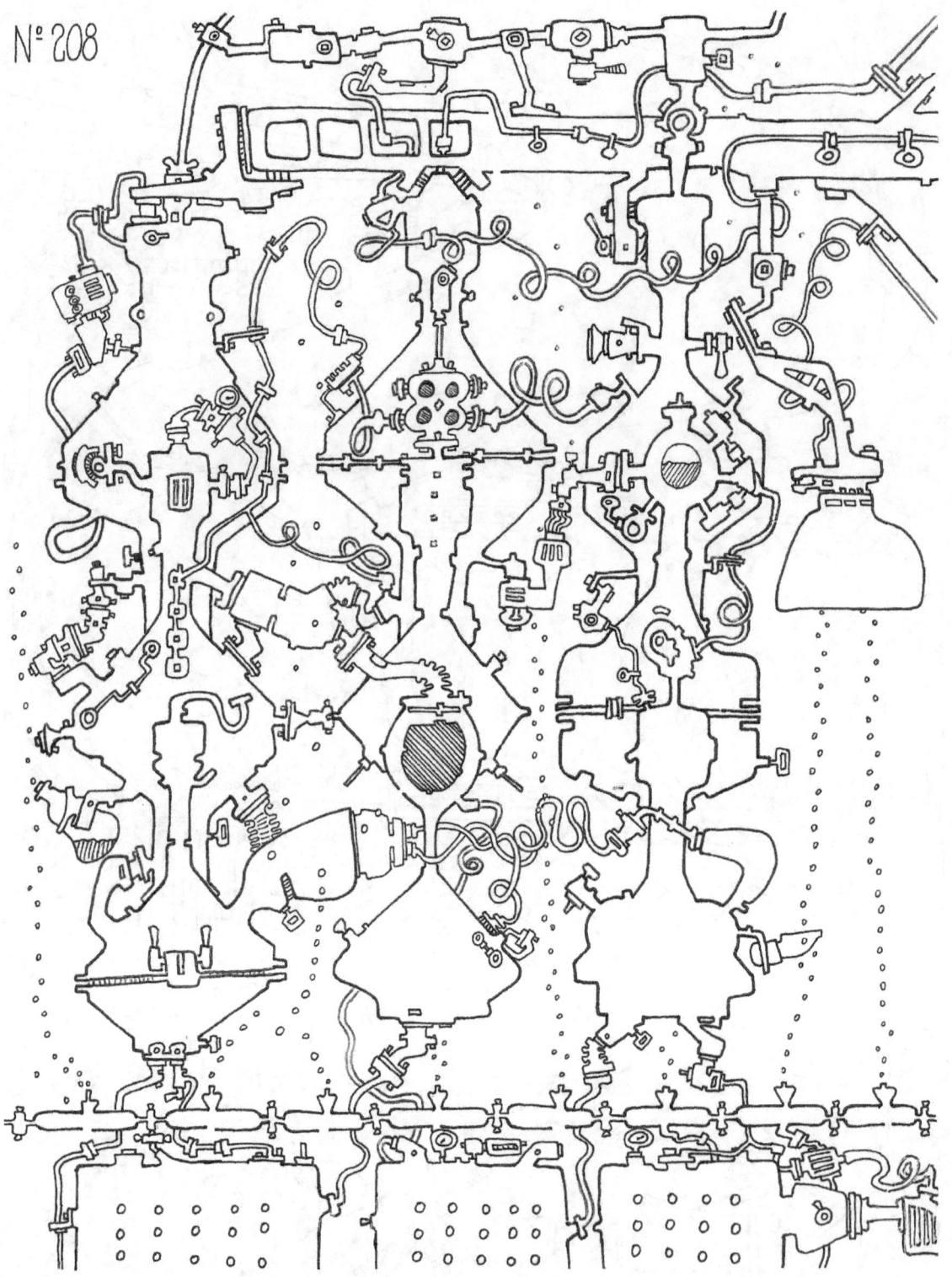

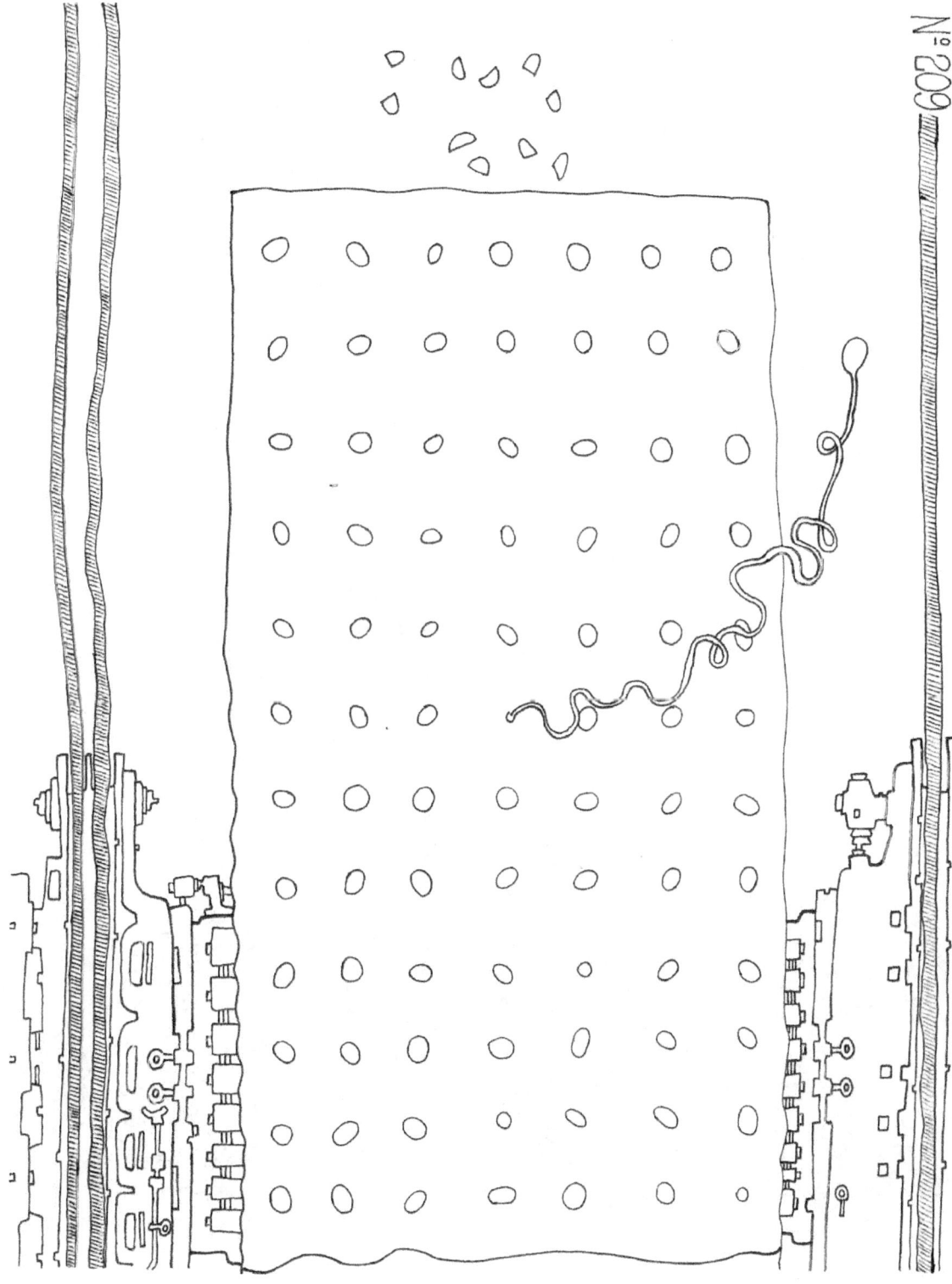

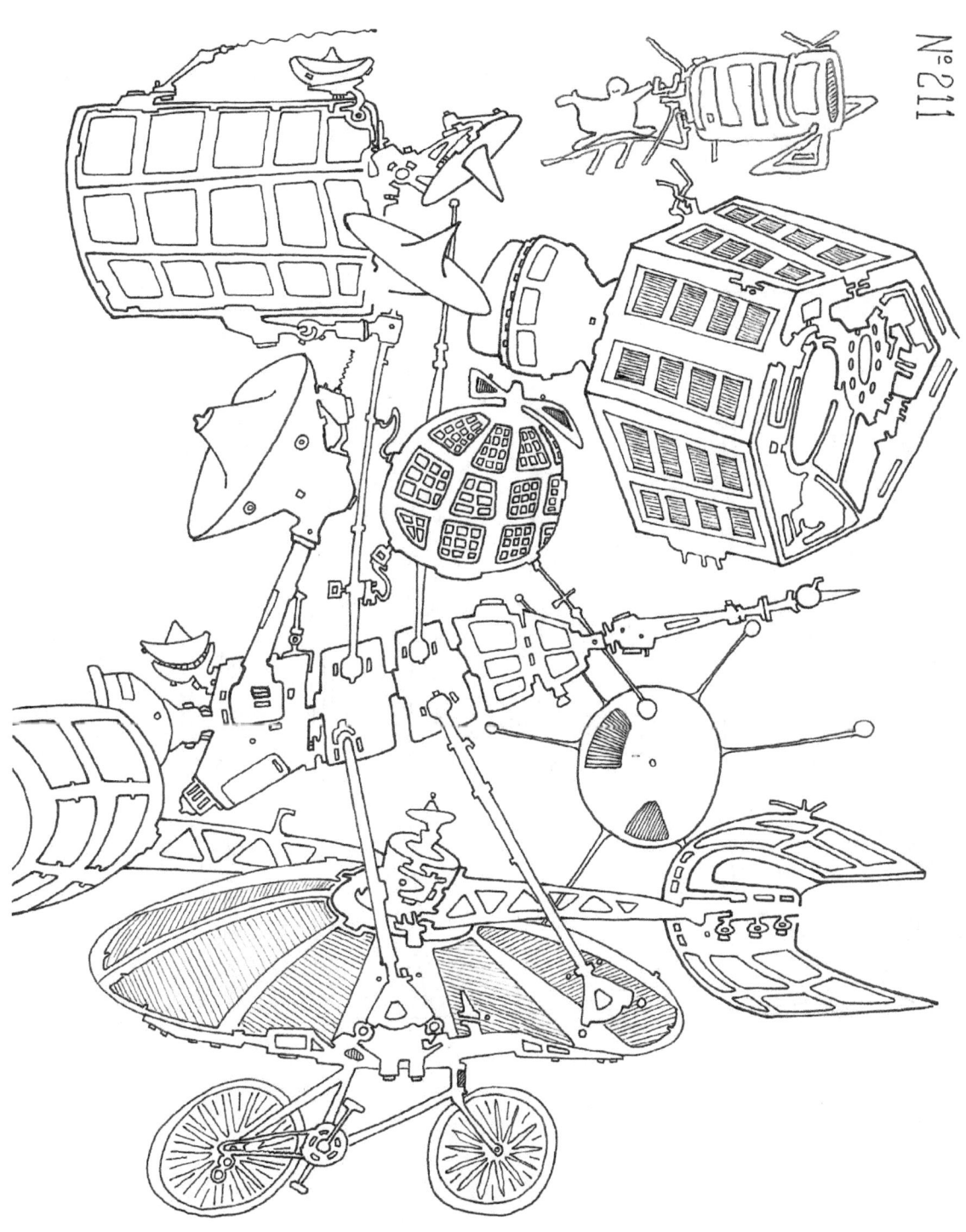

Nº212

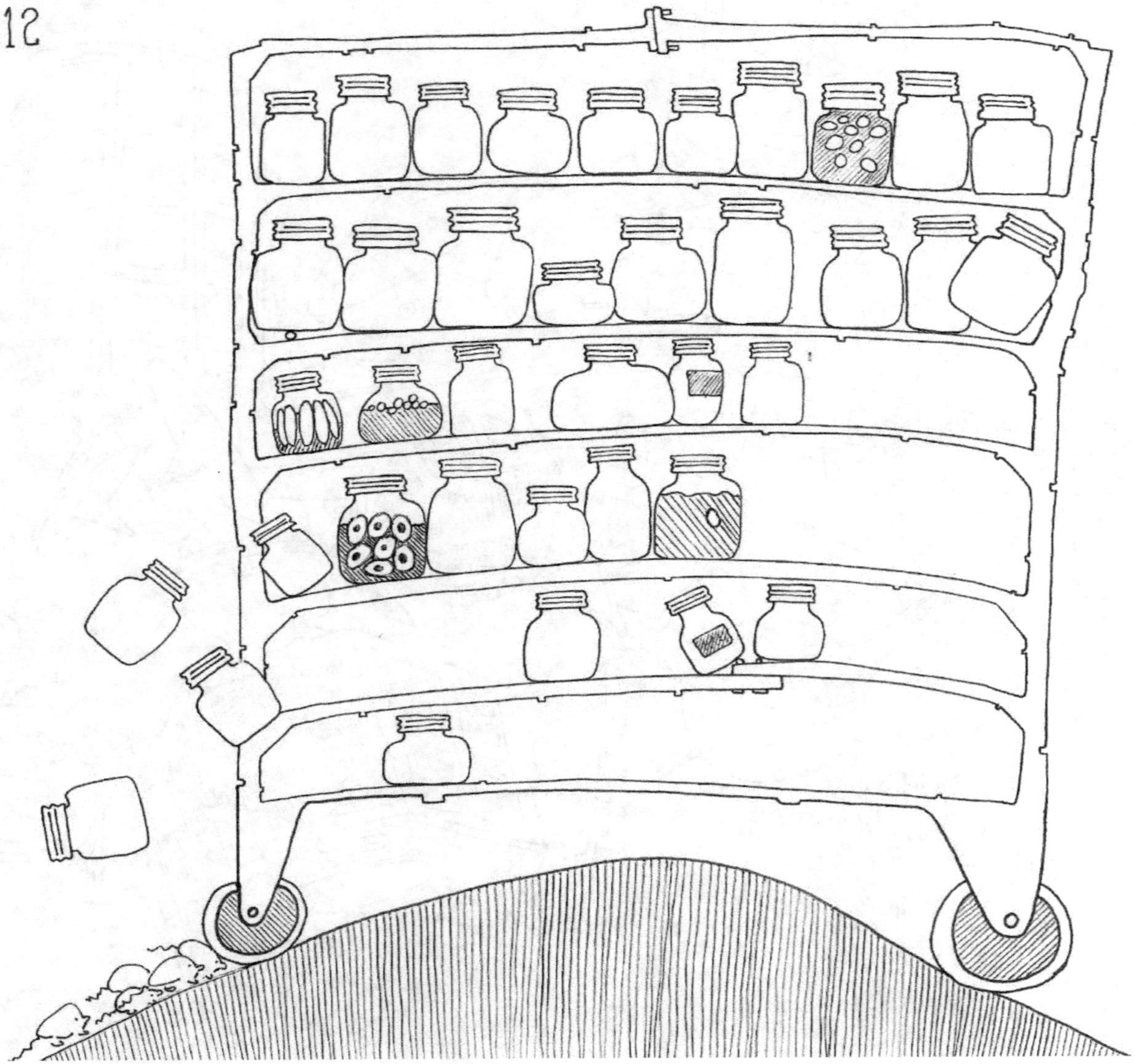

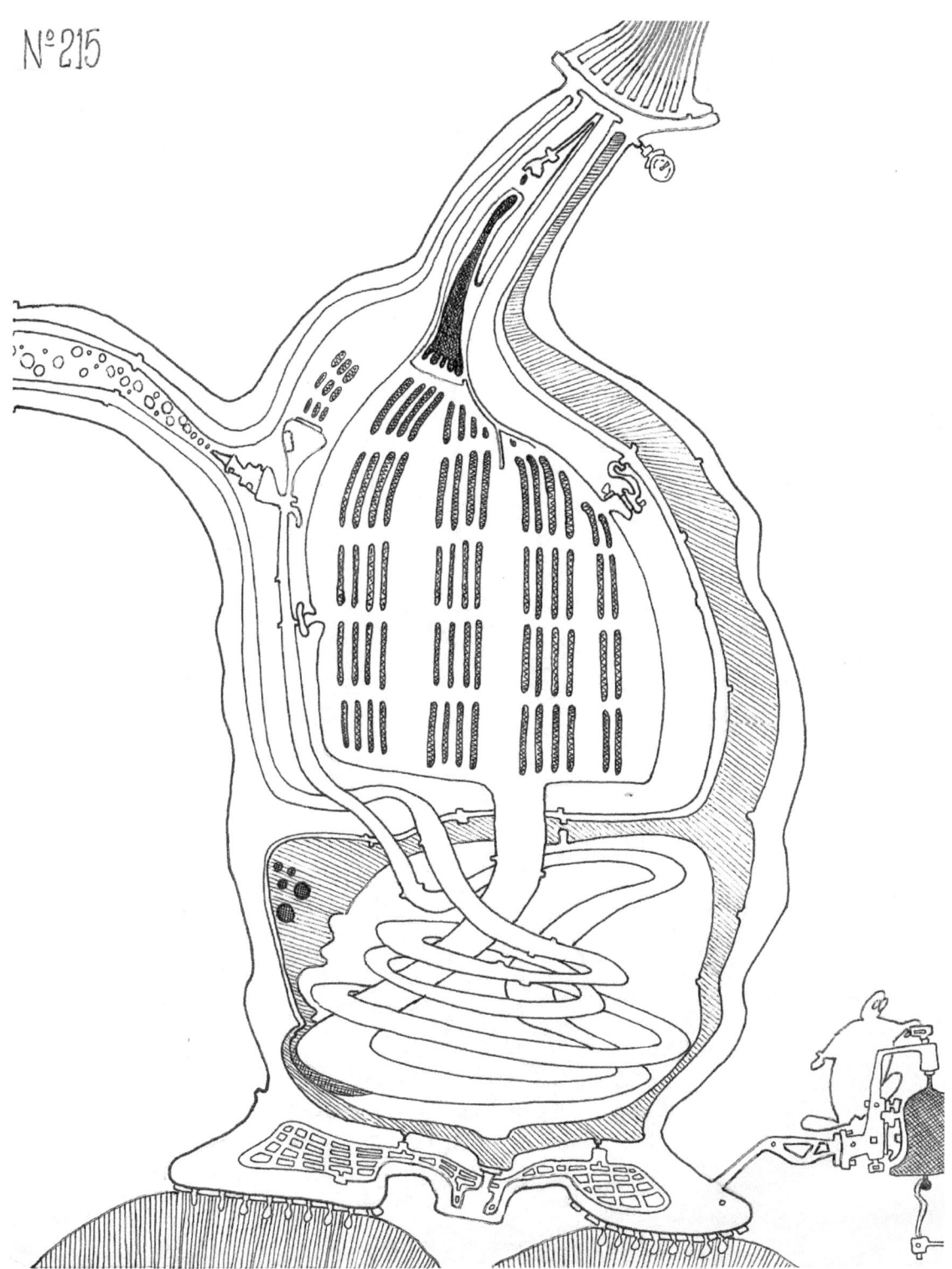

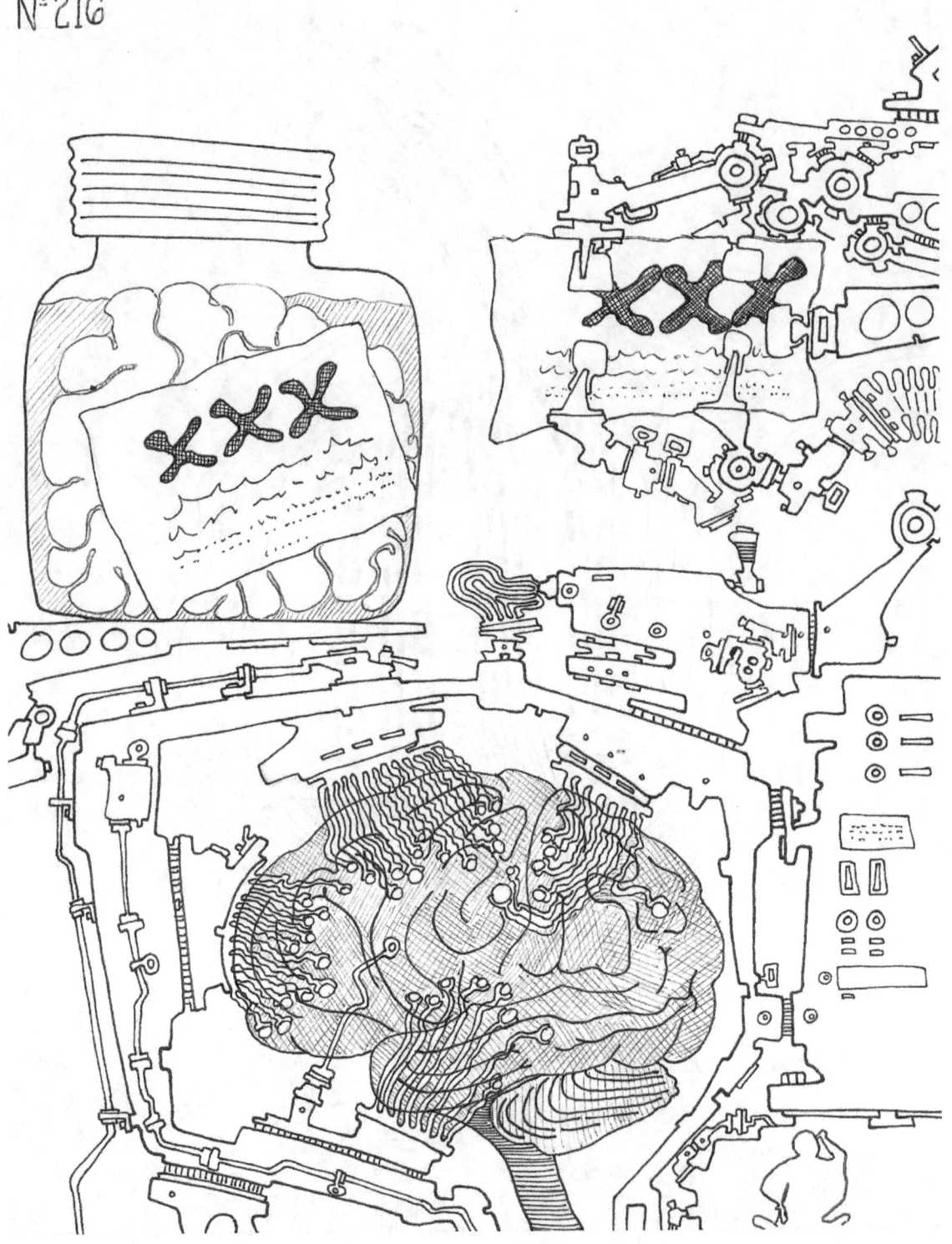

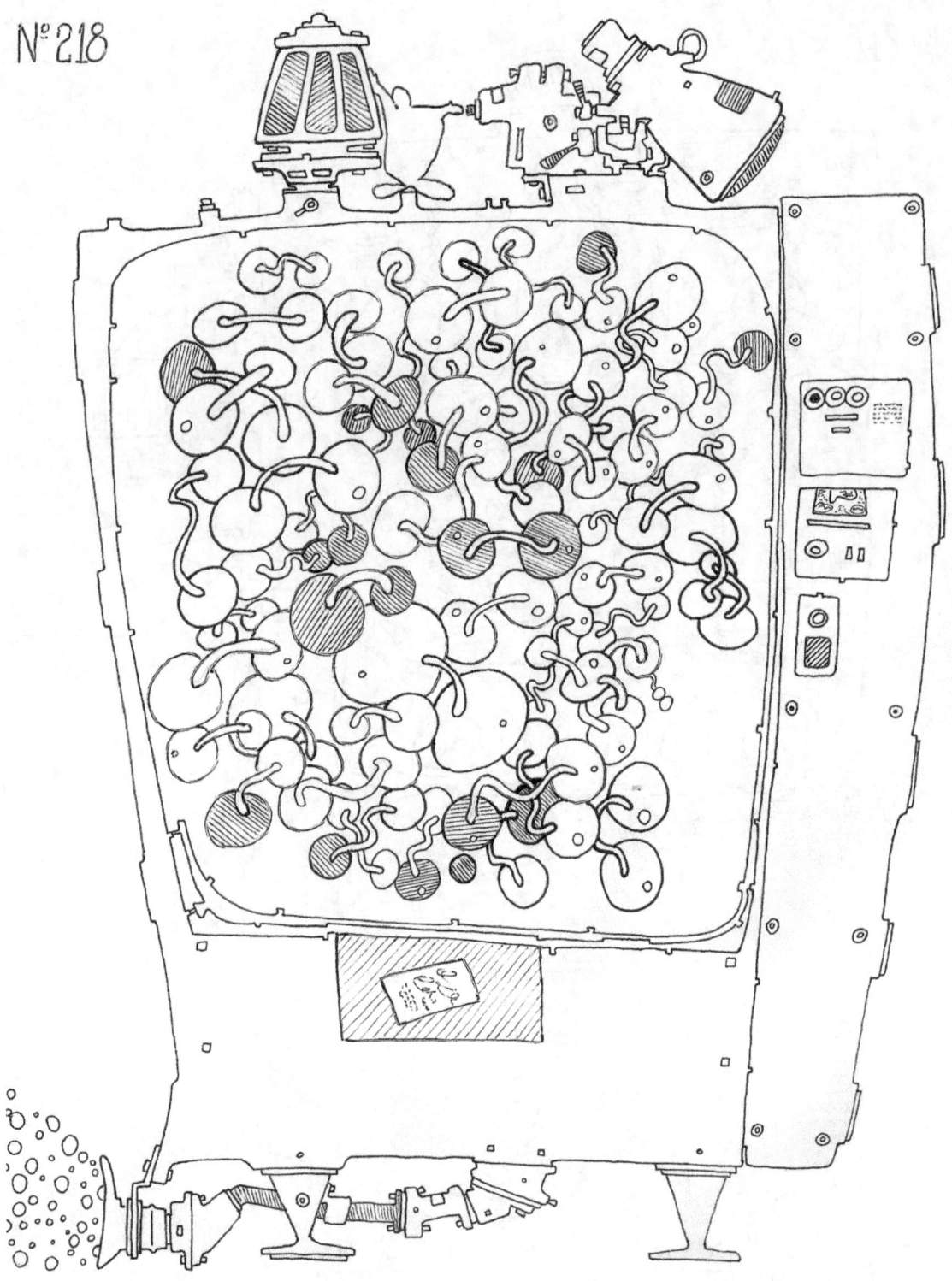

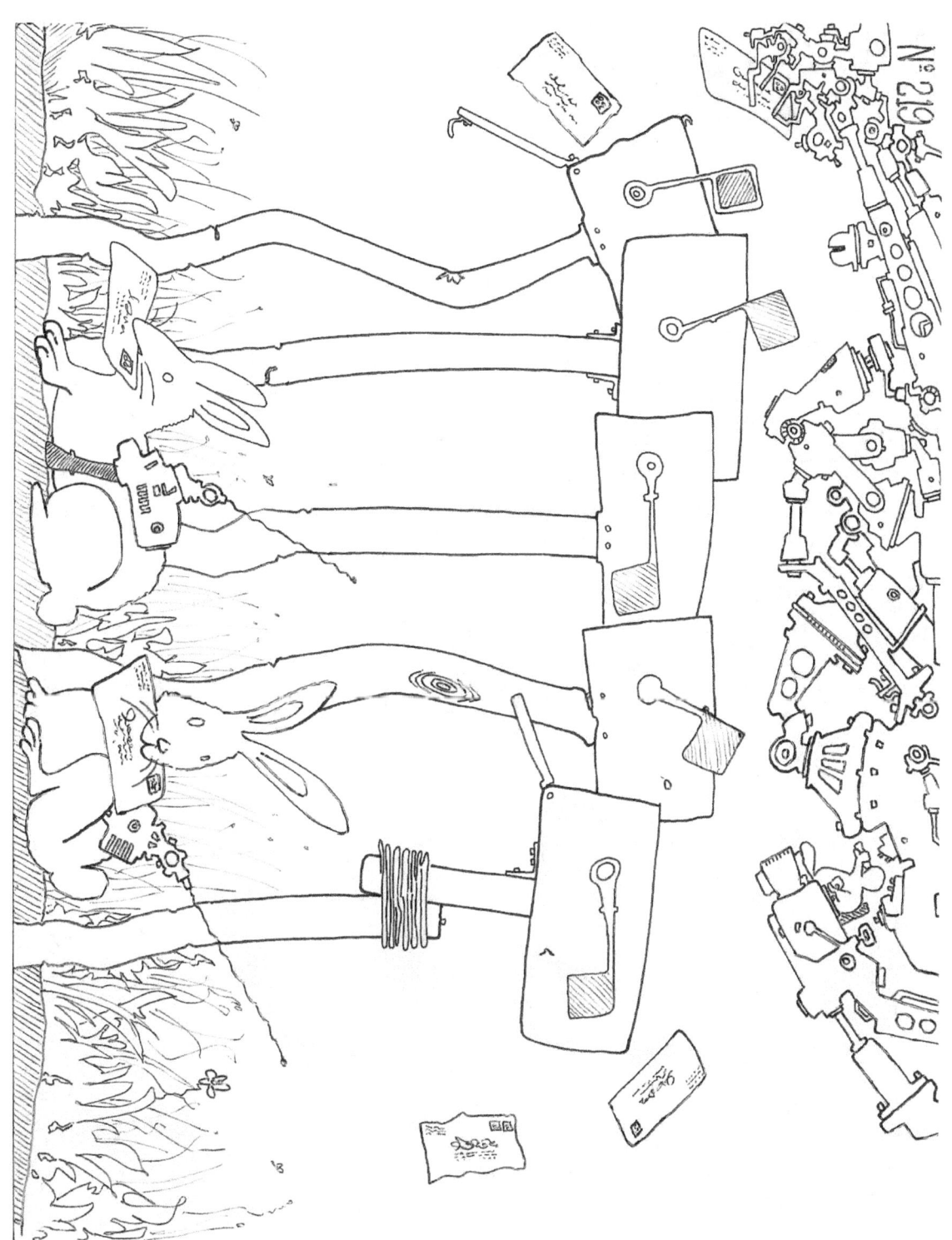

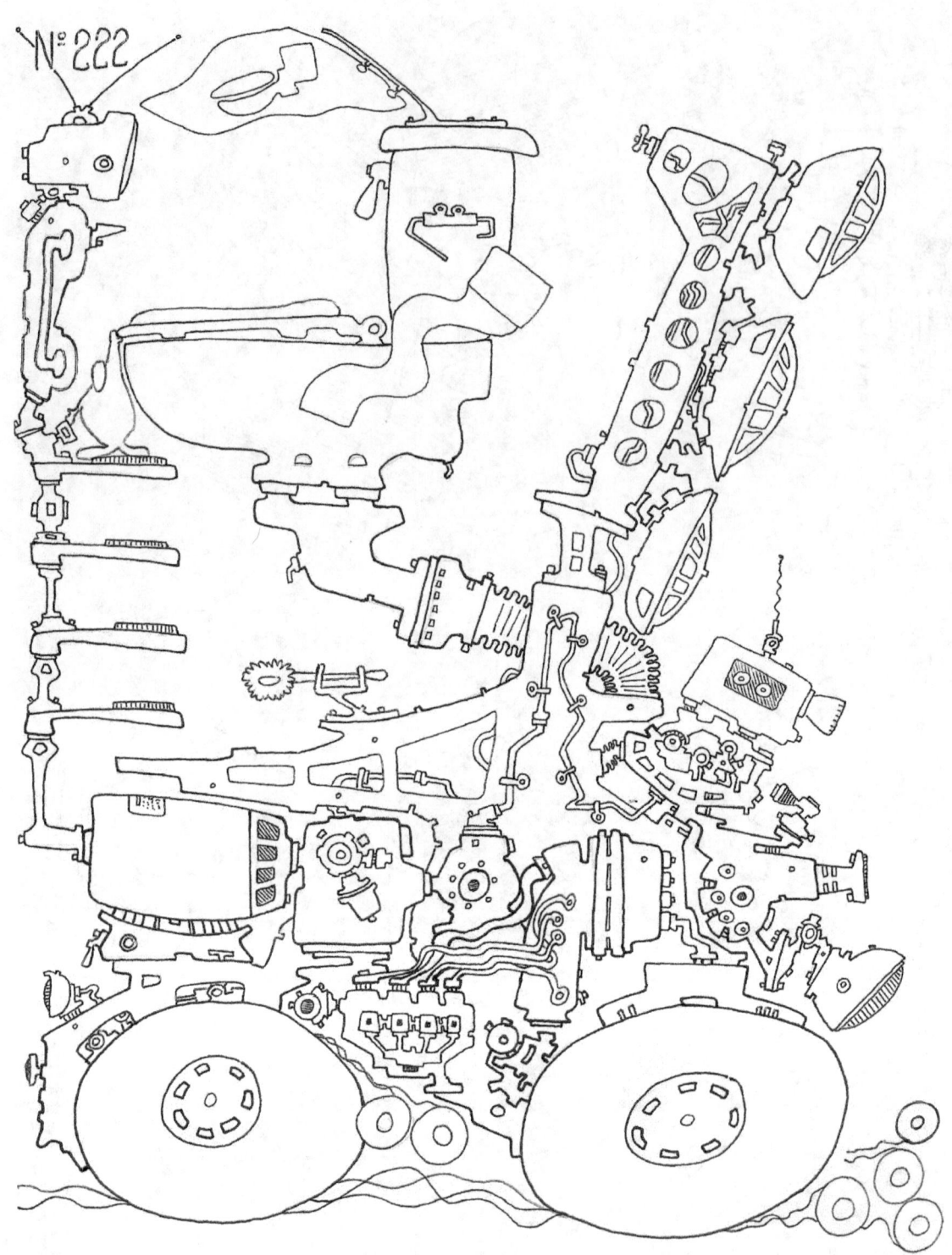

Nº223

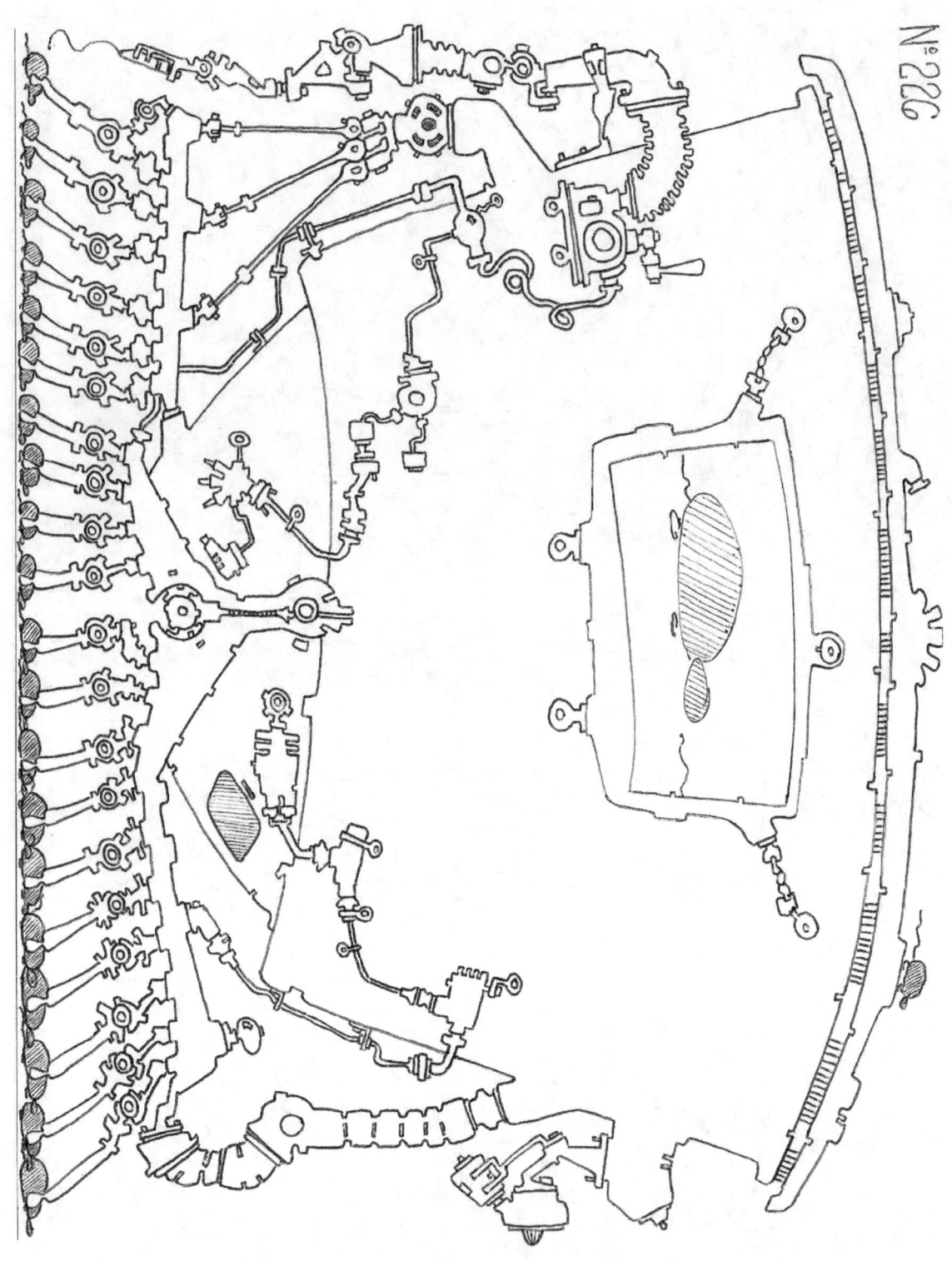

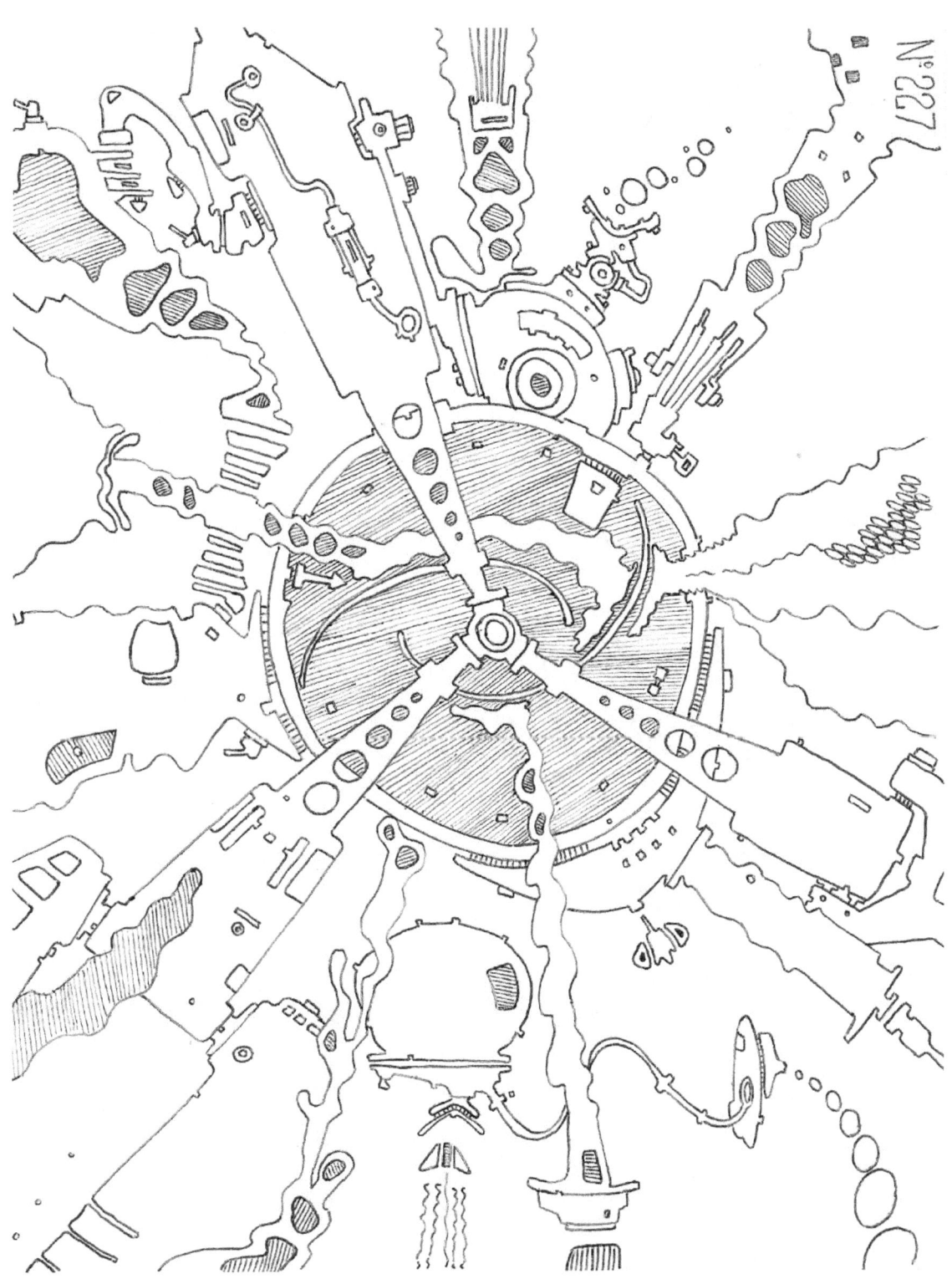

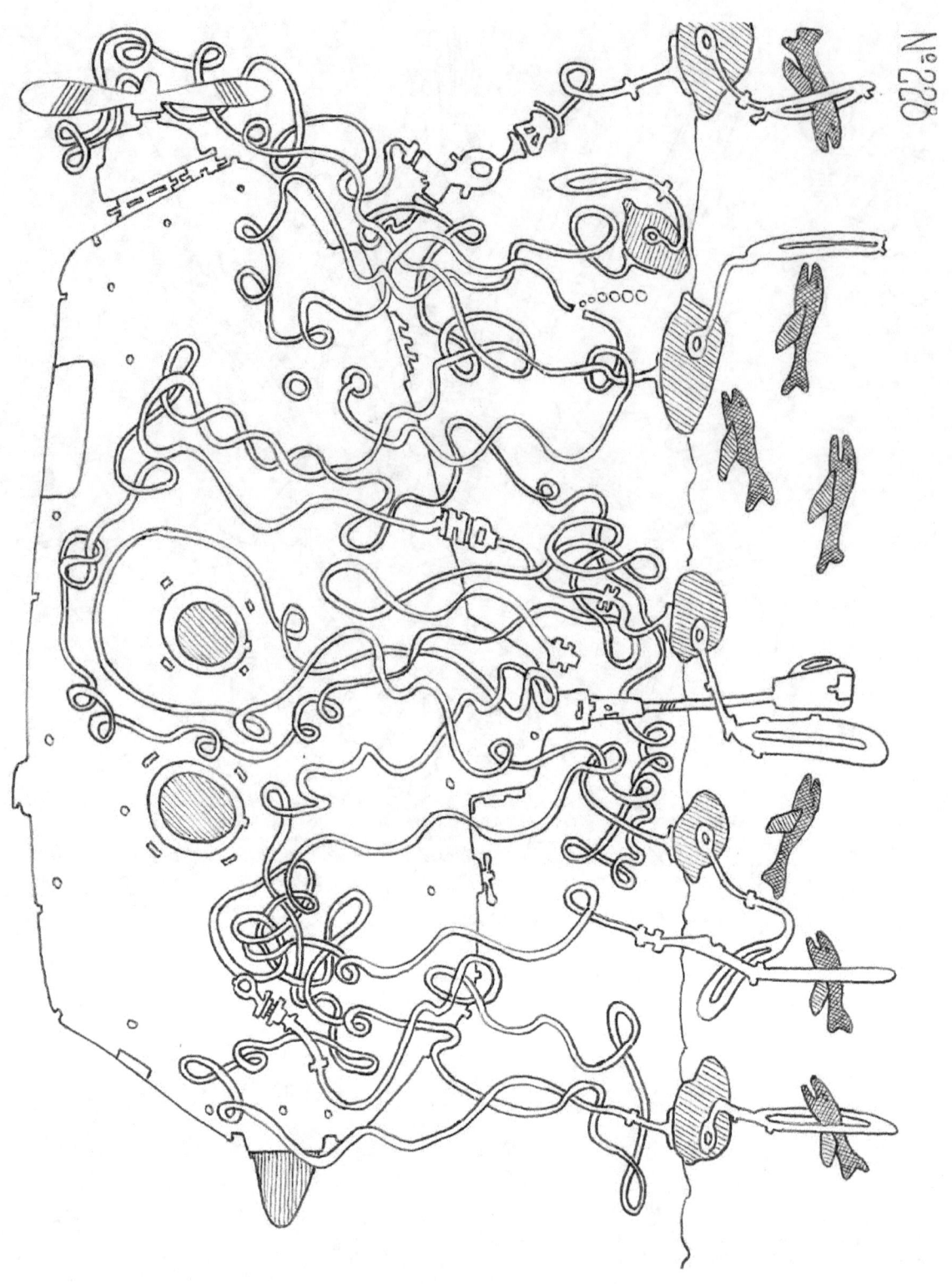

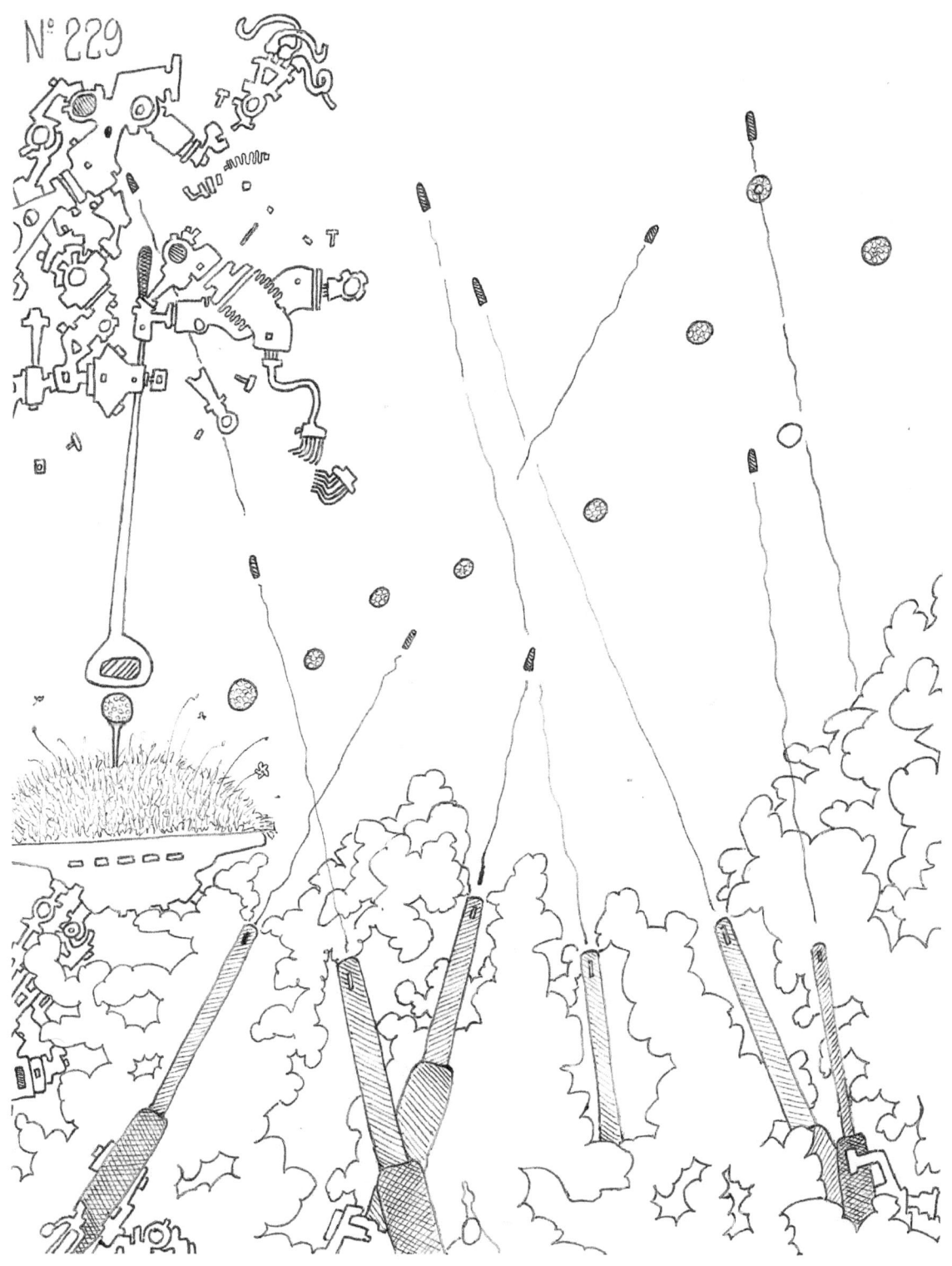

N° 229

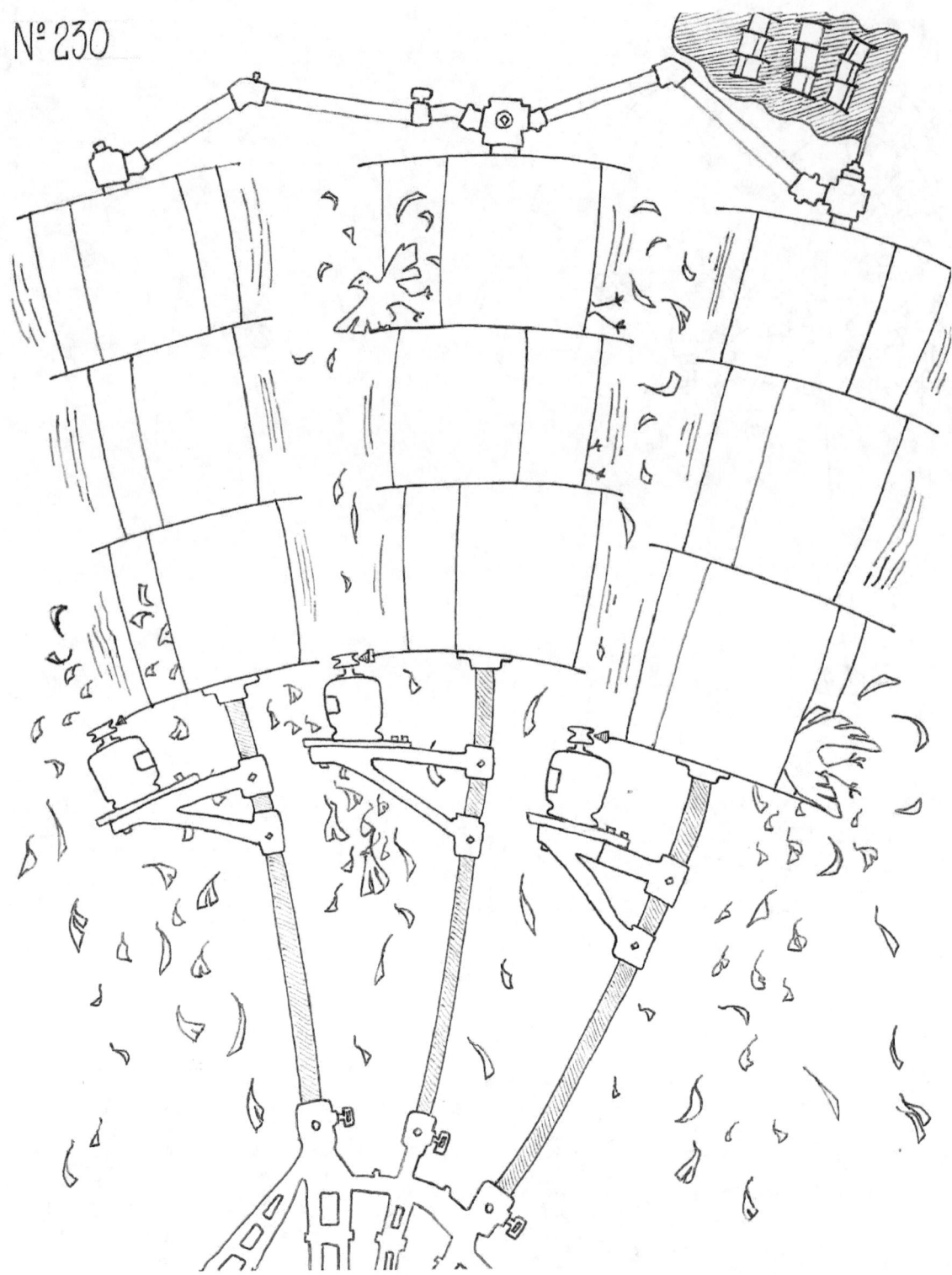

Nº 232

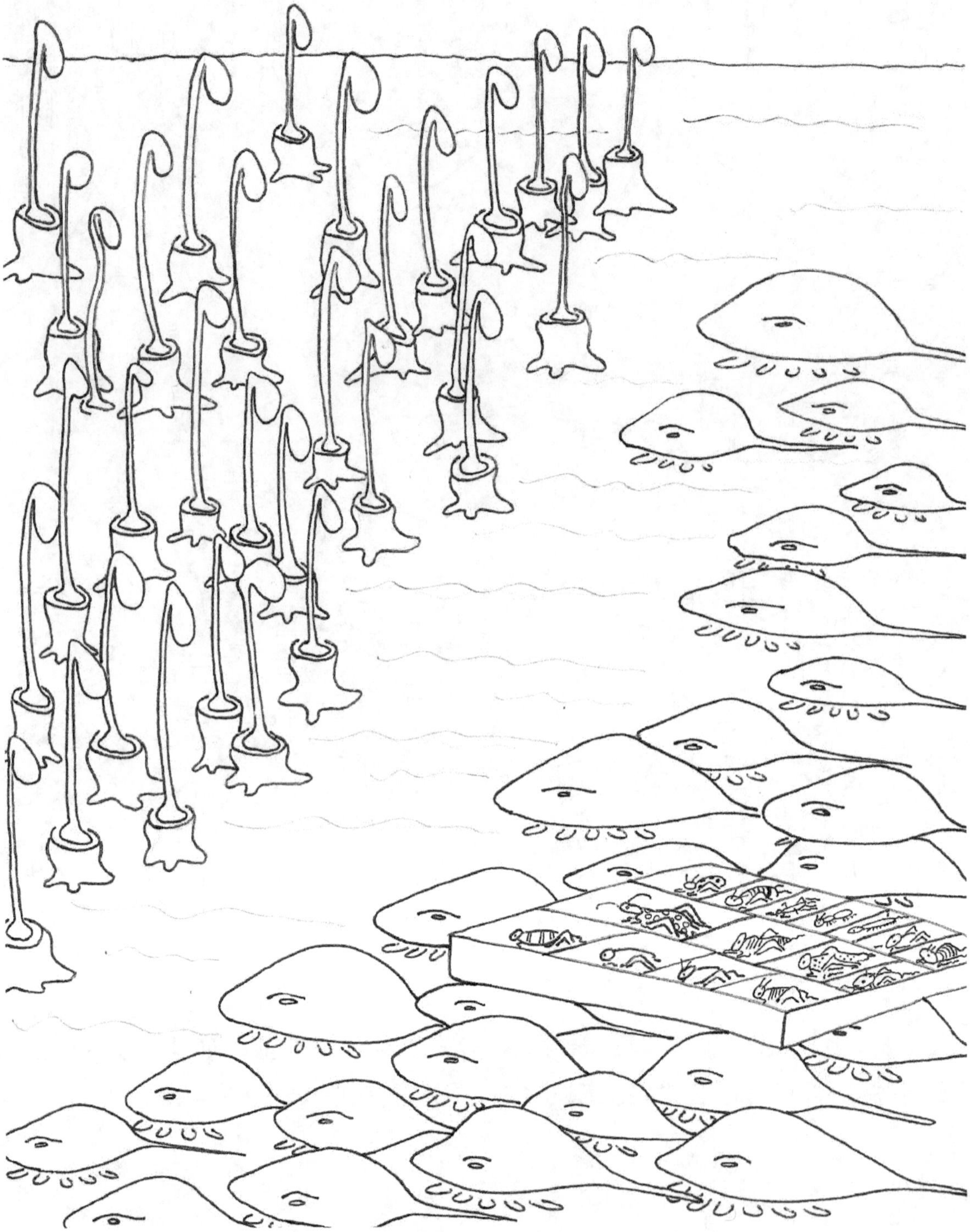

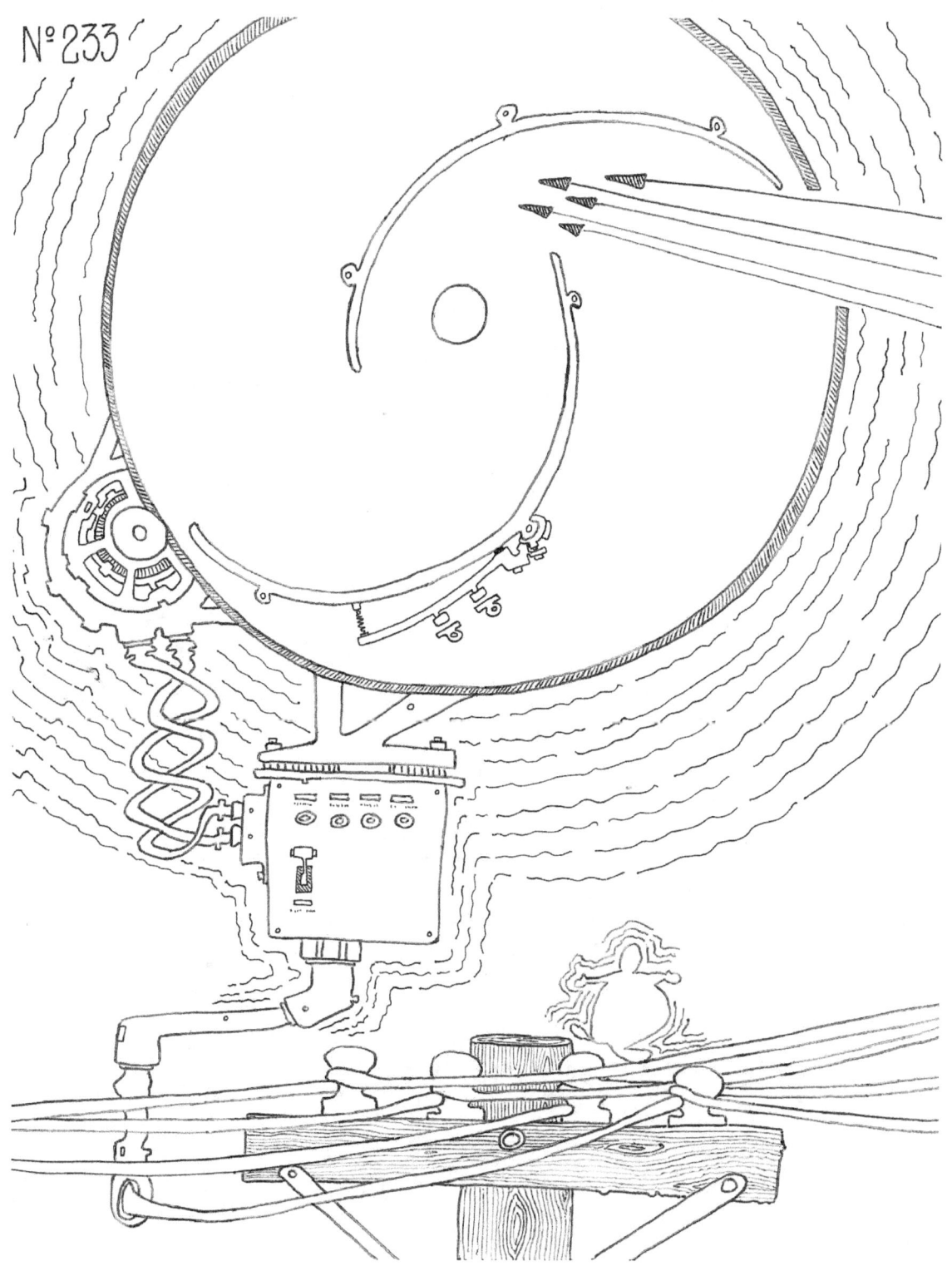

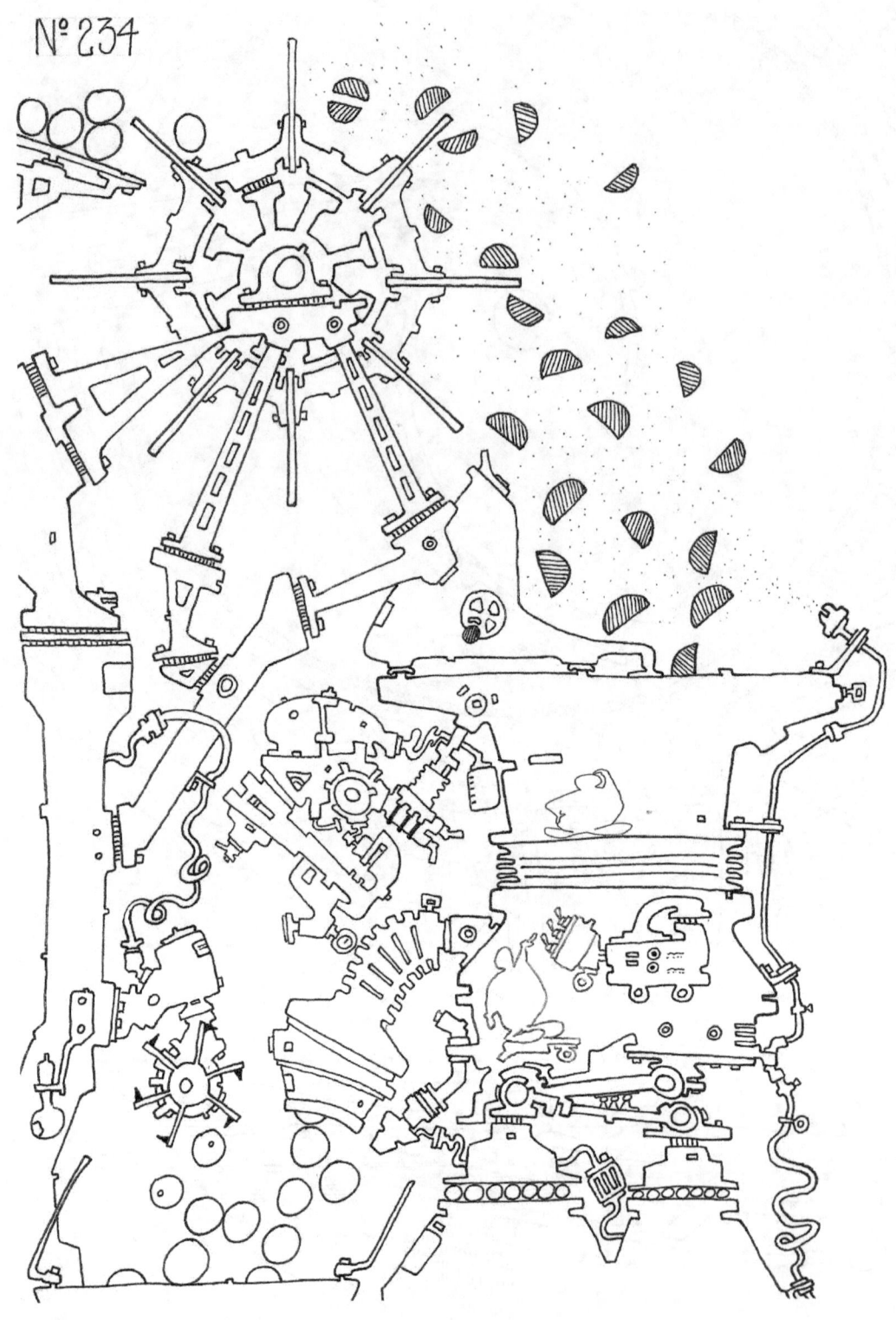

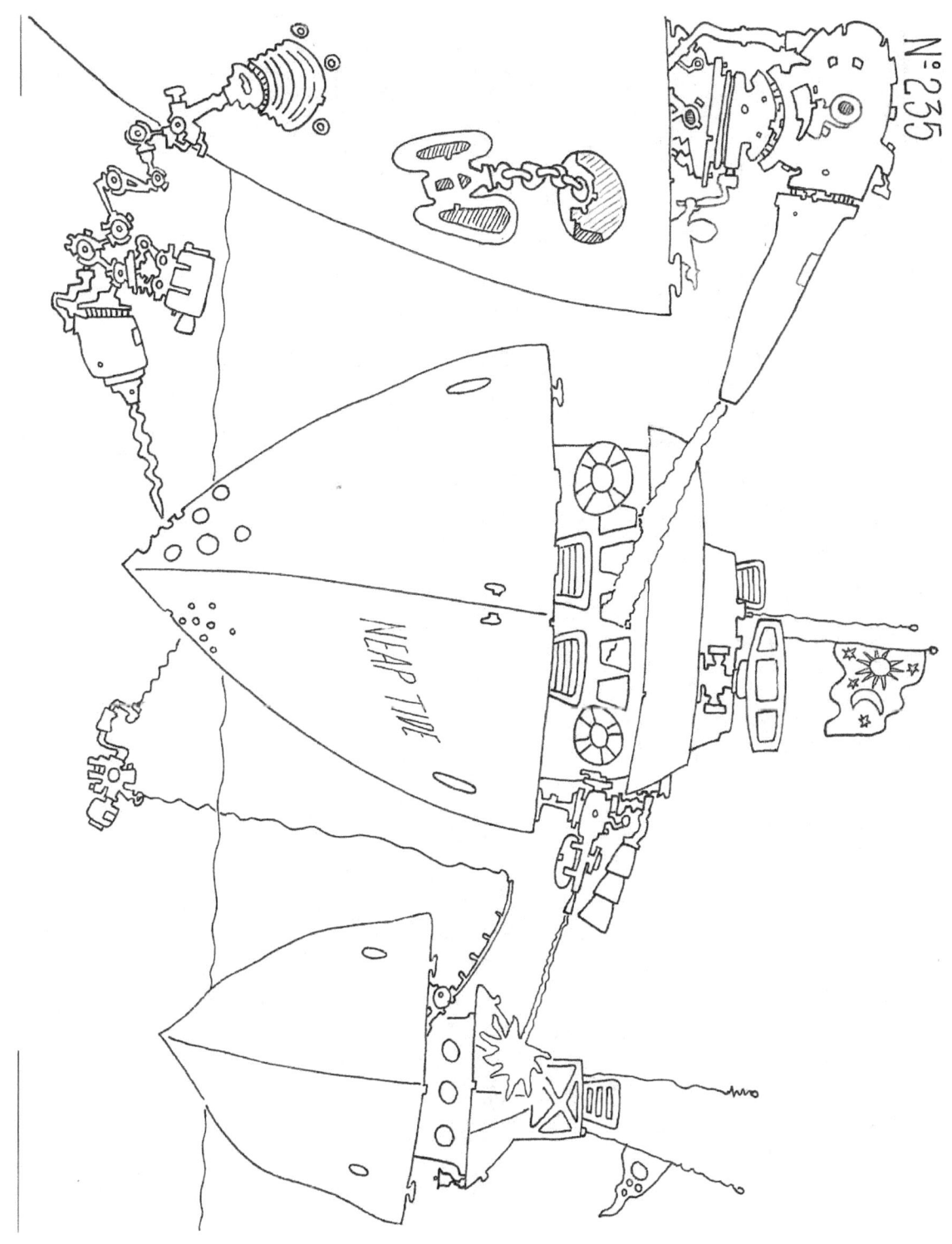

NEAP TIDE

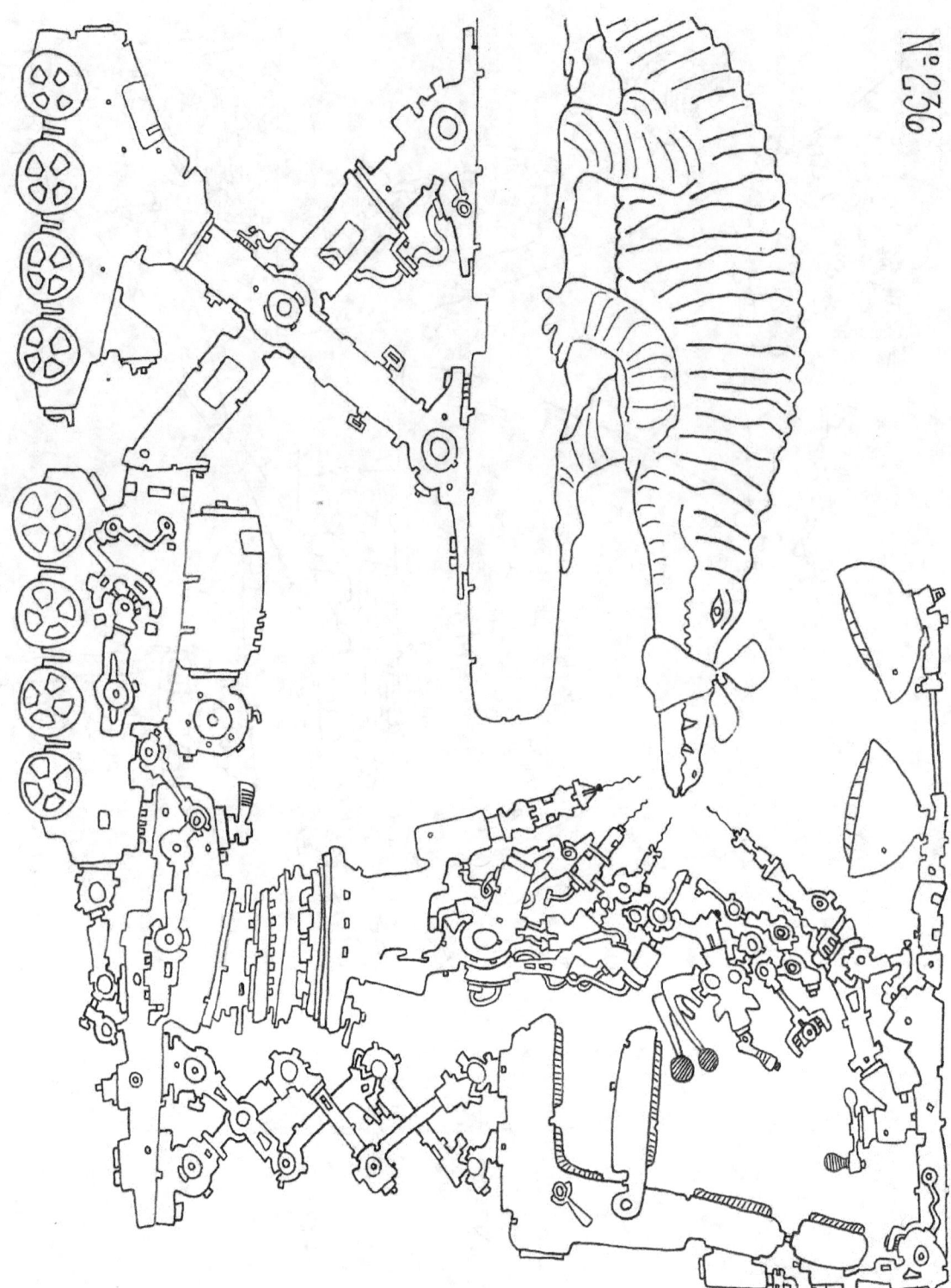

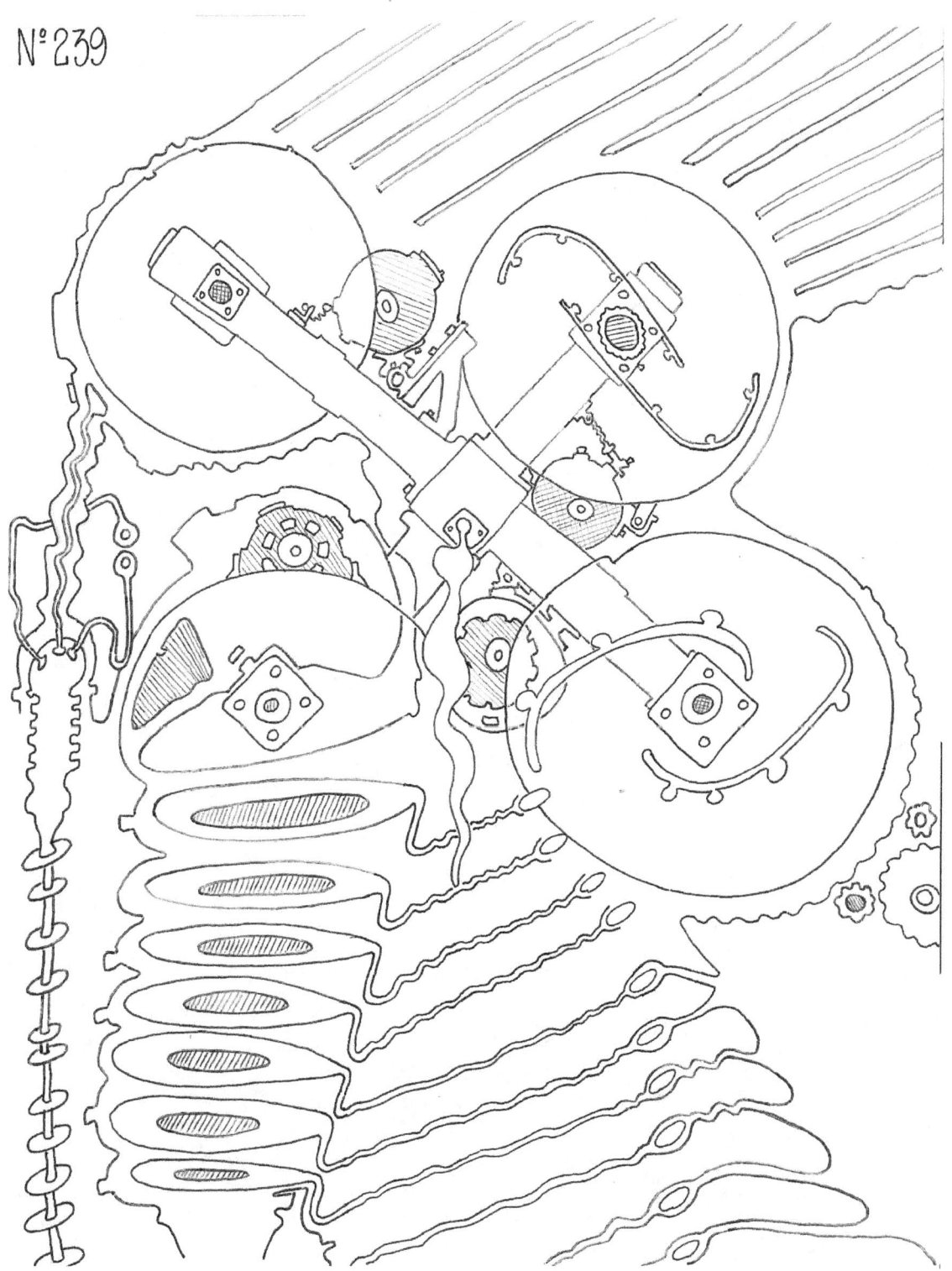

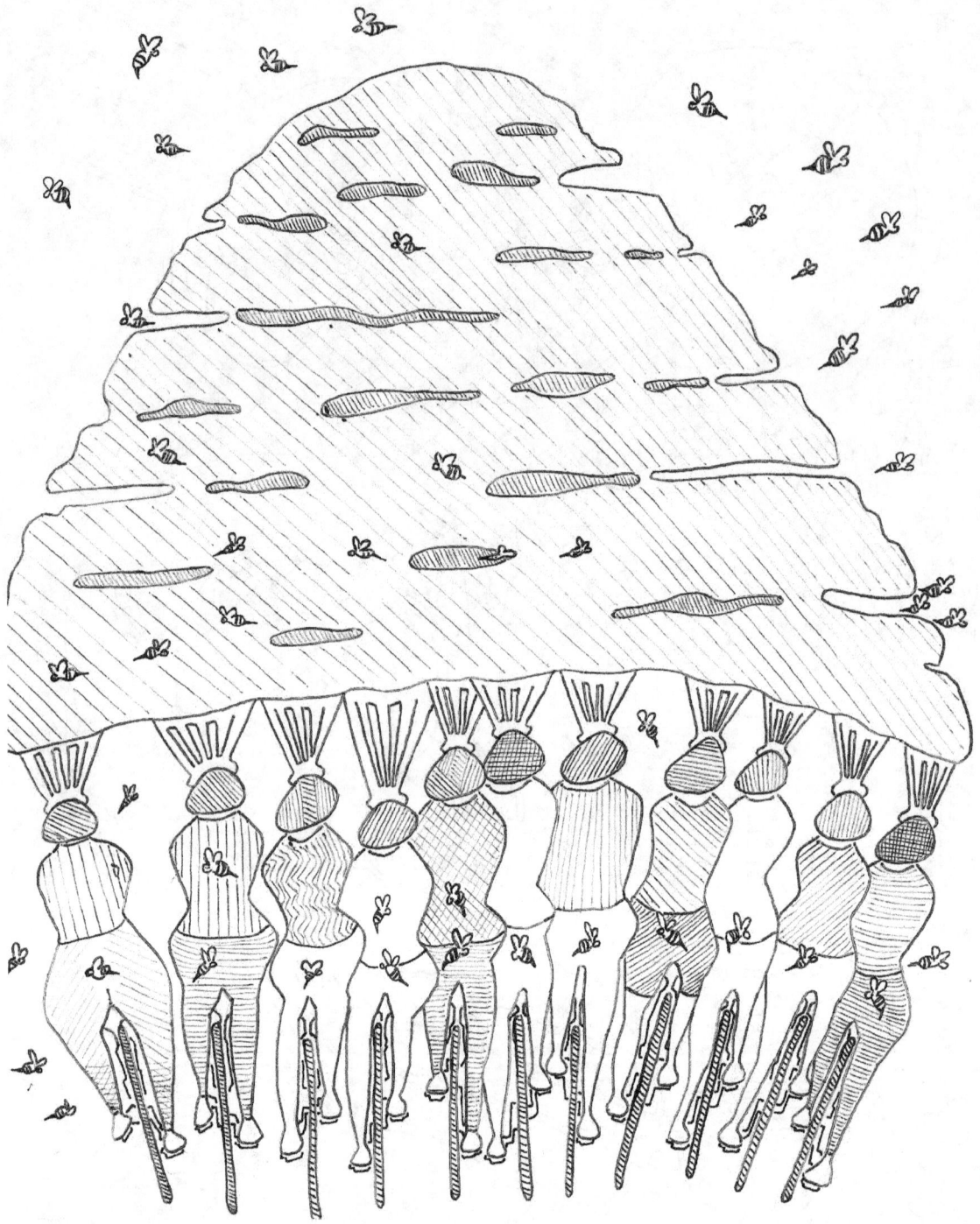

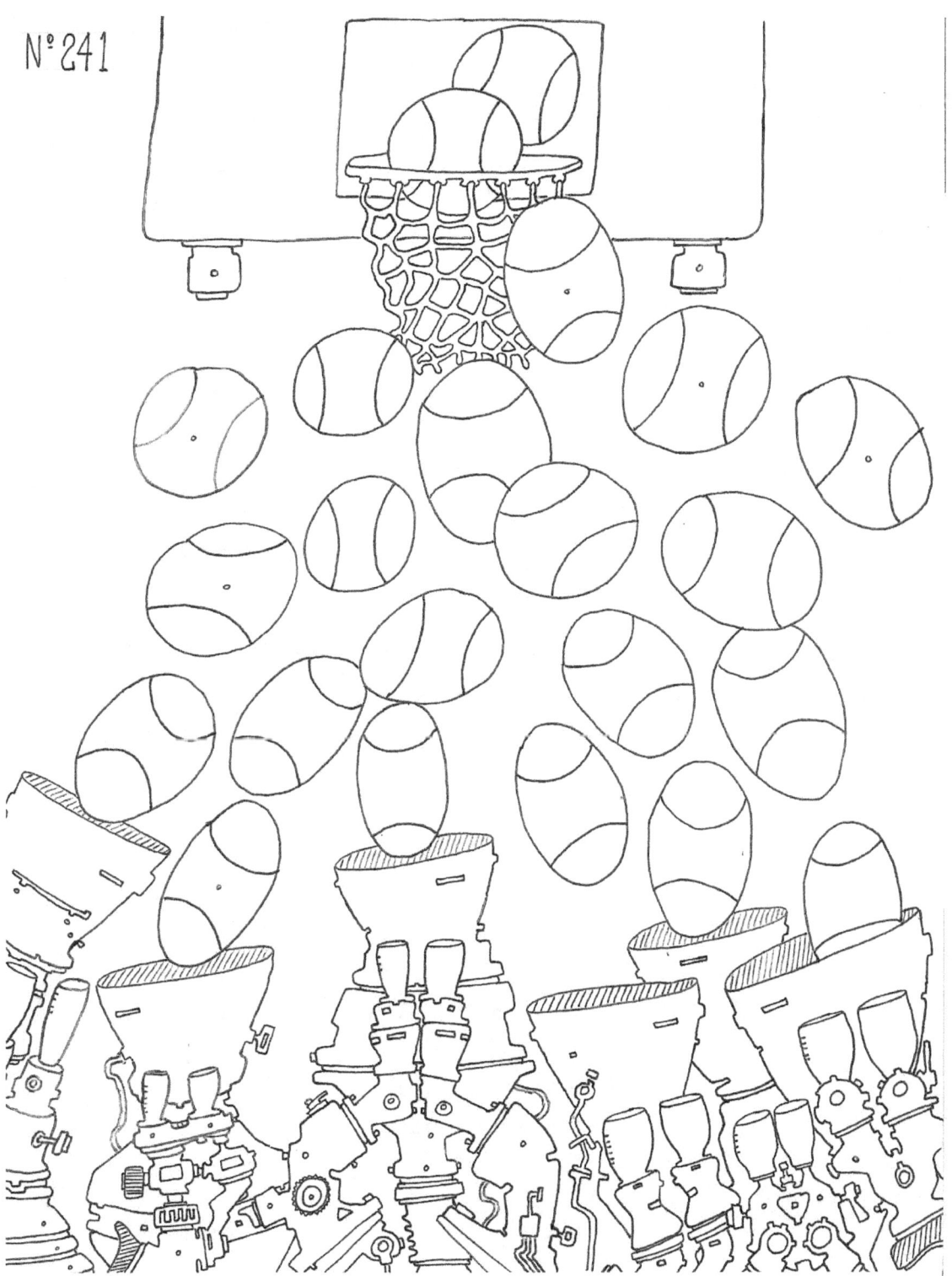

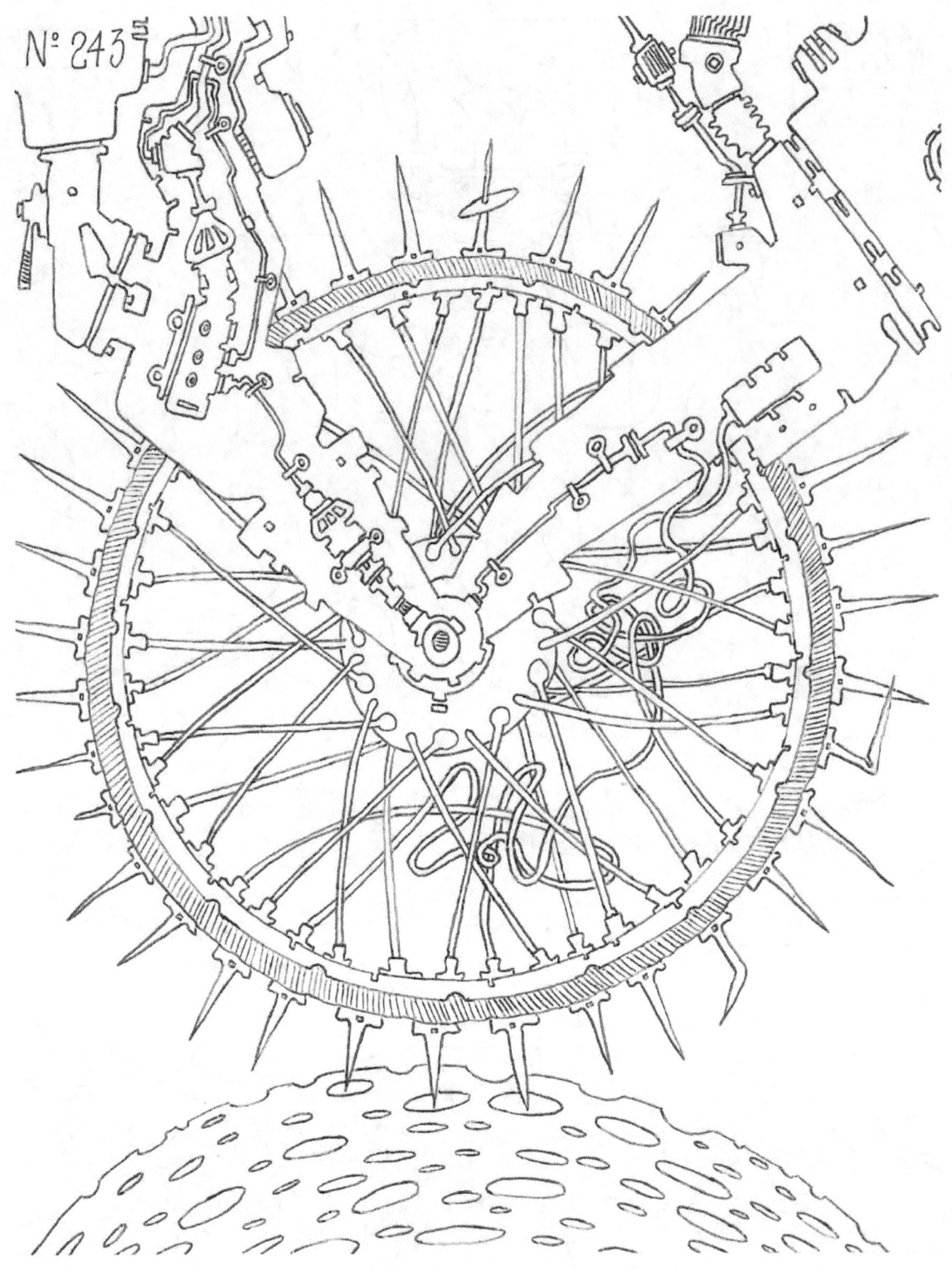

Nº 243

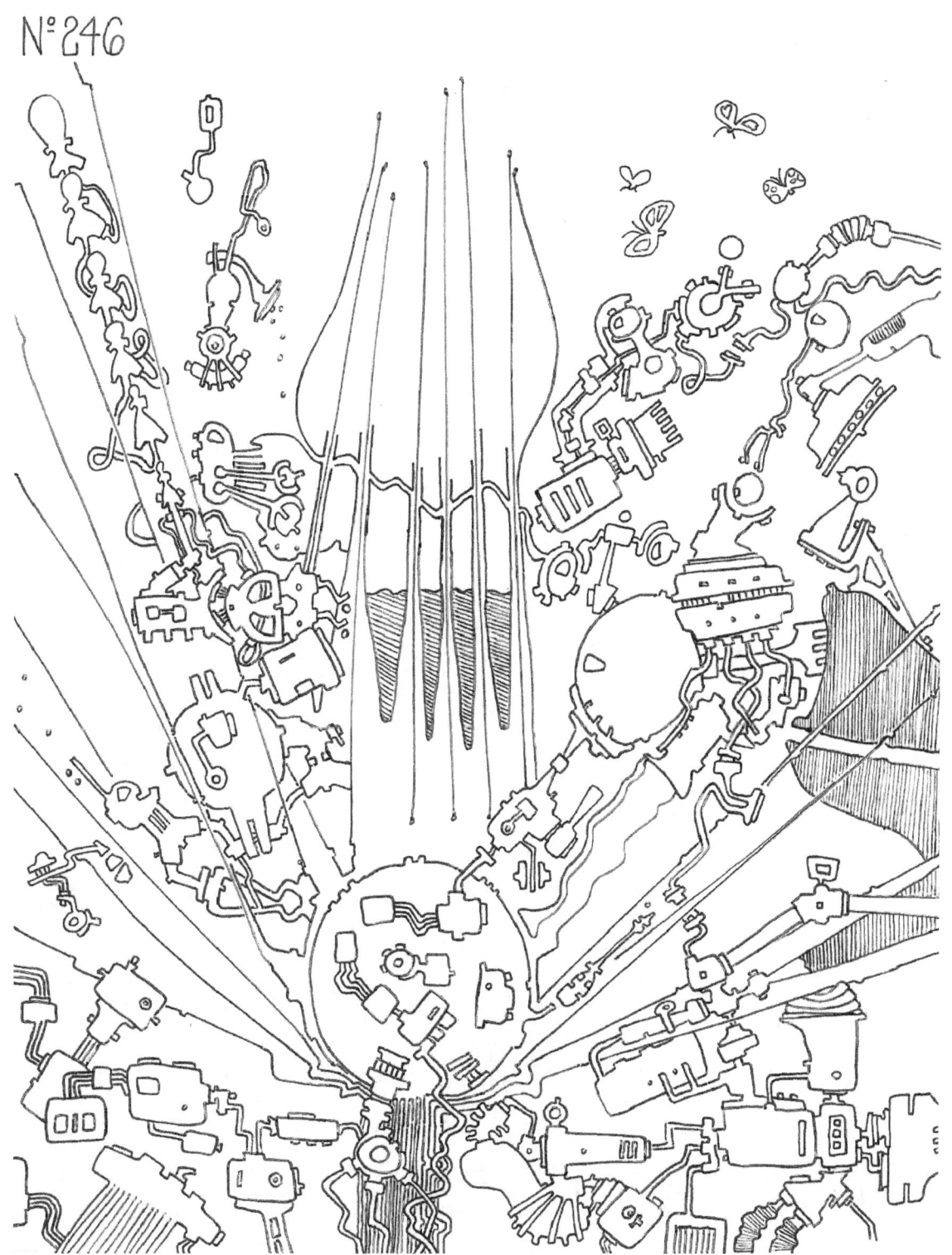

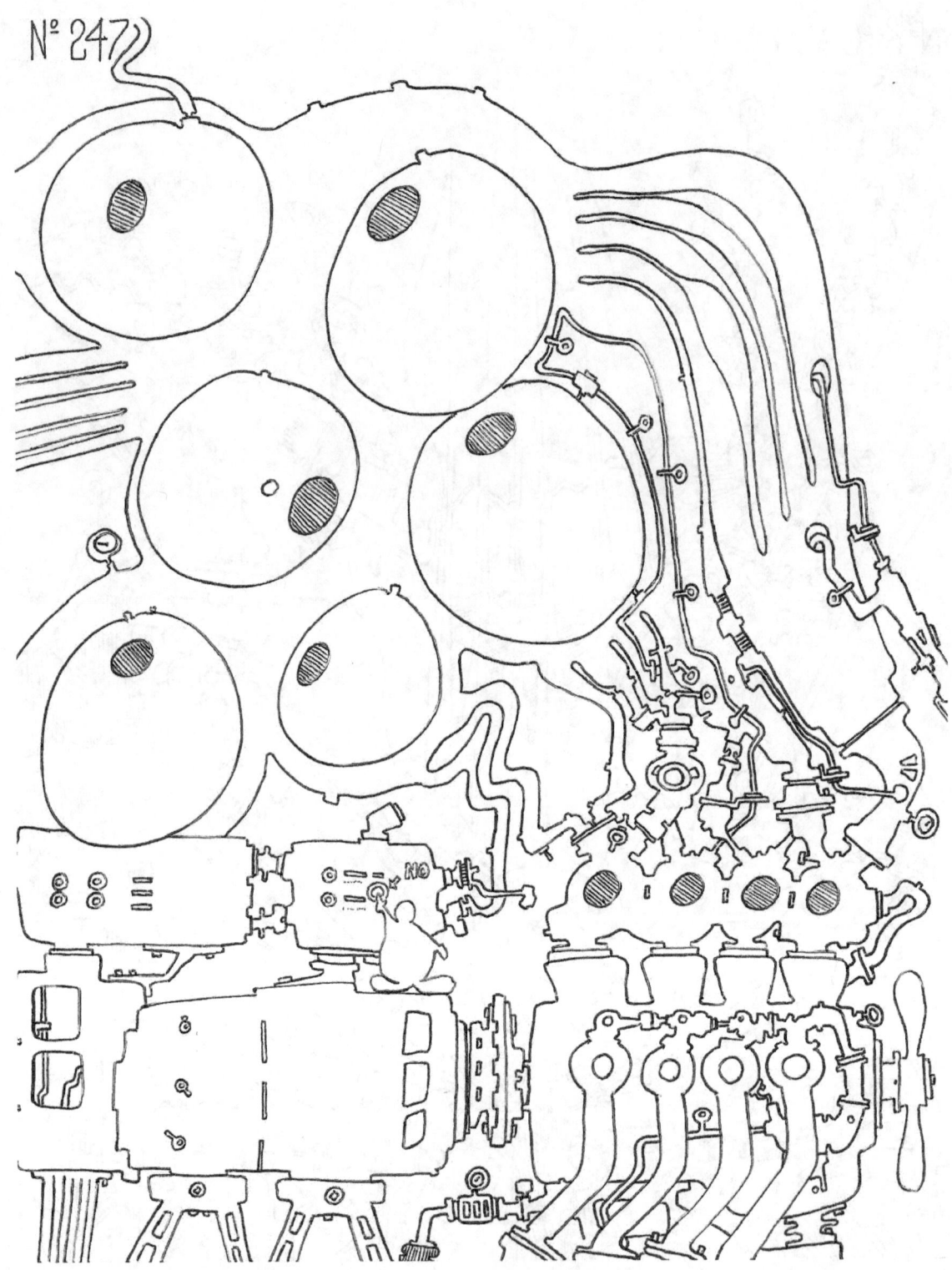

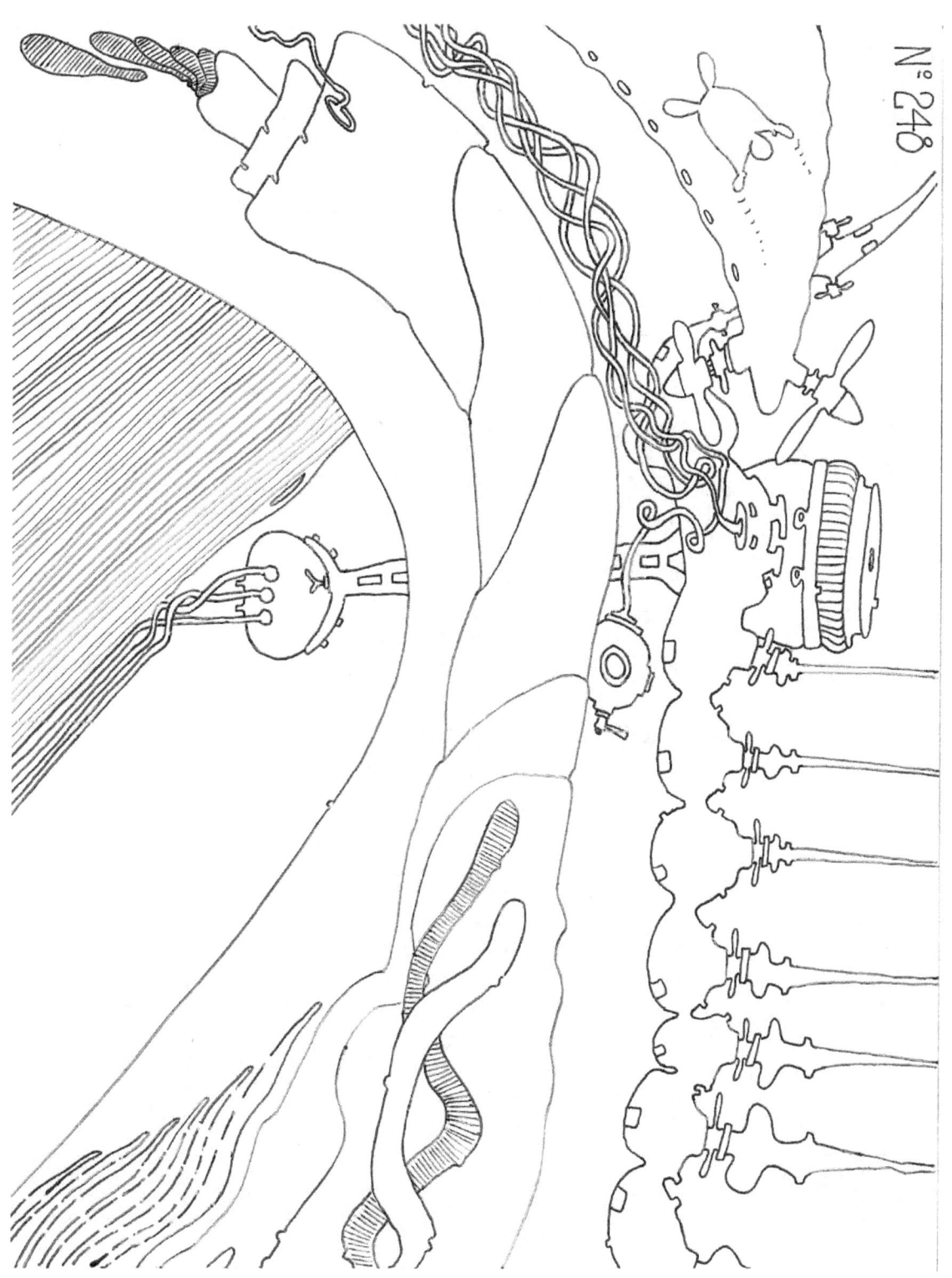

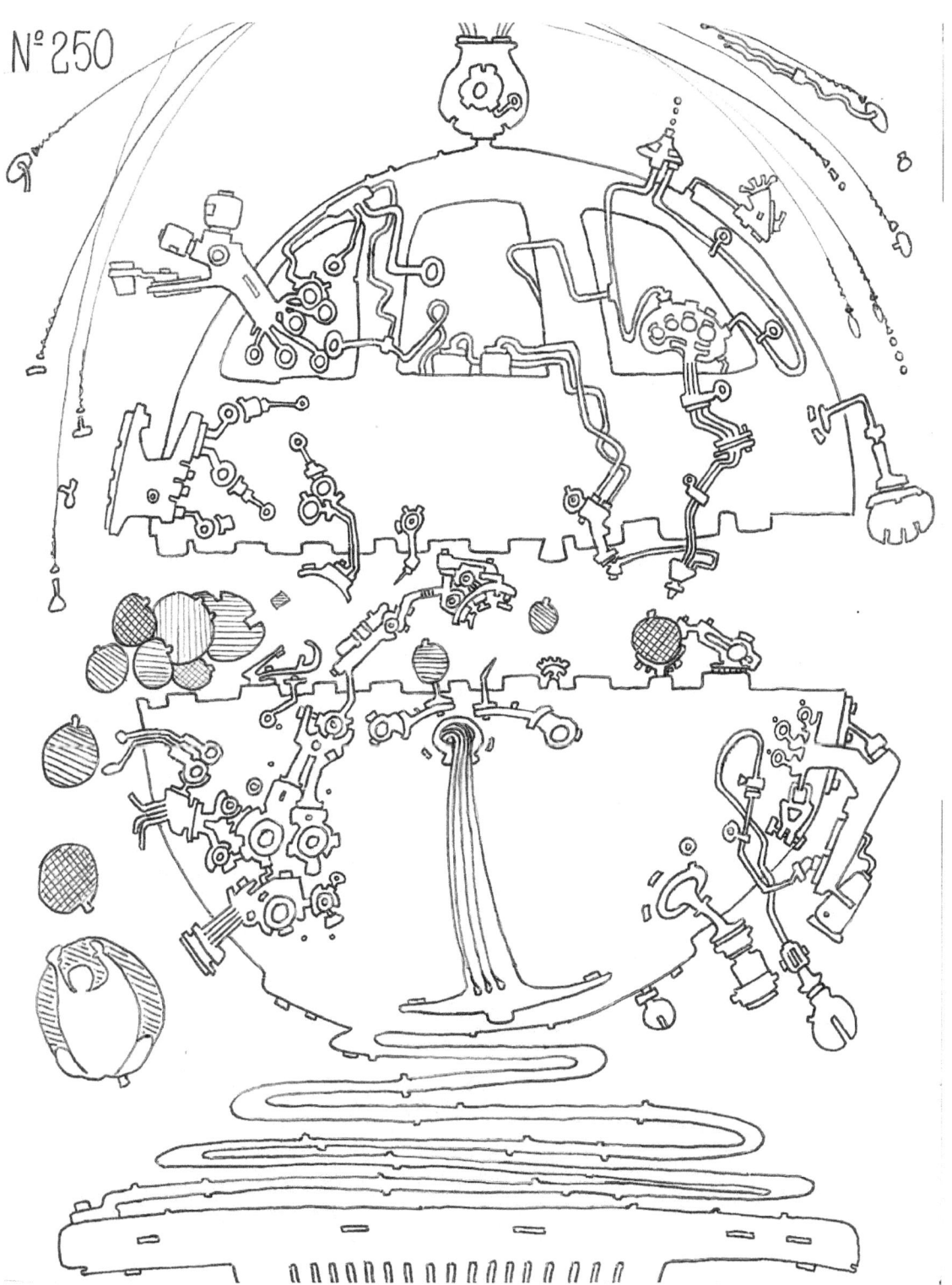

www.ingramcontent.com/pod-product-compliance
Lightning Source LLC
Chambersburg PA
CBHW080819250626

47159CB00011B/3441